Suffolk
kirsty

GW01071874

A SECOND PATH

By G A Wilson

. . . .

The lanrels   Saturday

1115   1154

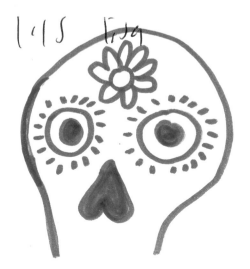

New Generation Publishing

For E.W.

My inspiration

CHAPTER 1

Slowly, Kate opened her eyes and immediately squeezed them shut against the shaft of blinding sunlight. With a soft groan, she raised her eyelids a fraction and blinked several times to clear her blurry vision. She realised she was peering through a mosquito net. It covered the hard camp bed where she lay, encasing her in a cocoon. A warm breeze blew around her face. A sudden gust of wind had loosened the laces which fastened the tent entrance and the flapping noise had woken her up. Kate sat up, disoriented. What was she doing in a tent?

Fighting off the mosquito net, she stood up and studied her surroundings. The tent appeared to be circular, with a conical roof. Most of the furniture was placed around the circumference of the tent. An oil lamp sat on a small table, along with a cracked porcelain bowl and a large jug. Her bare foot knocked against a pile of books on the floor. Two large battered trunks rested on a faded rug which felt gritty under her feet. Everything was covered in a thin layer of dust. The air was thick and smelled slightly musty. There was a hammock near the bed, hung precariously between two packing cases. Surmising that she shared the tent with another person, Kate looked for a clue as to their identity. She walked over to a small folding table, littered with papers. A leather-bound notebook lay open, its pages filled with beautiful handwriting and miniature sketches. A small rock, acting as a paperweight, held down a stack of papers. Some of the papers were accounts while others looked like lists of provisions and equipment. A large, well-worn map lay open on the centre of the desk, and Kate recognised a map of Egypt. Absently, she traced her finger down the River Nile. A smaller, hand-drawn map depicted an area called Akhetaten. It looked to be halfway between Luxor and Memphis, on the east bank of the Nile. Kate's eyes returned to the diary, remembering that she had seen the word 'Akhetaten' on its open pages. Perhaps there would be more clues there.

'Good morning,'

Kate jumped, dropping the book back on the desk and turning quickly towards the entrance to the tent. A man stood silhouetted by the glaring daylight behind him. He stood there for a moment, clearly appraising her, before walking slowly towards her. He was at least a head taller than Kate, with broad shoulders tapering to a lean waist and long legs. His dark hair looked unkempt, as if he had been running his fingers through it. It fell over his dark brown eyes. The sleeves of his white linen shirt were rolled up to reveal tanned muscular arms. He looked dusty, as if he had been digging in the sand. The beautiful smile he bestowed on Kate revealed perfect teeth and his eyes shone with love as he looked at her. Kate was rooted to the spot, her throat suddenly dry, her voice lost. She became aware that she was dressed only in a long nightdress, which barely covered her shoulders and was held in place by a knotted ribbon. She felt exposed and vulnerable. *I'm like a heroine from a romance novel*, she thought. *What a cliché!*

He held out a tin cup. 'I brought you some coffee,' he said, his voice deep and low. He held her gaze as he set the cup on the desk behind her. 'But I think it can wait.'

His hands slipped around her waist, and he pulled her gently towards him. Her body seemed to recognise his touch and she melted against him, her arms sliding around his neck of their own accord. She lifted her face to him. His eyes dark and smouldering, he lowered his lips to hers…

Kate's eyes snapped open, the screeching of the alarm clock ripping her from sleep. Forcing herself into the present, she sat up in her rumpled double bed. The dream, however, was still vividly playing in her head, and she longed to go back to sleep. Her body slowly returned from its state of gentle arousal, leaving Kate bereft. The man in her dream had appeared before. For many years, Kate had been aware of a shadowy male figure, dark-haired but otherwise featureless, a comforting presence in times of need. In the last few weeks, however, his presence had taken on a much more sensual form. And yet, she was sure she had never met him.

A mug of coffee was wafted under her nose. Still distracted, Kate took the mug then smiled her thanks to Mark. Her husband was already dressed for work in one of his overly expensive suits.

'I have an early morning meeting with a client,' he informed her, his face impassive. 'I might be late tonight. I'll text you and let you know.'

He left the room, without a kiss or even a word of goodbye. But Kate was still thinking about other lips, warm and demanding...

Kate's mobile phone rang as she was coming out of the shower. Cursing, she hastily wrapped herself in a towel and ran back to the bedroom to answer the call. It was her old friend, Gemma Walker.

'Hi, sweetie!' Gemma gushed. 'How are you?'

'Fine, Gemma,' Kate replied, trying to hide her irritation. 'I'm just getting ready for work. How are you?'

'Don't be cross with me, sweetie - I'm swamped at work, and I can't make lunch today. Can we reschedule?'

Kate kept the exasperation from her voice; this was not the first time Gemma had cancelled a lunch date at short notice. 'Okay. Let me know when you're free, and we'll set something up. Take care!'

'Love you, Katie! Bye!'

As Kate dressed for work, she contemplated her friendship with Gemma. They had both studied journalism at university, and had spent three years sharing a small flat in Marchmont. Gemma had been a wild child, enjoying drunken nights out and numerous affairs. Kate had lived a fairly sheltered life at home before flying the nest to live with Gemma. For a while, she enthusiastically adopted the student lifestyle, beguiled by Gemma's vivacious and adventurous nature. By the final year of the course, however, Kate started to find some of her fellow students shallow and idiotic. They had no ambition, no plans for the future. Kate socialised less frequently and spent more of her time studying in the library.

Ironically, it was Gemma who secured a coveted job at a large Edinburgh newspaper. Nowadays, she mingled with many of the city's well-known high-flyers. But the demands of her job had hardened Gemma and made her cynical. She wasn't beyond bending the rules to catch a good story, often using her sultry beauty to manipulate people. The truth was, Kate thought sadly, that she and Gemma no longer had much in common.

Kate's reverie continued as she rode the crowded bus to work. Her own path had taken her in a completely different direction. Kate's father, Christopher, had been a doctor. During his successful career, he had worked for various medical charities in Africa. Kate's mother, Elizabeth, had been a photo journalist whose work had taken her all over the world. As a result of their parents' frequent absence, Kate and her older brother Benedict had spent much of their childhood living with their father's only sister. Margaret Grahame had never married and doted on her brother's children. She welcomed them into her cosy home in Garscube Terrace, which had once belonged to her parents. Kate had always felt closer to her aunt than to her parents; Margaret's home had been Kate's sanctuary.

Not long after the final exams, Kate's beloved aunt was diagnosed with terminal cancer. Against her parents' wishes, Kate moved into Margaret's house. She nursed her aunt until Christopher decided to move his sister into Saint Columba's Hospice. Two weeks later, Margaret was dead. Her will provided a generous bequest for Benedict, who was studying medicine. Margaret bequeathed her house and the rest of her considerable savings to Kate.

Margaret's estate was handled by a large Edinburgh law firm, who appointed Mark Forrester to fulfil Margaret's wishes. Deeds and savings accounts were transferred to a grieving and overwhelmed Kate. The ambitious young lawyer suggested that Kate invest her sizeable legacy, but Kate demurred. She knew very little about the stock market, and had always been afraid to take risks. She saved her money in the building society where it earned a reasonable amount of interest. Mark was kind and patient with his young client, who seemed cast adrift by her aunt's demise. After they had met in his office a few times, Mark invited Kate out for coffee. Coffee progressed to a lunch date, then dinner. Before long, they were a couple. After ten months of dating, Mark proposed to Kate, brandishing a large diamond ring. Without much deliberation, a dazzled Kate accepted. Mark persuaded her to arrange an extravagant wedding, but most of the guests were Mark's friends and colleagues.

The first year of their marriage had been a whirlwind of trips to exciting cities such as Paris, Rome and Amsterdam. Mark had been extravagant, booking first-class hotels and restaurants. He had spoiled her as if she were precious to him. Occasionally, he would suggest that Kate invest in some new scheme he had heard of at work, but Kate stubbornly refused to risk her aunt's money.

Mark's work became more demanding, and he frequently had to work late or travel to the London branch office. He was a successful lawyer with his heart firmly set on a partnership. Gradually, the luxurious holidays stopped along with Mark's profligate displays of affection. In the last few months, Kate had noticed an increasing indifference; they were becoming distant, and both were to blame. As Kate stepped from the bus at George IV Bridge, she tried to recall how she had felt in the first flush of love. The feeling eluded her.

Kate had never become a journalist. As she had approached her final term at university, she had begun to suspect that journalism might not be a suitable career choice. She had entertained a fanciful notion of being a crusader for the truth, a champion of the unjustly treated and oppressed. In reality, Kate had too much compassion to be an effective journalist. She had no appetite for probing into people's private lives and causing distress. Kate lacked the quality all journalists honed, the ability to be persistent and aggressive in order to get the best story. She had confided her fears to Margaret. As always, Margaret had listened attentively before advising Kate to follow her heart. Kate had snorted derisively, retorting that her life had been spent following her parents' hearts. They had relentlessly pushed Kate towards journalism, asserting that the profession would utilise her talent for creative writing. Kate had always tried to please them, but it seemed that none of her accomplishments had ever been quite good enough.

Her aunt's illness had caused Kate to postpone looking for a job. After Margaret's death, Kate spent time alone in her aunt's house, grieving and sorting through Margaret's belongings. Eventually, Kate took on some temping work and was offered a job in a life assurance office which made no use of her writing skills at all.

In 2011, Christopher passed away, also from cancer. Kate had grieved, but not as deeply as she had for her aunt, and this made her feel ashamed.

Mark had been content with Kate's working arrangements, as they allowed her to shoulder the responsibility for all the housekeeping chores. In short, she attempted to fulfil her husband's wishes to have a marriage straight from the 1950's.

Finally, Kate got bored and frustrated with her mind-numbing duties at the life office, and was ecstatic to begin a new job at the National Museum of Scotland. The museum held a special place in Kate's heart. As children, she and Benedict had spent many hours exploring the beautiful building. She was now in the third month of her probationary period. Her job was varied and enabled her to interact with people of all ages, from all over the world. She currently spent most of her time with the vibrant Events team, helping to organise workshops for school children. Her supervisor made use of Kate's literary talents by giving her the additional task of updating worksheets and other documentation. As Kate's experience grew, so did her confidence, and so did the distance between her and Mark.

'Oi, missus!'

Startled out of her unhappy contemplation, Kate turned in the direction of the voice and grinned at her friend and supervisor, Jess Mortimer. Jess's red corkscrew curls were confined under a woollen hat this morning, her neck protected by a thick scarf. She lived in a flat in Tollcross and had walked to work in the bracing March air. Kate had been assigned to Jess's team on her first day, and the women had quickly become friends.

Together, they rounded the corner into Chambers Street, and Kate felt a warm glow inside her at the sight of the magnificent building which housed over four million exhibits from all eras and parts of the world. She smiled brightly in anticipation of the day ahead.

'Hasn't the novelty worn off, yet?' Jess teased affectionately.

Kate chuckled. 'Not yet.'

Every time she went to work at the museum, she felt as though she were coming home. The museum was currently holding a fascinating exhibition on ancient Egypt. Kate had bought her ticket as soon as they had become available and had spent an enjoyable morning with some of the most beautiful artefacts she had ever seen. She had been thrilled to spend time in the exhibition hall as part of the security team, making sure no harm came to the exhibits and assisting the many visitors who shared Kate's admiration of the relics.

The security guard unlocked the door for Kate and Jess, and they stepped gratefully out of the cold and into the large entrance hall. This new entrance to the museum was breathtaking. It had been the storage vault until the recent refurbishment. Now it created a memorable first impression for the many visitors who stepped through the museum's wide glass doors. It was a long room with a vaulted ceiling and walls of pale stone, which were warmed by low-level lighting. The gift shop was situated at one end, the Museum Brasserie at the other. Leather-topped benches nestled in the recesses which lined one wall. There were also meeting rooms where the Events team entertained school groups.

Their footsteps echoed loudly on the stone floor as they crossed to the stairs which led to the Grand Gallery. Only a few of the lights were on, as the museum did not open for another ninety minutes. The staffroom and offices were at the back of the building. Kate and Jess were evidently the first to arrive, as the area was silent. They placed their belongings in their lockers, situated in one corner of the staffroom. Just as Kate was switching off her mobile phone, she received a text from Mark to say he would be working late and would be dining out with a client. Jess did not notice her friend's look of disappointment. She kept up a constant stream of chatter, mostly about a television programme she had seen the night before. Finally, she noticed that Kate's thoughts were elsewhere.

'You're quiet this morning,' Jess remarked, her hazel eyes full of concern. She knew Kate's marriage was not entirely blissful, and had often observed an air of melancholy about her. 'Is everything okay?'

Kate hesitated, unused to sharing confidences. 'Yes. It's just that I had the weirdest...' As if by magic, she felt his lips on hers again. She blushed.

'The weirdest what?' Jess probed. She tilted her head to one side, waiting for a reply.

'Weirdest dream,' Kate muttered, looking sheepish.

She moved towards the coffee machine in the small kitchen area, intending to prepare some for her colleagues. A full pot of fresh coffee already steamed on the hot plate. Fleetingly, Kate thought this was strange, as there seemed to be nobody else about.

'Tell me about it,' Jess encouraged her. 'I might be able to interpret it for you.'

Kate gave a derisory snort; Jess had a keen interest in all things paranormal. She had an open mind about virtually everything, which Kate often envied. As she prepared two mugs of coffee, Kate reluctantly revealed the barest details of her dream.

Jess was unappeased. 'What was he like, the man of your dreams?'

'An archaeologist, I think.'

'Indiana Jones, then?' she smirked, grinning salaciously.

Kate narrowed her eyes sternly at her friend. 'As far as I could tell, he didn't have a bullwhip. He *was* handsome, though...' Unconsciously, Kate touched a finger to her lip.

Jess eyed her speculatively. 'Was it good?'

Kate returned to the present. 'Was what good?'

'*It.*'

Kate blushed to the roots of her dark brown hair. 'I don't know,' she replied, flustered. 'I woke up.'

Jess considered for a moment as she sipped her coffee. 'Perhaps the universe is telling you that your needs are not being met...'

Kate knew Jess was only teasing her, and began to laugh. 'Then the universe should mind its own business!'

The Events team sat at the conference table fidgeting with pens, paper and iPads. They were anxious to get on with the busy day ahead, and were impatiently waiting for the deputy director. Some members of other departments arrived and sat down and finally Adam Gray appeared wearing his trademark grey suit. His snooty personal assistant followed close behind, carrying a cup of tea for her idol. The meeting came to order. Gray wanted to review the week's schedule, particularly the duties of the Events team. There were a number of school visits looming, and he liked the planning and execution of these visits to be perfect. The team consisted of outgoing and humorous historians who always provided enjoyable and educational visits for the schoolchildren; they didn't need Gray's constant supervision and 'input'.

Kate listened to Jess patiently explaining how she and her team would be liaising with other departments to plan the school visits, just as they always did. She succinctly outlined the plan for that day's visit by a class of primary five children who were learning about the Romans. Kate's attention wandered. Feeling a draught on the back of her neck, she shivered. Shifting slightly in her seat, she made a mental note not to sit with her back to the open door in the future.

'As you all know,' Gray was saying, in his slightly pompous tone. 'The Easter holidays are imminent. I would like us to expand our programme of children's' activities. I thought we could organise some sort of treasure hunt.' His flat grey stare slid around his staff and settled on Kate. 'Kate, I would like you to work on this.' Kate nodded dutifully and made a note in her reporter's notebook, her mind already working on the problem. 'In the same vein, I would like us to think about ways to attract more visitors to the museum. Does anyone have any ideas?'

'What about a ghost tour in the museum?'

All heads swivelled to Nick Robertson, a member of the Events team. He grinned mischievously at his colleagues, some of whom were clearly unimpressed with his frivolous idea.

'Edinburgh ghost tours are hugely successful, especially the one which includes Greyfriars Cemetery. Apparently this area of the city is a hotbed of spiritual activity. We work in an old historical building full of mysterious artefacts from around the world. I'm pretty sure that, with a little research and imagination, we could concoct enough spooky stories for an evening tour.' Nick paused for effect, scratching his bristly black beard. 'Besides, I'm sure I'm not the only one who has had a strange experience in this place. The building has a weird atmosphere, especially in places like the research library or the basement offices.' Nick fixed his twinkling brown eyes on Gray. 'I hear that the filing cupboard next to your office is prone to blown light bulbs…'

Everyone was silent for a few moments, the room divided. Nick's suggestion had inspired the members of the Events team, but some of their more staid colleagues appeared almost disdainful.

Gray sat up in his chair. 'I believe some of the city tours employ people in costume to bring their tales to life,' he said to Nick, who nodded encouragingly. 'Perhaps some of your team could do the same - in a tasteful manner, of course -' Gray swore suddenly and hastily stood up. His teacup had capsized and spilled its contents all over his trousers. Kate suppressed a snigger as Gray's assistant jumped up and fetched some paper towels to dab her master's trousers. Nick looked at Jess as if to say 'I told you so.' Brushing off the somewhat intimate attentions of his assistant, Gray sat down and prepared to end the meeting.

'Right...well...if anyone has any other suggestions, please email me. Nick, I'll think about your idea. Carry on, everyone.' Gray hurried from the room, his assistant running after him. Everyone rose from their seats, and prepared to embark on the day's assignments.

'Before you all go, can I have a minute?' They all turned to look at Professor David Young, the museum's Egyptologist. He was English, softly-spoken and very reserved. He divided his time between the museum and a teaching post at the university, where he had an office. When he was working at the museum, he shared an office with Kate, Jess and Nick, but rarely involved himself in their conversation. Although he was courteous to his colleagues, Young never attended social functions. His co-workers knew nothing of his private life, and so some malicious members of staff took pleasure in circulating rumours about him. Kate had heard that the professor was homosexual. Someone else had claimed Young was bisexual, while another gossip implied he was a fan of bondage. Whatever his preferences, they were all keenly aware of his blond good looks and green eyes. He was tall, lean, and clearly very fit.

David's face flushed slightly under the scrutiny of the people in the room. 'I'm giving a lecture in the museum tonight,' he explained. 'Unfortunately, my assistant for the evening is unable to attend. I wondered if anyone would be willing to take his place. It would mean working until about seven this evening. I know that it's short notice, but I'd really appreciate it...'

Some of the people in the room looked uncomfortably at their feet, while others muttered about being too busy. Kate spoke up clearly, her voice warm. 'I can help, Professor Young.'

The Egyptologist looked grateful. As everyone else slipped from the room, he gave Kate a rare smile. 'Are you sure you don't mind?' He knew she had a husband, and David got the impression from conversations he had overhead that Mister Forrester was quite demanding.

Kate returned his smile and shook her head. David caught an undeniable sadness in her smile. 'I don't have any plans. And besides, I'm fascinated by ancient Egypt. What is your lecture about?'

David eyes sparkled with zeal. 'Amarna.'

The class of twenty-six children sat agog as Nick paced back and forth in the costume of a Roman soldier. Re-enacting the life of a centurion, he had described his duties at the Roman fort at Cramond - or Caer Amon, as it had been called. The children had already seen the remains of the fort, but had been unaware of the Roman bath house nearby which had been excavated many years ago, then buried again in order to protect it from the elements.

Nick's tale moved north to a new posting at one of the sixteen forts which guarded the Antonine Wall, parts of which can still be seen near Falkirk. The wall had taken twelve years to build and stretched sixty-three kilometres from Old Kilpatrick in West Dunbartonshire to Carriden near Bo'ness. The Romans called the land north of the wall Caledonia. They spent twenty difficult years being harried and attacked by the native Caledonians, before finally withdrawing to Hadrian's Wall.

Nick was in the midst of telling the children about the ferocity of the Caledonians' attacks when Jess came shrieking into the room, dressed like an extra from the film 'Braveheart' and brandishing a fake broadsword. The children jumped and cried out in surprise, before erupting into gales of laughter. Nick and Jess engaged in a mock skirmish, Nick clearly losing the fight.

'Take that, ya pizza-eatin' pansy!' Jess shouted in a broad Scots accent, before pretending to stab Nick with her sword. She passed the weapon smoothly under Nick's arm and he treated the children to a dramatic death scene, complete with fake blood. Jess, meanwhile, did a victory lap of the room waving her blood-stained broadsword over her head to tumultuous applause. The pair then stood together and took a bow. Kate clapped as loudly as the children, unable to stop laughing at her friend's straggly matted wig and blue-painted face.

After the enactment, the class was taken to the Early People gallery, and Kate brought out the object handling box. The Roman box contained many interesting items, including a replica sword, a toga, wine cups, gaming pieces and some coins. Nick and Kate answered questions and supervised the handling of the items. By the time they left the museum, Kate was on first-name terms with many of the children. Some of them had even asked if they could 'friend' her on Facebook.

David's negligent assistant emailed Kate with all the information she would need for the Amarna talk that evening. Her first task was to print off an informative handout for the twenty guests to refer to during the evening and take home at the end of their visit. Once Kate had processed the paperwork she arranged refreshments for the evening, and then went to organise the room. David had requested some items from storage, which Kate collected and set up on a long table at one end of the room. One of the items was a statue of the head of glamorous Queen Nefertiti. According to the handout, the ageing bust was a replica of the one found in Amarna in 1912. Crafted in 1345BC by the sculptor Thutmose, the original had been found by a German archaeological team and was now on display in Berlin. As a child, Kate had been enchanted by Nefertiti's beautiful face and strong but feminine features. Ancient Egypt had dominated a corner of the museum's top floor back then; Kate and Ben had loved to sequester themselves in the dimly lit gallery, admiring the rows of sarcophagi and jewellery. Kate had even painted a portrait of Nefertiti for her Higher Art course at school. The new Egyptian gallery occupied more cramped quarters on the first floor, with fewer items on display.

Kate gently smoothed the queen's sculpted cheek with her hand and felt a corresponding stroke on her own face. Smiling at her vivid imagination, Kate continued setting up the display of artefacts, ensuring that Nefertiti had pride of place.

Half an hour before their guests were due to arrive, Kate changed from her lime green Events shirt back into her own clothes, hoping she looked smart and professional. As she approached the seminar room, she heard David talking on his mobile phone. She stopped short when she heard his tone change from placatory to quarrelsome. It sounded as though he was in trouble for working late. Kate took a deep breath and stepped into the room, just as David's caller apparently hung up on him. She busied herself with straightening the pile of handouts, carefully keeping her back to David and his frown of consternation.

'You've done a great job of setting up the room,' he said at last. David was using his laptop to project illustrations and additional information onto the screen mounted on the wall which faced the audience. Kate felt relieved that she would not be responsible for that particular task; in her experience, computers always decided to misbehave at the least opportune moments.

David walked towards her and handed her a clipboard. 'This is the agenda for the evening.' he explained, his tone brisk. Kate refrained from pointing out that his assistant had already provided this information. She wondered if the professor had trust issues with his staff. 'Welcome and seat the visitors. I'll do my presentation, and then we'll take them on a tour of the gallery. Back here for questions and refreshments.'

Kate nodded. 'I persuaded one of the night security staff to bring the refreshments at around six thirty. Is that okay?'

'That sounds fine. I'd like you to keep an eye on our guests when we're roaming the building. Round up any stragglers.' David gave her an apologetic half-smile. 'I'm sorry if a lot of this is menial.'

'It's not menial, Professor,' Kate assured him. 'I'm looking forward to hearing about Amarna.' A scene from her dream flashed once again into Kate's mind, a vision of a dark-haired archaeologist dusty from the desert. She dismissed it quickly, telling herself that now was not the time.

'Please, Kate, call me David,' he urged. 'There's one more thing. I don't mind answering questions from people at the end of the evening, but could you maybe keep an eye out for anyone who seems too...'

'Intent on monopolising your attention?' Kate finished, grinning at David's attempt at diplomacy.

David looked abashed. 'Exactly,' he muttered.

'I'll look out for signs of your discomfort, then,' she teased, just as the first visitors wandered into the room.

Kate welcomed them with a wide smile, as David returned to his laptop. The group of three young girls introduced themselves as David's second-year students. Kate gave them name tags and handouts and invited them to sit. She watched them rush to the front row, their eyes on David. Dressed somewhat provocatively for a lecture on ancient Egypt, the girls arranged themselves on their chairs in poses Kate guessed were meant to look alluring. David seemed not to notice, his face hidden behind his laptop, and his eyes intent on the screen. Kate smiled wryly, understanding why David had asked her to prevent him from being cornered by his guests.

The remaining attendees were a mixture of David's students and interested members of the public who had purchased tickets for the lecture from the museum. Once all twenty were seated, Kate sat at the back of the room. David introduced himself and Kate and briefly explained the agenda for the evening. Then he began to talk about an archaeological site which he clearly held close to his heart.

'The city has had many names,' David began, his eyes sweeping over his audience. 'Tell el-Amarna, El-Amarna, Akhetaten...'

Kate's ears pricked up at the mention of Akhetaten. The name had been on the map in her dream and in the page of the diary she had read.

She felt disconcerted; she was certain she had never heard Amarna called Akhetaten before today. Pushing the thought from her mind, Kate returned her attention to David. Like the others in the room, she soon became captivated by the sound of David's smooth voice, and his extensive knowledge of the city.

Amarna was built by the heretic pharaoh Akhenaten, also known as Amenhotep IV or Khuenaten. Married to the beautiful Nefertiti, he rejected the multiple gods of Egyptian theology in favour of one all-powerful deity: the Aten, the Light of the Sun. In the fifth year of his reign, he abandoned Thebes (also known as Luxor) and constructed the city of Amarna, three hundred and twenty kilometres to the north on the east bank of the Nile. Built from whitewashed mud bricks and local stone, Akhenaten's utopia occupied a wide semi-circle of desert, the river to the west and cliffs to the east. The city stretched for twelve kilometres and was five kilometres wide. It was not the most ideal site to build a city for thirty thousand people; it was isolated, there was very little agricultural land and fresh water was not always readily available. The pharaoh built a glorious shrine to Aten and lived in his new capital city for about thirteen years.

Unfortunately, this new utopia was based on a dictatorship, and upon the king's death, his subjects left Amarna and returned to Memphis and Thebes. Gradually the city was abandoned, after only around twenty years of occupation. The people also abandoned their new religion and resumed worship of multiple gods. In many places, images and literature relating to the pharaoh and his wife were destroyed or mutilated. No other pharaoh was tempted to live in Amarna, so the city was never used again, making it one of the best-preserved sites in Egypt.

David illustrated his talk with his own impressive photos of Amarna, taken from the air to show the layout of the city; apparently, exploring it from the ground did not convey just how impressive it was. Kate was mesmerised by artists' reconstructions of the Grand Palace, temples and gardens. She marvelled at the beauty of the statues and stelae, and admired the spectacular wall illustrations found in the cliff tombs. She absorbed every detail of David's own trip to Amarna. David told his audience about the work of Flinders Petrie, the ground-breaking Scottish archaeologist who had led an expedition to Amarna in the late nineteenth century.

Akhenaten's tomb was officially discovered in 1892, although it is thought that it was found by locals much earlier. Akhenaten's mummy was not found in the tomb; it is possible that his son Tutankhamen may have moved Akhenaten to another resting place in the Valley of the

Kings. In the nineteenth century, a number of mummies were found by French archaeologists in the tomb of Amenhotep II. Using cutting-edge forensic techniques, Egyptologists had recently identified one of these mummies as Nefertiti. David ended his presentation by claiming that the jury was still out on that particular judgement.

David received loud applause for his eloquent and informative lecture. Kate's heart warmed when she saw him flush self-consciously as some of the audience gave him a standing ovation, including the girls in the front row. Raising a hand to quieten them, he informed the group that they would now tour the Egyptian gallery, where they would see exhibits from Amarna. Surrounded by his three groupies, David led them from the room.

Their footsteps echoed in the silence as they walked to the empty gallery. As David entertained his guests with his extensive knowledge of Amarna and its treasures, Kate stood at the back of the group, unable to see through the huddle of people. Her eyes wandered to the display of the Qurneh burial items, an exhibit she felt inexplicably drawn to. Out of the corner of her eye she thought she saw someone in a white shirt move quickly past the arched entrance at the far side of the gallery. When she turned to look properly, the figure had moved out of sight, and a head count confirmed that the entire group stood in front of her. Kate assumed it had been a member of staff and dismissed it from her mind.

To end the tour, David took everyone down to the ground floor to look at the sarcophagus and wrapped mummy of Iufenamun, Third Prophet of Amun-Re at the Temple of Karnak, and Chief of Works in the Estate of Amun-Re. Even in the muted lighting the heavily-decorated wooden sarcophagus looked stunning, the figures and hieroglyphs as vibrant as if they had been freshly painted. As always, Kate averted her eyes from the body within. It saddened her that the poor priest had come to rest in a glass case surrounded by loud voices and prying eyes. Instead, Kate turned to the magnificent portrait of Frances Teresa Stuart, allegedly the inspiration behind the image of Britannia. She avoided looking too closely at the foreboding tower of the Millennium Clock, for although it attracted many admiring visitors, the monument to human frailty filled her with a disgust she was unable to articulate.

When they returned to the seminar room, people pounced on David with questions. He answered them in a manner which was courteous yet impersonal. After a while, a member of security arrived to escort the guests out of the museum. All of them left except one young woman, who had waylaid David. By her body language, Kate deduced that the woman knew David quite well, so she busied herself tidying up the room. After some minutes, however, Kate felt a slight tension in the air. Turning to where David and the woman were still talking she noticed that, while the woman was animated and smiling, David's stance was anything but relaxed. Kate watched the girl stroke her long blonde hair, bat her eyelashes and touch her throat. *Classic signals,* Kate thought with amusement. When the woman reached out to touch David lightly on the arm, Kate caught him recoil slightly before collecting himself. His eyes sought Kate's and pleaded for help. Kate walked purposefully over to the pair.

'I just can't get the dynasties straight in my head, Professor!' the woman whined in a childlike voice. 'I get them so muddled!'

'It's all in your textbook, Amy,' David explained tersely. 'The explanation provided in the book is quite comprehensive. Keep reading it over to yourself and you'll get it eventually.'

Kate touched David's elbow. This time he did not flinch, but turned to give her his undivided attention. 'Professor Young, security need to lock up the room.'

Kate gave Amy a pleasant smile, and then saw her face fall when David draped his arm around Kate's shoulders. The touch of his warm hand on her upper arm sent a spark of energy through her neglected body. Kate did not show her surprise, but casually hid her left hand from view so Amy would not see her wedding band.

'Yes,' David agreed, favouring Kate with a dazzling smile. 'We need to get home.' He looked pointedly at Amy. 'Perhaps we can discuss your difficulty in class, Amy. Some of your classmates may be having the same problem.'

Conveniently, one of the security team appeared at the door and meaningfully cleared his throat. 'This gentleman will see you out.'

Amy muttered a hasty goodnight, firing Kate a venomous look as she left. Once she was gone, David breathed a sigh of relief and ran his fingers through his hair.

'I apologise for that, Kate,' he said ruefully. 'I hope I didn't offend you. Amy is very…persistent.'

'I'm sure she's not the only one,' Kate teased.

'No, but she's definitely the worst!' David packed up his equipment as Kate finished tidying the room.

'Do you need me to do anything else?' Kate asked, surveying the room.

'No, you've been perfect,' David replied earnestly. 'But it's long after seven, and I've kept you later than I said I would.'

'It doesn't matter, David. I really enjoyed your lecture.'

'I'll take you home.'

'You don't have to - I can get a bus across the road.'

'No,' David insisted. 'It's late, it's dark, and it's probably cold. I'm driving you home.'

Kate was amused by his sudden bossiness. 'Yes, Professor,' she replied obediently.

Fifteen minutes later, Kate was securely ensconced in David's very masculine Land Rover Freelander. The inside of the black car was spotlessly clean and smelled seductively of the black leather upholstery. As they wound their way through the town centre and numerous diversions, David's phone rang insistently from its cradle on the dashboard. He quickly hit the 'decline call' button, but moments later it started to ring again. Kate noticed David's hand tightening on the steering wheel, his expression grim. Keeping his eyes on the road, he reached over to silence the phone.

Kate started to feel uncomfortable. 'David,' she began hesitantly. 'You don't have to take me all the way home. You can drop me off -'

'No!' he snapped impatiently and was immediately apologetic. His voice softened. 'I'm only driving five minutes out of my way. And besides, it's not as if tonight was unplanned. I've had this lecture in my calendar for weeks.' He glanced at Kate. 'Unlike you.'

Kate shrugged and said nothing, but the tension in the car increased insidiously the closer they got to their respective homes. Worried about Mark's reaction to his wife being brought home by a strange man, she asked David to drop her off at the end of the road. Raised to behave like a gentleman, David insisted on driving her to her front door.

'Thanks again for all your help, Kate,' he said, as she looked up at her dark windows and guessed that her house was empty.

Kate turned to David. 'If you need help again, will you ask me? I would love to hear more about Egypt, and you make it sound so fascinating!'

David grinned shyly, revealing perfect white teeth. 'I could give you a timetable,' he offered. 'You're more than welcome to attend my lectures.'

'I'd like that very much.' Now it was Kate's turn to feel shy as David gave her a warm smile. 'Would you recommend some books I could read, too?'

David nodded, delighting in her enthusiasm. He climbed out of the car to open Kate's door, then waited until she had stepped into her hall and switched on the light. Once Kate assured him she was alright, he climbed back in his car, and reluctantly drove home.

Kate stood at the top of the curved staircase, smoothing her silk evening gown. The fabric was a soft, iridescent blue. When she moved, the silk shimmered fleetingly with tones of pink and blue. The maid fussed with the train behind her, then stood back and admired her mistress. Kate pulled up the low, lace-trimmed neckline to a more modest position and smoothed her hair. Lifting her train so as not to trip, she carefully descended the stairs.

He was standing at the bottom, tall and handsome in a black evening suit, a white waistcoat and shirt, and a white bow tie. He looked up at her with adoration plain on his face.

Kate blushed, her eyes dipping shyly to the carpet. Running up to meet her, he gently took her arm to escort her down the remaining steps, his eyes never leaving her face. Once she was safely standing on the tiled floor of the vestibule, he lifted her gloved hand to his lips and kissed it, his warm brown eyes fixed on hers.

'You look beautiful,' he breathed.

'Thank you,' she replied demurely.

He took the blue velvet cloak from the maid, who tactfully made herself scarce. Moving behind Kate, he laid the garment sensuously over her shoulders. Kate jumped as she felt his warm lips on the nape of her neck. When she turned her face towards him, he cupped her face in his hands, and kissed her waiting lips. Turning her round to face him, he slid his hands possessively around her small waist. She revelled in his touch, her own hands resting on his chest.

The sound of voices and approaching footsteps forced them apart. The kiss had taken Kate's breath away; her lips felt hot and swollen, her cheeks were flushed, and her eyes sparkled.

He fastened the cloak about her neck, his fingers grazing her throat deliberately to see her tiny shiver. 'I can't wait to marry you!' he whispered, his eyes full of promise.

Kate sat in a seat upholstered in red velvet, ensconced in a Grand Circle box in the Royal Lyceum Theatre. She was intensely aware of him sitting on her right. An older couple shared the box with them. The woman was elegantly dressed and bore a resemblance to Kate. Her dark auburn hair was now turning grey, but she was still beautiful, with soft brown eyes and a serene expression. The man next to her looked very distinguished, with a bushy grey beard and twinkling dark eyes accentuated by laugh-lines. The couple discreetly held hands under the lady's programme.

Looking down at her own hands, Kate's gaze fell on the theatre programme on her lap: 'La Bohème'. Focusing now on the drama unfolding on the stage, Kate realised the opera was nearing its end. Mimi and Rodolfo were singing their final, heart-rending duet. Kate became captivated by the scene before her. The singing was so beautiful, the story so sad. When Mimi coughed, Kate held her breath and unconsciously touched her throat. A tear trickled down her cheek. And then her fiancé took her hand and squeezed it gently. Kate looked up into his handsome face and saw his love for her in his expressive eyes. He took her hand to his lips for a kiss then rested it against his cheek…

Kate woke up with a start, and found she was crying. Her consciousness recalled the dream in minute detail. She had felt surrounded by people who loved her, sitting in that dark box in the theatre. She could still sense the ardour of the man who wanted to marry her. And in her dream she had felt passionate about him, too.

Kate yearned for him, longed to be held and kissed by him again. Hot tears of frustration and grief flowed down her face, and she wept silently. Turning carefully, she curled herself around Mark's back, seeking solace from her real husband and feeling guilty about dreaming of another. She could smell whisky in the air, and deduced that Mark had consumed a sizeable quantity of his favourite drink.

Mark snored softly, lost in his own dreams and unaware of his wife's despondency.

'So you don't mind if I attend the lectures on Egypt?' Kate asked, as she sat on their bed watching Mark hurriedly pack his briefcase. 'Last night's talk was really interesting.' She picked up her statuette of the Egyptian cat goddess Bastet and stroked its smooth black contours.

'No, I don't mind,' Mark replied distractedly. 'Email me the timetable when you get it.' He frowned when he caught her looking misty-eyed at the ornament. Kate had recently rescued the cat from a box of her aunt's belongings, and it now watched him balefully from Kate's bedside table. 'Do you have to keep that by the bed? It's creepy.'

'Bastet is a goddess of protection. And hope.' Kate refrained from adding that the feline goddess was also linked to fertility, unwilling to provoke Mark with an already thorny issue in their marriage.

Kate watched as Mark packed his laptop and plane tickets. 'I could come to London with you,' she suggested tentatively, knowing that they needed to spend quality time together to refresh their flagging relationship.

Mark stopped what he was doing and looked at his wife. His gaze became guarded, as if a veil had been drawn across his frosty blue eyes. 'I'll be working today and Saturday. You know that. And anyway, I thought you were working at the weekend?'

'I am, but I'm sure I could arrange some time off. I haven't used any of my holiday allowance yet. I could travel down on Saturday evening and spend Sunday with you...' Kate hated to hear herself sounding needy.

Mark sighed impatiently. 'I'll be expected to schmooze the client on Saturday night. And I promised to spend time with my brother in on Sunday, since I'll be in his neck of the woods.' Mark saw Kate look away, deflated. 'I'll be back on Monday, for our anniversary.' He gave her a swift, impersonal kiss on the lips. Before he could move away again, Kate caught him in an embrace.

'I'll miss you,' she offered.

Mark gently disengaged himself, snorting as if he didn't believe her. 'I'm sure you'll be far too busy to notice I'm gone. What have you got planned for today?'

'Lunch with my mother,' Kate replied, and made a glum face.

Mark smiled knowingly and gave a mock shudder. 'Have fun. And patience.'

'Will you call me?' Kate asked as he carried his bags to the front door.

'I'll try,' he said without turning round.

Kate stood at the door to wave him off. She felt lonely and empty. But then, she thought dejectedly, I feel like that a lot of the time.

Once Jess discovered Kate would be alone all weekend, she insisted they go out for dinner that night. They also arranged a shopping trip in the town centre on Saturday afternoon, after Kate had finished her morning shift at the museum. Although Kate was pleased to have these outings to look forward to, she couldn't shake the nagging concern that she was becoming an object of pity among her colleagues. Her concern grew when Nick invited them out for a drink that evening.

After a busy morning with a group of pre-schoolers in the Imagine gallery, Kate cleaned paint and glue from her face, hands and shirt and met her mother for lunch in the Museum Brasserie. Elizabeth Grahame was already standing in the entrance hall, reading a leaflet about a future exhibition.

Kate's mother was tall, slender and elegant. Her greying brown hair was cut in a chic shoulder-length bob. Today she was wearing a navy trench coat over a white blouse and navy trousers. Her clothes and make-up were immaculate as usual. Elizabeth still grieved for her husband, but refused to resign herself to the potential loneliness of widowhood. She was a strong and independent woman, who now filled her days with a variety of pursuits. She smiled in greeting as her daughter approached, and held out her arms for a hug. Kate embraced her, feeling inadequately dressed as always. Once they were seated in a corner of the restaurant, Elizabeth surveyed her sometimes reticent daughter, and was instantly reminded of her husband. Kate shared Christopher's dark looks and also some of his character traits. She was a Grahame to the core. Straightaway Elizabeth noticed Kate had a slightly haunted look in her tired eyes.

Kate braced herself for a gruelling interview, and immediately started the conversation by asking about her mother's health and recent activities. This kept Elizabeth talking until their lunch arrived. While they ate, Kate warily answered questions about her health, her husband and her work. Elizabeth was relieved to see Kate perk up at last as she began to describe David's lecture. She smiled to see Kate's brown eyes light up and colour come to her cheeks as she revealed what she had learned about Amarna and Akhenaten. Her daughter was an excellent storyteller, Elizabeth thought. *What a pity she didn't follow a career in writing.*

'You know,' Elizabeth began. 'I think one of your father's ancestors had something to do with Egyptology…'

Kate stopped eating. 'Really?' she asked, her senses suddenly alert. 'Who? When?'

Elizabeth waved her hand in a vague gesture. 'I don't recall. In Victorian times or thereabouts. There was a connection to this museum, too. It might be mentioned in the Grahame family tree.'

'Do you have it?' Kate asked urgently, unaware that such a document even existed.

Elizabeth's eyes widened at the eagerness in Kate's voice. 'No,' she replied, and saw Kate's disappointment. 'But your aunt had one. Look in her papers.'

Kate smiled gratefully. 'Thanks, Mum. I'll do that -'

Kate stopped mid-sentence, her eyes looking over her mother's shoulder. Turning to follow her gaze, Elizabeth saw a good-looking young man with dark blond hair buying something at the counter. Picking up a brown paper bag he turned to go, then caught sight of Kate and approached the table. Kate groaned inwardly, but gave David a tight smile as he greeted them.

'Professor Young,' Kate began. 'This is my mother, Elizabeth Grahame. Mum, this is Professor David Young.'

24

David politely extended his hand to shake Elizabeth's. 'It's a pleasure to meet you, Mrs Grahame,'

Kate saw her mother eye David shrewdly as she shook his hand. 'I hear you've been keeping my daughter working late. I trust you will ensure that she's paid for the extra hours.'

Kate gasped, mortified. '*Mum!*' she hissed under her breath, her face turning red. She looked at her plate in embarrassment.

David shuffled his feet, his face colouring slightly under Elizabeth's direct scrutiny. 'Of course, Mrs Grahame. I put in her overtime claim this morning.' He looked sympathetically at Kate. 'If you'll excuse me, I'll leave you to your lunch. Enjoy your day.' With a slight bow to Elizabeth, and a nod to Kate, David hastily retreated.

Elizabeth watched him through the window, and then turned to her blushing daughter with narrowed eyes. 'He does know that you're married?'

Kate passed her hand over her eyes in exasperation. 'Of course, Mum.'

'Hmm...' Elizabeth thought she had seen David look at Kate with more than friendly interest.

Kate watched the wheels turning in her mother's brain - in completely the wrong direction. 'Besides, people believe he's gay,' she whispered.

Her mother speared a piece of food with her fork. 'Really? He doesn't look like it!'

Jess laughed as Kate regaled her with an exaggerated account of her lunch with Elizabeth, which had ended with Kate promising to attend a family lunch at her brother's house on Sunday.

'David will probably want nothing more to do with me now!' Kate moaned, as they tidied the Education Centre after another class visit. 'I can't believe how she behaved! I didn't help out with the lecture for extra money.'

'I'm sure David knows that,' Jess consoled her. 'And how was our esteemed professor anyway?'

'He's extremely good at his job,' Kate said vaguely, avoiding eye contact. 'And he was really nice to me.'

Jess grinned at her friend's back. 'Did he reveal anything?' she asked, and spluttered with laughter at her own innuendo. Kate gave Jess a look of disdain and shook her head.

They worked quietly for a while, before Jess asked, 'Have you had any more dreams?'

Kate recounted her last dream in all its glorious detail, down to the scent of her dream fiancé's skin. She related the events of the dream to Jess, who thankfully did not look at her as if she were insane. When her tale was over, Kate sat on one of the hard chairs and stared wistfully at the floor, filled with longing for this mysterious man with the seductive smile and fathomless brown eyes.

Jess sat down next to her and patted Kate's knee sympathetically. Clearly these dreams were troubling Kate, and Jess had long suspected that her friend's emotional needs were not fulfilled by her husband.

'Do you think you're remembering a past life?' Jess inquired, out of the blue.

Kate looked at her friend and saw she was in earnest. 'I don't know. My Mum said we may have had an ancestor who had something to do with the museum, archaeology and Egypt. But I don't know anything about that. Apparently I have to look for my aunt's family tree. I hope it's with her papers and not buried with the spiders in the attic bedroom.'

'Would you consider trying past life regression?' Jess asked gently. 'My sister's a practitioner.'

Erin Mortimer had qualifications in a number of healing techniques, including hypnotherapy and Reiki. Far from being a New Age hippie, Erin worked from a comfortable office in her home in Great King Street. She dressed for work in comfortable, professional clothing which did not include flowery fabrics or sandals. Although she was fond of scented candles, Erin shunned heavily-perfumed incense sticks in her workplace. Kate had met Erin several times and had immediately warmed to her. She knew she would be safe in the care of this woman, who projected an air of calmness and practicality. Kate nodded mutely.

'Then let's set up an appointment,' Jess decided.

Kate sighed at her reflection in the bathroom mirror. She was dressed in her own clothes again which, although smart, were not what she would normally choose to wear for a night out. She had put on a little make-up and brushed her shining hair, but the ability to look effortlessly chic like her mother seemed beyond her grasp. A lock of her softly curling hair fell forward onto her cheek. For a moment, Kate looked deep into her own eyes. As she gazed searchingly at her reflection, the bathroom door opened slightly. Kate supposed someone had opened another door in the short hallway outside which led to the Egyptian gallery. The resulting draught caressed her cheek and blew the lock of hair from her face.

Sighing again, Kate put her make-up back in her handbag and returned to her office to lock up her desk. David had left a pile of books on her chair, along with a lecture timetable. A hand-written note lay on the top of the pile. 'It was nice to meet your mother today,' Kate read, wondering if his words held a note of irony. 'I'll pass along lecture notes when I have them. I hope you enjoy the books. Let me know if you want to discuss anything.' Kate's gaze softened as she looked at his elegant handwriting. Handling the books reverently, she locked them in the bottom drawer of her desk. Folding the timetable into her bag, she switched off the lights and headed off to meet her friends.

Kate longed to lay her head on the cloakroom reception desk and feel its coolness on her aching forehead. Instead, she sat up straight and pasted a convivial expression onto her pale face.

The night before had started innocently enough with a glass of wine at a bar in the Grassmarket. A very boisterous Nick had then persuaded Jess and Kate to go for a curry with him at a local Indian restaurant. Lots of rich and spicy food followed, with more alcohol. By the time Kate caught the bus home, it was very late. Although the alcohol she had consumed made her fall asleep as soon as her head hit the pillow, Kate tossed and turned restlessly for most of the night. She woke feeling exhausted and bloated from rich food her stomach was not accustomed to.

Kate had to spend the first hour of the morning on cloakroom duty. She valiantly tried to project an upbeat demeanour for the hordes of visitors who approached her with their coats and bags, but she was heartily glad when she was relieved from her post and could go and have some water and two more paracetamol. Thankfully, she was able to spend the next two hours working on the treasure hunt assigned to her by Adam Gray. Her target audience was eight-to-eleven year-olds, and the aim was to inspire them to explore as much of the museum as possible. The questions should encourage them to engage their brains, but not prove impossible to answer. Each answer should lead the explorer to the next clue. Clutching her trusty notebook and pen, Kate wandered around the museum and started to construct her clues. Her headache and indigestion were soon forgotten, as she became engrossed in her task.

At the end of her shift, Kate hurried to meet Jess at the National Gallery of Scotland. Jess had arranged for them to go to Erin's house later that afternoon for Kate's first session of regression therapy. As Jess explained to Kate what would happen at the session, Kate received a text from Mark. She was thrilled to learn that her husband had booked dinner at her favourite Italian restaurant for Monday evening, their wedding anniversary. Hearing the news, Jess dragged her friend around the shops to buy a seductive new outfit for her dinner date.

The afternoon passed quickly amid constant chatter and laughter. Kate loved Jess's company, finding her warm, vivacious and funny. Always keen to encourage Kate to step out of her comfort zone, Jess persuaded her to buy an outfit she would never have considered had she been shopping alone.

After a small snack in a department store café, the pair walked down the hill to Erin's flat in Great King Street. Erin greeted them with a wide smile similar to that of her younger sister. She ushered them into her warm and comfortable treatment room, painted in soft neutral tones. There was a tidy desk, two armchairs, and a healthy cheese plant in a large pot by the tall window. The Georgian fireplace housed a modern gas fire, and Erin had placed large crystals of various shapes and colours along the mantelpiece.

Erin put Kate at her ease very quickly, encouraging her to relax on the comfortable therapy couch. After asking questions about Kate's lifestyle and medical history, the therapist explained that she would record the session for Kate, so she could listen to it at home. Erin then asked Kate about her dreams. Kate glanced nervously at Jess, who sat on a chair beside the couch. As Jess nodded encouragingly, Kate relayed the details of her dreams in a halting voice. She was unaware that Erin was imperceptibly leading her into a trance state. As she answered Erin's questions, Kate felt as though she were being transported back into the world of her dreams.

And so, the story began...

CHAPTER 2

Katherine Grahame walked obediently behind her elegant mother, gazing distractedly at Eleanor Grahame's swishing navy skirts. As they crossed the Grand Gallery of the Edinburgh Museum of Science and Art, a group of suited men greeted them respectfully. Eleanor inclined her head in acknowledgement, sweeping past like an empress.

Nothing could be further from the truth. Kate's mother was a kind and loving woman who adored her husband and two children. Several times a week, she and Kate brought James Grahame lunch in a basket, prepared by Eleanor herself. Nevertheless, they were the museum director's wife and daughter and so had a certain image to maintain. The two women made their way between the neat rows of glass display cases and walked purposefully through the museum to the director's office.

Tom Flannigan, the director's Irish assistant, was working industriously at his desk in the outer office. He stood up hastily as Eleanor entered the room in her usual business-like fashion. 'Good morning, Mrs Grahame,' he stuttered, and glanced bashfully at Kate. 'Good morning, Miss Grahame. I'll just tell Professor Grahame that you're here.' He walked quickly to the oak door and knocked, before entering James Grahame's office. Kate adjusted her emerald green velvet hat, the pins pulling uncomfortably at her auburn hair. She smoothed a stray lock behind her ear just as Tom beckoned them into the office. Kate smiled in anticipation; she loved the wood-panelled room, with its globes and maps and countless books. Her father's massive desk was always cluttered with papers and little artefacts he had collected on his travels across the world. The room smelled of warm wood and cigar-smoke. As she stepped through the doorway, she noticed her father had company.

The other man in the room stood swiftly as the women entered, took Eleanor's proffered hand in greeting as her father introduced them. Kate's eyes widened, and she was rendered immobile. At nineteen, she had not met many young men, except for her brother's friends. Her parents had sheltered their sometimes headstrong daughter, so Kate was unprepared for the effect this tall, handsome man had on her. He quite took her breath away. In the same instant, she remembered that her hair was falling out of its artful arrangement under her little hat, and she had stepped in a puddle outside the museum and dirtied the hem of her dark green skirt.

'Katherine, are you coming in?' Her father's deep voice sounded faintly amused, and she spotted the same glint of mirth in her mother's eyes.

'Yes, Father.' Kate clutched the lunch basket in front of her like a shield and walked carefully into the room. Her father moved from behind the desk, kissed his daughter's cheek and took the basket from her. He smiled kindly at her over his bushy grey beard.

'This is my daughter, Katherine, lately finished at the Ladies' College,' he told the stranger. *Oh Lord, what did Father say his name was?* 'Katherine, this is Mister Edwin Ford.'

She held out her hand and the young man politely took her gloved fingers, bowing slightly. When he raised his eyes to hers, she noticed they were the darkest brown, like melting chocolate. His hair was almost black and neatly combed. She imagined it falling becomingly over his eyes, if only she could run her fingers through it...

Eleanor discreetly kicked Kate's ankle, unseen by the men in the room. Kate was staring, but so was this enigmatic young man. Eleanor glanced at her husband meaningfully.

'Mister Ford has just arrived from London with some of the new Egyptian artefacts,' he told the ladies, his hand on Edwin's shoulder. Kate noticed he had strong, broad shoulders but looked trim and athletic. Unlike the other men who worked in the museum, he was not wearing a suit and tie. His collarless shirt was open at the neck, with the sleeves rolled up to reveal tanned, muscular arms. He looked as though he had been on an archaeological expedition that very morning.

'Have you been in Egypt then, Mister Ford?' Eleanor asked.

'Yes, Mrs Grahame,' he replied. 'I work for the Egypt Exploration Fund, and I was fortunate enough to take part in an expedition to Southern Egypt. The standing monuments are much better preserved in the south of the country than the north.' He looked at Kate. 'They are quite breathtaking...'

'Isn't that because of the drier climate?' Kate asked, flushing under his direct gaze. She was delighted to see his surprise at her understanding of the Egyptian climate and how this affected the preservation of the country's ancient architecture.

'You are exactly right, Miss Grahame! An archaeological survey team is currently recording all the ancient monuments of the area before they are destroyed altogether.' Kate wondered where Edwin was from; his accent seemed both English and Scottish. He was well-spoken, his voice deep and soft.

'And will you be returning to Egypt?' Eleanor asked.

'I may return in a year or so, Mrs Grahame. My latest assignment was to escort the shipment of artefacts from Egypt to Edinburgh. I will remain here to help arrange their exhibition, but I will also spend some time working in London. I hope to join an expedition to Akhetaten in the future.' His eyes moved back to Kate.

'Is that not the city built by Akhenaten the heretic pharaoh?' Kate inquired.

Edwin was obviously impressed by Kate's knowledge. 'Yes! Some of the city has already been excavated, but the tomb of Akhenaten has yet to be located.'

'We can hope, then, that it has not been destroyed by raiders,' James sighed. He exchanged another meaningful look with his wife; they had work to do, and Kate was starting to squirm under the intense gaze of Edwin Ford.

'Well, Mister Ford, you must join us for tea. Would tomorrow at two o'clock suit?' Eleanor asked crisply.

'I would be delighted, Mrs Grahame,' he replied, smiling disarmingly at Eleanor.

Eleanor said farewell to the men, then swept out of the room. 'Come along, Katherine!' she commanded her daughter from the doorway.

Kate kissed her father quickly on the cheek. 'Enjoy your lunch, Father.' She lowered her voice so her mother wouldn't hear. 'I slipped in some Dundee cake.'

'Thank you, my pet,' James smiled, patting her cheek.

Kate turned to Edwin but couldn't quite meet his burning gaze again. 'Goodbye, Mister Ford.'

'Until tomorrow, Miss Grahame.'

Cheeks flaming, Kate hurriedly followed her mother out of the museum, down the imposing flight of steps which led to the street.

'He seems to be a very nice young man,' Eleanor commented. She cast a sidelong glance at her daughter. 'He's certainly very handsome.'

'Do you think so?' Kate replied, trying to be nonchalant. 'I didn't notice.'

Eleanor covered her mouth and coughed to stifle her laughter.

Kate was unable to concentrate on anything the next morning. She wandered down to the kitchen with the intention of baking something for afternoon tea. Mrs Riley, their cook, was in turn amused and alarmed as the nervous young woman spoiled first one batch of scones, then another. Finally, she suggested Kate try a simple Victoria sponge before they ran out of flour and currants altogether. At one o'clock, Kate rushed to her room to change, but each outfit she dragged from her wardrobe seemed unsuitable. Eleanor carried on with her morning's duties unflustered as always, but observed her daughter flying about the house looking wide-eyed and flushed. She sent the maid into Kate's room to help her to dress, and checked on their progress after twenty minutes had passed. She found Kate dressed and sitting at her dressing table, looking critically at her reflection. Taking up Kate's brush, she pulled the boar hair bristles through Kate's long tresses with soothing strokes.

'You've had a busy morning,' Eleanor commented drily.

'I wanted to bake for Father,' Kate said defensively. 'It's not often he joins us for tea. And John will be coming, too.'

Eleanor smiled perceptively. Kate loved her older brother but had never so much as made him a sandwich before. 'Are you sure you can breathe in that dress?'

Kate had chosen a simple lavender day dress but had asked the maid to pull her corset laces as tightly as possible. Her waist was now tiny, but Kate hoped desperately that she wouldn't faint. She would have some tea, but no cake. Eleanor pinned up Kate's silky locks and secured them with a mother-of-pearl comb. She sat back to admire her beautiful daughter, whose eyes were like saucers.

'You look very beautiful, dear,' Eleanor told her, as she heard her son calling up the stairs to them. *Thank goodness,* Eleanor thought to herself. *John will distract her.*

Eleanor stood to greet her husband as he entered the parlour. Edwin came in behind him, looking smart in a dark grey suit. Eleanor watched his eyes sweep the room in search of Kate. Edwin frowned when he saw her giggling with a curly-haired young man in the corner of the room, her hand resting on his arm.

Eleanor cleared her throat. 'Mister Ford, it's nice to see you again. You haven't met our son, John.'

Edwin looked relieved as he shook Kate's brother's hand, seeing the family resemblance after all. John was studying law at Edinburgh University, though James often commented that there seemed to be more high jinks going on than attention to the Scottish legal system. Before Edwin could turn his attention to Kate, Eleanor bid them sit down. The maid brought in the groaning tea tray and set it on the sideboard. As Eleanor handed round cake, commenting wryly that Kate had insisted on baking for her father and brother, she nodded to Kate to pour the tea.

With a great deal of concentration, poor Kate managed to pour the tea into cups and add milk and sugar. *If I don't look at him, I won't be nervous.* Holding her breath, she handed the first cup to Edwin, her hand trembling. The china cup rattled traitorously against the saucer. She glanced at him from beneath her lashes as he smiled his thanks, his fingers lightly brushing hers. As she handed the next cup to her mother, Eleanor smiled sympathetically and patted her daughter's hand. Kate quietly finished her duties and sat down next to John, who was smirking at her discomfort.

Afterwards, Kate had little memory of what was discussed at afternoon tea. The weather, surely, and the upcoming museum staff dinner at the Merchant's Hall. Eleanor had mentioned the spring ball at Major Ramsay's house. John had talked about his studies and his grand plans for the future. James and Edwin had discussed ideas for the future Egyptian exhibition. Kate sat quietly, dutifully letting the men talk and wishing her corset wasn't so tight. She sipped her tea, thankful that her mother refreshed everyone's cups. She couldn't remember everything Edwin said, but she remembered the sound of his rich, velvety voice. She remembered his deep brown eyes and his long fingers gently holding her mother's best china. He made her so nervous and unsettled that she was glad when he and her father returned to the museum.

As they were saying goodbye, Eleanor invited Edwin to dinner the following week. Gazing at Kate, Edwin readily accepted. He held out his hand to Kate to wish her farewell. This time he bowed his head over her fingers, and Kate thought he might kiss them. But no, he was unfailingly polite. As James and Edwin left the room with Eleanor following behind them, John whispered, 'You can breathe now!'

Edwin Ford became a regular visitor to the Grahame house on Heriot Row, especially since he had conveniently rented a room on nearby Hanover Street. His job was to help the museum create a memorable and accessible exhibition of ancient Egyptian artefacts from their own collection, as well as persuading other collectors to lend pieces for display. James and Edwin attended many meetings to negotiate with these collectors, and also persuaded members of the press to advertise the exhibition which was set to open in May. Edwin supervised the members of staff who were responsible for preparing the artefacts for display, and liaised with the carpenters who were commissioned to build special display cases. In addition, he had compiled a precise directory of each item in the exhibition. He was supposed to use this information to create an interesting catalogue for visitors. As a man who thrived on activity, he found this the most difficult task of all.

Edwin and James spent many hours sequestered in the study in Heriot Row, and Edwin was invited to dinner several times a week. James introduced him to friends and colleagues, and so Edwin became very popular with other families, too, especially those with eligible daughters. This did not escape Kate's notice, but she was far too proud to vie for Edwin's attentions. She quietly continued with her usual activities when he was in the house, although he seemed intent on drawing her into conversation at every opportunity, and she often caught him watching her. Nevertheless, she was frequently surprised to find she was thinking about him; his handsome face would appear uninvited in her mind's eye. He adopted the habit of hanging his coat on the newel post of the staircase, and Kate could never resist touching it as she passed, her fingers caressing the soft dark wool.

By the beginning of March, the ice had gone from the streets and Eleanor took to walking out once again. One of her regular activities was to help at the soup kitchen for the poor at Greyfriars. She and Kate walked up through Princes Street Gardens to the Grassmarket and spent the morning handing out hot food. At lunchtime, Eleanor sat down with a cup of tea and a scone, and asked her daughter to take James's lunch basket to him at the museum. She claimed that the steep hill of Candlemaker Row might still be icy, and she feared she might fall. Kate knew her mother was no fragile old lady, but she smiled her assent, picked up the basket and strode up Candlemaker Row and across the road to Chambers Street.

Neither Tom nor James was in the director's office. Kate set the basket on the desk, intending to leave her father a note. Her eyes fell upon an open atlas on the desk, its pages displaying a map of the world. Kate traced her fingers pensively over the deep blue of the Indian Ocean, the icy white of the North Pole. Scotland was a tiny green patch, Edinburgh not noted at all. The top of Kate's head prickled, and she looked up. There he was, standing in the doorway watching her. Edwin Ford, looking crumpled with his sleeves rolled up. She wanted to

34

remark haughtily that it was rude to stare, but decided instead to appear demure.

'I was looking for your father,' he began. Kate shrugged, gesturing at the empty room. 'Just you?'

'Just me,' she replied with a sigh. 'I was going to leave a note, but then I began admiring this beautiful atlas.'

Edwin remained in the doorway; at this stage in their acquaintance, it would not be considered appropriate for him to be in a room alone with her. Then again, he could see Tom advancing on him from across the gallery floor. Moving quickly to stand next to her, he looked at the page which had caught her attention.

'Where would you like to go?' he inquired, admiring the delicate architecture of her ear.

Kate pointed to Italy, gazing wistfully at the boot-shaped peninsula. 'I want to visit Rome, and Florence, and Venice. Perhaps Sicily, where there are fewer people and the sea is turquoise blue.' She longed to swim in the ocean.

'Where else?'

'I might like to visit Paris, to put all those boring French lessons to good use.' She smiled timidly as Edwin chuckled.

Edwin was pleased to find she had a sense of humour; he had met so many young women who were seemingly bereft of wit. He noticed her smile lit up her perfectly oval face, and she had the sweetest dimples at the corners of her beautifully curved mouth.

A resolute bachelor, Edwin had indulged in several dalliances over the years, always with open-minded women who cared little for convention. In his travels, he had sampled the carnal delights of the Orient and Paris. But no woman had ever distracted him from his work - until now. Katherine Grahame was barely out of school pinafores and hair ribbons, but she was never far from his thoughts. Something about her tugged at his heart strings...

'I love the sea best, I think.' Kate's sweet voice interrupted his thoughts. 'It would be wonderful to swim in the sea - if it weren't too cold. Where have you travelled to, Mister Ford?'

He pointed to China, then Egypt, then Greece, then Italy, his fingers walking ever closer to hers where they rested on France. He inhaled deeply, greedily breathing in the faint smell of violets which emanated from her.

James cleared his throat loudly as he strode into the room. 'Now, Katherine, I hope you're not keeping Mister Ford from his work!'

They had done nothing wrong, but both Kate and Edwin managed to look guilty.

'No sir,' Edwin spoke up. 'It was rather the other way around. I interrupted Miss Grahame -'

'I was looking at this wonderful atlas, Father. I brought your lunch...'

'Where's your mother, child?'

'She's at Greyfriars. She was concerned about ice on Candlemaker Row.'

James pursed his lips at his wife's deviousness. 'You should get back to her, then.' He leaned down so she could kiss his cheek. Kate nodded her farewell to Edwin, and then started for the door. 'Lass!' James called after her. She turned. 'Is there anything nice in here?' He indicated the basket.

Kate smiled broadly. 'Aye, Father,' she replied, imitating his Scots brogue. 'A wee bit clootie dumpling.'

Edwin looked mystified, and James grinned. 'Ach, you're a lassie after my own heart!'

Edwin was once again in James's study that evening when Kate brought her father a cup of tea. She nearly walked into him as she backed through the study door carrying the cup and saucer on a small tray. He quickly apologised as she set the tea on her father's desk.

'Would you like some tea, Mister Ford?' she asked dutifully. Edwin declined, equally polite. She saw that he had been running his fingers through his hair, as some of the dark strands had fallen over his eye. He looked a little exasperated.

James looked slyly at the pair over his teacup. 'Perhaps you should let Katie have a look at your catalogue. I'm sure she will have an opinion,' he suggested to Edwin.

Kate looked flustered. 'No,' she stuttered, plucking imaginary lint from her skirt. 'I'm sure I won't be much help at all.'

James snorted; the girl was more opinionated than any man he'd ever met. 'Edwin's having trouble compiling his catalogue,' James explained.

Edwin was looking at Kate hopefully, brandishing several pieces of paper. 'Please, Miss Grahame, I would welcome any suggestions you may have. I'm more at home digging in the desert than writing at a desk. Words do not come easily to me - especially when I have to write them.' He grinned ruefully.

He pulled up a chair so that she might sit, and set the papers before her. Kate scowled at her father, but began to read. Edwin had beautiful penmanship, although many of the words had been scratched out and there was a lot of scribbling in the margins of each page. He had itemised each item in the collection, but what he had written was as dry as the desert he apparently called home. Kate absently picked up a pen from her father's desk, twirled it between her fingers. Edwin watched her put the pen to her lips, deep in thought. She stood up and looked at the men uncertainly.

Here it comes, James thought to himself.

Kate took a deep breath. 'This sarcophagus you mention here,' she pointed to the page. 'To you, it's an "anthropoid coffin with black-painted lappet wig, gilded face, black painted eyebrows and inlaid stone eyes." To me, it's a wondrous, mysterious work of art which tells a story. It held the body of an important man - who was he? What did he do? What was his life like? You wish to attract visitors from all over the country and from all walks of life, do you not?'

'Yes,' he replied with a helpless shrug.

'Then you must make your catalogue more attractive and accessible to everyone, not just stuffy archaeologists.'

He was visibly nettled by her comment. 'Are you saying I should romanticise the catalogue? It was not my intention to produce a lady's periodical!'

Kate refrained from rolling her eyes, but caught her father hiding a smile behind his cup. 'Well, perhaps you should consider romanticising it a little. People should know something of ancient Egyptian life, in order to place the items in context. Otherwise, they are simply looking at objects from a long time ago, nothing more. You have to find a way to bring each item to life, so that people also see the relevance and beauty in each piece.' Kate sat on the edge of her chair, embarrassed because Edwin was looking dumbfounded, and possibly a little offended. 'I'm sorry if I have spoken out of turn,' she mumbled.

James looked up at Edwin, who was struggling to find something to say. 'Katie could maybe help you,' he suggested, grinning impishly at his daughter. 'She has a way with words.'

Kate groaned silently. 'I already have duties to attend to for Mother,' she protested.

'Your mother could spare you for a while, lass. There's only so much tea and gossip a woman like you can take.'

That much was certainly true. Kate looked down at her hands, and waited modestly for Edwin to decide. Edwin decided not to waste the opportunity. 'I would greatly appreciate any help Miss Grahame could provide, if she can spare the time. '

'Well that's settled,' James said happily. 'Katie, I'll ask your mother if you may come to work with me in the morning. All our best

Egyptology books and manuscripts are in my office at the museum. You can use them for reference.'

Kate looked up, her eyes wide with pleasure. 'I can work in your office?'

'Aye, I'll get you a desk. But you only have a week before the catalogue needs to go to the printers.'

Kate's eyes were aglow at the thought of going to work. Edwin's eyes lit up for quite a different reason.

Although Eleanor grumbled about Kate working at the museum, she sent the pair off in the morning with a basket of food. Kate was quickly installed at a desk in a corner of her father's office, and James made sure she was settled before going off on his daily rounds. Edwin had left his notes with Tom, along with his own detailed sketches of the exhibition pieces. Kate would not have access to the artefacts until they were unpacked and ready for display, but the information she had would be sufficient. She set to work immediately and enthusiastically, using James's books to research ancient Egyptian history. Although she kept to the facts about each piece's provenance and use, she wove history and speculation around each object to try and capture the imagination of the reader. Words flowed quickly and easily from Kate's pen. She hardly registered Tom bringing her a cup of tea halfway through the morning, lingering near her desk in the hope that she might look up and smile at him. Instead, she murmured a distracted 'thank you' and continued to write.

At around lunchtime, Kate heard a deep voice outside the office and the subsequent shuffling of feet.

'Have you boys nothing better to do than stand around out here?' Edwin barked. 'Go on about your duties!' He stuck his head around the open office door. 'Have you been holding court, Miss Grahame? It's like Waverley Station out here!'

Kate was indignant. 'I can assure you I have been working all morning, Mister Ford. I've not even had lunch!'

Edwin strolled in carrying two mugs. He set one down before her. 'Then it's time you stopped. I made you some tea.'

Kate sniffed. Whatever Edwin was drinking had the most delicious, spicy smell. She pointed at his mug. 'What are you drinking?

'It's Arabic coffee. I bought it in Cairo. Would you like to try it?' He held out the mug to her and watched as she inhaled its strong aroma. Closing her eyes, she took a sip. It tasted bitter but was deliciously smoky and almost syrupy. Edwin raised an eyebrow in admiration;

ladies generally turned their noses up at the strong taste of Arabic coffee.

'Thank you, Mister Ford.' She handed him the mug, careful to avoid touching his fingers.

'Did you like it?' He sounded incredulous.

'I liked it very much.' She watched, wide-eyed, as he deliberately drank from the edge of the cup where her lips had been. 'Have you come to check on my progress?'

'No, I came to drive the wolves from your door.' He gestured towards the hallway. 'But I'm happy to read what you have written.'

She gave him several sheets of paper, and he started to read. His brow furrowed as his eyes moved over her neat writing. Kate watched him carefully as she drank her tea, looking for signs of disapproval. He was near the end before he said, 'Item 52a, the small alabaster pot. We cannot assume the pot belonged to a queen and held "an intoxicating exotic perfume".'

'Can you say emphatically that it did not?'

'No, but -'

'Have you smelled the pot?'

'No.'

'Was the pot not found in a royal tomb? Belonging to a queen?'

'Yes, but we don't know for sure that the pot belonged to her!'

'You would rather I just called it "item 52a, small alabaster pot", then?'

Edwin knew he had lost, and sighed in defeat. 'I bow to your superior knowledge of what will appeal to the imagination of ladies.'

Kate gave him a sly, sideways look. 'From what I hear, Mister Ford, you know a great deal about the things which appeal to ladies.'

'Apparently not all ladies find me so appealing!' he huffed, and left the room. Kate giggled and went back to work.

James was on his way to have lunch with Kate when he met Edwin in the hallway. He noticed the young man's pained expression. 'You've been to see Katie?' he asked.

'Yes,' Edwin replied tightly. James nodded, understanding. The Grahame women were a handful.

'Mrs Grahame expects you for dinner.'

'It's no intrusion?'

'Not at all!' James looked slyly at Edwin. 'Katie has a dinner engagement with Alastair Scott and his sister.'

Edwin's expression darkened ever so slightly. 'Oh?'

'Miss Scott is a school friend of Katie's. Her older brother works in a bank. Nice young fellow. Good prospects.' James could tell Edwin was troubled by this news. 'Between you and me, I think he has hopes for our girl. Poor lad! Of course, John will be acting as Katie's chaperone tonight. So, Edwin, we'll see you this evening at the usual time.' James continued to his office, leaving a contemplative Edwin in his wake.

The next morning Kate was walking along the corridor to her father's office when she saw Edwin sitting in the office next door. The room was barely bigger than a broom closet and contained only a desk, two chairs and a small bookcase. Edwin sat with his back to the door, his long legs perched on the corner of the desk. He was sketching with a piece of charcoal, his hand moving confidently across the paper.

'Good morning, Mister Ford,' Kate called in as she passed. Edwin stopped his work immediately and followed her into James's office. As she unpinned her hat, Kate noticed a small vase of yellow crocuses and an apple on her desk. Tom came rushing in with some tea, bidding her a shy good morning before hastening out again under Edwin's dark glower. Kate blushed, flustered under Edwin's accusing stare.

'Looks like you've gained at least one new admirer,' he commented sourly. Kate felt secretly disappointed that he hadn't been the one to leave the offering on her desk. 'How was dinner?' he went on, sarcasm heavy in his tone.

'It was very nice, thank you.' She refrained from providing details of her evening, wondering why he was being so objectionable. And why couldn't the man wear a suit to work like her father and the other employees? Once again he was wearing a shirt open at the collar, the sleeves rolled up to reveal those strong, suntanned arms…

'I'll leave you to your tea. Please let me know if you need help with anything.' Once again, he strode crossly out of the office. Kate sighed, shook her head in bewilderment, and took up her pen.

Kate asked Edwin to inspect her notes that afternoon. They sat in the office while James worked quietly at his desk, but Kate and Edwin started bickering almost immediately. Edwin took issue with what he termed Kate's fanciful ideas. Kate argued that her work might allow people a brief opportunity to escape their everyday lives and engage their imagination. She claimed she was attempting to bring a civilization to life, while he seemed intent on merely itemising artefacts as if he were writing a shopping list. James could barely contain his mirth, but it was clear that Kate and Edwin were angry about something other than an exhibition guide.

Thankfully, Edwin was called away to attend to his duties and did not reappear for the rest of the day. She did not see him the following day, either, so Kate took her work home and spent the evening rewriting the guide. She toned down the language to make it less 'fanciful' and included more of the facts as Edwin had written them. In the morning, she sat in the director's office with the door closed and finished the guide completely. Then she gathered up the stack of papers and, safe in the knowledge that Edwin was elsewhere in the building, she placed them neatly on his desk.

He had left his sketch pad face down on the desk. Kate listened for footsteps in the hall, before turning over the pad to look at his work. Her own face stared back at her, her eyes soft and glowing, a teasing smile on her full lips. Her expression was serene and loving. Kate's breath caught in her throat. Edwin had caught every detail of her features, right down to the lock of hair which never stayed in place, and the sprinkling of freckles across her nose. He had made her look so...beautiful. Did she really look like that? Had Edwin seen her looking at him with such tenderness? Kate blushed with embarrassment at the thought of her possible indiscretion.

Perturbed, Kate returned to James's office and closed the door. She paced restlessly for a while, wishing she could go home or talk to Sarah. Scanning her father's shelf of first editions, she pulled out a copy of 'Jane Eyre' and sat down. Although she tried to read, her thoughts were scattered and kept returning to Edwin's skilful fingers lovingly creating her image on paper. She wondered then about his feelings for her, and why they kept irritating each other. She was so intent on trying to control her churning mind, that she didn't hear the quiet knock on the door, or the door opening. When she finally glanced up from the page, she saw a steaming mug of coffee being set on the desk before her by a familiar, long-fingered hand. Edwin sat on the edge of the desk and quietly gazed down at her as he sipped from his own mug. She looked pensive today, and her cheeks were flushed. He glanced at the title of her book.

'You're reading Bronte?' he asked. 'A story of unrequited love and stifled passion, by any chance?'

'Only until the end,' she murmured sheepishly. She looked up and saw he was holding a plate.

'I thought you might like to share my lunch,' he said kindly, and set the plate down. The sandwich consisted of two slices of bread like doorstops with a wedge of cheese in the middle, but he had cut it into four pieces to make it more manageable. She thanked him, and bit into the soft bread.

41

'I read your guide,' he said evenly. 'You re-wrote it.' Kate's stomach tightened; would he know she had looked at his drawing? Should she say something?

'Did you like it?'

'Very much.'

They ate silently for a while and drank the hot coffee. Both were contrite.

'Friends again?' Edwin asked softly, although he was beginning to realise he wanted much more than friendship.

James walked into the room and raised a bushy eyebrow at the scene before him, curious as to what he had interrupted. 'Katherine, you have visitors,' he told her, busying himself at his desk.

Sarah Scott floated into the room, her brother following sedately behind her. Kate rose immediately and went to embrace her friend.

'Here you are!' Sarah exclaimed. She smoothed Kate's errant hair back from her face and wiped affectionately at a smudge of ink on her cheek. 'We've come to rescue you from this stuffy place!'

'We thought you might care for a walk in the Gardens, Miss Katherine,' Alastair Scott spoke up in his soft voice. He was an affable young man of twenty-three, with blond hair and moustache, and bright blue eyes. 'It is a particularly fine day.' Alastair looked pointedly at Edwin, who stood looking dark and brooding behind Kate.

Following his gaze, Kate remembered her manners and introduced them. James watched the two men size each other up like a pair of young stags, while an oblivious Kate chattered to Sarah.

'We've just put a new suit of armour on display,' James spoke up. 'Why don't I take you two to see it while Katie finishes up here? She can meet you at the front of the building.' He led Sarah and Alastair from the room.

Kate turned to Edwin. He was looking cross again. She tilted her head enquiringly.

'I've been referred to as "stuffy" twice in one week!' he grumbled.

'Oh, stop doing your Heathcliff impression, for goodness sake!' Kate exclaimed. 'I'm sure that Sarah was referring to the building,' she continued, in an attempt to mollify him. 'And you know perfectly well that I did not refer to you as being "stuffy".' He looked unappeased, so she said, 'Thank you for lunch. Please tell me if you need me to make any alterations to the guide. If not, I'll not need to return. I'm sure Father will be pleased to have his office back.'

Edwin watched her pull on her coat and hat, and check her appearance in the small mirror in the corner of the room. Her cheeks were pink, her eyes shining. *Is that the effect Alastair Scott has on her?*

'I'm sure you will be missed,' Edwin replied. She smiled up at him as she walked past, leaving the faint scent of violets in the room.

At the end of March, Eleanor decided to host a dinner for some of their friends. Unlike many of her peers, Kate willingly accepted domestic duties, and spent the day helping the household prepare for the event. The Grahames, though comfortably well-off and respected in Edinburgh society, kept only a small staff. Eleanor had accompanied her husband on expeditions around the world and had been both housewife and companion. She had learned to cook, launder, iron and sew, and wanted her daughter to learn the same. The Grahame women did not fill their days with idle pursuits, although both enjoyed strolling to Princes Street to eye the latest fashions in the window displays of Jenners. Kate offered her services to Mrs Riley, and was instructed to knead bread dough. The cook hoped that the restless girl would benefit from the repetitive, almost meditative action. When that was done, Kate started to peel potatoes, until Eleanor found her.

'Katherine Grahame!' Eleanor scolded. 'You'll have hands like a navvy! Come upstairs and help me lay the table.'

After a few words with Mrs Riley about the meal, Eleanor took Kate to the dining room, where their elderly butler Andrews was polishing the cutlery with a white cloth. Kate counted ten places at the long oak table.

'Who's coming, Mother?' she asked distractedly, as she prepared the place settings.

Eleanor sighed impatiently, as she had discussed the guest list with Kate only hours before. Her daughter had been behaving in a decidedly airy-fairy way, of late.

'Alastair Scott and Sarah will be joining us, along with Major and Mrs Ramsay and their daughter, Louisa.'

Kate grimaced. Louisa was only two years older than Kate, but acted as if she were the height of sophistication. Whenever she met John, she simpered coquettishly. *All powder and no common sense,* Kate thought.

'And of course, Mister Ford,' Eleanor continued, casting a sidelong glance at her daughter. 'He has become very popular since his arrival in Edinburgh. The Ramsays have all but adopted him, it seems. He has been at their house for dinner several times, and attended a concert at the Lyceum with them two nights ago. His efforts to bring those artefacts to Edinburgh instead of them ending up in London have impressed all the right people. Your father says he will go far.'

'That's nice...' Kate replied vaguely. Her thoughts turned again to Louisa. She knew the Ramsays were searching for a suitable match for their daughter, and would obviously be looking for a young man with promising prospects.

'Where shall I sit you, Katherine?'

Kate looked blankly at her mother. Usually Kate sat where she was put. 'Between you and John,' she suggested wilfully.

Eleanor frowned at her peevishly. 'You know very well I cannot do that. It would be impolite to our guests. You can sit next to Mister Ford or Mister Scott.'

Kate narrowed her eyes suspiciously. 'Put me next to Mister Scott, then.'

John arrived an hour before dinner, in order to update his father on the progress of his studies. He was a gregarious young man of twenty-four who earnestly wished to become a lawyer, and did not want to disappoint his loving parents. He willingly submitted himself to these interviews in order to reassure his father that he was working. Not that it was necessary, as John's tutor knew James from their own schooldays. When he saw Kate in her old day dress, he laughed.

'Is that the latest fashion, Katie?' he teased. 'You must be sure to tell Louisa!'

Kate poked out her tongue at him. 'I'm just going to get ready, and I'm sure I couldn't tell Louisa anything about the latest fashion that she doesn't already know.'

John took his sister's hand and pushed a stray hair from her face. 'Come now, Katie. You are more beautiful than her, even dressed as a scarecrow!'

'John, please don't tease me today. My head already aches.'

'I'm a law student - I speak only the truth. And there will be those here this evening who would heartily agree with me.' He saw her blush. They both knew that Alastair Scott had a crush on Kate. He had a good position in the bank, and Kate knew her parents would think him a good match. To Kate, Alastair's position in society was irrelevant. She had no intention of encouraging him, even though Sarah was her best friend. She had tried to show him that she was only interested in his friendship, but he seemed undeterred by her polite indifference.

'Don't do your laces so tight this time!' John warned her, as Kate climbed the stairs to her room. 'You have to eat tonight!'

Kate spent too long in the bath, enjoying the warm water and allowing her mind to drift. By the time she climbed out, the water was nearly cold. Her gown was already laid out on the bed in her bright and airy room. Her mother had asked her to wear her rose-coloured gown, which showed off her shoulders and slender arms, and complemented her colouring. She took John's advice and asked the maid to tighten her corset just a little, wryly supposing that Louisa's waist would measure a hand's span, and she would look like a heifer by comparison. She added a very simple necklace and earrings. Her hair was pulled gently from her face and fastened at the back of her head with small pearl pins, the tresses left to sit over one shoulder in a silky rope. Kate heard voices in the vestibule as the maid finished arranging her hair.

She dismissed the maid and sat at her dressing table a few moments longer, preparing herself. Despite her intelligence and ready wit, Kate was not confident in social situations. Her opinions had led her into trouble in the past, so she tried now to sit quietly and simply make small talk when necessary. But she hated to appear submissive and mindless. *Every young man's dream,* she thought dryly. Sighing, she slipped on her ivory evening shoes, with the little heel and the bow at the front. She loved the shoes, but they would be hurting her feet by the end of the evening. *Thank goodness I'll be sitting down. Men are so lucky!*

The maid appeared at the door again. 'Miss, your mother says you've to come down directly.'

With a final look in the mirror, Kate left the sanctuary of her room and hurried down the curved staircase to the parlour, where the guests had already assembled.

John was waiting at the bottom of the stairs for her and greeted her with a wide grin. 'Did you fall asleep in the bath again?' he whispered, earning himself an elbow in the ribs. He saw she was nervous; Louisa Ramsay always managed to intimidate his little sister. 'I can tell you with all certainty that you are the most beautiful girl in the house tonight.'

She gave him a grateful smile and kissed his cheek. Arm-in-arm, they entered the parlour.

The room was warm, the cosy atmosphere enhanced by candles and a roaring fire. The crystal sherry glasses sparkled in the light. The room was alive with chatter and laughter. Kate and John slipped in unnoticed by everyone except Major Ramsay, who immediately involved John in a discussion about the latest law passed by Parliament. Kate moved as far into the corner as she was able, using John's imposing height as cover. Andrews had finished pouring sherry and brought the decanter to the small side table where Kate stood. He helpfully stood beside the table in readiness, providing Kate with a little more shelter.

'Thank you, Andrews,' she whispered. Andrews nodded once in acknowledgement.

Kate surveyed the room. Her mother was gossiping with Sarah and the supercilious Mrs Ramsay, while James had joined John and Major Ramsay. Over by the fireplace, Kate spotted Edwin, barely recognisable in a dark dinner suit. He was talking with Louisa. They were laughing, she batting her eyelashes and touching her bare throat. And he, all intense brown eyes, giving her his full attention. Kate felt enraged, jealous and defeated all at once. *Perhaps he sketches lots of young women,* she thought. *I expect I'm not the only one who looks at him all doe-eyed.*

'Miss Katherine, are you hiding?' a gentle voice asked. She turned to Alastair Scott, immediately adopting her role as supporting hostess. She smiled at the young man, who tried in vain to impress her at every opportunity.

'Merely surveying the territory, Mister Scott. Are you and Sarah well? How are your parents?' Her façade in place, she allowed Alastair to lead her into dinner.

Kate sat between Alastair and Mrs Ramsay, with John's reassuring presence opposite her. He touched his toes to hers in a gesture of camaraderie. He had been placed between Sarah and Louisa, and Kate noticed that Sarah frequently glanced at John with shy admiration; John was attentive and entertaining, and he looked very handsome in his dinner attire. Kate tried her best to be amicable, without being controversial. At James's end of the table, Louisa reigned as queen. She hardly spoke to John at all, but lavished all her attention and considerable charms on Edwin Ford. Although Kate occasionally glanced in his direction, Edwin never once looked her way. Resignedly, she accepted that she was no match for the older girl. After all, Louisa had travelled all over Europe, and probably had much in common with the globetrotting archaeologist. And there was no doubt she had been graced with a more womanly figure than Kate. Louisa was, indeed, more sophisticated than she. Kate ate her meal but found the food tasteless.

After dinner, the men followed tradition and congregated in James's study for port and cigars, while the ladies returned to the parlour. Sarah and Kate sat quietly, occasionally trying to converse with one another. The Ramsay women had a lot to say, however, about their recent trip to Europe. They passed on the latest gossip, tutted at so-and-so's daughter who had found herself 'compromised'. Louisa was looking immensely pleased with herself, Kate thought, like the cat who had eaten all the cream.

When the heat and endless chatter finally became unbearable, Kate turned to her mother. 'Please, Mother, may I be excused?' she asked, her voice low and her gaze imploring. 'It's late, and I have a horrible headache.'

Eleanor instinctively placed her hand on her daughter's hot brow. 'Yes, of course, dear. Put some lavender oil on your pillow. I'll come and see you later.'

Kate said goodnight, embracing Sarah and promising to visit her soon. As she left the uncomfortably stuffy parlour, the men drifted out of the study, still busy putting the world to rights. John, who had grown bored with their discussion, spotted Kate crossing the hall and making a hasty dash for the stairs.

Catching up with her, John caught her arm and pulled her out of the line of sight. 'Are you all right?' he asked, concerned. 'You look pale. Why are there tears in your eyes?'

She quickly wiped her eyes. 'There are no tears, John. I'm tired, that's all, and I have a headache. Mother has excused me. I'm hardly needed to keep the conversation going, in any case. I have nothing sensational to say...'

John embraced her gently, kissing the top of her head. 'You're still the most beautiful girl in the house. And tonight you were even the quietest. A first for you.'

'John, can't you ever just give me a compliment?' Kate chided, smiling in spite of herself.

'I'm sorry, sweet. Can I escort you to church tomorrow, milady?'

'Thank you, sir. That would be lovely.' She kissed his cheek as he let her go.

Kate looked up at the sound of footsteps. Edwin had wandered out of the study behind the others and had overheard Kate and John at the foot of the stairs. His face stern, John nodded to Edwin as he walked past him and took up a position in the doorway of the parlour, where he could pretend to listen to their guests and at the same time keep a brotherly eye on Kate.

Kate was on the second step of the stairs, now at Edwin's eye level. They were silent for a moment, Edwin's gaze devouring her while she looked down at her aching feet. Even pale and tired, she was stunning. No rouge or powder coloured her face. When she had first come into the parlour that evening, her cheeks had been pink, and her eyes had sparkled. She needed no cosmetics or adornments to enhance her loveliness. Anywhere would be made more beautiful by her presence there. He wished he could say those words to her, but all he could manage was, 'You're not well?'

47

Kate kept her expression neutral. 'I have a headache, that's all. I'll be better in the morning.'

'Mister Scott is a very agreeable gentleman.' His eyes narrowed slightly, gauging her reaction.

'You seem to find Miss Ramsay agreeable also, Mister Ford!' Kate snapped.

'She is quite vivacious,' he replied tactfully.

Kate's blood boiled. 'Yes, all the young men seem to think so! Please excuse me, Mister Ford. I would like to retire to my room now.' She began to climb the stairs, carefully lifting the hem of her gown. Edwin stretched out his hand and lightly touched her arm to stop her. John stopped leaning on the door frame and swiftly moved towards them.

'Miss Grahame,' Edwin said softly, hearing John's approach. 'I would consider anything you had to say to be of great interest, even if it's not sensational -'

John reached for Kate's arm. 'If you'll please excuse us, Mister Ford, I'll take my sister to her room now. Come along, Katie.'

Once John delivered her to her room, Kate slumped on her bed and cried herself to sleep.

CHAPTER 3

Kate always tried to listen attentively to the sermon, but failed miserably every Sunday. The minister had a melodic, soothing voice which made her very drowsy indeed. Reverend Phillips usually preached kindness and tolerance, with hardly ever a mention of Hellfire and Brimstone. Every week Kate felt awash with guilt when she felt her eyelids grow heavy. This Sunday, however, she felt much worse. Eleanor had gone to check on her daughter after their guests had departed the night before, finding her asleep on her bed and still wearing her gown. Deciding not to wake Kate, she carefully loosened her daughter's dress and corset and covered her with a blanket. This morning, Kate's body ached from having slept in her constrictive clothing. She looked tired and pale, her complexion made starker by the dark blue outfit she wore to church. She sat between her father and brother, hiding behind her hymn book. If only she could rest her head on John's or her father's shoulder, she could go back to sleep.

After the service at Saint John's Church the family always took a walk in Princes Street Gardens, often joined by friends who shared the same habits. This Sunday was no different, with Eleanor joining a group of matrons to stroll along the upper path by the dormant rose beds. James joined some colleagues by the railway bridge near the bandstand. John took Kate's arm and led her past the empty bandstand to look at the glorious fountain, the water sparkling in the pale spring sunlight. Kate turned her face to the sun and looked up at Edinburgh Castle, the imposing guardian of the city atop the jagged peak which had never been scaled. They walked along the lower path between the trees and shrubs, where snowdrops and crocuses waved gently in the breeze. Early blossom drifted down from the trees and fell on the grass.

'We're going to keep walking, Katie,' John said quietly, his hand at her elbow. 'For Louisa Ramsay is not far behind and my ears are still ringing from last night.'

Kate looked over her shoulder and saw Louisa some way behind them, walking with Edwin. She was talking animatedly and laughing a lot. Kate's heart sank. Was the man absolutely everywhere? Louisa was carrying a lacy parasol, even though the sun was intermittent. Kate knew the accessory was just a tool, like a fan or a glove, or a dropped handkerchief. Such items could be artfully used to distract or ensnare a suitor, or impart a message. *I would like you to follow me. I would like you to call on me. I am willing to accept your attentions. Look at my eyes, my throat, my wrist. I want to be kissed...*

'Katie, is there something between you and Edwin Ford?' John asked curiously.

'Look behind you, John. Does it look as though there might be?' Kate sounded resigned and weary.

'Louisa craves the admiration of all young men. She's like a spoiled child with a new toy. But she tires very quickly. Not a month ago, I was her pet. I'm relieved she has grown bored of me!'

'Father has high hopes for Mister Ford. Apparently his prospects are very good. The Ramsays will surely pursue such a good match.'

'You must be relieved our parents are not so intent of purpose.'

'I am. But I wish I could find some purpose of my own. I'm not Sarah. I have no wish to be someone's wife and mother to a brood of children.'

'I don't think Louisa wants that, either. But she does want to be pampered and adored. I pity the poor man who finally wins her hand!'

'It's not all Louisa's fault, John. A woman sits on the throne of Britain, but those of us without that privilege have little choice in life. So many advances have been made in other areas such as science, medicine and industry. But we women are still at the mercy of our father's wishes, then our husband's.'

'You make it sound like slavery, Katie!'

'And is it not, in a way? I only ask to make my own choices and not be judged for them. I want to see the world, John. What can be wrong with that?'

He patted her hand where it rested in the crook of his arm. 'Well, why don't you come on the Tour with me after university?' John was to make the Grand Tour after his final term. What safer way for Kate to see Europe than to travel with her brother? Kate beamed up at him adoringly and nodded enthusiastically. 'It's settled then. You'll see Europe with me - unless Father marries you off first!'

Someone called John's name from the other side of the little railway bridge under Castle Hill. A group of jovial young men waved at John, inviting him to join them.

'They are my classmates from the university,' he explained. 'Do you mind if I go? I can take you up to Mother, first...'

'There's no need. I'll stay on this path through the trees and join her at the end of the Gardens. A walk on my own will do me good.'

John kissed her cheek and trotted off to join his friends. Kate carried on walking, even though the grass was a little muddy. She looked at her feet and sighed; mud on her boots again.

'Good day, Miss Grahame!' Kate turned to see Edwin Ford closing the short distance between them with long strides. Louisa had disappeared from view, no doubt to flirt with some other unsuspecting man. Kate suddenly wished she had brought a parasol to hide her pale face. Her hair had decided to escape from the confines of her hat as it always did, and she could see a tendril hanging at the corner of her eye. She pushed it back under her wispy little veil.

'Are you feeling better today?' Edwin asked, with genuine concern.

'Yes, thank you. You attended church with the Ramsays?'

'No. I attended church on my own. May I walk with you?'

'I'm not sure it would be considered proper, Mister Ford.'

'Your parents and brother are within shouting distance, Miss Grahame.'

He offered his arm, but Kate did not take it. Instead, she turned and continued on the pathway, coming off the grass in case she got the heel of her walking boot stuck in the damp earth. As he drew level with her, she felt his hand graze hers as if he would hold it. Instead, he drew his finger down her gloved palm from fingertip to her bare wrist. Kate's breath caught in her throat. What was she supposed to do now? Had he done that on purpose? She decided to ignore it, and began to talk about the impending ball at the Ramsays. Every April they hosted a huge dinner at their house in the elite district of the Hermitage, near the Braid Hills. After dinner, guests adjourned to the grand ballroom to dance under magnificent chandeliers imported from Paris. At the mention of dancing, Kate's face adopted a glum expression.

'I thought young ladies liked to dance,' Edwin commented, amused at her expression of distaste.

'Not all of us.'

'And why not?'

Kate frowned as she tried to explain. 'I lack the...finesse of experience. I seem unable to float across a dance floor like a butterfly.'

She pouted. 'I'm more like a hesitant moth!' Then she giggled, remembering that she always stood on her brother's toes when she danced with him. Sometimes, it wasn't accidental.

Edwin smiled. 'Did they not teach you to dance at the Ladies' College?'

'Yes, but I did not learn.' She shook her head in mock regret.

'What did you learn?'

'I learned to climb the wall.'

Edwin burst out laughing, and Kate smiled shyly at him. 'Kate, you are extraordinary!' he grinned. Kate's eyes widened. He had called her Kate. Nobody had ever called her Kate before, and he certainly shouldn't be using her Christian name at all. *I should be telling him off for the liberty,* she thought. *I'll ignore it.*

'What about you, Mister Ford?' she asked, pointedly enunciating his name so he would know she was aware of his impropriety.

'I'm afraid I was climbing walls when I should have been learning dance steps, too. I dance very little and never voluntarily. Perhaps,' he gazed down at her intently, willing her to look up at him. 'We could not dance together?'

She turned her head to look at him and realised he was being serious. They stopped as they reached a fork in the path.

'I must leave you here, I'm afraid,' he sighed. 'I have to go to work.'

Kate's eyes widened. 'On a Sunday?' she teased. 'Did you sleep through the sermon on following the Ten Commandments?'

He grinned back impishly. '*Me?* I noticed *you* were on the verge of nodding off a number of times, Miss Grahame!' Kate blushed at the thought of him watching her in church, and looked away. 'There is still a lot to do for the exhibition,' Edwin explained. 'The carpenters have still to make special cases for the sarcophagi, and I still have to send a precise inventory to the EEF. I want to do a good job for your father. And the Prince of Wales has shown an interest.' She saw his eyes shine with pride. 'So I'm sure I'll be forgiven for working on a Sunday until all is as it should be. Besides, the museum will be open this afternoon, so I'll not be the only one working today.'

'Then I hope your day goes well.'

'If my day ends as it has begun, it will be a very good day indeed,' he said quietly, holding her gaze until she blushed again. Kate held her hand out to him, feeling suddenly daring. Taking her hand in his, he carefully peeled back the soft leather of her glove and tenderly kissed the back of her hand.

The following week brought great excitement to Edinburgh society, as a group of Italian archaeologists arrived with some Egyptian artefacts from the museum in Turin. Their leader was Armando Rossellini, a man who considered himself a 'bella figura' and who soon became the main topic of conversation in every well-furnished parlour in Edinburgh. Kate heard her own mother discussing the Latin Dandy (as John was fond of calling him) at one of her tea mornings at home. Eleanor, Mrs Ramsay and Sarah's Aunt Jocelyn gushed about Rossellini's charming gallantry, fine figure and fashionable clothes. Sarah and Kate glanced at one another with raised eyebrows and laughed into their teacups.

'Of course,' Mrs Ramsay squawked in her stentorian voice. 'Louisa is not impressed by such posturing. She has her heart set on another archaeologist altogether.' Kate's ears pricked up. Surely she didn't mean Edwin? Edwin who had called her 'Kate' and then kissed her hand? She couldn't hear the question Jocelyn asked in her soft, timorous voice, but she clearly heard Mrs Ramsay's response. 'Oh yes!' she crowed. 'We expect a proposal within the month.'

Sarah saw Kate's stricken face and put a hand on her friend's arm. Kate had told Sarah all about her encounters with Edwin. Of course, Sarah found it all very romantic, but Kate wondered if it had all been some sort of game which she was too naïve to understand. Kate felt sick, and suddenly very young and stupid.

Sarah leaned towards Kate. Sitting on a settee in a corner of the parlour, the girls went largely unnoticed by the gossiping matrons. Sarah's voice was uncharacteristically firm. 'If you want him,' she murmured. 'You should fight for him.'

The Ramsays boasted about living in an exclusive part of town, but the roads to the Hermitage needed serious attention. The carriage rattled over every pothole, causing Eleanor to cluck her tongue with impatience. At last they approached the long drive to the grand mansion. The drive was lined with flaming torches, the huge Georgian house lit with hundreds of candles and lamps. It would be very hot inside, Kate surmised, as John handed her down from the carriage. Kate looked at the ground. *No puddles, thank goodness.*

Sarah and Alastair arrived behind them, and the party entered the house together. John and Kate were quickly separated from their parents in the throng of guests who gathered in the marble foyer. As Kate slipped her blue velvet cloak from her shoulders, she heard Alastair gasp. Her gown was new, and the most beautiful dress she had ever owned. It was made of a rich peacock blue satin, the sleeves and low neckline delicately edged with lace. The skirt had a train at the back, subtly embroidered with flowers in green, blue and silver thread. Kate's hair was adorned with pins decorated with tiny silver flowers which shimmered in the candlelight. Her arms were modestly covered with silk gloves, and she wore her mother's sapphire earrings. For the first time in her life, she felt beautiful and feminine. Alastair's open stare made her flush, and she modestly looked down at the tiled floor. She turned hastily to Sarah, resplendent in golden yellow, and put her arm around her friend's waist.

'You look like sunshine and daffodils!' she exclaimed, and the pair giggled girlishly. Someone handed them dance cards with a little pencil and a cord to fasten around their wrists. Kate surreptitiously tried to hide hers in her glove; she would not spend the evening with a price tag hanging from her arm. She was surprised when Alastair boldly took it from her and started to write in his own name.

'I always have the first dance with John,' she stuttered.

'I can make an exception tonight,' John declared. Kate threw him an irritated glance and pouted.

'And I have the second dance with Father,' she continued. Sarah started to laugh.

Alastair gave her a stern look; the girl was infuriating. 'Miss Katherine, I believe you are trying to put me off. I have filled in my name for the third dance, which is a polka. Please do not disappoint me.'

'Dio, che bella!'

Kate looked over Alastair's shoulder. The Italian archaeologists had arrived, Rossellini leading the other two. He was very richly dressed, making all the other men in the room seem dowdy by comparison. Rossellini was not as tall as Edwin, Kate observed, and he had a slight paunch. His black hair was oiled and combed back, his moustache curled foppishly at the ends. He stared at Kate in such a way that she felt like a piece of meat in the butcher's window; his eyes travelled slowly from her face down the length of her body, lingering at her bosom and hips. A slow flush started to creep up her throat as the Italian brazenly took up her hand and kissed it. He had brown eyes like Edwin, but his gaze was calculating, and lustful.

Rossellini bowed extravagantly to Sarah and Kate. John moved to stand between the two women and formally introduced them, his expression polite but watchful. He and Alastair then led Kate and Sarah into the reception room and away from the three Italians.

'The man who ignites that one's passions will be very fortunate indeed!' Rossellini remarked salaciously in Italian, believing none of these unsophisticated Scots would understand him. The three men laughed loudly. John heard the comment as he walked away, but decided to ignore it. He wanted to practice law, not break it. And it was likely that no one else had heard the exchange. Unknown to John, Edwin had entered the foyer in time to see Kate's departure and hear Rossellini's lewd comment.

The dinner guests were seated at two very long tables set with dazzling white linen, fine crystal and polished silverware. The Ramsays were renowned for their hospitality, and also their ostentation. Kate sat with Sarah, Alastair and John, and conversation flowed easily between them. The Italians sat some way down the table, and were enthusiastically entertained by Louisa and some of the other young ladies. As his host at the museum, James was also seated near Rossellini. Edwin sat next to James, at the opposite side of the table from Kate. She glanced at him several times, watching him as he engaged in a somewhat stilted conversation with Rossellini. Edwin looked bored, slightly harassed and a little cross. At last he looked at her, and his eyes lit up with a wondrous smile. He waved a fork at her but was distracted by conversation again. *Poor Edwin,* she thought, *he's not a social butterfly either.*

They seemed to dine for hours, but at last the guests moved to the ballroom and the dancing began. Kate danced with John, then James, and then was swept off by Alastair for his promised polka. *He's such a lovely man,* she thought. *He deserves a nice, quiet wife who will love him unconditionally and not give him any trouble.* The next dance was a waltz, and she had just agreed to dance it with Alastair when Rossellini swooped in and danced her to the middle of the floor. Kate was outraged at the man's lack of decorum. Her anger quickly became discomfort as he kept his eyes on her face. His piercing eyes peered over an aquiline nose, giving him a hawk-like appearance. His breath was hot, and he was holding her too close. Kate cringed as she realised that people were staring at them.

'What is your name, Principessa?' he asked, in heavily-accented English.

Kate stared at him, suddenly defiant and determined that those around her would see she had not invited this attention. 'My name is Katherine Grahame,' she said, her voice strong. 'My father is the director of the museum.'

'Ah yes, the honourable Professor James Grahame. You have his eyes.'

'I have my own eyes, sir.'

He laughed loudly and danced her out to the terrace. 'It is very hot in there, no?'

It *was* hot in the ballroom and much cooler out in the evening air. He led her to the stone balustrade, overlooking the manicured gardens, which were lit by twinkling lanterns. He kept hold of her hand, tightening his grip when she tried to pull her hand free.

'If you will excuse me, sir, I must return to my parents. In this country, ladies are not permitted to be alone with gentleman they do not know.'

He smiled wolfishly, his eyes roaming hungrily over her exposed flesh. 'In my country, Bellissima, if a man sees something he likes, he takes it.' He took a step towards her. She finally managed to pull her hand free and stepped back, her eyes flashing with anger. At the edge of her vision, she could see that a man was approaching from her left, and another from her right. Both were carrying glasses of fruit punch. Edwin and John, with faces like thunder.

'Here you are, Katie,' John said breezily, handing her the glass. 'Sorry it took me so long.' He deliberately stepped between Kate and Rossellini.

'Ah, Signor Grahame,' Rossellini said, his arms wide in a sign of friendship. 'Your sister is quite the bewitching beauty.'

Edwin had come up behind the fellow archaeologist. Kate heard him speaking softly in Italian, but could not understand the words. Whatever they were, they made the older man hold up his hands in mock apology, nod politely to Kate, and return to the ballroom.

'What did he say?' Kate whispered to John.

'I don't know,' he lied, but John knew very well. Edwin had told Rossellini that the lady was spoken for.

John left Kate and Edwin standing at the balustrade, looking out at the gardens. Kate was embarrassed, and therefore angry. 'I see I now have *two* over-protective brothers to watch over me!' she said tartly.

'I would not want you to think of me in that way, Miss Grahame.' His irritation was obvious. 'You should not be out here alone with a strange man!' he said reproachfully. She saw his eyes flash with anger, his sensual mouth a grim line.

'I did not invite it!' she replied defensively. 'In any case, I can take care of myself!'

'Yes, I have no doubt you would have struck him had he stepped any closer!' he quipped, in an attempt to lighten the atmosphere between them. But Kate was still angry with him; if he was to marry Louisa, why was he out here with her?

'Is your dance card not full?' he asked testily, his gaze falling on the rapid rise and fall of her bosom then flicking upwards to her tense face. He wanted desperately to hold her and comfort her, to keep her safe from predators like Rossellini.

'I threw it away. And in any case, that man would not have been on it!' she snapped. 'Should you not be directing your attentions elsewhere? You are correct, it is improper for me to be alone with a man I do not know, yet here you stand.'

'I expect your brother is lurking nearby, out of sight.'

'I expect he is.' In spite of her pique, Kate smiled. 'He's like the bulldog we never had.'

'He's separating the chaff from the wheat.'

She glanced at him, puzzled. 'I don't understand.'

Edwin focused his gaze on the gardens. 'John no doubt sifts through any possible suitors before introducing the best ones to your father. He will ensure you find the best possible husband.'

Kate was indignant. 'My father has no intention of finding me a husband!' But she couldn't be sure, and the thought of John choosing her spouse was not at all comforting. Would John betray her in that way? 'And I certainly have no intention of marrying anyone at the moment! You overstep yourself, Mister Ford!'

'Then I apologise. Forgive me.' Hesitantly, Edwin moved his hand next to hers on the balustrade.

Kate moved her hand away, loath to encourage him. She watched a moth fly too close to one of the lanterns, the bright flame luring the creature to its doom. Full of compassion for the hypnotised insect, Kate leaned over the balustrade and attempted to save it by blowing in its path. The moth changed direction and Kate leaned back, glad that it would be free for a little longer.

Edwin studied Kate intently, his eyes smouldering in the soft light. 'Marriage is not a death sentence,' he murmured gravely, although he had held the same belief until very recently.

Kate looked up at him. 'It would be, for me,' she said quietly. An awkward silence followed, the air around them charged with tension. Unsettled, Kate attempted to change this most uncomfortable subject. 'You speak Italian?' she asked.

'A little. Enough. My mother was Italian. She died when I was eight.'

Kate felt a surge of sympathy, at the same time realising that he must have inherited his dark good looks from his mother. She wondered if he had also inherited a Latin temperament. 'I'm sorry,' she murmured, sad for his loss.

Edwin shrugged. 'It was a long time ago.' They stood in silence once more, listening to the distant call of an owl.

'Rossellini called me something,' she said at last. 'Princi-' Kate struggled to recall the pronunciation.

'Principessa.' Edwin caressed the word, gazing at her with smoky eyes.

'And he called me bel-'

'Bellissima. I heard.'

'What do those words mean?'

'Princess.' His eyes burned into hers. Kate's stomach fluttered. 'Beautiful.'

Kate looked away. 'The man has no sense of propriety,' she muttered. *Either man.*

'His are a passionate people.'

'You are excusing his behaviour?'

'No, but perhaps I can understand it. He saw something so beautiful, it took his breath away. An Italian does not let such a thing pass without comment.' He lowered his voice. 'No man should.'

Edwin's brown eyes rested on her lips. Unconsciously, Kate reached up to touch her mouth. *I want to be kissed...*

'You should warn Louisa about Rossellini,' Kate said suddenly, hearing a tremor in her voice. She swallowed.

'Why? I wasn't talking about Louisa...' His hand slid over to hers again, his fingers reaching to cover hers. She moved a step away from him. 'Mister Ford, please - I have to go inside. My parents may be looking for

me.' Picking up the train of her dress, she turned and walked towards the ballroom.

'Dance with me,' he called. She looked back and saw he was smiling at her, asking forgiveness for upsetting her.

'We agreed not to dance,' she reminded him. 'You told me you never danced voluntarily. Besides, given the circumstances, it wouldn't be appropriate.'

'John!' Edwin called into the night. 'May I have the next waltz with your sister?'

'You may, Edwin,' John's disembodied voice replied. Kate exhaled in a rush, exasperated. *Where is he hiding now?* 'But then she's going home.'

'You lied to me, Mister Ford,' Kate told him reproachfully. 'You claimed you couldn't dance.'

'And you claimed not to be able to float across the dance floor like a butterfly,' he retorted playfully. 'Perhaps we bring out the best in one another - on the dance floor at least.'

Tired of the verbal sparring, Kate closed her eyes momentarily and succumbed to the sensation of floating, conscious of the feel of her hand in his, his other hand resting lightly on the bodice of her dress. The contact made her body tingle.

'What? No reproof?' he teased. Kate kept her eyes closed a moment longer. He led divinely; she hardly had to think about her feet at all.

'I'm tired, Mister Ford.' But she longed for him to dance her out to the seclusion of the terrace.

'Edwin,' he corrected her. She sighed, and opened her eyes to see Louisa glaring at her from across the room as she danced with a captain from the castle garrison.

'You know very well I can't call you by your name.'

'Don't you get tired of all this propriety nonsense?'

'It makes me very weary indeed. But as a woman I have no choice but to observe the rules in order to preserve my reputation. Of course, if a man should acquire a questionable reputation it just makes him all the more exotic - apparently.' She kept her eyes fixed on a spot below his ear, unable to look him straight in the eye. For his part, he couldn't take his eyes from her face. He committed every little detail to memory, admiring her arched brows, long dark eyelashes, and the fire in her large brown eyes. Her sweet little nose was kissed with freckles which spread to the top of her pink cheeks. A mouth soft like rose petals, a stubborn chin. There were copper tints in her dark, silky hair. His gaze travelled to the delicate sweep of her throat and shoulders. The expanse of creamy skin exposed by her gown was smooth and unblemished. The teasing scent of violets crept up his nostrils, but only because he had lowered his head towards hers.

'Kate,' he murmured throatily in her ear. 'You're so beautiful...' His hand tightened round her back, pulling her a little closer. Her eyes flashed a warning.

'Please,' she said softly. 'Just dance.'

A heavy silence pervaded the carriage on the journey home. James, Eleanor and John all wore serious, thoughtful expressions. Kate kept her eyes lowered, and her mouth closed, and wallowed in her misery. She had let them down - again - through no fault of her own. John had tried to protect her, but it seemed he had failed. Once home, her father kissed her goodnight and retreated into his study. Kate looked at John in anguish, but he merely squeezed her hand, shook his head and followed James. Eleanor declared she was exhausted, and retired to bed, directing Kate to follow suit.

Kate woke to the rattle of rain on the window. Forcing herself to get out of bed, she recalled with a sinking feeling the events of the night before. She would surely be hauled over the coals for her misdemeanours this morning. As she dressed, she composed her defence in her head. Hearing the doorbell chime, she looked out of the window but could only see the top of a large black umbrella. Who would call at this early hour? Was her mother even out of bed yet?

As if Kate had summoned her with the thought, Eleanor knocked on the door and then entered her daughter's bedroom. Her face was serious but not unkind, although her eyes showed concern. Eleanor sat on Kate's bed and patted the space beside her. Obediently, Kate sat down, her bare feet just touching the thick rug. Eleanor took a deep breath, gathering her thoughts.

'Katherine,' she began quietly. 'I want you to tell me what happened at the Ramsays' party, exactly as you recall it.'

Kate obediently related her version of the evening's events, from meeting Rossellini in the foyer of the mansion, to her last waltz with Edwin. There was little point in lying to Eleanor, as she could read her daughter like a book. Taking Kate's hand, Eleanor asked, 'Think carefully. At any point in the evening did you do or say anything which may have given Mister Rossellini the impression that you were...interested in him?'

'No! John and Alastair introduced Sarah and me to Mister Rossellini and his colleagues. I did not speak to him or even catch his eye at dinner.'

'Did you try to catch his eye?'

'No, Mother, I did not! I did not like him at all! Mother, what has happened? What did I do wrong?'

Eleanor stroked Kate's hand. The child was so unworldly and guileless. 'It seems that news of your unfortunate encounter with Mister Rossellini has spread, and the tale has grown arms and legs. Mister Rossellini has quite a different story to tell. He claims he acted under encouragement from you.'

Kate was horrified. 'But Mother, that's not true! And who else could have witnessed what happened on the terrace? Apart from me and that awful man, there was only John and - and Mister Ford.' *Surely not?*

'No, Kate, someone else was there, too. Someone who feels a great deal of spite towards you, it seems. But that brings me to the second topic we must discuss.' Kate looked at her mother with a growing feeling of dread. *Please don't ask me about Edwin!* 'Mister Ford.'

Kate sat in silence, not knowing what to reveal, unsure of his intentions. She wasn't even sure how to interpret some of the things he had said to her. She didn't want to confide the whole agonising tale to her own mother.

'Do you have feelings for him?'

'Is he not going to marry Louisa?'

'Please try and answer my question, dear.'

Oh, Mother, I believe I love him with all my heart! 'I would never try to steal someone else's beau.'

'Oh, good Lord, child! I have seen with my own eyes the way he looks at you, and the way you moon over him when you think no one can see!' Eleanor started to laugh, while Kate squirmed and bit her lip.

'Mother, please don't laugh! I am very perplexed by him. I don't want to see him if he is to marry Louisa. I can't bear it!'

'Has he said sweet words to you?'

Kate squeezed her eyes shut, cringing, and nodded. 'I think so. I don't know...'

Eleanor shook her head. Had they taught Kate nothing at that fancy finishing school? 'Have there been any...improprieties?' Kate looked blank. 'Has he kissed you?'

Shocked by the bluntness of her mother's questions, Kate mutely pointed to her hand. Eleanor patted her daughter's knee and rose from the bed.

'Mother, you're not going to tell Father?' Kate's eyes were wide.

'About hand-kissing in the Gardens? No! I was young once, too, you know. But that lying Italian snake will wish he had never met me by the time he leaves Edinburgh.'

'Thank you, Mother.' Kate wrapped her arms around Eleanor. 'I love you very much.'

'Come now, put something on your feet and we'll get you some breakfast.'

Eleanor led Kate down the back stairs to the kitchen. *Curious,* Kate thought. *Why not the main house stairs?* There was a pot of porridge on the stove, so the pair sat by the kitchen fire with a bowl each and some tea. Soon after they had finished, Kate heard the front door slam. She glanced at her mother, who sat in her chair looking nonchalant. Still, Eleanor had a steely glint in her eye. Kate asked to be excused, and when her mother nodded, ran upstairs to the vestibule.

The study door was closed, and all was silent. When she heard Eleanor climbing the stairs, Kate slipped into the parlour and closed the door, just as Eleanor entered the study. Opening the door a crack, she

61

noticed her mother had left the door slightly ajar. Had she done that deliberately?

'It is as I thought, James,' Kate heard Eleanor's firm voice. 'Katie is as artless as a new babe. She gave no encouragement to that awful man. She tried to rebuff him, but he persisted. If John and Edwin had not arrived when they did, heaven knows what he would have done to her! We must put an end to these spiteful rumours, James. Our daughter has behaved with dignity, unlike that other madam!' *What other madam?*

James spoke up, sounding weary. 'Aye, you're right as always. Rossellini must be persuaded to forget the incident. But we must be careful how we do it, for he could make things very difficult for Edwin. And that brings us to the other problem...' There was silence for a few moments.

'She has told me everything,' Eleanor assured her husband. *Oh, Mother, please don't tell him everything!* 'I am certain she has done nothing wrong. He, on the other hand, needs a skelp round the ear! What has he to say for himself?' *Oh God, they've spoken to Edwin?*

James's voice was gruff with discomfort. 'The laddie admits he loves her. He's sorry if he has caused her - or us - any offence. He says she will not have him.' Kate slithered to the floor, unable to believe what she had just heard.

'He has asked her?' Eleanor sounded shocked.

'Apparently not outright, but in conversation our wild lassie made it clear she's not for marrying. In fact, John tells me he's taking her to Europe with him!'

'Does Edwin intend to propose to her properly, instead of persisting with all this dancing around and ambiguity?'

'If he was going to, I doubt he will now. You know that Katie has strong views about marriage. She craves freedom and independence, neither of which she will find in matrimony. And if your next question is, did he ask my permission to try again, the answer is no. I'm not sure what I would have said to the laddie, in any case.'

'Did you ask him about the Ramsay girl?'

'Your son took it upon himself to ask that question. He got all het up about Edwin trifling with his sister while almost betrothed to another lass.' James guffawed. 'Our young lawyer was brought down to earth with a bump!' James laughed again.

'Well?' Eleanor urged impatiently.

'Edwin was completely dumbfounded! The Ramsay women need their ears and eyes cleaned oot, for there hasnae been a proposal, nor is there likely to be one anytime soon!'

Kate covered her face and started to laugh with relief and weep with despair all at the same time.

'What should we do?' Eleanor asked, and Kate imagined her wringing her hands.

'There's nothing we can do, lass. Those two lads have stormed out of here in a fine temper, on the hunt for Mister Fancy Pants. We can hope they will act with dignity and common sense. The Ramsays will see the error of their ways in time and will soon be back on the husband hunt. Miss Louisa will smart for a while, but she'll recover. Though she may lose a few friends, once people find out it was she who spread the rumours about Katie and Rossellini. Those that matter know Katie for the good, kind lassie she is.'

'But James, they love each other!'

'Aye, Ellie, that may be so. But the lad is not rich by any means, nor does he have a stable job here in Scotland. He'll be going back to London within a month or two, and he's desperate to go back to Egypt. It's no life for a lassie.'

'It was good enough for me.'

'Ah, but do you not remember how your own father felt about it?' Eleanor murmured something Kate could not hear. 'No, Ellie, we must not interfere. Katie knows her own mind, and we must trust her to make the right decision. Edwin claims she was quite adamant on the subject. Let it run its course, my love. Once he's gone from Edinburgh, all will be well again in time.'

CHAPTER 4

Kate stayed at home for the next week, afraid to go out into the world for fear her reputation had been ruined by gossip. She worried for her parents, too, lest they were hurt by scandal, but James and Eleanor carried on as normal. They were confident of their daughter's innocence and convinced that there would be no slur on her reputation. James showed Kate detailed drawings of the new Egyptian artefacts and the floor plans for the exhibition, which was almost ready for public view. In four weeks' time, a dignitary from Buckingham Palace would open the exhibition on behalf of Queen Victoria.

Kate's twentieth birthday passed quietly, at her request, with a family dinner at home to mark the occasion.

Rossellini and his group returned to Italy, but not before many of Edinburgh's society had closed their doors to them. James behaved with dignified civility towards the man and his colleagues, but he had felt a grim satisfaction when Rossellini visited the museum two days after the ball sporting a black eye and a cut lip.

Despite the rumours spread by Louisa, people still called at the house on Heriot Row and were welcomed as always with tea and cake. At first, Kate was afraid to appear in front of the old hens of Edinburgh. She kept to her room, or the garden. At length, Sarah persuaded her friend to brave the parlour. But although Eleanor's friends treated her kindly, Kate was still reluctant to appear in public.

During her second week of self-imposed isolation, Kate was returning from a walk in Queen Street Gardens when her mother called her into the parlour. 'Father wants us to go to the museum to see the Egyptian treasures before they are put out on display. He said you wanted to look at them without the glass case in the way. Well, it seems all the cleaning and cataloguing is done, and they're ready for display.'

Kate smiled wanly. She had told James how she longed to see the artefacts she had written about, to feel the history under her fingertips. Her smile vanished. 'Will Mister Ford be there?'

'I expect he will, dear. But don't fret. Just behave as you always do, and you will be fine.'

'I'm not sure that behaving like I always do will be fine at all!'

Eleanor put her arm around her daughter's sagging shoulders. 'My beautiful girl, you can't change who you are. And nor should you, for any man. Now, go and make yourself presentable and I'll send out for a cab.'

The young woman who stepped down from the cab was very different from the girl who had run to the museum from Greyfriars carrying a basket all those weeks ago. Ashamed of the trouble she had caused her beloved family, she had stifled her wilfulness and outspoken tongue. Since John was studying for his final exams, Kate had spent less time with her brother. Eleanor had seen this as a good thing, as John had always brought out the tomboy in Kate. Time in the company of ladies had improved Kate's temperament, and she now behaved sedately whenever she was in company. Although still opinionated, she saved her enquiring mind for discussions with James in the privacy of his study, where she would not incur the disapproval of others. Kate spent many hours in her father's sanctum, reading his books while sitting in his old leather wing chair. The most interesting books were kept in his office in the museum, but Kate had not visited her father at work since the incident at the Ramsay house.

Kate had made every effort to avoid Edwin Ford. Since her encounter with Rossellini, Edwin and John had become as thick as thieves. They had spent a lot of time together until John sequestered himself in the university library to study. When Edwin was expected to call at the house for John or James, Kate made sure she was busy elsewhere. She convinced herself that she had merely suffered an immature infatuation. Edwin's feelings were unimportant. More than ever, she eschewed the idea of marriage, intent on travelling to Europe with John. Girlish emotions were of no use to her. If she had the misfortune to meet Edwin Ford again, she would behave in a dignified and reserved manner.

Eleanor studied her daughter as Kate rearranged her skirts. The girl was transformed into a woman. She looked remarkable, graceful and slender, her corset sensibly laced to show off her hourglass figure. Kate wore a skirt and fitted jacket in teal green, the lapels and narrow cuffs trimmed with velvet. The white blouse beneath the jacket was edged with white lace, which peeped out at her wrists and throat. The v-shaped neckline of blouse and jacket showed off a throat unadorned by jewellery. Her hat was also teal green, with feathers and a little veil, set at a jaunty angle on her immaculate head. No stray hairs fell over her face. No mud caked her boots or the hem of her skirt. Kate stood straight, holding a parasol to shade her from the sun. She looked serene, almost ethereal. Eleanor thought she had never looked as beautiful, but missed the fiery girl she adored. Eleanor fervently hoped they would not meet Edwin Ford today. She had not told Kate that Edwin had declined the opportunity to join an expedition to Memphis at the end of the year. Nor had Eleanor mentioned that Edwin constantly inquired after Kate's health, and would certainly be aware that Kate was trying to avoid him.

The Grand Gallery was devoid of exhibits. Instead, new custom-built glass cases stood empty and waiting. Painters and carpenters had created backdrops for the new exhibition. Scenes from ancient Egypt covered every available wall. Attendants flitted to and fro like industrious ants as Kate and Eleanor made their way to the director's office. James led them to the workshops at the rear of the building. They stepped into a large white room where the sun shone through the tall windows. Two men worked quietly at a table in the corner. The room was dominated by two long trestle tables which were covered in artefacts. The edges of the room were crowded with statues and several sarcophagi of varying sizes. Kate's eyes widened in awe and delight as she propped her parasol in a corner and removed her gloves. She donned a pair of the white cotton gloves used by staff when handling precious artefacts.

James led his wife around the trestle table to inspect some jewellery and left Kate to wander on her own. Kate was astounded at the detailing on the sarcophagi. The colours were so fresh they could have been painted the day before. One of the sarcophagi was still sealed, its occupant still resting within. Kate felt uneasy; the poor soul should not have been disturbed, let alone packed onto a ship and brought all the way to Edinburgh. She hoped he would be left inside his sarcophagus and spared any further indignity.

Kate smoothed the head of an alabaster statue of Anubis which was almost the size of a real dog. She crouched down carefully to look at a large stone tablet which depicted a scene from everyday Egyptian life. Running her finger over the hieroglyphs which surrounded the scene, Kate wished she could interpret the symbols. Another stela showed the story of the great god Osiris. As a child, Kate had loved the story and still held Isis, the wife and sister of Osiris, in great esteem. She smiled as her fingers traced the outline of Isis stretching out her mighty wings, wishing that she, too, could fly.

The workshop door opened, causing a draught to blow at Kate's feet. She heard a familiar voice. 'Atkins, have you got the - oh! I apologise, Professor Grahame, I didn't realise you were in here. Mrs Grahame, how are you?'

Oh, good Lord, it's him! Kate's heart sank then rose again to pound wildly in her chest. She remained in her crouched position behind the table. She wasn't very tall, so it was entirely possible he would not see her and leave with whatever he came for. She resolved to stay in her crouched position and gather her strength and dignity to her like a shield. But Edwin was now talking with her parents, and her knees were starting to ache. *Blast it, I need to stand up!* As Kate began to rise as gracefully as she could, she felt a hand gently support her elbow. *The man creeps about like a cat!*

'Miss Grahame.' His eyes sought hers but she would not look up at him. She stood very still.

'Mister Ford...' *Please leave me alone!* Kate glanced imploringly at her mother for help.

'Edwin,' Eleanor called. 'James tells me you found this piece in Egypt yourself.' She indicated some item at the other end of the room.

Edwin reluctantly moved away to tell Eleanor the history of the item, leaving Kate to her own devices once more. Ignoring her quivering stomach, Kate began to examine the objects on the table.

There were tools and pieces of weapons. Long papyrus scrolls were protected between panes of glass, the beautiful writing so clear she fancied the ink might still be wet. Several canopic jars had lids carved in the shape of animal heads to symbolise which internal organ should be stored within. A partially broken stone tablet was carved with the handsome face of King Akhenaten wearing the blue crown with its rising cobra. Kate traced her fingers over the young king's features, lingering on the curve of his full lips. She sighed wistfully and moved along to some children's toys, marvelling at a little woven ball and a spinning top. Many charms littered the table, made of alabaster, wood and faience. There were miniature gods, animals, scarabs, and fertility symbols. Hopes and dreams. A black marble statuette of the goddess Bastet held court amid the charms, depicted as a sitting cat. Kate stroked the cat's smooth curved back, tickled it under the chin and smiled to herself.

At last she found the little alabaster pot itemised as number 52a. It was beautiful in its simplicity, its surface creamy and smooth. She didn't notice Edwin turn to look at her as she carefully picked up the pot and held it to her nose. Kate was certain she could detect a hint of Frankincense.

As Kate moved to the next table, she noticed that Edwin had joined her parents in their inspection of the artefacts. Eleanor kept him busy with questions, allowing Kate to properly study the exhibits. Kate was lost in her own world, increasingly unconcerned by Edwin's presence. She had transported herself back to ancient Egypt, recalling every fact she had read on the era, understanding the significance of everything she touched. She admired a beautifully carved box which was filled with shabtis. These little human figures were placed in the tombs of wealthy Egyptians, and members of the royal family. The Egyptians believed the little people would be reanimated in the afterlife in order to serve their master or mistress. Some of the figurines even held their own tools, so that they would be prepared for work.

The jewellery was fascinating. Kate remembered Edwin explaining that the bright yellow gold was almost completely pure. The craftsmanship was intricate, the colours of the gems still dazzling. The earrings, however, looked heavy and uncomfortable. Kate absently touched the tiny pearls in her own ears. The jewelled collars were impressive, but looked as if they might cause neck strain. *The sort of thing Louisa might wear,* Kate thought, and tittered to herself. She conjured up an image of Louisa in a lappet wig and headdress, sporting an array of ornate collars, her cold grey eyes ringed with kohl. Helplessly, she started to giggle.

Eleanor looked up. 'Are you all right dear?' she asked. James smiled, always happy to see his daughter's mirth.

'Yes, Mother, I am quite well,' Kate replied, still giggling. 'I'm sorry.'

Edwin's eyes were alight. It had been too long since he had seen those irresistible dimples. He took a step in her direction, but Eleanor moved to join her daughter.

'What amuses you?' she asked gently, slipping her arm around her daughter's slim waist. The two men began talking again, moving to the table where the two members of staff worked steadily. Kate quietly described Louisa, Queen of Egypt. Her mother shook her head in mock reproof, secretly pleased to see that Kate had not completely lost her wicked sense of humour.

Kate and Eleanor finished looking at the exhibits, then joined Edwin and James at the small work table to watch the work in progress. The two members of staff were painstakingly cleaning a small scarab brooch of bright blue faience. Kate looked on, spellbound, as the men used small paintbrushes to remove the vestiges of grime which clung to the beetle's back. Edwin stared in fascination at Kate's parted lips, silently cursing everyone else in the room. He wanted to be alone with her, to have her all to himself...

All too soon, Kate had seen every object in the room. The next time she saw these items, they would be resting in their display cases and scrutinised by all of Edinburgh. Edwin held the door open for Eleanor and Kate, while James had a final word with the two men at the table.

Kate turned to her mother. 'If you're not too tired, may we stay for a while? We haven't looked around the museum in such a long time.'

'Katherine, you know every inch of this place!' her mother laughed. 'Why, you probably know it better than Father! But if you wish, we can wander for a little while.'

'Well, Edwin, we must get back to work,' James said briskly. Edwin looked disappointed but nodded compliantly. He shook Eleanor's hand, but Kate busied herself with her gloves and parasol and merely nodded politely in his direction. And then he was gone. *See how easy that was, Katie Grahame? You can behave like a lady, after all!*

Eleanor professed a desire to see a new collection of china. Kate did not much care for plates, but followed her mother to the first floor gallery and feigned interest. For her, it was satisfying enough just to be in the building, with its elegant curved ceilings and high arched windows. Once Eleanor had finished admiring the Napoleonic porcelain, they moved to the Costume Gallery. They both enjoyed examining the clothes from ages past. The suits of armour and unwieldy-looking swords did not impress them, however, so they wandered back downstairs. Kate suggested the natural history section, but Eleanor professed weariness.

'I'll go and sit in your father's office,' Eleanor decided. 'I'm sure Tom can fetch me some tea. You carry on here, and meet me in a while. No more than an hour, though.'

Kate roamed between cases of stuffed animals. She remembered the many hours of her childhood spent running around this section with John, inventing adventures and safaris. Kate made her way to the rotunda, her favourite place in the museum. The sun shone through the circular skylight onto the tiled floor. The display cases were built into the walls, and showed birds perched in trees or on their nests. Kate climbed the narrow steps to the upper floor, where the light did not quite reach the magnificent golden eagle, set to swoop on some unsuspecting prey. Kate closed her eyes, imagining herself as that mighty bird, soaring with the sun behind her and the wind at her back. Except it was a breath on her neck she felt, and the prickling of the downy hair at her nape. Startled, she looked over her shoulder.

Edwin stood behind her, lost for words. Something had changed in her, and it suddenly felt inappropriate to tease her as he had done before. She had studiously avoided him for weeks but perversely, his feelings for her had only strengthened. After the Ramsays' ball, he had angrily sought out Rossellini, accompanied by John. Undaunted by the possible penalties of his misconduct, Edwin had punched Rossellini twice before John intervened. His passion for Kate was all-consuming, and he could no longer bear to waste time observing the restrictive rules of propriety.

She had turned back to the eagle and was waiting calmly for him to speak.

'It's a beautiful display,' was all he could think to say.

She nodded slightly in agreement. 'She is a beautiful creature...' Kate's voice was wistful. *Undoubtedly shot down by some selfish man in search of a trophy. And now she's in a glass case.*

'Do you think you might like to fly?'

'Oh yes, without a doubt.'

'Would you come home again?'

Kate did not reply.

'You must have spent a lot of time here as a child?'

Kate smiled reflectively. 'Yes. In here, the only limitations are in one's own imagination. And it has the best hiding places!'

Edwin was encouraged as he saw her relax slightly. 'Did you enjoy looking at the artefacts from Egypt?'

'They are truly wonderful...'

'And have you read the finished catalogue?'

'Yes.' As she had expected, there had been some alterations to her work. But she was happy with the end result. 'I found it very concise. And not stuffy at all.' She glanced sideways at him and her lips twitched as she saw him frown in consternation.

They walked on from the golden eagle and reached a small alcove next to a display of two magpies nesting in a tree. Edwin gestured for Kate to sit on the small bench set into the alcove, folding his tall frame next to her.

'Kate,' he began, then immediately corrected himself. 'Miss Grahame -'

Kate lifted her hand slightly to stop him. Politeness was wearying. 'It's alright, Edwin,' she said quietly. 'Please continue.'

'The night of the Ramsays' dinner -'

'I caused everyone a lot of trouble. I know.'

'But you were not to blame! I heard all the rumours, Kate. I know you did not encourage Rossellini that night. If you hadn't been trying to obey the stupid rules of polite society, you would not have been placed in that situation.'

'I was very naïve, and you were right to scold me. I'm glad you and John were there.' She glanced up at him. 'You were angry with me...'

Edwin frowned. 'I wasn't angry, Kate. When I first saw you with him, I was jealous.'

'I thought you and Louisa -'

'I know that now. I never gave her any reason to think I was interested in her -'

'Then perhaps you are also naïve.' She looked down at her tightly clasped hands. He stretched his fingers towards hers, gently stroked her knuckles, and then at last took her hand in his. She didn't protest.

'Kate, I'm leaving tomorrow.'

Her eyes flew to his face, and she pulled back her hand. 'Why?'

'My father has called me home to Kelso.'

'Is he unwell?'

'He seemed fine when I last saw him on my way to Edinburgh, but he has summoned me urgently and so I must go.'

'But you've worked so hard on the exhibition. It seems unfair that you will not be at the opening ceremony, to receive recognition for your efforts.'

Edwin smiled at her. 'I don't need recognition or rewards, Kate. I'm not a treasure hunter - I leave that to the Italians. This is your father's museum. He and his staff should enjoy the admiration of the public, and of the Palace. They do important work here all the time. I am but one tiny cog in the wheel and my work here is done. The exhibition will be a success whether I'm here or not.'

Kate stood up quickly, her eyes growing hot with tears. He was hurting her again with his inability to be forthright. Was he implying that he would prefer a new assignment away from Edinburgh? *I don't understand - why can't he make up his mind!* She walked quickly past the magpies to the next alcove where a narrow passage led behind the subsequent display cases.

Edwin caught up with her in two strides and pulled her into the passageway. In the half-darkness, he pulled her to him. 'Please don't walk away from me, Kate,' he commanded, his eyes burning into hers. 'There are things I need to say to you -'

'Edwin, please let me go!' Kate hissed. 'If anyone sees us, I'll be ruined. Please, Edwin!'

'No, Kate. I'm finished with this propriety nonsense. I don't care who sees us, and I'm not playing this game any longer - listen to me, Kate!' She was struggling to break free, terrified in case someone

71

entered the rotunda below them. 'I love you.' Kate stopped struggling immediately, not sure if she had misheard. She turned her face up to his, her eyes questioning. 'And I think you love me.'

His brash assumption brought a spark of defiance to her eyes. 'Oh, you do?'

Edwin cupped her face in his hands, his gaze intense. 'You can't deny the connection between us, Kate. I know you felt it on the first day we met.' His eyes softened. 'All my life I've felt…incomplete. When I met you, I felt as though I had found the missing piece of my soul. I love you, my darling. Don't push me away.'

Her lips were close, her scent curling around him. Encouraged by her stillness, Edwin kissed her softly on the lips. Once, twice. The third time he kissed her, Kate closed her eyes and slipped her arms around his neck. *Oh my, he kisses even better than he waltzes!* Her legs felt weak. Had he not been holding her so tightly, she felt she may have fallen down altogether. His lips left hers to kiss her cheeks, her nose, and her eyelids. She stroked his rough cheek, her fingers tracing his warm lips. He kissed her fingers, her hand, and her wrist. She felt dizzy and hot. She wanted to sit down, but he held her against him.

'Marry me, Kate,' he murmured against her ear, before turning his attention back to her lips. 'I know we haven't known each other long,' he continued. 'But I know in my heart that we're meant to be together.'

An inner voice shouted at her to flee, reminding her that marriage would be akin to imprisonment. Her heart fought back, crying out its need to love him, and be loved in return. Kate struggled to find the right course. 'Edwin, I'm much too young for you!'

Edwin leaned back. 'I'm not an old man, Kate! I'm twenty-eight!'

'You must ask my father,' she said weakly as his hands caressed her back, causing shivers to race up her spine. The tenacious inner voice was becoming fainter, but still nagged.

'I don't want to marry your father,' he quipped. 'I would very much like to marry you.'

'Edwin, I cannot…'

He looked into her eyes, searching for the truth. 'Do you not love me then?'

She sighed in surrender. 'Yes, I love you.'

'Then I don't understand.'

Kate moved away, as standing so close to him made her head fuzzy. 'Edwin, you will be going back to Egypt.'

'I may not be sent back to Egypt.' *Especially after causing a diplomatic incident with a fellow archaeologist.* 'There are plenty of things I can do here.'

'But you're an Egyptologist.'

'Not exclusively.' He took her back into his embrace. 'I'm adaptable. Marry me.'

Kate put her hand to her forehead. 'Oh, I need time to think!'

'Then you have until I return from Kelso.' He kissed her, his lips demanding. 'But when I return, Kate Grahame, I will require your answer. There will be no more games between us.' He kissed the corners of her mouth, where the dimples hid. Her fingers had wound themselves into his hair where it curled at the back of his neck.

'I have to go,' Kate whispered feebly. 'Mother told me to stay only an hour. She'll be cross with me...' Kate tried to pull away, but he made no effort to release her.

'In a minute,' he told her firmly, and leaned down to kiss her lips once more. For a further five minutes, he kissed her so thoroughly she thought she might faint from lack of air. At last she put her fingers over his lips and pulled away. Without another word, she ran down the steps and hurried to her father's office.

Eleanor jumped as the office door banged open. Her daughter stood in the doorway, a strand of hair falling over her ear, her hat slightly askew. 'I'm so sorry I'm late, Mother!' she said, sounding shrill. 'I got quite carried away! You know, with the golden eagle.'

Eleanor took one look at Kate's flushed cheeks and swollen lips and thought it was a good thing the eagle couldn't talk.

The Ancient Egypt Exhibition was a roaring success. People came from all over Scotland to gasp at the magnificent exhibits. Newspapers described it as one of the finest exhibitions of Egyptian artefacts in Europe. James Grahame was proud of his staff and his museum. He was also proud of his daughter, who arrived at the museum each morning to lead tours for groups of ladies. She had memorised Edwin's catalogue and, armed with her knowledge of ancient Egyptian history, wove tales of intrigue and romance around the pieces on display. Some of the ladies came back several times, just to hear Kate's stories. Kate entertained groups of children by including magical adventures and great battles in her descriptions of the artefacts. James wrote regularly to Edwin, and always included news of Kate's invaluable contribution in his correspondence.

When Edwin returned to his family home in Kelso, he found his father bedridden with pneumonia. George Ford had been a hearty man in his prime, a well-respected and successful wool merchant. Edwin was distraught to see him so frail.

George had always known that his only son would not follow him into business; the lad was a dreamer as his mother had been. George had met the lovely Isabella when he had travelled to Rome as a young man, and the pair had embarked on a passionate affair which had resulted in their marriage. She had fallen pregnant soon after their return to Kelso. Isabella had been a doting mother to Edwin, imparting her love of art and music. Unfortunately, the cooler climate proved to be her downfall. A particularly harsh winter brought an epidemic of influenza which cruelly took poor Isabella's life when she was barely thirty years of age.

After Isabella's death, a grief-stricken George sent his son away to school in the north of England. Although devastated by his mother's death and the seeming abandonment by his father, Edwin accepted his new situation. He studied conscientiously and made his father proud when he was offered a place at university. George focused his attention on maintaining his successful business, although he mourned Isabella for the rest of his life. Finally, he retired and sold the business for a small fortune. He lived quite simply, pleased that he would leave a sizable legacy for his son.

Edwin tended his father day and night, insisting that the doctor visit daily. Sadly, all they could do was make George comfortable in his final days. Edwin read to the weak old man, told him about his travels, his work in Edinburgh, and finally about Kate. George laughed to hear of Kate's wilful nature, but the laughter made him cough and wheeze. After four days, George passed away peacefully with his son at his bedside. Edwin smoothed his father's wispy white hair, kissed his brow, then sat by the bed and wept for both his parents.

Edwin wrote to James, and separately to Kate, to inform them of his father's death and let them know he would remain in Kelso to settle his father's estate. At around the same time, a letter from the EEF was redirected to him from Edinburgh, summoning him to London for a disciplinary interview. Rossellini had formally complained about the marking of his arrogant face. Once Edwin concluded his business in Kelso, he immediately travelled to London, where he received a very firm reprimand from his superiors. It was uncertain whether he would be given a place on future expeditions to Egypt, but Edwin's only desire was to return to Kate. He would be content to spend the rest of his life in Edinburgh, as long as she was his wife.

By the end of June, James felt it was time he took his family on holiday. The museum had plenty of capable hands to keep it running smoothly for a week. John had passed his exams and was immediately

74

offered a position with an Edinburgh law firm. So, instead of making the Grand Tour, John satisfied himself with a week's holiday with his family. The trip to Europe would have to wait, and John knew that his sister would not be going with him anyway. He could tell by the way she serenely floated about the house - her face lit by a secret smile - that Kate would travel to Europe as Edwin Ford's wife. James rented a small house in North Berwick, for Kate and Eleanor loved the sea, and the family travelled down the coast by train. The weather stayed fine for most of the week, allowing Kate and John to ride in the countryside, and for the family to take a trip on a boat to the nearby Bass Rock. They strolled around the little harbour - James and Eleanor sharing a poke of mussels - and wandered around the pretty gardens with the aviaries of chattering birds.

Every afternoon before dinner, Kate strolled alone through the sand dunes and down to the water's edge. Sometimes she would just stand looking out to sea, her eyes following the Fife coastline before moving to the southern horizon. Every day she sent out a wish for Edwin to come home, but she did not feel forlorn. He would return, when he was able.

Kate had adopted the habit of removing her stockings before her walks and putting her boots on her bare feet. She would walk along the beach to an outcrop of very large rocks and slip behind them. Her back was sheltered by a high sand dune, providing almost complete privacy. And so, if no one else walked on the long stretch of clean sand, she would slip off her boots and dip her feet in the icy water.

On the last day of the holiday, Kate sneaked furtively to her private paddling spot. The sky and sea were a uniform grey, but it was not cold. A strong breeze plucked at the velvet ribbon holding back her long hair. She scanned her surroundings for other people, but the beach was empty. Gleefully, she kicked off her boots and ran towards the sea. The cold water lapped her feet, and she gasped, but stayed until she got used to the exhilarating bite of the cold. Kate lifted her skirts a little higher, certain she was still alone. Stepping a little further into the water, she squealed and retreated quickly as a small wave rose up her shins. She splashed along the shoreline, away from North Berwick and towards Edinburgh. The sea water felt pleasant around her feet and ankles, and the sound of the gentle waves was soothing. She loved to feel the breeze on her face, tousling her hair. Without thinking, she lifted her skirts to her knees and inched a little deeper into the water.

'*Katherine Grahame!*'

Kate nearly jumped out of her skin and anxiously looked around the beach, completely forgetting she was still holding her skirts to her knees. She would be in trouble now, for sure.

Edwin walked through the dunes towards her, his face shocked and delighted at the same time. She stood transfixed in the water, not believing her eyes. He had been gone a month, and she had almost grown used to the sweet torment of his absence. He had been too busy to write more than one letter, but she had understood and so had not written to him either. She had no desire to be considered a lovesick girl who could not survive without letters from her beau. He looked unbearably handsome in a dark suit and tie, a shining watch chain tucked into his waistcoat pocket. Her fingers itched to tangle themselves in his neatly combed dark hair.

'Where are your stockings?' he asked her sternly. 'You look like a fishwife.' He raised a dark eyebrow suggestively, his gaze piercing even though he stood several feet away.

Kate was scandalised. 'Edwin Ford! Stop shouting about my stockings! Someone will hear you!'

'Are you coming out of there?' Edwin eyed her bare legs appreciatively. 'I imagine it's quite cold.'

Obediently, she waded out of the sea, dropping her skirts when she reached the shore. Well, he'd seen her legs, no point in making a fuss. They stared at one another, suddenly shy.

Kate spoke first. 'I'm so sorry about your father, Edwin.'

'Thank you, Kate. He led a good life, and he passed peacefully. No one can ask for more than that.' He continued to gaze at her, his eyes a little forlorn as he contemplated his loss.

'Have you just come from London? How did you know we were here?'

'Your father has kept in touch...'

Kate wondered if his comment was a reproof; she had not written because she had not wanted to intrude on his grief, or his business in Kelso and London. Furthermore, she had needed time to consider his proposal and the ramifications of marrying him.

'I arrived on the train two hours ago,' he continued, unable to take his eyes from her beloved face.

'Two hours ago?' Now it was Kate's turn to adopt a tone of reproof.

'Yes. I've been speaking with your father.' He saw that she understood the connotation.

She pouted resentfully. 'Oh, have you been bartering for me like a pair of market traders, then?'

'A trio of market traders, actually. Your brother was also present.' Edwin watched her draw herself up to deliver a sharp riposte. 'Are you going to come over here and kiss me, then? Or do I have to come and get you?'

Hmm, I think I might prefer the latter. Kate stood firm, her eyes glinting with devilment. He strode towards her, his boots splashing through the water's edge. Taking her hand, he pulled her behind the tall outcrop of rocks and kissed her very firmly. As Kate tilted her head back, the breeze finally whipped off her hair ribbon. Edwin caught it in his hand. With his other hand, he caressed her long silky hair, pulling her so close she couldn't move. All she could do was gaze up at him and submit to his kisses. At last he released her, to pull a small blue velvet box from his pocket. He opened the box and presented it to Kate. Kate's eyes widened at the beautiful solitaire diamond ring sparkling in its nest of velvet.

'Say you'll marry me, Kate.'

Kate looked from the ring into his sparkling eyes. There was not a doubt in her mind.

'I will marry you, Edwin.' Kate smiled, and heard him sigh with relief.

His hands trembled as he took the ring from its box and slipped the delicate gold band on her finger. It was a perfect fit. She held up her hand so that the diamond caught the light, and then threw her arms around his neck. His lips moved to a spot below her ear which made her shiver.

'Edwin, I need to sit down,' she told him breathlessly. She pushed him away gently and sat down in the shelter of the rocks and the sand dunes, her breath slowing, the rock cool against her back. He sat down next to her and raked his hand through his hair, itching to kiss her again. Kate looked at her exposed feet. Pulling up her knees she hid her feet under her petticoat. *Now he's seen my petticoat, too. Why can I not behave with decorum?*

'Where are you staying?' she asked him, in an attempt to pull his gaze away from her toes and the white lace peeping from below her skirt.

'I have a bed at the hotel,' he replied softly, twirling a lock of her hair around his fingers. She looked out towards the Bass Rock so he wouldn't see her blush. He put his arm around her shoulders, and she leaned against his chest.

Bravely, Kate looked up at him. 'I missed you,' she told him and kissed his cheek, before burying her face in his neck. After a while she asked, 'When shall we be married?'

77

Edwin looked into her eyes, smiling mischievously. 'There will be no long courtship,' he told her decisively. He had given this a lot of thought. 'No walking out. No scrutiny. No fevered kisses snatched in dark corners when we're left alone for ten seconds.' Kate looked disappointed. 'Oh, don't mistake me, there will be fevered kisses aplenty. But they will not be the result of unrequited passion.' Kate's face turned scarlet, but her body trembled with anticipation. 'We will be married in unseemly haste.'

Kate stared at him in shock. 'But, Edwin, people might think I'm...' She hesitated, embarrassed to say any more.

'With child?' His steady gaze told her he would be more than happy to arrange that condition. 'It doesn't matter what people think.'

Kate shook her head. 'I don't think my parents will approve.'

'Your father has told me that his own courtship of your mother was...unconventional.' *Yes,* Kate thought. *John was born barely nine months from their wedding.* 'My own parents married within weeks of meeting,' he informed her. 'So, as soon as the banns are read, Miss Grahame, we will be wed.' He took her face in his hands. 'Now then, my wife-to-be. I am reliably informed that girls dream of enormously ostentatious weddings.'

'Then your informant has misled you, Mister Ford. My preference is for a smaller affair, with only my family and dearest friends around me. However, in my limited experience it is usually the girl's parents who organise the wedding.'

He bent to kiss her ear, his hand sliding round her waist and his voice low and husky. 'We could elope to Gretna this very minute...'

'Mother would throw a fit! I think I would like a *little* wedding.' Her eyes danced as she gave him a smile which was unwittingly seductive. 'And I will also enjoy making you wait a little longer.'

His eyes were dark with longing. 'Kate Grahame, for your own sake, you had better put on your boots so I can take you safely back to your mother.'

They were married less than a month from that day, amid the disapproval of Edinburgh's Old Guard. Eleanor was undeterred, however, and arranged her daughter's wedding in accordance with Kate's wishes. Although she grumbled about not having enough time to buy a suitable trousseau, Eleanor packed a trunk of beautiful clothes for Kate to take on her honeymoon. Kate and Edwin were married at Saint John's Church, with Kate's family and friends in attendance. They then enjoyed a sumptuous wedding breakfast at the Royal British Hotel, before the guests wished them well and departed. John had arranged for them to stay in the bridal suite that night, while he transported their luggage to the station to await their departure for Liverpool the following morning.

As the porter carried their overnight bags to the bridal suite, Kate started to quiver with nerves. Over the last few weeks, she had tried to push thoughts of her wedding night out of her head. This had proved a very difficult task indeed, not helped by Edwin pulling her into empty rooms and dark corners at every opportunity so he could kiss her with an almost indecent passion.

Her anxiety generated a memory from only three days before, when she had taken her father's lunch basket to his office. In an effort to practice being a dutiful wife, Kate had taken a sandwich and a piece of cake to Edwin in his little room. To her astonishment, he had locked the door behind her then pinned her against the wall and kissed her protesting mouth. His hands had encircled her waist but had grown bolder, sliding possessively up her bodice towards her breasts. Even through the layers of her clothing, she could feel the heat of his wandering hands as though they roamed her naked skin. Feebly, she had tried to push him away, but he had only grown more insistent. His lips had moved to her throat and kissed every inch of flesh he could reach. Kate had found herself almost panting, shocked and thrilled at the same time.

'Please stop!' she had gasped against his dark hair, as one hand snaked down her back towards her bottom. '*Edwin!*' A shove on his shoulder had brought him back to his senses. Edwin's eyes had been full of hunger for her.

'I can't wait any longer...' he rasped.

'Only three more days,' she had reminded him, in an attempt to placate him even as her body ached for his touch. 'Please, Edwin, open the door.' He had kissed her sweetly then, and apologised for his lack of restraint.

Now that she was on the verge of being alone with her husband, Kate started to feel a degree of apprehension. He would expect much more from her than kisses and clearly, he was a passionate man. What if she was unable to please him? She began to recall whispered conversations among the matrons of Eleanor's acquaintance, telling of their own dreadful experiences in the marriage bed. Eleanor had remained resolutely silent on the matter, and Kate had felt too embarrassed to seek her mother's advice and reassurance.

As the porter approached the door of their room, two giggling maids came out. They curtsied to Kate and Edwin, and gave Kate a knowing look which made her face flush scarlet.

The suite was opulent, with thick carpets, pale green walls, velvet drapes and a massive canopied bed. As Edwin tipped the porter, Kate wandered into the bathroom and gasped. It was beautiful, and clearly designed with a lady's comfort in mind. A vanity unit was laden with creams and potions and scents. Kate examined the bottles, sniffing the contents. Then her eyes fell on the large roll top bath in the centre of the room, and concerns about her wedding night evaporated. The maids had poured a steaming bath, and infused it with a concoction from a bottle which rested on the vanity unit nearby. Kate sniffed the milk and honey bath tonic, wishing she could look as alluring as the portrait of Cleopatra which adorned the bottle's label. The maids had sprinkled rose petals on the surface of the water. Kate absently began to remove her ivory lace veil and the pins which held up her hair, at the same time kicking off her satin slippers.

'You're taking a bath?' Edwin asked incredulously as he stood in the doorway.

Kate pointed at the water. 'It would be a shame to waste it after they've gone to so much trouble,' she replied, shaking out her hair. The dark brown coils cascaded sensuously down her back.

'It's a very large bath,' Edwin remarked meaningfully.

'Yes, it is much bigger than the one at home.'

Edwin was unsure if she were being deliberately facetious. She had reached behind her back and was now unhooking her beaded ivory wedding dress. He had rather hoped to do that himself. 'Do you need help with that?'

In her haste to get into the bath, Kate had acted without thinking. Mortified, she immediately stopped unhooking her dress. 'No, I do not! And I think you should go!'

He lingered for a minute more, then turned away and closed the door. She heard him muttering, 'I'll go and…recite my times tables or something.'

When Kate finally emerged from the bathroom, the drapes were closed, and the room was lit by a cluster of candles by the bed. Edwin was sitting up in bed, reading. His chest was bare, the bedcovers pushed down to his waist. Kate was mesmerised. She had never seen a man in any state of undress before. His olive skin glowed in the candlelight, his brow furrowed as he read. She admired the taut muscles of his arms and torso. Kate remembered a censored picture she had once seen of Michelangelo's David, but the statue of apparent male perfection paled in comparison to her husband. Kate experienced an unfamiliar ache rising from deep within her. She moved quietly to the bed, clutching her white silk robe over her chest. The silk nightdress beneath was almost transparent, barely held up by a ribbon tied above her bosom. What was her mother thinking of, buying her daughter such a flimsy garment?

Sensing her presence, Edwin looked up. Putting his book on the floor, he blew out all but two of the candles and pulled back the covers on her side of the bed. As Kate slipped off her robe, Edwin stared in wonder at his wife. She didn't look at him, but turned to place her robe carefully on the chair beside her. Her lithe body was silhouetted through the nightdress, which slipped off one shoulder as she moved. Her shining hair fell in soft waves over her smooth creamy shoulders. She reminded Edwin of a Rossetti painting. She looked exquisite, but Kate felt sorely inadequate as she slid into bed next to him, careful not to touch him. She lay on her back with the covers clutched to her chin.

Edwin smiled encouragingly as he pulled the covers a little way down so that her shoulders were exposed. He propped himself on one elbow and gazed at her lovingly. She looked like a frightened rabbit, her breath rapid, and her eyes like saucers.

'Are you frightened?' he asked softly.

'No,' she squeaked. 'Yes. A little... '

He stroked her hair and then with his fingertips stroked her cheeks, her jaw, and her throat. She watched his eyes grow darker, heard his breath quicken just a little.

'There's nothing to fear, my love,' he told her tenderly, coaxing her to relax. His fingers moved over her shoulders, caressing her smooth skin. He traced the neckline of her nightgown where it rested above the swell of her breasts. She made a tiny noise in her throat, and her body trembled. 'We'll do this very slowly,' he murmured, pulling gently on the ribbon which fastened her nightdress.

'Can we put out the candles?'

He shook his head. 'No, Kate, we will leave them on.'

Edwin kissed Kate's naked shoulder. 'Sweetheart, wake up.' Kate groaned and snuggled further under the covers. Edwin smiled. 'We have to get up for the train.'

'No,' she murmured obstinately, her eyes still closed. 'I'm still sleepy. Go away...' She turned her back to him, so he began to kiss the back of her neck and continued down her spine until Kate's body quivered in response. Now fully awake, she stretched languorously and turned towards him in the half darkness.

'What time is the train?' she asked, yawning.

'Nine o'clock,' he replied, grinning roguishly. His hand slid over her naked hip and down her smooth thigh.

'And what time is it now?'

'Half past five.'

'Planning to eat a big breakfast, are you?' she teased, draping her arms about his neck. She pressed her body against him, no longer afraid. She was thrilled to hear him moan as she pressed her lips against his throat.

'I am,' he replied. 'But not yet…'

As Kate sat down at the breakfast table, the middle-aged woman sitting at the next table gave her a look of obvious sympathy. Kate noticed glances from other diners, too, and kept her eyes lowered. Edwin watched her intently as she ate her eggs and bacon and drank her tea. Kate's eyes fell on her husband's long fingers as they curled around his coffee cup. Her gaze followed the cup as he raised it to his lips. Oh, the things he had done with his fingers and his lips…A rosy flush crept up Kate's throat as her breath caught at the memory of the night before, and the fresher memories of this morning. Her wide eyes locked with his, and she caught his small smirk of satisfaction. As if he could read her thoughts, he slowly raised her hand to his lips and tantalisingly kissed her palm. His eyes glittered with his desire for her as he held her gaze.

'What are you staring at?' she hissed.

He shrugged, grinning. 'You. Sitting there. Looking…prim.' He lowered his voice to a seductive murmur. 'When you're anything but…' His lips moved to the inside of her wrist, where he lightly kissed her racing pulse.

'Edwin, stop it!' Kate pleaded, keeping her voice low. 'People are watching us.'

'They're watching us because we're newlyweds. We have a kind of glow.' Edwin continued to stare covetously at his beautiful wife.

'Let's go back upstairs,' he suggested quietly. The eavesdropping woman at the next table spluttered into her teacup. Kate was mortified, though she couldn't wait to be alone with him again.

'Edwin Ford, eat your breakfast!' she scolded. 'We'll be late for the train.'

Edwin leaned across the table. 'I love you, Kate Ford,' he told her, and returned to his food.

'When you open your eyes, Kate, you'll remember everything. You will feel perfectly safe, and totally relaxed…Open your eyes, Kate.'

Kate returned to the present, and the sound of Erin's soothing voice. Her mind was full of the memories she had unleashed. She flitted from one scene to the next, but most prevalent was the memory of Edwin's lips and hands on every inch of her body. She could still feel him...

Kate looked up slowly, blushing as she fretted over what she may have revealed to Erin and Jess. She remembered Erin saying she would record the session for her, and resolved to listen to the recording later to make sure she hadn't humiliated herself.

'Are you alright?' Jess asked anxiously. Kate nodded distractedly.

Erin was preparing some herbal tea in a corner of the quiet room. She brought Kate a mug, which Kate held to her chest. Heat radiated through her.

'I was Kate Grahame before...' Kate mused, a wistful look in her eyes. 'I married him...' She was filled with a sudden, desperate longing. She wanted to go back to that place where she had been loved.

Erin patted Kate's leg where it rested under the blanket. 'It certainly seems like you're recalling a past life,' she agreed. 'Do you know anything about your family history from that time?'

Kate shook her head. 'My mum recently told me we had a family connection to the museum, and Egypt. My aunt had a family tree - I'll have to find it.'

'Has anything happened recently which may have triggered your dreams about Edwin?'

Kate reflected while sipping her tea. 'When I was a teenager, I remember having dreams about a dark-haired man. He was a kind of guardian angel, I suppose, appearing when I needed comfort. He would hold me, and make me feel protected.' Kate drew in a shuddering breath. 'But recently, his appearances have taken on a more...intimate quality.' She blushed again, but Erin and Jess looked unperturbed.

'Forgive me for asking, Kate, but what's your marriage like - in that respect?'

Kate looked decidedly uncomfortable, and Jess rose respectfully to leave the room and give Kate some privacy. Kate waved her back down on her chair; she trusted these two women implicitly. And she longed to talk to someone.

'Mark is very ambitious,' she began hesitantly. 'He works hard, and he's tired when he comes home.' Her voice became little more than a whisper. 'But in the last few months, it seems he's lost interest in me altogether. We hardly ever...you know...'

Jess's heart went out to her friend, whose eyes sparkled with unshed tears.

'It's not uncommon for marriages to experience a dry spell,' Erin said, comfortingly. 'Do you still hug each other and maintain a connection in other ways?'

Kate looked into her mug, ashamed. 'Not often. As I said, he's very wrapped up in his work. Sometimes he works at home late into the night and gets up early to go to the gym or to work. He travels, too.' Kate shrugged and gave a self-deprecating half smile. 'He works with a lot of clever, glamorous women. How can I compare to them?

CHAPTER 5

Kate sat up in bed and drew her fingers through her unruly hair. She had been dreaming again, vividly, and was once more filled with the aching yearning which engulfed her whenever she sampled life with Edwin Ford. This time she had experienced a long and passionate honeymoon. They had travelled to Liverpool, and from there had sailed to Italy, spending most of their time in their small cabin. Edwin had taken her to Venice, and Kate's lips tingled at the memory of him pulling her into shadowed doorways and stealing kisses as they hid behind her parasol.

They had wandered around the major sights of Florence, Rome and Naples, but found idyllic seclusion in Sicily. Edwin had rented a small cottage which nestled in its own little bay at the bottom of a hill. It was owned by a farmer who lived a mile away, and whose wife visited the newlyweds once a day to clean the house and bring enormous baskets of food and wine. Apart from these brief visits, Kate and Edwin were left completely alone in their isolated paradise.

Once the farmer's wife had gone home, Kate took great delight in swapping her heavy clothing for one of Edwin's shirts. His shirts reached her knees, and so she felt comfortable enough to wander around the house barefoot, or lie on the beach under the warm sun. Although nervous at first, Kate soon plucked up the courage to join her husband in the sea. They swam together in the azure water of the Mediterranean, Edwin cavorting like a playful dolphin before catching her in his arms again. In the evenings, she would curl up beside Edwin on the porch seat, and they would drink the farmer's homemade wine, watching the fireflies dance in the air around them. They felt as if they were the only two people in the world, and they had never been happier.

Kate sighed; her own honeymoon with Mark had been much less decadent and sensual. It had been more about taking advantage of the facilities offered by a luxurious Roman hotel than indulging in the delights of getting to know one another on a deeper level.

Allowing herself to savour the memories of her past life with Edwin Ford, Kate floated through Sunday as if she were still in a dream. In the late afternoon, she retrieved the cardboard box of her aunt's paperwork from the spare bedroom. Our alleged nursery, Kate thought sadly. Taking the box to the living room, she set it down on the thick rug in front of the fire and began to sort through the numerous papers, notebooks and diaries. In time, she came across a rolled up piece of thick paper tied with a red ribbon. Carefully, Kate unrolled the scroll, realising she had found her family tree. It was beautifully written in ink, names and dates cramming the page in different handwriting styles. At the bottom of the page, she found her aunt's name, and her father's: Christopher and Margaret Grahame. Both names had their dates of birth below, but not the dates of their death, or Kate's mother's name. With her finger, she traced the 'branch' to her grandfather's name: Michael John Grahame, who married her grandmother, Mary Fuller. Kate followed the tree to her great-grandfather, James Edwin Grahame. He had married Susannah Harper. As well as Michael, their union had produced two daughters, Rebecca and Amelia. They had married and produced children of their own, their tree branches spreading to the edges of the paper. Her great-great grandfather, John Grahame, had married Sarah Scott. James Edwin had been their only child. Kate gasped in astonishment. John's father, James Grahame, had married Eleanor Richards. As well as their son, James and Eleanor had raised a daughter. Katherine Grahame, born in April 1870, had married Edwin Ford in August 1890.

Kate's fingers shook as she held the paper, noting the dates of birth and death, although not all of them were mentioned. She read it several times, until it finally sank in. Her brother in Edwin's time was her own great-great-grandfather. John had married kind and gentle Sarah, and they had produced a son. Kate smiled wistfully when she saw that John and Sarah had named their son after John's father, and Edwin. They must have loved her husband, too. Kate felt inexplicably relieved that there were no dates of death for any of her Victorian family.

Carefully rolling and retying the scroll, Kate put it to one side. She would take it downstairs and have it framed. It would have pride of place somewhere in her home.

'Kate!'

Kate jumped in her seat, returning violently to the present. She looked up to see Adam Gray glaring at her impatiently over his spectacles, his secretary rolling her eyes in disdain. Kate squirmed under the scrutiny of everyone in the room.

'I asked you for an update on the treasure hunt,' Gray repeated tetchily.

Kate thought fast. 'I have written up the clues,' she told him, trying to sound efficient. 'I know where I'll place them. The worksheets are printed. I just need someone to try it to make sure it's going to work.'

Gray nodded and continued on to the next item on his agenda. Kate's mind wandered again; despite her best attempts to stay focused on her work, she couldn't erase Edwin from her thoughts. Thankfully, the Monday morning meeting ended swiftly, and people dispersed to their duties. Kate stood slowly, gathering her notepad and pen. Jess approached her and laid a comforting hand on her arm.

'Are you okay this morning?' she asked gently.

Kate was aware that Nick and David were still in the room. David shot her a quick look of concern, before turning his attention to his phone.

'I'm fine,' Kate replied softly. 'Tired, that's all. And I have a lot on my mind, obviously.' Inhaling deeply to try and wake herself up, Kate looked over at Nick. 'I need a volunteer to do the treasure hunt sometime this week, to make sure it's at the right level for our target audience.'

Nick looked indignant. 'Why are you looking at me?' he asked, spotting David hiding a smile as he listened to their exchange.

Kate grinned impishly. 'I need someone with a child-like mentality...'

Kate picked the garment bag from the back of the office door and hurried to the ladies' toilets. She only had half an hour before she was due to meet Mark at the restaurant in the High Street. Her day had been busy, affording her little time to contemplate anything other than her duties. Mark had left her no time to go home and dress for dinner, so she had brought her outfit with her.

She undressed in the cramped cubicle, using baby wipes in lieu of a preferred shower, and slithered into the dress she had bought on the shopping trip with Jess. The dress was black, sleeveless, with a lace panel at the low neckline which was lined with skin-coloured satin. It was quite fitted and showed off her curves. *A dress for a goddess*, Kate thought. *Not a mouse.* Tonight, however, she wanted to feel bold. She was wearing new black lace lingerie and silky hold-up stockings with lace tops. Hopefully, Mark would be impressed.

Kate slipped on high-heeled courts, hoping she wouldn't get them stuck in a hole in the pavement, or slide on the restaurant floor. Stuffing her work clothes into a bag, she left the cubicle to fix her hair and make-up at the sinks. Generally, Kate disliked wearing too much make-up, although she had bought a new lipstick in a bright berry shade in a bid to step even further out of her comfort zone. A spritz of her new perfume and she was done. She stepped back to survey her handiwork, then grimaced and turned away. She had just enough time to put her work clothes back in her locker so she wouldn't have to turn up at the restaurant clutching a carrier bag.

Jess and David were in the staffroom when Kate rushed in. They gaped at this unfamiliar Kate, with the hourglass figure, shapely legs and luscious red lips.

'Bloody hell!' Jess exclaimed. 'What have you done with *our* Kate?'

Kate held the carrier bag self-consciously in front of her body as she hurried to her locker. She slid the key into the lock and turned it, but the door was stuck. Again. Rattling it in frustration, Kate cursed under her breath. The locking mechanism had worked until a couple of weeks ago, when it had begun to stick intermittently for no reason other than to make her angry.

'Here,' David said, reaching for the key. 'Let me try.' Naturally, when he turned the key the door opened. Kate thanked David as she tossed in her bag of clothes and removed her black wool coat and handbag. She stood in front of her colleagues.

'Tell me honestly,' she asked. 'Do I look alright? I'm meeting Mark for dinner in the High Street.'

'Not just for dinner, apparently,' Jess quipped, nudging David. The archaeologist's face turned red, as did Kate's. Was that what she looked like - a desperate housewife?

'Kate, you look really lovely,' David said sincerely.

Jess eyed him curiously, always looking for evidence to back up the gossip about his sexuality, even though she knew some of the rumours had been concocted by a woman whose attentions he had spurned. At this moment, however, his eyes were on stalks as he gazed at Kate.

'I'm just leaving,' he continued. 'Shall I walk up the road with you? It might be a little icy.'

'I can come, too, and take your other arm!' Jess chimed in.

'Yes, please,' Kate nodded. 'I'm scared I'm going to fall over in these heels!'

Mark was waiting outside the restaurant, and looked pointedly at his watch as Kate hurried to meet him, five minutes late. He greeted her a little curtly and ushered her into the small, dimly-lit Italian restaurant. The waiter led them to a small table near the back of the busy room, and courteously helped Kate with her coat. Kate felt miserably deflated when it became evident that Mark had not noticed her new outfit. She sat down and held the menu in front of her face to hide her disappointment. What did she have to do to be seen by her husband? Sometimes Kate felt he wasn't even aware she was a woman, even though she always tried to look her best.

The waiter returned, and Mark ordered wine and his own food. When the waiter turned to Kate, she ordered her usual pasta and lowered her eyes to her cutlery. Their conversation was stilted. Kate dutifully asked about his trip to London, but Mark was vague and did not disclose many details, even about his visit to his brother. He did not hold her hand across the table as he had done when they were dating. Neither wished the other a happy anniversary. Although Mark ate heartily as always, Kate picked at her food, her appetite and enthusiasm gone. She tried to tell herself she was being stupid for getting upset. Men hardly ever noticed what their wives wore, did they?

'Well, fancy meeting you here!' Kate's nostrils were assaulted by the heady scent of Poison perfume, and Gemma leaned over to air-kiss her cheek. Kate noticed her friend was wearing beautiful earrings; sparkling diamonds nestled in white gold. The design was intricate and unusual, the gold forming a 'G' shape around the diamonds.

Gemma looked over at Mark, who smiled politely but only with his mouth. His blue eyes were glacial, although Kate could see him appraising Gemma in her tight red dress which didn't leave much to the imagination.

'Romantic dinner for two, then?' Gemma asked.

'It's our anniversary,' Kate replied, forcing a smile and trying not to feel ugly. 'Are you here with friends?'

'Only the one,' the journalist replied, turning to wave at a man sitting at a nearby table. He appeared to be in his forties, and was wearing an expensive-looking suit. In the subdued lighting, Kate thought he looked very like one of the city's Labour councillors. Gemma turned to Mark, and Kate saw her adopt her seductive 'come hither' stance. 'How's the hotshot lawyer?'

'Very well, thank you,' he replied crisply. Kate saw his nostrils flare as if he were inhaling Gemma's scent.

'Did I see you in the High Court today?' she asked, her eyes narrowing slightly. Kate saw the shift from femme fatale to seasoned reporter. 'Are you on the defence team for the accountant who's been charged with bank fraud?'

'Yes, I am,' Mark said. 'And I have nothing to say about it - on or off the record.'

Gemma laughed and turned back to Kate. 'I still owe you a coffee, sweetie. I'll call you soon. Enjoy your dinner!' She kissed Kate's cheek properly this time. 'Happy anniversary!' she said without sincerity, more to Mark than Kate, then sashayed back to her companion.

Mark's face was like thunder. 'I wish you would stop seeing that woman!' he muttered. 'Does she spray-paint on all her clothes?'

Oh, so you noticed? Kate thought to herself, feeling hurt and resentful. 'I don't see her very often,' she answered, pushing her food around her plate. 'We don't have much in common anymore. But she is an old friend.'

'Well, sometimes we have to de-clutter our friendships,' Mark retorted gruffly.

Mark seemed so tense and grumpy that Kate was glad when the meal was finally over. He had left his car in his company parking space, so Kate had to walk into the town centre in her untried high heels. When she reached for Mark's arm for support, she heard him give a sigh of impatience. *God, he's beastly tonight!* Kate felt her own irritation grow, but she was determined to make an effort. When they finally got home and through the front door, Kate put her arms around Mark's neck and gave him a lingering kiss. Her heart sank when he didn't respond, but gently extricated himself from her embrace.

'I'm sorry, Kate, I have to work tonight.'

'But it's our anniversary!' Kate hated herself for sounding plaintive.

Mark quickly kissed her forehead before stepping away. 'I know. I'll make it up to you.' He removed his coat and started to unpack his briefcase, leaving her to take off her own coat and gratefully slip off her shoes.

'Is that a new perfume you're wearing?' he asked, as he gathered paperwork to take to his home office.

'Yes,' she answered, surprised he'd noticed.

'It's a bit heavy. Can you shower before you go to bed? The smell might give me a headache.'

'I'm only suggesting you wear something more ladylike!'

'I'm not wearing skirts in this heat!'

Kate marched ahead of her husband, her jaw set. 'Besides, these trousers are very loose, so nobody can see anything. And look - I'm wearing a very ladylike hat!'

Kate stopped to tie the silk sash which kept her straw hat in place. She had coiled up her long dark hair and pinned it atop her head, where it would be concealed by the hat. Edwin came up behind her and placed his hands on her shoulders to make her stop. Out here, among his staff and the local workers, he tried to remain aloof and in command. Kate wasn't making it easy.

'Kate, you are the most infuriating woman! I'm only -'

'Fine! I'll go back to the hut then!'

Kate was angry. How dare he tell her what to wear, just so she wouldn't scandalise men who were more interested in digging in the dirt than in her attire! She started to march back towards their living quarters, where only an hour before she had lain contentedly in Edwin's arms.

Edwin groaned to himself in frustration. Hoping they were not being observed by the workers scuttling about the site, he strode after her. Catching her wrist, he pulled her behind the lean-to where the cooks were already preparing lunch in a huge copper pot over an open fire. He turned her to face him, holding her hands captive behind her back.

'I'm living in a room made of mud bricks, Edwin,' Kate snapped. 'I think a little leeway is in order.' She looked up at him defiantly, her lips pressed together. Edwin felt his resolve crumbling, as it always did as soon as he had her in his arms.

'Where did the clothes come from?' he asked, already guessing. 'They seem to fit very well.'

'John got them for me,' she replied, a little too smugly. 'I gave him my measurements, and he went to the gentleman's outfitters.'

Edwin closed his eyes in exasperation. 'So now all the men working at the outfitters know the measurements of Mrs Edwin Ford?'

'Oh, Edwin, we all have measurements! And I'm not ashamed of mine.' She changed tactics, slid her arms around his waist and reached up to nuzzle his neck. 'Have I ever told you how delicious you smell?'

Edwin wasn't fooled by Kate's attempt to befuddle him. He was well aware that his astute wife had quickly learned how to use her feminine charms. 'Yes. Usually when you're trying to distract me.' He had to admit it nearly always worked, too.

Kate stepped back in order for him to assess her appearance. 'Do I look so bad?' she smiled, placing her hands on her hips. She fixed him with a seductive stare.

Edwin pulled her against him. 'Are you always going to be this much of a handful?' he asked. Looking into his eyes, she could see his exasperation, but his love for her also shone there. She reached up to touch his unshaven cheek, and smooth his dark hair.

'I expect so,' Kate replied. 'But I would live anywhere with you. And I promise always to let you kiss me...' She tilted her head up brazenly and pouted.

'Into submission?'

'Never!'

He kissed her firmly, his arms wrapped tightly around her back. His hands swept down her back and over the curve of her rounded hips. She pressed her body against him, and he suddenly pulled back.

'I can feel...*everything*!' Edwin breathed, his voice holding a hint of dismay even as his body betrayed him.

'Yes,' Kate replied tartly, dropping her arms from about his neck. 'I'm not wearing a corset, either.' She poked out her tongue at him and ran off, giggling at his shocked expression. She could hear him muttering as he walked behind her, catching up when they reached the site where she was to work that morning.

From her vantage point several feet above the dig site, Kate could see from the layout of the excavated stone walls that buildings and roads were beginning to appear from the sand. The lost city of Akhetaten was rising again, preparing to reveal its treasures to the world once more. Since there had been no building work carried out since the city was abandoned by the heretic pharaoh's court, the site was very well-preserved, and the expedition was proving very successful. The location of the pharaoh's tomb, however, still eluded them.

A young man with blond hair waved up at them from below. Edwin waved back and turned to his wife. 'Down the ladder,' he commanded, his masculine pride still marginally wounded by her inability to do as she was asked. It seemed to Edwin that his wife never missed an opportunity to flout convention, which could be downright inconvenient at times. He pointed to the nearby ladder which led into the site. It was a descent of about ten feet. 'I'll go first.'

Edwin climbed down then held the somewhat rickety ladder for her. Determined to hide her apprehension, she stepped onto the first rung, then began her careful descent.

'Stop there a moment!' Edwin called up. Concerned, Kate looked down at him over her shoulder, her knuckles white where they gripped the rung above. She was astounded to catch him smirking because he had been ogling her backside! Ignoring him, she climbed down the rest

92

of the way, firing him an outraged glance as her feet settled on the hard dirt floor.

'That's a sight I won't forget in a hurry,' he murmured, grinning wickedly. His grin was infectious, and Kate turned away to hide her smile. It was impossible to stay irritated with him for long.

'What would you like me to do?' she asked, looking around at the industrious workers. Some were employees of the Egypt Exploration Fund, while others were local men wearing traditional long robes. They all kept their eyes studiously on their work and avoided looking at her.

Edwin led her to a corner of the site, which was marked out in the usual grid pattern by canes and twine. They were sheltered by three walls of a building, possibly the remains of a house. A large basket lay on the ground, holding small picks and trowels. Edwin bent down and picked up a small trowel and a paintbrush.

'Start digging in this corner - you'll probably find a lot of pottery. Don't dig any deeper than the blade of the trowel. Carefully brush the dirt from whatever you find, put it in the basket for identification and cataloguing. Jackson will be here all morning if you need him.' He indicated the young man who had waved to them, busy working in another part of the grid. 'Be sure to drink enough water - and keep your hat on!'

'So you want me to find little bits of things with these itty bitty tools?'

Edwin put the brush and trowel in her hand. 'It's this or our quarters. You said you were bored cataloguing and wanted to help with something more "exciting". I want to keep you safe. I'll be busy over at the cliffs, looking for the pharaoh's tomb. The archaeologists from the EEF arrived this morning, and I have to show them what we've found so far. We're close to finding the entrance - I can feel it. I'll be back, so no flirting with the locals.'

At that moment one of the local Egyptian workers cantered up on horseback, leading a second horse by the reins. The man called down to Edwin in the local dialect. Edwin replied in what Kate supposed was perfect Arabic, his tongue caressing the strange syllables.

He turned back to Kate and smiled. 'Last chance to go back and put some decent clothes on.'

She stepped towards him, her fingers tracing the waistband of his trousers. Standing on tiptoe, she nipped his earlobe with her teeth and dropped her voice to a whisper. 'Mister Ford, when I hear you speaking Arabic, I want to take my clothes *off*!'

Edwin bit his lip; she never played fair! Bending down, he kissed her nose. 'You are a saucy minx, Mrs Ford, and I won't forget you said that. I'll see you later.'

He took up her hand and kissed her knuckles, and then clattered up the ladder like a mountain goat. 'Jackson!' he called. 'You're in charge here this morning. Be sure to look after my wife.'

Jackson had kept his eyes on the ground during their exchange. The intensity of the Fords' relationship was a frequent topic of discussion in the camp. Blushing, he looked up at Edwin and grinned. 'Of course, Mister Ford,' he replied. 'But I believe Mrs Ford is more than capable of looking after herself.'

Edwin looked down at Kate, feeling a rush of pride. 'Aye,' he growled softly, so only she could hear. 'She's a feisty wench!' Kate watched him swing effortlessly into the saddle of his horse, and he was gone.

Kate spent three hours kneeling in the dirt, but she didn't notice the heat or the dust. She even became oblivious to the constant noise around her, the chatter of voices speaking English, Arabic and the local Egyptian dialect. Methodically, she had divided her own grid, measuring nine square feet, into smaller sections. Starting in one corner, near the wall, she carefully removed the top layer of gritty sand. Each time her trowel skimmed across something hard, her heart fluttered. She was frequently disappointed when her find turned out to be a stone. Occasionally, however, her efforts were rewarded with a piece of pottery or tile. As instructed, she carefully brushed the dirt from these pieces and placed them gently in the basket. Just before the team were due to stop for lunch, Kate hit something with her trowel.

Kate scooped and brushed the sand away from her find, and then felt gently for the edges. This was larger than the pieces she had unearthed so far. A little more work revealed a stone tablet of some kind. It was about the size of a large book, and she could make out some of the hieroglyphs carved into its surface. Kate placed her hand on the tablet, feeling excitement in the pit of her stomach, but also reverence for the piece of Egyptian history under her fingertips.

'Jackson!' she called urgently. The young man was instantly at her side. 'Can you help me lift this out?'

They gently levered the tablet out of the ground and held it between them, studying the characters still visible. Jackson brushed the sand from the tablet to reveal lines of hieroglyphs. Silently, he scanned the symbols, intent on his translation.

'What does it say, Jackson?' Kate badgered, and was intrigued to see his ears turn red.

'Well...it's - it's either a love letter or a romantic poem, Mrs Ford.'

'A love letter? To whom? Who wrote it? Tell me what it says!'

'I think it's to Queen Nefertiti...'

'*Never!*'

'Yes, look, this is her cartouche,' Jackson pointed excitedly to the symbols near the top of the tablet. 'The author's name isn't mentioned, though. Probably anonymous, as he would have been executed if he'd been discovered wooing a queen. He may just have admired her from afar, of course.'

'Can you read it to me?'

Poor Jackson's ears were flaming now, the flush creeping up his youthful face. He couldn't read words of love to Edwin Ford's wife! In fact, he had never uttered any words of love to any female. But Kate was insistent, gently pleading, and he found it hard to resist her large brown eyes and kind smile of encouragement.

'You are more dazzling to my eyes than all the stars of heaven, the sun and the moon. You are my heart, my life. I enslave myself to you for all eternity, my Queen.'

'That's very good, Jackson. Your translation skills are improving.'

Kate and Jackson hadn't noticed the shadow looming over them, and both looked up into Edwin's stern, disapproving face. Jackson heartily wished the sand would swallow him up. Shamefaced, he dropped his gaze to the tablet.

'Put the tablet in the basket and go and take your lunch break. Work resumes at three o'clock.'

Jackson stood up to leave, avoiding eye contact with either of them.

Kate rose stiffly and touched his arm briefly with her fingertips. 'Thank you, Jackson,' she smiled, and watched sympathetically as the poor man scooted up the ladder and disappeared. She turned to her husband. 'That was cruel, Edwin,' she chastised. 'I asked him to help me lift the tablet out of the ground, and I insisted he translate it for me. The words are beautiful, are they not?' Kate sighed theatrically, enjoying another opportunity to tease him. 'Men just don't have a way with words these days...' She sauntered off to the foot of the ladder and since they were the only two left on the site, made a show of climbing up very slowly as Edwin stood frowning below.

The sun was almost at its zenith when they reached the lean-to where lunch was being served. An Egyptian woman who helped with cooking in the camp handed Edwin a plate of what looked like stew. Kate had learned not to look too closely at what was in their food. It was always hot, and nobody had yet died from food poisoning. The elderly woman offered Kate a plate of food, but Kate declined. She didn't feel like tackling the food today, and she was suddenly exhausted. The woman muttered something which sounded like a reprimand, her dark gaze studying Kate's face. Handing the plate to another worker, she handed Kate some warm flat bread and a flagon of water instead. With a knowing smile, she lifted her fingers to her lips in a gesture which was meant to encourage Kate to eat. She then lightly touched Kate's belly before moving on. Kate flushed, looking around to make sure nobody had witnessed the scene. Edwin was conversing with a colleague and had his back to her. But Doctor Cummings had seen the exchange. He raised a quizzical eyebrow, but Kate imperceptibly shook her head and looked away.

Munching the bread, she followed Edwin back to their dark little brick house with the wooden door and roof made of corrugated iron. With the sun at its merciless peak, they would have to stay in the shade for the next four hours. Kate's stomach flipped in anticipation of spending all that time alone with Edwin, but was sadly disappointed when he settled down at his desk to read some paperwork whilst eating his stew.

Kate understood Edwin's dedication to his work, and his ardent desire to uncover Akhenaten's tomb - not because he wanted to find treasure which would make him rich, but because he wanted to reveal Egypt's secrets for the rest of the world to see. Following his instincts, he had moved some of his workforce a little way outside the city boundary, near the cliffs which sheltered the city. Still, Kate thought, it was hard to look at his muscled back and not lust after her irresistible husband. To distract herself, Kate read for a little while, but she felt uncomfortably dusty and hot in her trousers.

For her benefit, Edwin had erected a modesty screen in a corner of their room. Behind the screen, a small table held a ceramic basin, a jug of water, soap, sponges and some scented toilet water. Kate quietly slipped behind the screen and undressed, tossing her dusty clothes over the top of the screen. She poured some tepid water into the basin and used the soap and sponge to wash herself. It felt pleasant enough, but Kate longed for a bath. She wrapped her body in a thin cotton towel and unbound her hair. Hanging her head over the basin, she made a clumsy attempt to wash her long hair in the confined space. But bending over the basin caused her to rattle the screen and disturb Edwin.

Given his sombre mood, Kate expected a sarcastic comment about the inability of women to cope with a little dirt. Without a word, Edwin rose from his seat, put the paperweight rock on his papers and came over to help. He moved the screen out of the way and took off his shirt so it wouldn't get wet. Taking the jug, he slowly poured water over Kate's head without spilling it on her face or the rug which covered the ground.

'Perhaps I should just cut it short,' Kate suggested meekly.

'Absolutely not.' Edwin sounded adamant. He bent to kiss the back of her neck. 'I love your hair.' He soaped his hands and massaged Kate's head. She closed her eyes, relaxing. All too soon he was rinsing out the soap and squeezing the water from her tresses. Taking up another towel he gently dried her hair.

Straightening, Kate reached for her comb. Edwin saw a momentary weariness in her eyes. He had seen that expression several times over the last week. At other times, he had seen a soft, faraway look. He took her hand, and led her to sit on their cramped wooden bed. Taking up the comb, he sat behind her and gently drew it through her thick hair. She sat quietly, uncomplaining as always about the conditions he was forcing her to live in. It was his fault she was here, in a land neither safe nor hospitable. When he had been offered a place on this expedition, he had refused to go at first. They had been married for less than two years - hardly long enough to bear being apart for nearly four months. But Kate had vehemently asserted that he would be foolish to forego such an opportunity. She had then fought with him until he had agreed to take her with him. They had been at camp for three weeks, and she had learned to live with the dust and the hostile desert creatures, the often unidentifiable food and brackish water. She had washed and mended their clothes, tried to make their stark quarters a welcoming sanctuary and silently borne the loneliness of being the only British woman in camp. She had to share rudimentary facilities with the Egyptian women in their separate camp. Every day he feared she would ask to return home. Not for the first time, Edwin was overwhelmed with love for his beautiful, brave and devoted wife.

'How would you like to spend Christmas in Cairo?' he asked, his fingers kneading the tense muscles in her neck and shoulders. The next moment, Kate had flattened him on the bed and was lying on top of him, her cheeks rosy with excitement. The narrow bed creaked in protest.

'Do you mean it?' she gasped. Christmas was only two weeks away.

'I've already arranged a room at a nice hotel, courtesy of the EEF.' He was interrupted by a shower of kisses all over his face. 'I'll have to work some of the time, but I believe there will be a traditional Christmas dinner for the European community and a New Year ball.'

'I can have a bath!'

'Thank God!'

Kate thumped his chest at the playful insult, but grinned and nuzzled his nose with hers. 'That's not a nice thing to say to a lady!' She kissed his bare chest, the sprinkling of coarse dark hair tickling her face. In one swift movement, Edwin rolled her beneath him and gazed hungrily at her lips. He apologised to her in Arabic, his lips close to hers. 'More…' she breathed, gazing at him from beneath her lashes. His eyes sparkled as he spoke again, his voice soft and caressing, the words strange and exotic. He kept murmuring against her lips as she reached down to pull away the towel.

'Kate. Kate! Wake up! You're having a nightmare!' Even as she was pulled from sleep she could hear the irritation in Mark's voice. *Damn, damn, damn!* Kate moaned to herself. *Why do I keep waking up when I really want to stay asleep? That* wasn't *a nightmare!*

'I'm sorry Mark,' she mumbled. 'I didn't mean to wake you.' She shaded her eyes from the glare of the bedside light above her head.

As he leaned over her, Mark saw something in her eyes which he hadn't seen for a long time. He had lain awake listening to Kate in the midst of her dream for five minutes before waking her, recognising her soft moans as sounds of ecstasy, not horror.

Perhaps because she was starting to feel guilty, she reached up to wind her fingers in Mark's tousled fair hair. Tentatively, she pulled him down towards her, at the same time arching her body to meet his. Mark was perplexed, and a little suspicious, but he had no intention of letting this rare opportunity pass him by.

CHAPTER 6

Kate woke before the alarm, and reached over to switch it off so her ears wouldn't be assaulted by its ear-splitting tone. Mark had already left for work, leaving a mug of coffee on her bedside table. Clasping the warm mug between her hands, she lay back against the pillows, feeling as though she hadn't slept at all. Her head felt foggy and muddled, her thoughts tumbling around inside her brain. *How is it possible to dream in such graphic detail? Why am I dreaming like this? What the hell does it mean? Why can't I just be happy in this life?*

Her breath quickened as memories returned. She could still feel the roughness of Edwin's unshaven cheek against her own. In her dreams he loved her so completely, and Kate felt she loved him. How could she have such intense feelings for someone she had never met? She recalled, too, the other event of the night and discovered her feelings about that were unclear. There had been little tenderness between her and Mark. She had felt a desperate need to connect with the man she had chosen to spend this lifetime with, at the same time yearning for the husband of her dreams. Who knows what Mark had felt about the encounter? Confused and unsettled, Kate got ready for work.

As soon as Jess walked into the staffroom, she knew something was amiss. Kate sat staring blankly into space, a mug of cold coffee in her hand. Swapping it for a hot cup, Jess quietly asked what was wrong. Kate divulged the latest instalment of her dream life. She had texted Erin on her way to work, asking for another appointment. Kate hoped that, once she had discovered all she could about her past life, she might gain some clarity and be able to put the whole, unsettling experience behind her. Erin had expressed her reluctance to perform another regression so soon after the first, but Kate had been persuasive, despite sitting on a busy bus filled with people who could overhear her conversation. Without revealing all to her fellow passengers, Kate had convinced Erin to see her that evening. Jess automatically offered to accompany her.

Just as Kate was finishing her coffee, her mobile phone rang, announcing a call from her husband.

'Hi, Kitty Cat,' he said, in a husky voice. Kate cringed at the pet name. 'I thought we might stay home and have dinner this evening, just the two of us.'

Kate bit her lip. 'I'm sorry, Mark. I'm going out with Jess after work for a little while, so I'll be a bit late. Could we have a late dinner?' She heard him sigh, peeved at not getting his own way.

After a second, he replied, 'Sure. I'll cook us something. Text me when you're on your way, okay?' Before she could respond, he had hung up.

'I'm going to put up the clues for the treasure hunt today,' Kate told Jess, who was tactfully washing their cups. 'See you later?'

Jess smiled and nodded. 'If I don't see you through the day I'll meet you back here after work. Good luck. Don't get lost.'

Kate gave her a lopsided grin. 'Don't kill any Romans.'

Kate ascended the stone stairs leading from the entrance hall to the Grand Gallery, carrying her box of clues for the treasure hunt. The wall beside the stairs was lined with fearful-looking spears and knives, brutal remnants of battles past.

'I don't fancy getting that stuck in my eye!'

Kate turned to see a small elderly man behind her. He pointed at a particularly nasty-looking spear as he smiled at her through twinkling blue eyes.

'I don't know...' he sighed, shaking his head. 'The things we humans make to hurt others. People can do terrible things to one another!'

'I know,' Kate agreed kindly. 'Give me animals any day.'

'Aye, animals are never vindictive. They'd never hurt us deliberately.'

The man followed Kate as she headed for the escalator, obviously hoping for a longer conversation. Inside, Kate was screaming for escape. She smiled at the old man and wished him an enjoyable visit, before stepping onto the escalator. As she ascended to the first floor, the Millennium Clock began to mark the hour of eleven. The accompanying organ music began, so that visitors could once again be reminded of the evil events which had taken place in the last century. When Kate passed the spire of the clock tower, she glanced at the eerie figure of a woman carrying a dead man. The image was supposed to convey compassion, and encourage observers to reflect on the past and contemplate the strength needed to move forward into the future. *How?* Kate wondered. *How should I do that?*

Kate pushed open the heavy glass doors of the Lady Ivy Wu Gallery and stepped into a different environment altogether. Compared to the bustle and noise of the airy, sunlit Grand Gallery, this room was dark, silent and pleasantly cool. Putting the box of clues on one of the square cushioned seats, Kate took a moment to look around the glass cases, studying the possessions of people long dead. She scrutinised a beautiful silk dragon robe and a pair of black satin boots said to originate from the Qing Dynasty. Faintly, Kate heard the Millennium Clock ending its hourly warning, and she shuddered involuntarily. The room suddenly seemed eerie, as if it were holding its breath, waiting, watching her. Kate moved from China to Japan, admiring the intricately-crafted regalia of a Samurai warrior. Reading the labels for the exhibits in the case, she noticed that 'Samurai' was Japanese for 'one who serves'.

Kate jumped at the sound of footsteps creaking on the wooden floor. A Chinese tourist had joined her in the gallery, all scuffing feet and rustling carrier bags. Sighing resentfully at the intrusion, Kate walked over to the box to pick out the clue for the treasure hunt.

Near the seating area there was a little alleyway, hidden from the main gallery - just the sort of hidey-hole kids loved. The display case here held items salvaged from the wreck of the Diana, a sailing ship which had sunk in 1817 in the Straits of Malacca on its way from China to Madras. Blue and white porcelain from the Qing Dynasty shone in the dimmed lighting. It was hard to believe the patterned plates and crockery had been found under the sea. Next to the tableware sat a beautiful wooden replica of a Dutch East Indian merchant ship from 1719. Kate crouched down to admire the intricate detail and immaculate condition of the model. As she straightened, she thought she saw a man's face reflected in the glass. For a split second, dark eyes gazed into hers and then vanished. Kate told herself it was probably the tourist, waiting for her to get out of the way. Quickly, she fixed the clue to the case and then hastily pushed her way through the doors. The gallery had left her feeling slightly spooked, or maybe it was the dirge of that awful clock.

Back on the bright second floor landing, Kate leaned over the railing and looked down. The refurbishment had seen the removal of the two large rectangular fish ponds which had graced the ground floor. A number of exhibits took their place, including a Victorian pavilion with a drinking fountain in the centre, the huge lens from the Inchkeith Lighthouse and an improbably large feast bowl shaped like a canoe from the nineteenth century Cook Islands. The exhibits were randomly scattered, but reminiscent of archive photos she had seen of the Grand Gallery during the Victorian era.

Right, Kate thought. *Where to next?* She had started by placing clues in the Science and Technology areas, where children generally made a bee-line for the interactive exhibits. From there, she had left a trail in the Animal World gallery, which led to the Earth and Space area. The aim was to encourage children to look at the less 'cool' exhibits, in the hope they would learn more about different cultures, and the history of the world they lived in. Kate recalled the ancient Peruvian pottery of the Nasca civilization. One of the knobbly vases on display was decorated with gruesome decapitation scenes. Older kids would delight in the grossness of these images, but the younger ones might be disturbed. Kate decided to place a clue in the Nasca area, but far away from any pictures of flying heads.

She walked along the second floor gallery, past sculptures of deities and busts of important men who seemed to steal a glance at her as she passed. After visiting a couple of the less popular areas, she stopped before the large tapestry of a handsome, copper-haired Saint George spearing a rather dopey-looking dragon. George's golden halo was resplendent, even though it had been stitched more than one hundred years before. Words lovingly sewn at the top of the tapestry read: 'And while his lady pray'd with one good thrust he pierced that false tongue.' *Hmm,* Kate thought. *There's a mother-in-law joke in there somewhere.*

Holding the near-empty box to her chest, Kate finally sought the tranquillity of ancient Egypt. It was her favourite place in the museum, a place she visited when she needed peace and solitude. As always, she fondly remembered the beautiful artefacts which were no longer on display, having been replaced with more educational items. Now visitors could see that Egyptian children had played with balls and spinning tops. Tools, storage jars and a bowl of desiccated food were undoubtedly interesting, but they could not fire Kate's imagination in the same way as past displays of intricate jewellery and hair combs. And of course, her beloved Nefertiti was nowhere to be seen. The queen had been removed from the gallery just as the ancient Egyptians had tried to remove her from their history.

Kate knelt to place her final clue on the iron railing near the display case of desiccated food. As she stuck the card on the curved upright post, a man's voice made her jump. 'What are you doing down there?' he asked curiously.

Kate spoke to the legs which had appeared beside her. 'I'm setting up a treasure hunt for the children. School holidays are upon us again!'

'What will the treasure be?' He sounded amused by the concept.

'A certificate.' It sounded lame even as she said it. 'Maybe a sweet and a pencil from the gift shop. And hopefully they will learn something about the world along the way.'

'That's an admirable intention.'

He had an indistinct accent, neither broad Scots nor blatantly English. His soft, deep voice was vaguely familiar. She looked at the man's feet, her eyes moving upwards. Black shoes - no, boots - with laces, dark wrinkled trousers, a white shirt with the sleeves rolled up, strong jaw - *Oh my God, it can't be, it just* can't *be!* Kate's fingers gripped the railings tightly, and she swallowed a feeling of nausea as her head started to spin. The man standing before her was the image of Edwin Ford! He looked a little older, his hair was a little longer, his face looked somewhat careworn, but it was him. Unable to speak, Kate strove to calm herself and not appear mentally-deficient. Standing, she crossed her arms in front of herself. His direct gaze made her feel naked. *No wonder, with the dreams I've been having!*

'You've cut your hair,' he stated, matter-of-factly. She touched a curl below her ear. She had made the decision to cut her long hair into a shorter style three weeks after starting work at the museum. Now her wavy hair just touched the top of her shoulders, but an errant lock still fell irritatingly across her face. She had always worn it long, and Mark had been less than pleased by the change. He had tactlessly told her that, in his opinion, her long hair had been one of her best features.

'Have we met?' she croaked, desperately trying to remember when and where it could have been - in this reality. And why she had apparently superimposed his face onto her husband from a past life. *Oh, God, none of this makes sense!*

'Yes, Kate. A while ago.' His lips curved into a gentle smile. She looked at his lips, remembering. From the look in his eyes, she felt that he somehow remembered, too.

'I'm sorry - I met so many people in my first few weeks, it's hard to remember everyone.' Kate knew she was babbling. She fought to get her breathing under control.

Her two-way radio suddenly squawked into life, and Kate jumped. 'Jess for Kate - are you there?'

'I'm here, Jess.' Kate's voice was strained.

'Will you be free for lunch at one?'

'Yes. I'm almost finished here.'

'Meet you under Bulldog?'

'Okay. Kate out.'

'Bulldog?' he inquired, a bemused smile playing on his enticing lips.

'Yes,' she replied. 'You know, the plane suspended over the rear entrance. It belonged to Angus, fifteenth Duke of Hamilton.'

He inclined his head, his gaze still fixed intently on her face. She tried to stop staring, busied herself with picking up her things from the floor.

'You like ancient Egypt.' It was more a statement than a question. She could feel her cheeks burning, like some silly schoolgirl with her first crush. She was mortified. He must think her an imbecile.

'I love ancient Egypt,' she prattled on. 'I come here all the time.' *Did that sound like a pick-up line? Oh, please go away so I can run and cringe in the loo!'*

'I know. I've seen you here before.' He followed her to the Qurneh corner. She looked blankly at the display cases, trying to get sensible sentences to come out of her mouth.

'Which department are you from?' she asked him.

'Art and Ethnography, with a sprinkling of Egyptology,' he replied evasively.

'That's not a department,' she chided gently. 'Have you been here long?' She walked further along to the stone tablet of King Akhenaten.

'Yes.'

'What are you working on at the moment?'

'China.'

She remembered the tableware from the Diana. 'Qing Dynasty?'

'Wedgwood.'

Kate looked up and caught him smirking. *Oh, he thinks he's funny. Very droll!* She smiled, relaxing a little. The old museum clock started to chime twelve but was quickly drowned out by the Millennium Clock. A shadow fell over Kate's eyes.

'You don't like the Millennium Clock,' he observed. 'Why?'

Kate hesitated, not sure her reply made sense. 'We all suffer at some time in our lives, don't we? We don't need a hideous clock tower to remind us of life's suffering every hour of every day.' Kate changed the subject, pointing through the glass at Akhenaten. 'I like this piece. His features are so detailed, and he looks so strong and purposeful. I wish I could touch it,' she said wistfully, her fingertips against the glass as she remembered caressing the king's lips in her past incarnation. When she raised her eyes, she saw the man watching her reflection intently. Their eyes locked...

The Millennium Clock's party piece ended, breaking the spell. Kate blinked, completely unnerved, but reluctant to leave him. Unfortunately, she had a job to do which didn't involve gazing into this man's eyes like a love-struck teenager. She did enough of that in her dreams.

'I have to go,' she murmured.

'I know.'

'Have fun with your china.'

He smiled, but she thought his eyes looked mournful. He moved to let her pass and she started to walk towards the landing, towards the sunlight, where people were no doubt gathering in the Balcony Café. She turned before she left the Egyptian gallery, but he had already gone.

Kate nearly dropped her box as a group of noisy French students pushed past her rudely. She descended the stairs to the ground floor and moved swiftly through groups of visitors, heading for her office. A couple with a baby in a pushchair headed towards her, obviously in the midst of an argument, and oblivious to their screaming child. The wheel of the pushchair clipped her foot as they passed, and Kate felt a stab of pain. She moved faster, keen to escape the visitors who wandered thoughtlessly with their eyes looking up instead of where they were going. Suddenly it was too hot, too bright, and too loud.

She slammed the door of her empty office and leaned against it, breathing deeply until her heart stopped pounding. Kate sat at her desk and rested her head in her hands for a few moments, reliving her meeting with the man from her dreams. The thrill of excitement she had felt made her feel guilty, as if she had been unfaithful. She pushed her confused thoughts to the back of her head and looked around her desk for something to do to fill the half hour before she could meet Jess. Given her current state of anxiety, she wisely chose not to embark on anything too complicated. Opening the bottom drawer of her desk, she drew out one of the books David had lent her.

Kate and Jess sat on a bench in Bristo Square, people-watching as they ate their sandwiches. The trees were starting to blossom, and the sky was blue, but Kate felt cold. She was content to listen to Jess talk about her family, her massive crush on her next-door neighbour, Steve, and what had happened to her at work that morning. Jess usually made her laugh with her ability to make even the mundane sound wildly entertaining. But today Kate was distracted and her silence was noticed. Jess poked her gently in the ribs and asked, 'Are you listening?'

'Of course I am! You just told me you dropped a whole box of files at the deputy director's feet. Just as well it wasn't china...'

'Why would I be carrying china?'

'Does the museum display any china other than the Chinese stuff?'

Jess gave Kate a puzzled look. 'Could you be a bit more specific?'

'Wedgwood.'

'It used to be displayed a long time ago, before Ikea. Nobody's interested in it anymore. Such exhibits "would not appeal to our target audience". There's a small display on the top floor. Why do you ask?'

'I met someone today who claims he's working on a Wedgwood project.'

'Well, there's probably loads of the stuff in storage. Some it might be on long-term loan from private collections. Perhaps he's involved in returning a collection, or conserving some of our own stuff. What's his name?'

'He didn't say, and I forgot to ask. I met him in ancient Egypt. He seemed to know me. He noticed I'd had my hair cut...'

'But you don't know him?'

Kate looked perturbed. 'Apart from having Mills and Boon-type dreams about him, no.' She saw Jess's incredulous stare. For once, her friend was stuck for words. 'Yes,' Kate continued. 'I'm fantasising about someone I apparently work with. How sad is that? He's the spitting image of Edwin Ford.' Kate passed a hand over her eyes in despair. 'I don't understand!' she wailed.

'Is he gorgeous?' Jess asked. Kate didn't want to admit out loud that he was possibly the most handsome, charismatic man she had ever laid eyes on, but Jess had already guessed. 'I'll take that as a yes, then. Poor you, was it awkward?'

'I acted like a teenager! How can I not remember meeting him, but have such detailed dreams about him as if we were man and wife?'

'He obviously made a big enough impression the first time!' Jess sniggered, and Kate finally smiled. It was a little funny, and surely harmless...

'Seriously, though, surely I would have seen him more than once in all these weeks?'

'Not necessarily. Some of the staff work away in the bowels of the building, and hardly see the light of day. Or he may work in one of the off-site offices, or one of the other museums. What department is he from?'

'Art and Ethnography, with a sprinkling of Egyptology.'

'That's not a department.'

Kate chuckled. 'That's what I said.'

'Kate, can you tell me where you are?' Erin's voice was soft and level. She and Jess watched as Kate smiled lovingly, as if she were looking at something or someone she adored.

'I'm on a train,' Kate informed them. 'I'm with Edwin. We're coming home...'

When Kate and Edwin stepped from the train at Waverley, John and Eleanor were waiting on the platform. John immediately enveloped his sister in a fierce hug which lifted her off the ground. Eleanor was rather more dignified in her embrace. As John greeted Edwin, she took Kate's chin in her hand and looked into her daughter's glowing face.

'How was Italy, dear?' she asked, smiling at her daughter's sparkling eyes.

'Oh, it was wonderful, Mother!' Kate sighed, grinning.

Eleanor lowered her voice. 'And how is your husband?'

Kate's cheeks flushed. 'Oh, he's wonderful, too!'

Edwin and John joined them, and Edwin leaned down to kiss Eleanor lightly on the cheek. 'Hello, Mother,' he said respectfully. Kate was astounded to see her mother blush.

'Now, now,' Eleanor sounded flustered. 'Is that the porter coming with your baggage? John, you must get them a cab.' She turned to Kate. 'Katie, darling, we can't come home with you. But we'll see you later?'

Kate was bemused, as her mother hurried her to a waiting cab. Their luggage was loaded, and Edwin handed her into her seat. He turned to John, his eyes questioning.

'It's all in hand,' John told him. Kate began to sense a mystery.

Edwin shook John's hand. 'I can't thank you enough, John. We'll see you soon?'

'Yes, of course. Oh, by the way, Father wants you to start work on Monday morning at nine sharp.'

'I'll be there.' Edwin turned to Eleanor and gallantly kissed her hand. 'Goodbye, Mother.' Kate giggled as she saw her mother blush again.

Kate expected the cab to take them to her parents' house. Although she and Edwin had viewed several properties before their wedding, they had not found anything suitable. She was surprised, therefore, when the cab stopped in front of a house at the end of Abercromby Place. She looked up at Edwin, mystified.

He regarded her hesitantly. 'Now, I don't want you to be cross with me,' he said firmly. 'But I've rented us a house.'

'But how?' she asked, trying to remember if she had seen him with any correspondence while they were on their honeymoon. She couldn't remember him having anything in his hands but her.

'It became available just before we left, so I asked John to look at it. In short, your family thought the property would suit us, and John handled all the necessary legalities on our behalf.'

As Edwin helped Kate down from the cab, the front door opened and Kate's maid from Heriot Row came to stand at the top of the steps. Beth was followed by a young girl and an older woman. They stood in a line as Kate climbed up the short flight of steps to meet them.

'Welcome home, Mrs Ford,' Beth smiled warmly. She gestured to her companions. 'This is Mrs Mackay, the cook, and Annie, the housemaid.' The two ladies curtseyed as Kate shook their hands. As Kate prepared to enter her new home, Edwin raced up the steps.

'Just a minute, Mrs Ford!' he called. She turned, and cried out in surprise as Edwin scooped her up in his arms and carried her over the threshold. He kissed her lightly as he set her down in the vestibule, gave her a boyish grin then raced off again to help the cab driver with their luggage.

Kate gazed around the welcoming entrance hall. The black and white floor tiles shone, reflecting the light from several wall sconces. An ornate chandelier hung from the high ceiling, which was adorned with equally decorative cornices. Kate wandered into the first room, which turned out to be a parlour. It was cosy, like her mother's, with soft sofas and a beautiful limestone fireplace. Occasional tables were artfully arranged over a massive Persian rug. Heavy brocade drapes hung at the sides of the tall windows which overlooked Queen Street Gardens. In the far corner of the room sat a small piano. Kate noticed some of their wedding presents in the room: silver candelabra on the mantelpiece, a crystal decanter and glasses on a silver tray. Kate left the parlour and investigated the large dining room, in the centre of which sat a long, polished table and twelve beautifully carved chairs.

Kate could not contain her excitement as she lifted her skirts and ran upstairs. The first floor held a more intimate parlour on one side and a wood-panelled study with a large desk and bookcase on the other. There was also a water closet. Climbing the curving stairs to the second floor, Kate stepped into the spacious master bedroom, which faced the front of the house. The walls were painted a warm rose colour, with two chairs and a love seat upholstered in dusky pink velvet. The bed was large, with a carved wooden headboard. Another door revealed a small dressing room, with a dressing table, a large mirror and hanging space for all Kate's clothes. Kate opened a second door and gave a soft cry of delight when she saw the cream marble bathroom, with indoor plumbing and a large bath.

Edwin came up behind her, slipping his arms around her waist. 'Well, Mrs Ford? Does this meet with your approval?'

Kate turned in his arms. She wanted to ask if they could afford such a palace, but she knew this would offend her husband. He had, rather unconventionally, discussed his income with her in order to allay any fears she might have about his ability to support her. She supposed that her sensible man would not rent a house he could not afford, just to make her happy. And so she gave him a glorious smile and nodded enthusiastically.

'It's not a large house,' Edwin said, almost apologetically. 'But it will do until we need something bigger.' He gave her a very direct look, which made her blush.

'Edwin,' she scolded. 'Is it your sole aim in life to fluster every woman you meet?'

When Kate woke on Monday morning, Edwin had already left for work. She sat up in bed, feeling slightly bereft; this was the first time she had woken up without him, and she missed him already. Kate wondered how she was going to fill her day, now that she was a wife. She tried to recall her mother's household duties, determined to be just as efficient and economical as Eleanor.

Rather than ring for tea, Kate dressed and went downstairs to the small, well-appointed kitchen. Her mother had employed the cook and housemaid on her behalf, as well as sending Beth to be her personal maid. The cook, Mrs Mackay, was a kindly woman of about fifty. She looked surprised to see Kate enter the kitchen, and immediately offered her tea and some breakfast. Before long, the two were like old friends. Mrs Mackay provided gentle guidance with menus and the ordering of provisions. In her younger days, she had worked in some of the grandest houses in Edinburgh. She now looked forward to working at a less punishing pace, in a smaller home. Kate found her to be a mine of information, and very easy to get along with. She did not feel at all embarrassed in admitting her lack of experience in running a household, and expressing her desire to learn how to do so competently. Like her mother, Kate wanted to help shop for their food and was quite prepared to get up early the following morning to go to the market with Mrs Mackay and Annie.

After numerous cups of tea and a fruitful discussion with Mrs Mackay, Kate decided to make some scones to take to Edwin. Mrs Mackay cleared a corner of the big wooden kitchen table for Kate then returned to her work, impressed by her new mistress. Kate Ford was no white-handed lady afraid of a little hard work.

While the scones baked, Kate wandered around her new home for the umpteenth time since her arrival two days before. The second bedroom was small, but still held a double bed and wardrobe. Its window looked onto the homes and gardens at the back of the house. They had a small garden of their own, which had been attractively landscaped. Edwin had already placed his few books on the tall bookcase in the study. A small statue of the Egyptian goddess Bastet sat on his desk. Kate sighed, besotted with their first home.

Kate checked her hat in the hall mirror before taking the basket from Beth. She had packed an enormous lunch for Edwin, before changing into her teal green suit and walking boots. It was nearly noon when she set out on the uphill walk to Chambers Street, and Kate hoped Edwin would not take an early lunch break. The sun was shining, though the breeze held an autumnal chill. The trees in Princes Street Gardens were changing colour and preparing to shed their leaves. Kate thought they were at their most beautiful with leaves of red, copper and gold. The Castle stood sentinel above the city, its grey rock blackened by the smoke from the trains below. As Kate walked up the Mound, she felt a pang of longing for the clean sea breezes of Sicily, instead of the sooty air of Edinburgh. She wished she could feel warm sand between her toes instead of the hard grey pavement under her boots. Although she loved Edinburgh, it suddenly felt a little too dirty, a little too crowded, and a little too cold. Kate fervently hoped that she and Edwin would travel abroad again in the not too distant future.

Outside the museum, Kate paused to smooth her skirts and hair. Her cheeks were already pink from her brisk walk. Straightening her shoulders, she climbed the steep steps. An usher opened the door for her, touching his cap. 'Good afternoon, Mrs Ford.' He gave her a courteous smile. Kate beamed at him, secretly proud to be addressed as Edwin's wife. As she walked between the exhibits on the ground floor, every member of staff she met greeted her the same way.

Edwin was still housed in the tiny office a few doors along from her father. There was no assistant to announce her, so she crept quietly to the partially open door and peeped inside. Her gorgeous husband sat writing at his desk, a pile of books at his elbow. Although he faced the door, his head was bent attentively over his work, and he did not see her. He held a pen in his fingers, the end tapping his lips in contemplation. His other hand fidgeted with a small rock which he absently rolled around under his palm. She thought she could hear him muttering, and stifled a giggle. Tentatively, she knocked on the door and was amused to hear him grunt in response. Quietly, she entered the room and stood before his desk. She watched him reluctantly look up from his work, his eyes moving upward until he realised there was a skirt in front of him. Hastily he rose from his seat, and grinned with pleasure when he realised it was his wife under a very large and decorative hat. He came around the desk towards her.

'That's a very fine hat, Mrs Ford,' he told her. She smiled wryly; Edwin had bought the hat in Florence, and then complained bitterly about having to cart its huge box all over Italy. He stroked his hands up her arms. 'And I remember this outfit, too...'

Kate brought the basket up between them. 'I brought you some lunch,' she said crisply and set the basket on the corner of the desk. She moved to his chair, leaning over to see what had him muttering to himself. He had been scribbling lots of notes. 'What are you working on?'

Edwin was unused to being rebuffed by his new bride. Piqued, he folded his arms and narrowed his eyes. 'Your father has asked me to give a lecture.' Kate looked up, impressed and pleased for him. 'He wants me to talk about my travels in Egypt. Apparently he thinks I would attract a...wider audience.' He bit the inside of his cheek to stop himself smiling as he watched her jaw tighten and her eyes narrow.

'Oh, did he?' she asked, her tone ominously quiet.

'Yes, and I believe your mother is already spreading the words among her friends.'

The office was too small to effectively flounce from the room, but Kate managed a fair interpretation as she strode with her chin in the air towards the door. Edwin's laughter finally bubbled up as he reached the door first and closed it before she could escape. He wrapped his arms tightly around her, but she did not return his embrace, choosing instead to stand rigidly and not look at him. Edwin wondered if perhaps he had gone too far, but he secretly enjoyed bickering with her; the reconciliations were well worth the exasperation.

'Will you read my speech when it's finished?' he asked, in a wheedling tone. 'You know you're a much better writer than I am.' He ducked under the hat to kiss her, but she turned her cheek and his lips missed their target. He took hold of her chin. 'No, Mrs Ford, that won't do at all.' He made another attempt to kiss her, but she stubbornly pressed her lips together.

'Well, that's all you're getting!' she snapped. 'Go and have your lunch.'

Edwin looked at the overflowing basket, covered with a red and white cloth. 'Anything nice in there?' he asked, just as her father did.

'I made some scones,' she replied huffily, looking as though she wanted to throw them at him.

'You know, if I'm going to be giving lectures, I'll have to keep my fine physique.' He stopped as she slapped his arm and wriggled away from him, something like a growl escaping from her throat. He grabbed her round the waist and set her down on his desk so that he could look at her without the troublesome hat getting in the way.

Kate was angry and jealous. She was a new bride, possessive of her husband, unwilling to share him and certainly not willing to allow all the women in Edinburgh to gawp at him, and then discuss his attributes amongst themselves. She did not want him exposed to women like Louisa Ramsay. She stared up at Edwin defiantly, unaware that he found her pouting lips irresistible. He swooped down to kiss her hard on the mouth and, as usual, she found herself melting. Still, she sat on her hands just to make him suffer a little, and forced herself not to respond to his kiss.

'Will you stay and have lunch with me?' he asked, nuzzling her neck. 'It looks as though you've packed enough for two.'

Kate gave an involuntary squeak as the tip of his tongue tickled her ear. 'No - I'm far too busy. Besides, you're at work.' Blast it, she could feel herself weakening.

'But I haven't seen you for *hours*...' His lips brushed the corner of her mouth.

With grim determination, she stubbornly turned her face away. 'Well, they say absence makes the heart grow fonder.'

He pulled her against him and kissed his way from chin to ear. 'In that case, you can expect me to be *very* affectionate when I come home for dinner.'

'Oh, so you're expecting dinner?' she said tartly.

'Yes. In reverse.'

'Whatever do you mean?' she asked impatiently.

Edwin lifted her face and looked at her meaningfully, his eyes alight with devilment. 'I want dessert first.'

There was a knock at the door, and Kate hopped down from the desk. She proceeded to unpack the basket as Edwin opened the door. James stood in the doorway, his face registering surprise and then embarrassment when he saw Kate in the room.

'I apologise if I'm interrupting -' James began.

'It's all right, Father,' Kate said tightly. 'I'm just leaving.' Kate was placing a wrapped sandwich on the desk with more force than was necessary. James thought his son-in-law would be left eating crumbs in a napkin by the time she was done.

'Your mother is at Greyfriars, Katie,' James offered, realising he had walked in at an inopportune moment. Edwin was wearing a hangdog expression and Kate was working herself up into a temper. She reminded James of Eleanor.

Kate picked up her empty basket and strode past Edwin to the door. Edwin reached out to touch her arm, but she stopped him with a flash of her dark eyes. 'Dinner will be at the usual time,' she told him, with a withering look. *'And in the usual order!'* As she passed her father, she shook her head and glowered at him. Kate swept out of the room, leaving the two men staring dumbly after her.

'Just like her mother,' James muttered, shaking his head. Edwin struggled to understand how his gentle teasing could have caused such an intense reaction in his wife. James looked up at him and smiled sympathetically at Edwin's bewildered expression. 'Well laddie, looks like you're in the dog house now!'

Of course, by the time Edwin returned home in the evening, Kate's anger had dissipated. The minute she heard him close the front door she ran into his arms and kissed him, sorry for being so jealous and petulant. Swiftly, Edwin swept her up into his arms and carried her to his study. Locking the door behind them, he indulged in half an hour of reconciliation with his wife before dinner.

When Kate returned to the present she was giggling, her eyes sparkling. 'Our first tiff as a married couple,' she reminisced. 'And over something so stupid!'

'Kate,' Jess began gently. 'Tell Erin what happened today.'

Kate looked alarmed, reluctant to tell Erin about the man in the museum. She didn't want people to think she was weak-minded, or hear Erin put all this down to a failing marriage and a crush on a co-worker. Erin squeezed Kate's hand and smiled encouragingly.

It's okay,' she soothed. 'You can tell me anything. It won't leave this room. Only your regression is recorded, nothing else.'

Taking a deep breath, Kate described her meeting with the man in the Egyptian gallery. She remembered every word, every expression on his face and every emotion she had experienced throughout their encounter. She had felt unaccountably drawn to him, as if they had known each other for years. Slowly, Kate began to get an inkling of

113

what this could mean, but she needed someone objective to voice what she only suspected.

'Could he be Edwin's current incarnation?' Jess asked at last. Kate closed her eyes in relief; if she was mad, at least she wasn't the only one. 'Or could Kate have simply met this guy when she started working at the museum, felt attracted to him, but denied her feelings and then forgotten him?'

Erin nodded slightly, deep in thought and following her healer's intuition. 'There's more to this than simply having the hots for a co-worker. The evidence indicates that they have some sort of soul connection.' She turned to Kate. 'It's possible that he's this life's incarnation of Edwin Ford and that you met him when you started work at the museum. Your family has a history in the museum; their energies will still be stored in the bricks and mortar, to a degree. You may be sensitive to that energy. Both of these things together could very well have triggered your dreams and your past life memories.' Erin smiled reassuringly at Kate. 'Don't be afraid of it and don't fight it. If you want to find out about your Victorian family, then do so. You can also choose to let it go, if you prefer. What you mustn't do is obsess about it so much that it affects your current life.

'In each lifetime, we have a lesson to learn and a lesson to teach. Perhaps you need to discover what your lessons were in that lifetime, and see if you learned and taught what you were supposed to. If you didn't, you may have to repeat the lessons in this lifetime. Perhaps your dreams are trying to show you the way forward in this life - to stop you from stagnating.'

Erin's last comment struck a painful chord within Kate. She looked down at her clasped hands, shame-faced.

Jess rose to make some tea, and Erin patted Kate's arm. 'You must remember, though, that this modern-day Edwin Ford may not remember anything about his past life. Any relationship you have must be based on what you share in *this* lifetime. Just because you had a wonderful marriage with him in your past life, don't assume you can have the same relationship with him in this one.'

'I can't have any sort of relationship with him,' Kate murmured, her eyes misty. 'I'm already married.'

Kate texted Mark when she left Erin's house, and by the time she got home he had set the table and prepared their evening meal. It did not escape Kate's notice that Mark's idea of cooking dinner was to prepare two ready meals in the microwave; had she attempted the same shortcut, he would have complained bitterly. Determined not to cause friction, she sat down at the dinner table and smiled at her husband gratefully when he put her plate in front of her and poured her some wine. He had even gone to the effort of lighting a candle in the centre of the table.

They chatted about work, Mark being his usual elusive self in the interest of client confidentiality. Both of them made an effort not to antagonise the other, Kate steadfastly keeping her mind in the present. After a pleasant meal, they cleared up the dishes then sat on the sofa and watched some television. When Kate yawned and snuggled against his arm, Mark rose and ran her a warm bath filled with the violet-scented bubble bath she loved. Kate was astounded by this loving gesture, and gratefully sank into the warm water and closed her eyes.

When she finally emerged clean and fragrant from the bathroom, Mark was in bed sound asleep.

CHAPTER 7

By Friday afternoon, Kate was exhausted, emotionally and physically. It was day five of the Easter holidays and the Events team had administered a nonstop programme of workshops, tours and talks for all ages. Apart from overseeing the treasure hunt, Kate had helped out with a range of activities from crafts for young children to robot making for pre-teens. She had also assisted on the museum floor, answering visitors' questions and offering assistance when it was required. There had been no time to mull over dreams, regressions or the altered behaviour of her husband. Mark had been unusually attentive for the last few days, had even put his work aside to organise a relaxing weekend for the two of them. Kate tried not to be suspicious, but she couldn't help but be wary of Mark's possible motives.

There had been no opportunity to look into her family history, or find any information on the mystery man she had met three days before. Kate had not seen him again, and was relieved to put it all out of her mind for a while. Her third regression was scheduled for Tuesday, and Kate hoped this would be her last, for she desperately wanted to put her past life where it belonged. Life in the present was challenging enough; she needed to focus on what she wanted from this life - a career she enjoyed; a way to advance her knowledge and use her skills; a successful marriage.

Once the museum closed for the day and the Events team had cleared up the mess left behind by hordes of children, Kate dragged herself to her office and collapsed gratefully into her seat. As she checked her emails, David strode into the office and slumped in his chair, his long legs stretched out under the desk. Kate scrutinised his face, seeing weariness in his eyes and irritation in his tightened jaw. Kate returned to her own work, listening to David battering the keys of

116

his laptop as he typed angrily. He exuded annoyance, and Kate instantly felt sorry for him.

'Can I get you some coffee?' she asked cautiously.

David looked up, embarrassed that she had witnessed his ill-temper. 'No, thanks,' he replied softly. 'I've had enough caffeine, I think.' He smiled self-consciously.

Kate took a deep breath. 'Do you want to talk?' She saw his look of surprise and wondered if she had been too presumptuous.

David was unused to having a confidante, but he was glad of the opportunity to vent his frustration on a sympathetic ear. 'My assistant has let me down again,' he grumbled, gesturing at the screen of his laptop. 'Apparently his social life is more important than career advancement.' He ran his fingers through his neat blond hair.

'I'm sorry, David,' Kate replied sincerely. She considered an idea for a few moments and then spoke up. 'If I would be of any use, I could help with Monday's lecture. I was going to come and listen to you, anyway. It's on hieroglyphics, right?'

David was once again taken aback by this woman's unconditional kindness. 'You wouldn't mind?'

Kate shook her head. 'Let me read your notes, so I know what to expect. I'll do all the preparation on Monday, just like I did before.' She flashed him a cheeky grin. 'And I'll protect you from over-enthusiastic admirers.'

As Mark had promised, he and Kate spent the weekend together. He drove them all the way to Pitlochry on Saturday for lunch and a walk by the River Tay, where they watched the salmon ascend the purpose-built salmon ladder. By the time they got home again, it was late afternoon, and they spent a lazy evening indoors. Although there were domestic chores to attend to on Sunday, it was a novelty for Kate to do them with Mark. Leaving their mobile phones at home, they walked in the woodland nearby and went to the cinema in the evening. Mark was considerate and generous but still noticeably physically restrained.

Monday morning arrived too soon, and Mark and Kate resumed their separate roles. Mark left for work early, untroubled by the knowledge that his wife would be working late because she was standing in for Professor Young's assistant. It was another hectic day for Kate and her colleagues, but Kate worked with a spring in her step; she had enjoyed her weekend and tentatively hoped that she and Mark had managed to repair some of the damage caused by apathy. She was also looking forward to helping David with his lecture.

Once again David was impressed by Kate's organisational skills and attention to detail. It allowed him to focus on explaining the characteristics of the different types of ancient Egyptian writing. Most people were familiar with the Egyptian style of sign writing known as Hieroglyphics, which was used in sacred texts. The style known as Hieratic was more like a running hand, in which the hieroglyphic signs were much debased and summarily executed. This form was used by the priests on papyrus paper but was not usually carved on monuments. Ordinary people used Demotic writing, which was even more abbreviated and cursive. During his lecture David explained the differences in the writing styles, and showed his audience examples of each.

After the presentation, they adjourned to the unusually cold Egyptian gallery to view examples of papyrus scrolls. The ink looked vibrant still, the characters beautifully executed. Then it was back to the warmth of the seminar room, where everyone enjoyed trying to write in hieroglyphics under David's patient tutelage. The evening passed without incident and was enjoyed by all participants. Although Amy attended the event, she wore a doleful expression throughout and left with the rest of the visitors. A grateful David drove his assistant home, and Kate was surprised and pleased to see lights on when he parked in front of her house; she had texted Mark before leaving the museum, but had not expected him to be at home. Kate ardently hoped life was changing for the better. For his part, David drove around the area for another twenty minutes before returning to his darkened house.

'Kate, can you describe your surroundings?'

Kate could hear Erin's soothing voice from far away as she looked around the room. 'I'm in a bedroom - it's old-fashioned. But it looks clean and bright.'

'What are you wearing?'

Kate spoke slowly, pausing between each sentence as if she were considering her words. 'A long blue skirt. It has a white petticoat underneath. Lovely ankle boots, with laces. They're new. I'm not dirty anymore. I can have a bath. I'm wearing a white blouse, but the lace is scratching my neck. My corset is tight - I want to take it off. My hair feels heavy - it's piled up on my head. I'm hot. I feel nervous.'

'Why are you nervous, Kate?'

'I have to tell Edwin something important. I'm afraid he's going to be angry with me.'

'Is Edwin with you?'

From her chair beside the couch, Jess saw her friend smile. Kate's face softened with adoration.

'Yes. Edwin, I have something to tell you...'

Edwin entered their hotel room to find Kate standing facing the door, waiting for him. She looked anxious, her hands tightly clasped in front of her.

'I've organised the supplies for our return to camp. Is there anything else you need to buy before we go back?' Her strange expression unnerved him. 'What's the matter, Kate?'

Kate looked into his eyes. 'I'm - we're - going to have a baby, Edwin.'

His face was unreadable. For a moment, he didn't even move. Kate felt sick. It was just as she had feared.

In Erin's treatment room, tears started to trickle down Kate's face, her expression distraught. Jess quietly moved to take her friend's hand, but Erin stopped her and shook her head, preventing interference.

Edwin stood gaping at his wife. 'When?' he blurted.

'August, or thereabouts.' Kate squirmed as she watched him working out dates in his head. His eyes widened, and she thought she saw a glint of anger, a slight tightening of his jaw.

'So you were pregnant before we reached Egypt? You conceived on the journey here?'

'Possibly,' she murmured, lowering her gaze to the floor. Kate knew exactly when she had conceived. They had spent one night in Naples before boarding the ship to Alexandria. The joy she had felt at returning to Italy had ignited her passion. She knew for certain they had made a baby that night. Kate smiled wistfully at the memory.

'Have you known all this time?' Edwin asked, silently chastising himself for missing the signs which were now obvious: the secretive, faraway look in her eyes; the slight filling-out of her body in the last few weeks; the cravings for foods she hadn't cared for before, and her revulsion for old favourites.

Kate still couldn't look at him. 'I wasn't sure,' she replied quietly. 'Not until I saw Doctor Cummings this morning.'

'Do you realise what a risk you've been taking?' His deep voice rose, causing Kate to look up sharply. 'How could you be so reckless?' Kate's eyes filled with tears and a sob escaped from her dry throat.

Sighing, Edwin took Kate in his arms and held her against him, his lips kissing her hair. She nestled against his chest. 'I'm sorry, Edwin,' she whispered. He leaned back, wiping the tears from her cheeks.

'You have no need to be sorry. I'm sorry I shouted. Kate, it's wonderful news.' Nonetheless, he didn't sound convinced. He pulled her to him again, but Kate suspected it was so she couldn't see his face. 'I'm just...surprised. We've been married all this time, and nothing's happened. It's not like we don't - I just assumed -'

She looked up at him, stunned by his revelation. 'You thought that I couldn't have children?'

'It didn't matter to me!' He was emphatic. 'Once I met you, my life was complete.' Kate clung to him and felt his back muscles tense. She knew she was about to hear what she dreaded most. 'I'll make arrangements for you to stay in Cairo - perhaps with the Hamiltons - until we can go home.'

'But I'm well, Edwin!' Kate protested. 'I don't want to stay here!'

Edwin released her, his mouth set in a grim line. 'No, Kate! You are not making the long journey back to camp. It's no place for you in your condition. You will stay here and look after yourself and the baby. I'll take you home to Edinburgh on the first ship going back to Britain. Our child will be born in a clean hospital, at home, with our family around us. I'm not going to argue with you about this!'

'But Edwin, I was already pregnant when we travelled to Cairo!' she argued. 'And one of the camp women gave birth in camp before we left. She and the baby are both fine!'

'They were fine when we left. We have no way of knowing what will become of them in the future. In any case, the Egyptians are born into this environment - you were not.'

'I'm not a piece of Wedgwood, Edwin!'

'No. You are my wife, and you are carrying my child. And you will be staying here until I can arrange for us to go home.'

He turned and stormed out of the room, the door slamming behind him.

Kate breathed a sigh of relief as she threw the corset resentfully on the chair; no more whalebone for her. She smiled fondly at memories of a time when she couldn't tie the laces tightly enough, all in the hope of impressing Edwin Ford. Her thoughts turned to the events which had brought her to this place.

Once the newlyweds had returned from their honeymoon, Edwin had worked at the museum on various projects, expanding his knowledge of ancient and modern art, and helping James in any way he could. He had given several lectures on archaeology, ancient Egypt and his travels, which had been very successful and increased the number of visitors to the museum. After a year, Edwin had received a summons from the Egypt Exploration Fund and had travelled to London. When he returned a week later, he announced that he had been asked to lead an expedition to Amarna that November to uncover the tomb of Akhenaten. After much agonising on his part, and cajoling on hers, they set out on their first expedition together.

They had been so happy, even living in a tent and then a dark brick hut in the desert for a month. And now she had ruined everything by falling pregnant at the wrong time, and Edwin was angry.

Kate changed into a long nightdress, climbed into bed and wept, her body shaking with sobs of sadness and despair. He was going to leave her here, and then he would be forced to accompany her home. Edwin would probably never forgive her for ruining this expedition. Exhausted, Kate finally fell asleep, her arms wrapped tenderly around the new life within her.

It was very late when Edwin crept quietly into their hotel room. Kate had closed the shutters, and the room was dark. The sound of the door closing woke her, but she kept her breathing steady so he would think her asleep. She felt him slide into bed beside her. His face felt cold as he kissed her cheek softly and curled his long body around hers. She felt his hand stroke her arm and move to rest protectively over her belly.

'I love you, Kate,' he whispered. 'And I love our child.'

She turned towards him, her voice weak from crying. 'Do you mean it?'

Edwin wrapped his arms around her. 'With all my heart. I'm sorry I walked out. I just needed time to think.' He didn't want to tell her how scared he was. He had immediately sought out Doctor Cummings and asked about Kate's health. The doctor had allayed Edwin's fears, asserting that Kate was as healthy as a horse. Their recent living conditions and days of travelling had caused no evident harm to either Kate or the child. However, the doctor recommended that Kate should not return to the site, and believed it would be prudent for her to return to Scotland as soon as possible.

Edwin had immediately telegraphed his superiors to advise them of the situation and request a replacement archaeologist to lead the expedition. He hoped they would reply in the morning, as he had no choice but to return to the site with his team the following day. He had then visited the Hamiltons, who had befriended the Fords when they had first arrived in Cairo, and asked if they might accommodate Kate until she and Edwin could travel home. They had agreed immediately, and assured Edwin that their own physician would check on Kate every day.

'Please don't leave me, Edwin!' Kate pleaded softly, unable to stop herself from crying again.

Edwin took her face in his hands and kissed her tears. 'Don't cry, Kate,' he soothed. 'Please don't cry. Everything will be all right, my love.'

Edwin received a reply to his telegraph the following morning. His replacement would be dispatched with all possible haste and should arrive in Cairo within a fortnight. Edwin was instructed to return to Amarna in the meantime to prepare to hand over his work to the new expedition leader. He rushed up to the hotel room to tell Kate the news, but refrained from telling her of the thorn in his side. The EEF was sending Rossellini to replace him.

Kate tried to put on a brave face, but she was frightened of being pregnant and without him.

He saw her forced smile and took her hands. 'We will go home together, Kate. We'll be home before the end of the month!'

'But what about your work? You've worked so hard, and accomplished so much!'

'Kate, I've dug up the possessions of people long dead. My work is not as important as our family! One day, in the future, we can all come back. There will be many other expeditions.' He knew he was running out of time; the boat was loaded with his men and supplies and waited at the harbour. Edwin knelt down in front of Kate and kissed her belly. She wound her fingers into his dark hair. 'Be safe, little one,' he murmured, and then stood to kiss his wife. Kate held him tightly, wordlessly, struggling to keep her tears in check. 'I love you, Kate Ford,' he said. Then he was gone.

When Erin brought Kate gently out of her trance, Kate was still weeping quietly. She had been pregnant and elated, and Edwin had initially been so cold and hard. *Just like Mark,* she thought. When she had broached the subject of children with Mark two years ago, he had told her he never wanted children. *They just get in the way of a fulfilling life,* he had said. *We can have so much fun together, just the two of us.*

Erin said very little to Kate, feeling that the young woman needed support and comfort, not a cold diagnosis from an impartial hypnotherapist. Kate was not suffering ill-effects of the therapy, she was simply sad and needed time to process her discoveries. Erin made them all a cup of tea, and they sat quietly in the treatment room, Jess's arm around Kate's drooping shoulders.

'Kate,' Erin began. 'Do you want children in your future?'

Kate looked up, dark circles under her eyes. 'Mark doesn't want a family. I should have spoken to him about it before we got married. I stupidly thought that when the time was right we would know, a baby would magically appear, and life would be perfect. I liked having the freedom to travel and socialise, but I knew that, in time, I would want to stop all that and settle into being a mum.'

Jess and Erin shared a knowing look; Kate had some difficult decisions to make in the future. They both felt that Mark was selfish, arrogant and immature. Jess also suspected that one of the reasons he had married Kate was because of her inheritance money. Kate leaned her head on Jess's shoulder, exhausted.

'Come on, you two,' Erin said briskly. 'I need to get some petrol. I'll give you both a lift home.'

Kate stood in the shower with her eyes closed, letting the warm water cascade over the top of her head and down her tired body. She wished she could just slide under the duvet and sleep a deep, dreamless sleep. At last she reluctantly turned off the shower and wrapped her slender frame in a large towel. When she looked in the bathroom mirror a pale face gazed back at her, the large brown eyes ringed with dark circles.

Kate shuffled to her bedroom and sat on her side of the bed, absently drying her hair with a towel. Mark was not at home and had provided no explanation as to his whereabouts. Kate contemplated calling him, but knew he would accuse her of being possessive and paranoid. She contemplated going to bed, but it was ridiculously early, even for her. She jumped as the little statue of Bastet suddenly fell off her bedside table. Kate chided herself for accidentally knocking the precious family heirloom to the floor. As she stooped to pick up the little black cat, she noticed something glinting in the thick fibres of the carpet. Kate picked it up, a sense of horror slowly filling her chest. It was an earring; glittering diamonds surrounded by white gold which curled around the stones in a 'G' shape.

Suddenly everything fell into place - Mark's constant absences, solo 'business' trips, and vague excuses. He was having an affair with Gemma. No doubt their paths had crossed continuously over the years as she covered high profile cases which he would have worked on. A hundred thoughts collided in Kate's brain, as her stomach churned queasily. What was wrong with her that Mark had to turn to Gemma?

Were Mark and Gemma in love? Was that why Gemma had appeared at the restaurant on their anniversary? Had she known they would be there and felt jealous? Had Mark taken Gemma to London? Had he been nicer to his wife recently because he was feeling guilty, or because he wanted to throw off suspicion? How long had this been going on in her home, her bed, under her nose? And what the hell was she going to do now?

A soft breeze from the open window brushed Kate's cheek, and she suddenly knew exactly what to do. She packed an overnight bag, then inexplicably tidied up before writing Mark a note: 'I will be back tomorrow after work. I expect you to be gone by then.' She placed the note on the kitchen counter where he would see it, with the earring on top. Then she left and walked the short distance to her mother's home in Murrayfield.

When Elizabeth saw Kate's overnight bag and her daughter's stricken face, she ushered her into the flat without a word. Elizabeth made up the spare bed for Kate and made her eat some dinner. When Kate finally felt ready to talk she told her mother about Mark and Gemma. Had she been in the company of her Aunt Margaret, Kate would also have confessed the details of her dreams and regression therapy, and the man she had met in the museum. But her mother was practical, not open to anything remotely supernatural; she may think Kate was suffering from a mental disorder. Elizabeth, however, surprised her daughter by listening patiently with her arm around Kate's shoulders. Kate was immensely grateful for her mother's comforting embrace, and Elizabeth's wise decision not to offer her usual parental judgement.

Inevitably, the next day at work was horrible for Kate. She was unable to focus on her duties, or muster her usual enthusiasm, so she was relieved to spend some of her shift in the research library on the first floor. It was seldom used by the public, although today a man sat at a desk with a laptop and a mountain of old books. The occasional curious tourist wandered in and quickly wandered out again. Kate took a little comfort from the peace and quiet. She returned books to the stacks, and handled requests for material from researchers. At midday, Nick arrived to send Kate for her lunch, but she could only manage an apple and some water. Lost in despair, she locked herself in a cubicle in the toilets, unable to talk to anyone. She didn't check her emails or voicemail messages; undoubtedly there would be messages from Mark and she wasn't ready to deal with him yet.

On the way back to the library, Nick called her on the radio to ask her to collect some books from the deputy director's office. Kate had never visited Gray's office, but as soon as she stepped through the door she experienced a strong sense of déjà vu. The décor was different, the wood panelling long gone, but Kate recognised James Grahame's office, and her eyes fell on the corner where she had worked at a small desk for a few wonderful days. She had experienced so much happiness in this room, with people she had cared about. She wished she could close the door and hide here for a while, but Gray or his secretary could return at any moment. Instead, she closed her eyes and sent her love to her Victorian father, along with a plea for his help.

Kate picked up the books Gray had left on his desk and walked back along the hallway. Impulsively, she stopped and opened the door of the filing room a few doors along from Gray's office. It was a small room which housed some filing cabinets, and it was no bigger than a broom closet...

Kate climbed the stairs to the first floor and walked along the landing. The books were heavy, the pile almost reaching her nose. As she passed ancient Egypt, she turned instinctively to look in the direction of the Qurneh burial site. There, leaning against the railing, stood the man from her dreams. Even in her melancholy state, Kate felt herself blush as he turned to smile at her sympathetically, as if he knew she was in pain. She offered him a sad smile, her eyes filling with tears at his tiny gesture of compassion.

Nick was sitting at the desk when she returned to the library. He handed her a large brown envelope. 'Jess left this for you,' he said quietly, so as not to disturb their only visitor. 'She says she'll call you later.' He got up from his seat, closed down the game of Solitaire he was playing on the computer, and went off for his lunch.

Kate returned the books from Gray's office to the library shelves and updated the computer system. The researcher thanked her for the use of the library and left her to put away his books. She tidied the desks, dealt with emails and requests for material. Once she had completed all the outstanding tasks, she settled down with the brown envelope. Jess had been working in the archives that week, and had volunteered to look for information on James Grahame. Kate hoped Jess had been successful in her search, as she was eager to have some tangible evidence, some proof that the people she had dreamt of had actually existed.

The phone on the desk rang quietly. It was the switchboard operator. 'Mrs Forrester?'

Kate baulked at the name. 'Yes,' she replied grimly.

'I have Doctor Benedict Grahame on the line for you.'

Kate smiled at the officious title. 'Please put him through.' There was a pause, before she heard her brother's voice saying hello.

'Are we using our professional names today?' she teased him, exceedingly glad to hear his reassuring voice.

'I wanted to make sure they put me through quickly,' he explained. 'Can you talk?'

'I'm alone for the moment.'

'I spoke to Mum.' Kate groaned inwardly but remained silent. She had always known that Ben and Mark disliked each other. She also knew that her brother, who was seven years her senior, could be excessively protective of her.

'Kate, I went to your house this morning and used my key. I hope you don't mind - I had your locks changed. I think Mark has moved all his stuff out.' Ben refrained from mentioning that, on his arrival, he had found Mark and Gemma leaving the house carrying boxes of Mark's possessions. Unable to contain his anger, Ben had swung his fist into Mark's jaw, causing the box and Mark to fall on the pavement. The adulterous pair had jumped into Mark's BMW and roared off down the road.

'You didn't have to do that, Ben, but thank you.' Kate forced strength into her voice, but had Ben been in the room she felt she would have fallen sobbing into his arms.

'Well, it put my mind at rest. Listen, my shift starts before you finish work. Is it okay if I leave your new keys at the museum security desk? I gave a set to Mum, and I've kept a set.'

'Yes, that's fine. I'll collect them at the end of the day.'

'Why don't you come and stay with us tonight? Daniela says you're more than welcome.'

'Daniela has her hands full with the kids, Ben. I'll be fine on my own.' *I'm used to it.*

'You could go to Mum's…'

Kate heaved an audible sigh. 'I will be fine on my own.'

'Kate - shall I text you the number of our solicitor?' Ben sounded hesitant, but Kate's voice showed no such uncertainty.

'Yes, please. As soon as you can.'

The afternoon was surprisingly busy in the library, and it was nearly five o'clock when Kate finally opened the envelope from Jess and drew out several sheets of A4 paper. Jess had scribbled a note to Kate: 'Edited highlights from the portfolio of James Grahame. Call me!'

Kate scrutinised a photocopy of a newspaper article about the Ancient Egypt Exhibition hosted by the Edinburgh Museum of Science and Art under the directorship of Professor James Grahame. The journalist had written an exceedingly favourable report, and complimented the concise and descriptive catalogue which accompanied the wonderful exhibits. There was also mention of an eloquent young woman, whose role had been to escort parties of ladies and children around the exhibition: one Miss Katherine Grahame, daughter of James Grahame.

Kate stared at the article, incredulous, and picked up another piece of paper. Jess had found a copy of the exhibition catalogue, and had photocopied some of the pages. The descriptions of the artefacts were excellent, and Kate recognised some of the items from the collection currently on display. Her eyes fell on one of the paragraphs.

'Item 52a: small alabaster pot, found in a royal tomb belonging to an unknown woman. Evidence suggests she may have been a queen, or a lady of royal blood. The pot may have been used to hold perfume and on discovery was found to smell faintly of frankincense.'

Jess had also made a copy of the inside cover of the catalogue, which listed the name of the printers, the publishing date and the authors: Miss Katherine Grahame and Mister Edwin Ford.

Shocked, her breathing becoming laboured, Kate looked at photocopies of old sepia photographs. One showed a distinguished-looking James Grahame, gazing proudly over his bushy grey beard. Another was a group photo, and Kate recognised her Victorian family. James stood behind Eleanor, who was as beautiful and well-dressed as Kate remembered. John stood next to James, tall and handsome with dark curly hair and a mischievous smile. He stood behind his sister, whose small hands clasped in her lap. Kate gasped at the similarity between herself and this young woman.

The third photo was of a young couple. The man was tall, ruggedly handsome, with dark hair. He was wearing a dark suit and gazing down at a young woman in a beautiful lace and silk wedding dress, her lace veil trailing down her back and hiding her dark hair. She looked up at him adoringly, her eyes holding his. Jess's scribbled caption told her what she already knew: Kate and Edwin Ford. But Kate looked almost exactly like the Kate in the photo, and Edwin was identical to the man she had met in the museum, the man in her dreams.

The last item was James Grahame's obituary in 1901. With tears in her eyes, Kate read about an eminent career in archaeology, which culminated in the directorship. She read about a loyal friend, a loving family man, a true scholar. She read about his early retirement due to ill-health. The writer speculated that James's health had started to deteriorate after the tragic death of his young daughter at the age of twenty-one.

Kate stared in disbelief at the words on the page until they blurred before her tear-filled eyes. Had this actually been her life? Had she been this Kate? Had she lost her life before it had truly begun? What about their baby? Questions filled her head even as the pain in her heart threatened to overwhelm her. *And what is the connection between my dreams, Edwin Ford, and the man who works here and could be his twin brother?* She cowered before the possibilities, not daring to believe what Erin had suggested and what her own heart told her was the truth.

The door opened, and one of the security guards stuck his head round the door. 'Closing time,' he announced and left again. Her hands shaking, Kate switched off the computers and gathered up the papers. She left the library and unconsciously walked to the deserted Egyptian gallery. Suddenly overcome with despair, she stumbled to the dark and secluded corner beside the Qurneh burial display and slithered to the floor. Hugging her knees, she lowered her head and began to sob quietly.

'Kate, don't cry.' She knew the voice, and lifted her face from her knees to see him sitting beside her on the carpet. He gazed at her tenderly, but there was a painful sadness in his expression. Kate swiped at the tears streaking her cheeks and sniffed loudly, feeling utterly shattered. Pulling a tatty paper tissue from her pocket, she blew her nose. Without stopping to consider the consequences of her actions, she took the papers from the envelope and spread them out on the carpet. Her instincts told her that she could trust this man. She felt as if she had always known him. Perhaps he could give her some of the answers she sought.

His eyes fell on the wedding photo. 'My Kate,' he whispered. 'My beautiful Kate.'

'I don't understand,' Kate stammered. 'I don't understand any of this.'

He looked at her intently. 'Yes, you do,' he said gently. 'You just refuse to believe it. You have such a fascination with ancient Egyptian history. Yet you don't believe in rebirth, or the afterlife?'

Kate stared at him dubiously as she struggled to think rationally, but the evidence was there before her on the carpet. It was there in her hypnotherapy sessions and in her dreams. She couldn't have imagined it all.

'You believe I was *her* in a past life?' she asked hesitantly, pointing at the wedding photograph.

'You know that you were, Kate. You remember. You and she are one.'

'Why am I only remembering now?'

'You returned to this place, which you loved. There were people here who loved you, too.'

'And you?'

'Kate, you *know* who I am.'

She faltered and looked into his dark eyes, as he offered a small smile of encouragement. 'You're the reincarnation of Edwin Ford.'

He shook his head. 'No, dearest one. I *am* Edwin Ford.'

Kate unconsciously inched away from him, suddenly fearful. 'That would mean you're a...' her voice sounded hoarse. *This can't be happening,* she told herself. *Am I dreaming again? Perhaps I'm mad.*

'Yes, Kate. I came back because you called me back. Or I sensed you, somehow. I don't know...' He looked pensively into the middle distance.

'How?'

'I don't remember. There was a smell of violets...and there you were, back in the museum. But you were unhappy because you had taken the wrong path. And now you need me.'

'How do you know that?'

Edwin shrugged and shook his head. 'Sadly, I don't have all the answers.'

Kate was silent for a while, her brain desperately trying to make sense of what was happening. A thought occurred to her. 'If I'm the reincarnation of your Kate, why haven't you come back in corporeal form?'

His reply was hesitant. 'The part of me which is here will remain for as long as you need me.'

Kate wondered if that meant he *had* been reborn, but whoever he was in this lifetime was somehow incomplete. She felt appalled at the thought of some poor person going through life with a part of their essence missing. 'Then I release you - don't stay because of me.'

He smiled sorrowfully at her. 'I made a promise.'

'Did you knock over the statue of Bastet beside my bed?'

'I confess I did. I'm sorry if I scared you.'

'You wanted me to find the earring?'

'You had to know the truth. That man is no good for you.'

'Have you been in my house at other times then?'

'Yes.'

Kate felt inexplicably embarrassed. 'Oh.'

'But only when you needed me,' he said quickly.

That would be most of the time, then, Kate thought. She looked at Edwin closely. He looked so...solid. And she could feel the connection between them. Not love, exactly, but a deeper connection of souls. *If I touch him, what will happen?* She started to reach out her hand, but quickly drew it back again. It was enough that he was sitting next to her, that she could feel his love for her and that she felt consoled by his presence. Slowly, Kate began to feel a calm acceptance of this new turn of events.

'What happened to Kate?' she asked tentatively, and saw the torment clearly etched on his face.

'I remember that day as if it only just happened,' he replied, passing his hand over his eyes.

Checking to make sure the gallery was empty, Kate shifted a little closer to him. All the visitors had gone home, and only some of the staff remained. They would be safe unless one of the security team happened to pass by.

Edwin took a deep, shuddering breath, and began to tell his story...

Edwin slid from his sweating horse, handing the reins to the Egyptian groom who hurried to meet him. He ran up the flight of stairs to the Hamilton's mansion, which was situated in the suburbs of Cairo. Pushing past the servant at the front door, Edwin ran up the central staircase and was met by Jonas Hamilton.

'Where is she?' Edwin roared. 'Where is my wife?'

'Lower your voice, Ford!' Jonas urged in a hushed voice. 'She's asleep. The doctor's just been to see her. Come into my study.' He led Edwin back downstairs and into his study. Edwin barely registered the details of the room, his panicked gaze fixed on Jonas.

'What happened?' he asked through gritted teeth, refusing to sit in the chair Jonas pulled up for him.

Jonas took a deep breath, reluctant to pull Edwin's world down around his ears. He spoke haltingly, his voice sombre.

'About a week ago, your wife was feeling uncomfortable due to her pregnancy and decided a bath might help. She refused to let one of the maids stay in the room with her while she bathed. Alas, when she was getting out of the bath, she slipped on some soap, fell and banged her head on the side of the bath. She lay unconscious for quite some time before the maid found her. We got her into bed and immediately sent for the doctor. I'm sorry, Ford, but she miscarried the child.' Jonas paused as he saw Edwin's stricken face. 'Katherine lost a lot of blood and was very ill. The doctor did everything he could, Ford, but she became very weak and caught an infection on top of everything else.'

'Why wasn't I told immediately?' Edwin spat, his eyes full of impotent rage.

'As we put her to bed, she was lucid enough to demand that we did not disturb you. She believed that your work was too important, and by the time you returned as planned, she would be well enough to go home. When her condition worsened with the infection, we thought it best to recall you.' Jonas looked away, his own eyes blurred with tears of sympathy. He poured himself a whisky and handed another to Edwin. Edwin set the glass untouched on the desk before him.

'And what does the doctor say now?' he asked. 'I would like to talk to him myself.'

'He has already left. Edwin, I'm sorry to have to tell you this, but Katherine is dying.'

Edwin slumped into the chair, his face white. He tried to make his body rigid, to stop the shaking. He stared at the rug under his feet, trying to regain some semblance of composure. At last he looked up with hardened eyes. 'Take me to her.'

Kate looked tiny in the large bed. The shutters had been closed against the glaring sunlight; the room was lit by a lamp in each corner. Amelia Hamilton sat vigilantly by Kate's bed. She looked up as Edwin stepped into the room, her eyes full of pity. Edwin approached the bed silently, and noticed that someone had cut off Kate's beautiful auburn hair. The remaining locks clung damply to her face and neck.

'You cut her hair?' Edwin growled.

'She had a high fever, Edwin. We wanted to try and cool her down. Cutting her hair was a last resort.'

And no doubt some wretched servant has already sold it. Edwin was furious. 'Please leave us, Mrs Hamilton. Thank you for your care.'

He waited until the door had closed behind Amelia before falling to his knees beside the bed and sobbing quietly into the coverlet tucked around Kate's fragile body.

At length, he felt a small hand stroking his head. 'Edwin, you need a haircut,' Kate said softly, her voice hoarse. Edwin looked up into his wife's dark, pain-filled eyes, and she smiled weakly. Immediately he rose to take her gently in his arms. He kissed her pale face, and tried to adopt a countenance which would not betray the panic and rage which tore at his heart. She felt so thin, as if the life had already been drained from her. Her breathing was ragged. But her eyes brightened a little as she looked lovingly into his face.

'You need a shave, too,' she teased feebly and sank against him with her arms around his waist. He released her long enough to fetch her a glass of water, then sat down next to her on the bed and held the glass to her lips so she could drink. He was afraid to speak, lest his voice revealed his heart-rending despair.

'You're cross with me,' she stated. He shook his head.

'I'm not cross,' he replied, his voice a hoarse whisper. 'But you should have called me back right away, Kate.'

'Your work is important, Edwin.'

'Nothing is more important than you!' Edwin bit his lip in an attempt to steady his voice.

Kate clutched his dusty shirt. 'Promise me you'll finish your work here after I'm gone.'

Edwin closed his eyes against hot tears. 'Please don't talk like that, Kate. You'll get well again, and we'll go home together.'

Kate shook her head sadly. 'No, darling. I heard the doctor talking to Amelia. I heard him say I had lost our baby.' Kate started to cry. 'I'm so sorry, Edwin!'

He could think of nothing to say, so he held her as she wept into his shirt, his own tears spilling onto her hair.

'Edwin, promise you'll take me home?' she pleaded. He nodded mutely as he stroked her face and kissed her clammy forehead. 'And promise you'll be happy?'

'Not without you.' His voice cracked. 'Please Kate - you *must* try. Don't leave me. I love you so much!'

'And I will always love you, Edwin.' She looked up into his poor haggard face. She had never seen him look so helpless and desolate. 'Remember the day in the museum when you proposed to me?' He nodded, a tear rolling down his cheek. 'You said we were connected.' She stroked his face. 'That connection won't be lost just because one of us is gone.' The sound of his sob felt like a knife twisting in her gut. 'Will you stay with me, Edwin? I'm a little scared...'

Edwin kicked off his boots and slipped under the covers, tenderly gathering her to him. 'I will stay with you, Kate,' he told her and kissed her dry lips. 'For as long as you need me.'

Edwin could not tell how long they lay together, for the room was in a permanent state of night. They spoke softly to one another, Edwin stroking Kate's back as she lay in his arms. They wiped each other's tears away and at length simply clung to one another until Kate fell asleep with her arms around Edwin's neck.

Jonas and Amelia Hamilton were sitting silently in front of the fire in their parlour when they heard a grief-stricken wail from upstairs. The sound was like the despair of a wounded animal. They knew then that Kate was gone.

'I brought my poor girl home, as she asked, and she was buried in the cemetery of Dean Parish Church.' Edwin's voice was distant and flat. 'Her parents wanted her to be buried in their own parish of Saint John's, but Kate had disliked the cemetery there because it never got the sun.' Edwin smiled sadly. 'I chose her a resting place in a sunny corner.'

Kate wiped her tears away with shaking fingers. 'Edwin, I'm so sorry.' It was all so...avoidable.

As if reading her thoughts, Edwin shook his head and murmured, 'My Kate never did a single thing she was asked. If only she had allowed a maid watch over her bath...If only she had asked for me right away...' He hung his head. 'If only I hadn't taken her to Egypt.'

'Edwin, Kate wanted to go to Egypt, to be with you. She would have endured anything to be at your side.' She reached her hand towards him, still not daring to touch. 'I can say with absolute certainty that she loved you with all her heart.' Edwin looked up at her then, as if in the hope of absolution. 'I can feel it, Edwin.' Kate placed her hand over her heart. 'In here. She didn't blame you. And she would not want you to be...roaming about in this place. She would want you to be at peace, with her.'

He was gazing into space again, as if listening to another voice. Kate wished she could hold him, that he could hold her as he had done all those years ago. Instead she asked, 'What did you do - afterwards?'

Edwin sighed. 'Kate's family were devastated, but they didn't cast me out. For a long time, I mourned in a darkened room, alone. After a long while, James persuaded me to return to work. He wasn't in good health, and he needed help. I worked as an assistant in the Art and Ethnography department and later became the keeper there. I helped out in other departments, and with loans and acquisitions, but mostly for things like the Wedgwood collections which were popular at the time. I no longer felt the drive of ambition, and I felt incapable of working on bigger projects. Each night, I went home and locked myself in that dark room, unless one of your parents or John made me come out to eat. I longed for my life to be over...'

'Kate wanted you to finish your work in Egypt.'

'I couldn't face going back to Amarna, but I was eventually asked to join an expedition to another dig site near Thebes.' Edwin pointed to the Qurneh burial display behind Kate. 'That was my last dig.'

'You were on the Qurneh team, with Flinders Petrie?' Kate was frankly a little star-struck by the revelation that Edwin had worked alongside the famous archaeologist. She had always been drawn to the Qurneh display, and now she knew why. Edwin had touched the artefacts in the very case she was sitting beside, as he must have touched many other pieces in the museum's collection.

'Yes,' Edwin replied. 'But by then a part of me hated Egypt. I started to feel unwell on the return voyage. A few weeks later I was buried next to my wife.'

'And you've been here all this time?'

'I don't think so. I remember my death. The next thing I remember is seeing you in the museum. But you were slow to notice me.'

'How so?'

'I saw you on your first day, and although I made myself visible to you, I remained unnoticed.' His voice had a slightly petulant edge to it, and Kate found herself smiling. 'I've tried a number of things to try and attract your attention.'

'Such as?'

'Oh, knocking things off shelves, hiding your coffee mug. You were in a meeting with that idiot Gray. His tea spilled all over his trousers.' Edwin snorted with sudden laughter.

'That was you?' Kate was incredulous.

'The man's a fool! Still, nothing seemed to arouse your suspicions. Not even my stroking your hair.'

Kate recalled the occasional tingling sensation, as if an unseen hand gently caressed her head. It made her shiver every time, but she had dismissed it as being the product of her own imagination.

'Then I heard you discussing your dream with Miss Mortimer, and I knew that something within you was waking up.'

'You didn't make me dream those dreams?' Kate blushed.

Edwin looked a little guilty. 'Not entirely, though I may have helped them along...'

'Hello there, Mrs Forrester!'

Kate jumped, startled by the voice from across the gallery. Scrambling to her feet, she saw one of the security men walking towards her. It was Stan, known by the female staff as Sleazy Stan. He was in his fifties, with sparse greasy hair and a round face which had a perpetually sweaty sheen. His shirt strained to cover his beer belly and Kate discovered he also had bad breath, as Stan moved up to stand closer than was necessary. Kate moved into the walkway so she couldn't be backed into a corner. Edwin was still sitting in the gloom, but Stan evidently could not see him.

'Working late, are you?' Stan asked, his eyes homing in on her chest.

Kate fervently wished she was wearing a baggy jumper instead of an open-necked white shirt, and crossed her arms defensively over her chest. 'I'm just leaving, Stan,' she replied, with a quick smile which did not reach her eyes. She bent down to pick up the contents of the brown envelope, careful to keep her backside away from Stan's leering stare.

'Good, because there's a man hanging about outside the front entrance who says he's waiting for you. Like to keep them waiting, do you?' His beady little eyes narrowed salaciously.

She bid him a hasty goodnight and headed for the stairs to the ground floor. Behind her, she heard a gasp from Stan, followed by a heavy thump. Kate kept walking, but whispered to the air, 'What did you do?'

'I tripped him up,' Edwin said indignantly from behind her. 'He was looking at your rear view.'

'And you've never done that?' she asked archly. 'I seem to recall you had a liking for a girl in trousers.'

Kate retrieved her belongings from her locker, placing the envelope from Jess carefully in her bag, and pulled on her coat. Edwin had apparently gone, as she no longer felt his presence around her, and now she felt cold and apprehensive. Her intuition told her that Mark was waiting for her, and she feared she wasn't strong enough to deal with him. With growing anxiety, Kate collected her new house keys from the security desk and walked out of the museum.

Mark leaned against the wall, the collar of his grey raincoat pulled up against the drizzle. Kate stood a safe distance away from him, and waited for him to speak. She kept her face impassive, but as she looked at him she could feel righteous anger rising from within. She wanted to slap him, but she noticed someone had already beaten her to it. Mark had a bruise on his cheek, and his lip was cut.

'What do you want, Mark?' she asked, surprised at the strength in her voice. He came towards her, his hand reaching out towards her arm. She moved away, her body language clearly telling him to keep his distance.

'I wanted to say sorry -' he began, but the words sounded hollow and meaningless to Kate.

'How long have you been with her?'

He looked shifty, and Kate realised that she had seen this expression many, many times in the past. Was Gemma his first infidelity, she wondered, or was their whole marriage a sham? She realised that she didn't care, that the details were unimportant. There was no longer any love between them - if it had ever been there in the first place.

'It started not long after you began working here,' he confessed, and had the good grace to hang his head.

'Was I boring?' she blurted, and hated herself for sounding so pathetic.

He looked up at her and lamely shook his head. 'It just all became so…flat. I tried, Kate, but it was just...' He shrugged, unable to find the words.

In other words, I was boring. Kate felt herself crumple inside, and struggled to keep her façade in place. 'I tried to do everything you asked, Mark. I tried to be the kind of wife I thought you wanted.'

'But in the end it wasn't what *you* wanted, Kate, and you resented me for it!' He became defensive. 'Is it any wonder I looked elsewhere? I bumped into Gemma when I was working on a case which caught her paper's attention. She listened to me; she was interested in what I had to say. It started off as just a bit of excitement -'

Kate held up her hand to stop him going further, fighting the tears welling up in the face of her humiliation. It was time to finish this for good. 'My solicitor will be in touch, Mark. Until then, there's no need for you to contact me again.' Kate turned on her heel and marched quickly along Chambers Street, where she ran the last few metres to catch the bus home.

The bus was busy, so Kate was unable to sit on her own and wallow in her misery. A large lady embarked at the next stop and slumped down beside her, placing a bulky carrier bag on her ample lap. Kate was edged further towards the window, where she looked at her own reflection and willed herself not to cry, or scream. She had been a boring housewife. Even though she had shaped her life to please Mark, she had not done enough to keep him. Despite his complaints about her returning to full-time employment, her job had turned out to be just the opportunity Mark had been waiting for to take a more attractive woman into their bed.

Kate began to think about the practicalities of divorce. Although their savings were in joint names, Kate still owned the house. Her aunt's will had clearly specified that the house be held in Kate's name only. Mark would undoubtedly ensure he got everything he was entitled to under the law.

Outside, Edinburgh was growing dark, and the rain became heavy. Rivulets streamed down the windows of the bus, obscuring her view of other people's lives. The traffic was busy, and the endless roadworks made the journey interminable. Kate could feel the irritation of her fellow passengers; a heavy sigh punctuated by tutting, the complaints about the council's constant need to dig up roads and reroute buses. The air seemed filled with negative energy, and the bus was very hot. Kate wished she could get out and walk, but home was a good way off yet.

Half an hour later, she closed her front door and drew the safety chain across it. She was filled with a sense of exhausted relief. Kate switched on a light in every room and drew the curtains. She moved about on autopilot as she ran a hot bath and poured herself a small glass of wine. She put on some relaxing music to drown out the silence and started to undress, deliberately leaving a trail of clothes behind her. Mark had liked everything in its place - including his wife - but this was now *her* home, and she would do as she pleased. She poured a huge amount of bubble bath into the tub and lit some candles in the bathroom. As she started to remove her bra, one of the candles went out. Kate stopped undressing immediately and looked around the room. Was Edwin here, watching? Kate wrapped her arms around herself protectively, but she was not afraid.

'I'm taking a bath,' she called out. 'Go away.' She waited a few moments before relighting the candle, and then she undressed completely, slipping quickly into the water. Kate closed her eyes and tried to control the sneering voices in her head which told her she was inadequate, unattractive and naïve. She reflected that all through her life, her family had babied and protected her - their helpless little girl - when they should have been preparing her for the harshness of reality. Nobody had ever warned her about deceitful men, or people who pretended to be your friend before they stabbed you through the heart. Tears fell down Kate's cheeks, and after a while she began to shiver in the water. She couldn't seem to get warm, even when she put on pyjamas and a bathrobe. Padding through to her bedroom, she halted when her eyes fell on her bed. An unwelcome image appeared before her eyes, of Mark making love to Gemma. Pulling back the duvet, Kate scanned the sheets. And there in the centre of the bed she found a long, blonde hair.

Kate's misery turned to rage, an emotion she had been taught not to display. With a scream of uncontrollable anger, she pulled the duvet and bed linen off the bed, throwing the pillows to the corner of the room. Sobbing, she picked up the statue of Bastet and threw it in the same direction. She whirled around to her dressing table, unaware that the little cat had paused in mid-flight and dropped gently to the ground without breaking. Kate picked up the framed wedding photo of her and Mark and smashed it against the wall. Her self-control lost, she swiped her arm across the surface of her dressing table, scattering bottles, jewellery and make-up all over the carpet. She let out a savage howl as she sank to the ground, sobbing and gulping air.

And then suddenly Edwin was there, kneeling beside her. 'Hush, Kate,' he murmured. His attempt to soothe her was taken as an attempt to encourage composure. Kate glared at him angrily; she did not want to be stifled into more 'acceptable' behaviour.

'It's alright, sweetheart,' Edwin soothed, ignoring her look of fury. 'Everything's going to be alright.' He stretched out his hand towards her, but the gesture was futile. 'Oh, Kate, I wish I could hold you!'

His words made her cry even harder, because she yearned for him across the gaping chasm between her world and his. She had always been his, so why had she not found him in this lifetime? Kate squeezed her eyes shut, feeling a pain in her chest from the effort to breathe between sobs. She felt Edwin stroke her hair, but instead of his fingers she felt a tingling sensation on her scalp. The tingling localised on a spot near the top of her head as he kissed her there. Her brain struggled to rationalise and interpret the phenomenon that was Edwin Ford.

'I see your temper is even worse than it used to be!' Edwin remarked. Despite her utter weariness, Kate chuckled weakly through her tears. She remembered he had always possessed the ability to defuse her anger, as well as ignite it. As she struggled to control her erratic breathing, memories surfaced from that other life. Kate cried from grief now, for that wonderful life lost so long ago and for the child they never got to meet. She cried for the wasted years of her current life, and for the children she had not been allowed to have. Her body shook with great racking sobs until she felt like a limp, wrung-out rag. All the while, he stroked her hair, her back, her face. His peculiar touch was soothing, but not enough. Kate wished she could cling to him like a lifeline, until she had no more tears to shed.

'Edwin,' Kate's voice was choked. 'I remember us being together...'

Edwin's pale fingers trailed down her jaw to her chin. She saw the sadness in his smile. 'I know, darling.'

Kate drew in a shuddering breath. 'What are we going to do?'

'Well...you need to get some sleep.' He sounded pragmatic.

Edwin stood, and Kate shakily got to her feet. Rubbing her eyes, she looked at the stripped bed.

'I can't sleep here. Not when they've -'

'Kate, there's nowhere else. Go and fetch some fresh linen.'

Obediently, Kate walked unsteadily to the linen cupboard in the hall. She returned with fresh bed linen and made up the bed, her mind shrouded in a thick fog of incomprehension. She gazed vacantly at the mess she had made in the room, then knelt to retrieve her belongings from the carpet.

'That can wait until tomorrow,' Edwin said gently. 'You must rest now. Get into bed.'

Gratefully, she lowered herself onto the clean, soft sheet and smiled tremulously at him as she pulled the duvet over her exhausted body.

'Close your eyes, sweetheart,' he told her, stroking her cheek. She complied, dimly aware that the lights were being switched off. The room was silent.

'Edwin,' Kate called softly into the darkness.

'Yes?'

'Can you stay with me for a little while?' She didn't care that she sounded desperate and pitiful. She could be strong and independent among the mortals tomorrow.

'Always, my love.' Kate felt his weight on the mattress, and his arm circling her tightly-curled body. She yearned for the warmth of his body but gratefully accepted his light, incorporeal touch. 'You smell of violets,' he whispered into her hair, as he kissed the top of her head.

Sighing, she drifted off to sleep.

CHAPTER 8

The next week passed in a blur, as Kate executed her duties at the museum like an automaton. At home, she couldn't muster the incentive to cook, so she lived on cereal and junk food. She hid behind drawn curtains and closed doors, her mobile phone switched off, and her answering machine switched on. Exhausted, she went to bed early every night, and tossed and turned until the alarm sounded in the morning. Her friends at work noticed Kate's haunted look and lethargy but said nothing. Instead, they offered their support by making her coffee and casually asking if they could get her something to eat.

At the weekend, she stayed at home, cleaning as if possessed. She wanted every trace of her husband and his mistress removed from her house. And she needed time alone, to process recent events and acknowledge her heartache.

Kate was aware, through the smog of her despondency, that Edwin was always nearby. Although she did not see him, she could feel him around her. Occasionally, she would catch the scent of Arabic coffee, or feel a loving caress on her hair or cheek. When she went to bed each night, she felt sure he kissed her head.

On Sunday morning, she woke to find him sitting on the bed next to her, leaning against the padded suede headboard. He was watching her, smiling fondly.

'Good morning, sleepyhead,' he murmured. 'You still pout when you sleep.'

Still drowsy, Kate wondered if her hair was a mess and whether there were pillow creases on her face. She sat up groggily and rubbed her eyes. 'Am I dreaming again?'

'No. It's Sunday morning, and time you opened the curtains. The sun is shining.'

Kate stared down glumly at the duvet, disinclined to face the world. She saw Edwin reach across to stroke her hair. She felt the strands shift as his fingers sifted through the unkempt tresses, but she did not feel his fingers. Her brain struggled to reconcile what her eyes were seeing with what her body was feeling.

'Kate,' he asked, stroking her cheek. 'Have you explored your attic room?'

She looked up at him, quizzically. 'I use it as a store room,' she replied. 'I don't spend much time in it.'

'You need to go and look. There are some family heirlooms of ours which you need to find.'

'What heirlooms?'

Edwin tapped her nose with a finger, and she experienced a tickling sensation. 'Go and find out for yourself! But do it soon.'

'Can you come with me?'

Edwin sighed regretfully. 'I can't stay, sweetheart.' He looked away for a moment. 'I'll try and come back later. Please eat something nourishing, Kate, and do something to nurture your soul.' With a light, tingling kiss on her forehead, he was gone.

Bolstered by his appearance, Kate hopped out of bed and pulled on old leggings and a t-shirt. She forced her tired body to practice yoga for twenty minutes, then made herself scrambled eggs and toast. For the first time in two days, she opened the curtains and windows to let in fresh air and sunshine. She tried to calm her turbulent mind by meditating, but ended up reading David's books instead. Kate passed the day in pursuits which let her body rest but stimulated her brain. It was early evening by the time she decided to brave the slightly spooky third floor room which was used for storage. Shafts of fading daylight spilled through the small windows, highlighting dust motes which floated around the room like tiny spirits. Kate had stored some of her own possessions in plastic boxes, which sat on one side of the room. The rest of the floor space was littered with a few cardboard boxes, some old pieces of furniture, and a couple of pictures. Thankfully her aunt had not been a hoarder.

'Edwin?' she called softly into the room.

Almost instantly, he appeared, standing beside an old-fashioned trunk which peeked out from behind some boxes in the far corner of the room. Kate joined him, sneezing from the dust. The trunk looked familiar, although Kate could not remember her aunt using it. Bending her knees, Kate pulled it out into the middle of the floor. It was dusty and battered, but the large key was still in the lock. Kate knelt on the bare wooden floor, Edwin kneeling silently beside her. The key resisted

141

a little as Kate turned it. She opened the lid, to be met with the smell of old lavender. Bags of the fragrant sprigs covered several layers of tissue paper. Removing them, Kate found some old clothes which smelled of mothballs. There were several old books, copies of classics such as 'Wuthering Heights' and 'Jane Eyre', which were two of Kate's favourite novels. She opened the front covers in the hope of finding an inscription, but was disappointed. A rolled-up scroll in the corner of the trunk caught her eye, fastened with a faded ribbon. Kate untied it and unrolled the curling paper. It was another family tree, but the branches ended with Katherine and John. She carefully rolled and tied it again and turned back to the contents of the trunk, anticipation rising within her.

Kate took out a shortbread tin filled with old photographs. They depicted her aunt's and father's childhood, but older pictures showed faces she did not recognise. Kate decided to take the photos downstairs and put them in an album. There were a few other mementoes which meant nothing to Kate, and then she was at the bottom of the trunk.

'Keep looking,' Edwin urged.

Kate gave him a puzzled glance, noticing that he looked very pale in the half-light and seemed to emit a faint glow. 'It's empty,' she told him.

Edwin pointed to the bottom of the trunk. 'Check the base. Trunks were often built with a secret compartment for valuables.'

Kate smoothed her palm along the base of the trunk then rapped the uneven surface with her knuckles. She discovered a small gap in one corner and was able to prise open the base panel, causing a cloud of dust to waft into her face. Sneezing, she set the baseplate on the floor and looked at the metal box nestling at the bottom of the trunk. It had some sort of pattern on it, darkened with age. The letter K was inscribed on the lid. She held her breath as she lifted the lid. The contents nestled in a delicate, gauzy fabric. Kate recognised the wedding veil immediately. She held the discoloured material next to her cheek, certain she could detect the faint scent of violets. Several sepia photographs fluttered to the floor. She gazed down at photos of her family from long ago, her loving parents and handsome brother. Her throat tightened when she picked up a photo of Kate and Edwin on their wedding day, not unlike the one in James Grahame's portfolio. *It's not me,* she reminded herself. *I'm a different Kate.*

Kate turned to Edwin and saw tears sliding slowly down his cheeks, his sorrow almost palpable. Kate reached out to touch his cheek, but he shook his head, and gestured for her to continue her examination of the box's contents.

Kate picked up a drawstring pouch of dark blue velvet. Carefully, she loosened the silken cord and emptied the contents into her palm. Stunned, she picked up the small tarnished gold ring with its single diamond. Dull and lifeless, it sparkled no longer. With an aching heart, Kate slipped it on the bare ring finger of her left hand. It was a perfect fit. Kate choked back a sob, grief-stricken for Edwin and his lovely young wife. Fate had struck them a cruel and unjust blow. Respectfully, Kate removed the ring and replaced it in the pouch. She picked up a gold, heart-shaped locket on a fine chain. Squinting in the gloom, Kate saw the initials K and E entwined on the surface of the locket. Using her fingernails, she opened it carefully, and a lock of hair fell out onto her lap. She held the lock up to the beam of light from the window. It seemed to be two different locks of hair, twisted together and secured with a fine silk thread. Both were dark, but one was more auburn. Kate knew the hair belonged to Edwin and his Kate. *My hair is darker than hers,* she told herself. *Her hair had more red in it than mine. We are not the same person.* She put the keepsake back into the locket and returned the necklace to the pouch.

'I gave it to you on your twenty-first birthday,' Edwin murmured. 'And the ring is your engagement ring.'

'I know,' Kate said, very quietly. *But they're not mine. They belonged to her.*

'Those things are yours,' he said vehemently. 'You should wear them.'

Kate shook her head. 'No, Edwin. They belonged to *your* Kate. I couldn't wear them. But I will clean them up, and keep them with my jewellery. If you think she wouldn't mind?'

Edwin stared at her as though perplexed, but didn't respond. Kate turned away from his tortured gaze.

The last item in the box was wrapped in a square of almost threadbare silk. Kate unfolded the silk to reveal a tatty, leather-bound notebook. She opened the pages carefully and found they were filled with Edwin's familiar script. It was Edwin's diary; Kate remembered seeing the little book in her dream. The book was only two-thirds full, and described the trip to Egypt which resulted in his move to Edinburgh. The last pages were of the trip to Amarna, but he had written nothing after he had rushed back to Cairo to be with his dying wife. As Edwin had told her, his life had ended with Kate's passing. Kate felt a deep sadness for them, and started to cry helplessly as she closed the book and kissed its battered cover. She noticed a loose piece of paper sticking up near the back of the book. It had been folded many times so that it would fit among the pages. Kate carefully unfolded the brittle sheet and smoothed it out, revealing a faded drawing of Katherine Ford's face. She was struck again by the similarities between herself and this other Kate. The likeness depicted a young woman, with long dark hair and wide dark eyes which were both innocent and mischievous. Her full lips curved into a teasing smile, her slender neck was adorned with a high lace collar. At the bottom right hand corner, the artist had scribbled his initials: EF. At the top left hand corner, he had written: 'My Angel'. She carefully folded the picture and tucked it back between the pages of the diary.

Kate looked up at Edwin, her eyes shining with tears. She smiled weakly at him and showed him the book. 'This is yours...'

Edwin's expression was one of profound grief, as though the memories were still raw. 'And now it's yours,' he told her.

Kate had tried to be discreet at work, telling only Jess about her separation from Mark and swearing her to secrecy. Unfortunately, Ben's solicitor could only see Kate during working hours, so she could not avoid emailing the Events manager to ask for permission to attend her appointment. She was still under probation, after all. Her attempts to keep her private affairs to herself were then thwarted.

On Monday morning, the cluttered, windowless office was a place of productive activity. Jess, Nick and Kate sat at Jess's desk to review alterations to the Vikings workshop, while David immersed himself in an acquisition assignment. Adam Gray strode into the room like a whirlwind, pulling up at David's desk.

'Professor Young!' Gray barked. David looked up from his work and raised an eyebrow expectantly. 'You have fired your assistant -'

David kept his gaze and his voice level, aware that his three roommates were watching the exchange. 'Lee was not doing his job to the standard I expect. He was unreliable and inefficient, with very little work ethic to speak of.'

Gray's face turned red. He had championed the appointment of David's assistant, and was displeased to hear of the boy's failure. Even more infuriating was the fact that Young knew this, but was not at all hesitant to list Lee's flaws.

'Do you have a replacement?' Gray asked frostily.

David glanced over at his colleagues, who were valiantly trying to continue their own discussion instead of eavesdropping on his. 'Perhaps we should discuss this in your office, Deputy Director.'

'We cannot. I'm on my way to the director's office now. He wants to know if you have a replacement in mind.'

144

'Not yet.' David's voice was equally icy. 'Until I find someone who can do the job properly, I'll manage by myself.' David glanced in Kate's direction. 'Kate has offered to help with evening lectures.'

'If you return to Egypt this winter, you will need an assistant with appropriate qualifications. Mrs Forrester is not an archaeologist.' Kate grimaced at the mention of her married name but did not look up from her notebook.

'Neither is Lee. And he has no hope of becoming one unless he gets his act together.'

'She does not work in your department, Professor.'

David stood up, aware that he towered over Gray. He lowered his voice so that only Gray would hear him. 'Kate is efficient and eager to learn. She has a positive attitude to her work and a nice way with visitors. Her presence at my lectures will surely represent the museum and its staff in a positive light.' The last comment weakened Gray's resolve, and David pounced. 'I would like Kate to take over some of Lee's duties, at least until I find a new assistant. A lot of his tasks were administrative, and Kate is more than qualified to tackle those.' David's green eyes narrowed. 'Should I contact the director with my request, or would you rather discuss it with him yourself?'

Gray pinched his lips together, realising he had been manipulated. 'There's no need to bother the director with such minutiae. I'll consider the matter myself and get back to you with my decision.'

'Thank you, Deputy Director,' David said, with a disarming smile.

Silently fuming, Gray turned to leave the room, but stopped midstride. 'Mrs Forrester,' he called to Kate. 'You have my permission to leave work for your solicitor's appointment on Thursday afternoon. Please don't make a habit of arranging personal appointments during working hours.' He looked over his glasses at Kate's reddening face. 'Remember, you are still on probation for another two weeks.' With a final sweeping glance around the room, he left.

Kate stared at her notebook, her face scarlet. She had not anticipated that the Events manager would mention her request to Gray. Jess swore under her breath, cursing Gray for his lack of tact and compassion. Nick threw Jess a curious glance, but she shook her head and turned back to Kate. She reached out to touch Kate's arm, but Kate stood up clumsily, her chair scraping the floor.

'Please excuse me,' she muttered and headed for the door. As she passed him, David noted her stricken face.

Jess threw her pen on the desk and rose to follow her friend. 'That man is such a bloody -' She refrained from spitting out the word on the tip of her tongue.

145

She found Kate in the ladies' toilets down the hall, splashing her face with cold water. Wordlessly, Jess put her arm around Kate's shoulders, reaching with the other hand for a paper towel. Kate dried her face and hands. Their gazes met in the large mirror.

'You know that we all care for you,' Jess told her firmly. 'No one in that room will judge you, or gossip. We all think highly of you, and we'll support you through this.'

'You're speaking for David and Nick, too?' Kate asked, with a weak smile.

Jess grinned back. 'I'll beat them up if they don't!'

Kate chuckled wearily and hugged her friend. 'I'm sorry I walked out of your meeting. Can I get some coffee before I come back in?'

Jess shrugged. 'We were finished anyway. I was dragging it out to make it less awkward for David. Not that it helped much. Take your time. Do you need anything?'

Kate shook her head, and Jess left her in peace. After a few more minutes of solitude, Kate made her way to the staffroom. Her fingers trembled as she washed out her mug, and she tried in vain to feel Edwin's strengthening presence. She felt annoyed at herself for lacking the courage to stay and face her colleagues after Gray's disclosure of her solicitor's appointment; Nick and David were probably quizzing Jess at this very moment. *On the other hand, I'm not the one who cheated. I have no reason to hang my head in shame.*

Clutching her mug in trembling hands, she turned to the coffee machine. Holding the cup tightly against her body, Kate willed herself to calm down. She closed her eyes, breathing deeply, forcing herself to relax. When she opened her eyes, David was standing before her. Gently, he rescued the mug from her rigid fingers and filled it with hot coffee.

'You take it black, right?'

'Yes,' Kate's voice was ragged.

David handed her the mug. She inhaled the rich aroma of coffee and felt comforted, both by the drink and David's equanimity. She watched him fill his own mug, discovering that he took his coffee black, too. He raised the mug in salute.

'Adam Gray, man of the people,' he toasted.

Kate stared vacantly into space, replaying her meeting with the solicitor the day before. He had been kind and sympathetic, an old-school lawyer. Not at all like Mark or his arrogant and sometimes sleazy friends. Mister Simpson had made everything seem very simple. If Mark did not contest the divorce then all their joint assets would be divided equally, and their divorce would be finalised fairly swiftly. Kate had felt ashamed when she had cited infidelity as the main reason for divorce, but the elderly lawyer had simply given her a sympathetic glance and continued to write. Now she would have to wait to see if Mark would be difficult. She worried that he would want a share of the house. Kate dropped her face into her hands and sighed, relieved and worried at the same time. When she looked up there was a mug of steaming coffee on the desk in front of her. David Young had entered quietly and sat down at his desk across from her. Kate thanked him, cupping the warm mug with her fingers.

One of the junior attendants came into the office, carrying two cardboard file boxes. He set them on Kate's desk. 'James Grahame's portfolio and all the stuff on Qurneh,' Lewis Smith announced, giving Kate his best smile. 'I'm afraid there's not much in the Qurneh box, though. It's only information pertaining to the artefacts acquired by the museum.'

Kate smiled at him, and was surprised to see him blush furiously. 'Well, I'll have a look at it anyway. Thanks, Lewis.'

'Let me know if I can help with anything else,' Lewis offered, and left the room.

'Are you advancing your education?' David asked curiously.

'Yes, I suppose I am,' Kate replied with a smile.

'You're interested in the Qurneh expedition?'

'I'm looking for some particular information on Qurneh and Amarna.' *I want to find out about the wonderful man who worked on both expeditions.*

David was intrigued, especially since he sensed Kate was being deliberately vague. 'What has James Grahame got to do with it?'

Kate hesitated under David's inquisitive gaze. 'I want to know more about an expedition to Amarna which took place around 1891, when James Grahame was director. Some of the museum staff were involved, including some of Professor Grahame's family.'

David racked his brains for a few minutes. 'Do you mean the Rossellini expedition?'

Kate paled. 'Rossellini expedition?' she repeated cautiously.

'Yes. As far as I remember, an Italian archaeologist led the expedition and received lavish praise for its success. Some of the artefacts are on display, and some are in storage. I think many of the other finds were sold to other museums...' David stopped talking when he saw Kate's crestfallen expression. He wondered why she was interested in this particular expedition.

He never said, Kate thought. *He must have known Rossellini was taking over the expedition, and he kept it to himself. If he'd been able to stay longer, he would have found the tomb himself. Poor Edwin!*

'There's not much in the archives about the Amarna dig,' David told her, sounding apologetic. 'Again, it's only information about the artefacts we hold here. But there's some information on the internet, although it can be contradictory.'

Kate looked up, and David's eyes narrowed when he saw tears in her eyes. 'Did Rossellini find the tomb?' she asked, striving to compose herself. David would surely wonder why she was becoming over-emotional about an archaeological expedition which took place more than a hundred years ago.

David shrugged, and tried to hide his bemusement. 'The Italians took credit for finding it, although some believe it was found by a local woman years before. The tomb was six kilometres from the city, built into the side of a cliff. It was found by chance.'

Adam Gray poked his head round the door. Seeing David at his desk he came into the room. 'Professor Young, I've been thinking about the primary five children who are visiting us next Thursday,' he began. David groaned inwardly; the deputy director had to stick his oar into everything. 'Perhaps we could do some sort of dramatization for them. You know, tell them a story to bring it all to life.'

David looked sceptical. He was already showing the children Iufenamun and explaining the hieroglyphs painted on the sarcophagus. One of his team was going to help them mummify apples to take home. Kids of that age were more interested in the gorier and hands-on aspects of his job than being made to sit and listen to a story.

'I'll do it,' Kate piped up. The two men looked at her. 'Fifteen minutes on a dashing young archaeologist from the nineteenth century, who found some of our artefacts. How does that sound?'

Before David could reply, Gray clapped his hands together. 'Excellent!' he said briskly.

'I might need to reorganise some of my duties,' Kate went on. 'I'll also need access to the archives, and I might need to work after hours tonight -'

'Do whatever needs to be done, Mrs Forrester. Let me see your work by next Wednesday. Carry on.' Gray strode from the room.

'Does this have something to do with your research?' David asked. Kate nodded, but her eyes were guarded. 'Can you find what you need in the archives?'

Kate gave him a mysterious smile. 'Don't worry, I'll find the information I need. I'll have something for you to read by Tuesday, okay?'

'Well, let me know if you need any help.' He curbed the urge to question her further and returned his attention to his work.

Kate pushed the file boxes to the corner of the desk, planning to examine their contents when she was alone. Taking a pen and some paper from the drawer, she began to write about the past life experiences she remembered which could enhance her story on Edwin. She recalled digging for artefacts in Amarna. She wrote about the objects she had seen in the museum workroom before the Ancient Egypt Exhibition. Her pen slid furiously across the paper as memories poured forth. She was glad to be able to put her recollections to good use, at last. When the flow of ideas slowed, she turned to her computer and perused the research library's database. She was disappointed to discover that there were no records of the expedition which had brought Edwin to Edinburgh with crateloads of treasure. She typed 'Edwin Ford' into the search box and felt discouraged when the message 'no matches' flashed belligerently across the screen. It was as though he had never existed, after all the amazing things he had seen and done. *Damn him,* she thought. *And damn his virtuous ideals about not needing recognition!* She had been so proud of him and yet he had felt no ambition, had held no desire to be praised for his achievements. She had sacrificed her last days with him in that lifetime so that he might accomplish his mission, and yet now he had vanished from history altogether. Kate felt the irrational urge to shout at him.

'Kate,' David's mellow voice pulled her from her internal fuming and forced her to look up from the unhelpful screen. 'I remember you once saying that you used to ride...' He was cautious, unused to interacting socially with his workmates. But something about Kate put him at ease. And she intrigued him...

Kate smiled wistfully at memories of cantering across the Pentland hills, the feeling of pure freedom, and the wind in her face. It seemed a very long time ago. 'I did, before I got married.' David saw a shadow cross her face, and Kate lowered her eyes. She didn't know David that well, and was unwilling to show him any sign of her vulnerability.

'I ride most Saturdays, out near North Berwick,' David told her, and tentatively asked, 'Would you like to come with me tomorrow?'

Kate's face betrayed several different emotions. She hadn't been on a horse for seven years - what if she made a fool of herself? Moreover, she had just split up with her husband, and it seemed inappropriate to go out with a man she barely knew in the same week as she had started divorce proceedings.

David watched her contemplate his offer, then realised the issue which troubled Kate the most. 'There's no agenda, Kate,' he assured her. 'I split up with my partner a couple of weeks ago, and I could do with the company.' He faltered, feeling that perhaps his behaviour was inappropriate. 'And I thought you might feel the same way...'

Kate's eyes narrowed; was she the subject of gossip after all? David seemed to be very intuitive, because he said, 'Don't worry - I didn't hear anything on the grapevine. On the night your husband was waiting outside for you, I'm afraid I came out of the building as you were talking to him. I walked in the other direction, but I heard enough. And then Gray was indiscreet about you seeing a solicitor. I just thought - I'm sorry, Kate. Forget I asked.'

Kate remained silent for a few moments, watching David as he pretended to read something on the computer screen. She was used to seeing the professor behave in a calm, tightly controlled manner. His awkwardness was almost endearing. She felt as though she could trust him. When he looked at her, there was only an open kindness in his gaze. Right now, she would accept solidarity from wherever it came. At last she smiled. 'You realise I haven't been on a horse for a few years?'

David gave her an engaging smile. 'Not a problem. We'll take it slow. Shall I pick you up at nine in the morning?'

'I'll be ready.' Kate gave him a wide smile, already mentally searching the depths of her wardrobe for her riding gear.

Kate spent the rest of the morning writing her story, surprising herself with how much information she could recall about Victorian archaeology. Writing what she remembered about the man she had loved proved bittersweet. Unfortunately, the only information about him online was gleaned from the census records. She found his date and place of birth, his parents' names, his addresses over the years. She stared at the screen with conflicting emotions when one census listed her name under his, at their address in Abercromby Place. She emailed both the Egypt Exploration Society and the British School of Archaeology in Egypt on the off-chance that they might hold some information in their own archives, either about Edwin's career or the 1891 expedition.

Jess dragged her outside at lunchtime to sit on a bench in the sun in Bristo Square. Summer was near, heralding the start of the Fringe and Edinburgh Festival. Soon, their favourite lunch spot would be teeming with tourists. They sat in companionable silence for a while, before Jess asked how Kate was coping.

'I feel relieved that Mark has gone,' Kate admitted, guiltily. 'It scares me how little I feel about the whole thing now. I'm not angry anymore, and I'm not upset. Does that make me a cold and unfeeling person?'

Jess snorted. 'With respect, Kate, you were a prisoner in your marriage. Now you're free. You can do whatever you want. With whomever you choose.' Kate nodded slowly and looked down at the ground. 'And it's okay to look forward to the future and feel hopeful.' Jess put her arm around Kate's shoulders and gave them a squeeze. 'Are you ready to talk about Edwin Ford, yet?'

Kate shook her head. 'No. I'm still processing.'

Jess nodded, understanding Kate's confusion and uncertainty. Jess had been shell-shocked when she had discovered the pictures of Kate Grahame and Edwin Ford. She had been raised to have an open mind, however, and had witnessed several strange events in her lifetime. Jess firmly believed in reincarnation and soul groups. From her own experience, she was convinced that the spirit world existed. 'Have you seen him again? In the museum, I mean?'

Kate looked at Jess, unsure of what to say. She wasn't ready to tell Jess that Edwin was a spectral presence in her life, not one of flesh and blood. She didn't want her friend to think she had lost her grip on reality altogether. Jess saw Kate's reluctance and nudged her in the ribs. 'He could be a great rebound guy!'

Outwardly, Kate laughed at the preposterous suggestion but felt a futile longing for Edwin's touch. Realising it was time to change the subject, Kate told Jess about her story-writing task and her plan to go riding with David. When her friend raised her eyebrow in speculation, Kate quickly reminded Jess of the suspicions regarding David's tastes. If David was indeed gay, Kate need have no fear of any potentially romantic entanglements.

Kate was scheduled to help in the museum shop that afternoon, and was kept so busy restocking shelves and helping customers that the time flew. At the end of her shift, she returned to the office and opened James Grahame's portfolio. She perused the documents within, glanced over the photographs, read newspaper clippings about the Ancient Egypt Exhibition, and finally studied the catalogue which Edwin and his wife had written. When melancholy threatened to descend upon her, Kate put the portfolio and its contents in her desk drawer. She gathered up her pad and pen, and walked briskly to the Egyptian gallery to look at the exhibits she remembered from the Victorian exhibition. Since the museum was now closed, the gallery was still. The sarcophagi seemed to be watching and waiting, their painted eyes following her as she passed. She stopped at the carved image of King Akhenaten.

'I see you've made a new friend.' Edwin's voice was gruff and made Kate jump.

He's peeved, she thought, remembering the tone. She also recalled that this used to be her cue to tease him. 'Who do you mean?' she asked innocently. She didn't turn around, but stayed facing the display case and hid her mischievous smile.

'The Egyptologist,' he grumbled. Their eyes met in the reflective glass of the display case.

Kate waited a beat before replying, 'Well, you know I've always had a soft spot for Egyptologists...'

She turned to look up at his pale face, which was tight with suppressed anger. 'Oh, Edwin!' she cried in disbelief. 'You can't be jealous!' He didn't answer. 'David is just being kind, that's all. We have no romantic objectives, I can assure you. You can't have a very high opinion of me if you think I would throw myself at a man just days after leaving my husband.' Her eyes flashed, and she was suddenly irritated with him. Did he spend his whole afterlife spying on her? He had the decency to look down at his feet in contrition.

Unable to stay annoyed with him, she told him about the story she wanted to write about him and how she had been unable to find any information about him or his work. Her information requests to the EES and BSAE had proved fruitless. He shrugged, unconcerned, which irked her again.

'How can you not care that you didn't receive any recognition for all you accomplished in your lifetime?' she asked, exasperated.

Edwin looked bemused. 'There were hundreds of archaeologists on expeditions at that time,' he told her. 'Teams from all over the world competing for dig sites. How many of them can you name?' Kate remained silent. 'I told you that my aim was to bring ancient Egypt and its treasures into the public eye. I wanted people to learn about the civilisation. I didn't want the f-'

'Don't you dare say "fame and glory", Edwin Ford!'

He shrugged again. 'It's the truth.'

Kate sighed and looked away, dismayed that nobody had ever acknowledged his worth, his intelligence, his noble crusade.

Edwin's voice softened. 'It was enough that I was special in your eyes...'

Kate looked into his dark eyes. 'Talk to me about your work,' she requested, and saw pain flit across his face like a dark shadow.

'I won't talk about Amarna,' he told her firmly. 'I can't.'

'No, I want you to tell me about the expedition which brought you to Edinburgh.'

Suddenly, Edwin's whole form seemed to glow brighter, and he beamed down at her. 'You mean the one which brought us together?'

She nodded, grinning at his boyish smile. Turning back to Akhenaten, she asked, 'Do you remember this piece?'

'I remember watching you trace his lips with your fingers,' he said wistfully. 'And wishing you would do the same thing to me.' He led her to another display case which showed small cosmetic pots of alabaster and stone. He pointed to a small round pot. 'Alabaster pot number 52a,' he announced. 'I saw you sniff it in the workroom, when you thought no one was looking. When we argued about it in your father's office, all I wanted to do was silence you with a kiss.' He moved to the case of jewellery, the gold and gemstones still bright. 'When you were looking at the jewellery in the workroom, something made you laugh. It was the most beautiful sound I'd ever heard. Next to you, all the gold just looked like old brass.' Edwin stepped closer. 'Do you remember our first kiss?'

Kate gazed up at him, forgetting for a moment that the man before her was not flesh, forgetting that she was not the Kate he had fallen in love with. She felt a familiar sensation of butterflies in her stomach when he looked at her with those smoky brown eyes.

'Edwin,' she breathed. 'You know I do. For me, it only happened days ago.' She started to shiver, suddenly cold. His hands rubbed her upper arms but did not have the desired effect.

'Let's go home,' he told her. 'Once you're warm, I'll tell you anything you want to know.'

Kate flexed her hand, her fingers sore from writing frantically in shorthand for over an hour. They sat on the rug in front of the fire, leaning against the sofa. Edwin had recounted the thrilling, atmospheric tale of uncovering the tomb of an Egyptian queen near Thebes. He had followed the team leader into the darkness of a winding tunnel which led them down into the earth. The air was thick and stagnant, and all they had to light their way were a couple of lanterns. Eventually, they arrived at a doorway blocked with rubble. Together the men toiled to clear the path, and eventually continued along the dark passageway until they came at last to a wide wooden doorway. After several attempts, it was finally levered open, and they peered into the silent, dusty darkness. As they held their lanterns aloft, the queen's burial chamber was revealed to them. The walls were heavily decorated with paintings and hieroglyphs. Furniture, statues and jars of all shapes and sizes surrounded the queen's ornate sarcophagus, which lay in the centre of the room. Edwin stepped into the chamber first, to ensure it was safe; they had encountered traps in other tombs, which had caused colleagues to be injured. The treasures they found in the tomb surpassed anything Edwin had found before. The sarcophagus was sent to Cairo, along with some of the larger statues. The expedition leader, a patriotic Scot, wanted to make sure that at least some of the artefacts would be sent back to Edinburgh for his own countrymen to see. Edwin was given the job of packing up these items and accompanying them to the museum.

Edwin fell silent, for they both knew what happened next in the story.

'Thank you, Edwin,' Kate said quietly, as he reached out to caress her cheek. It was so easy to believe she was his wife, that he was really here and that she could love him as before. She needed him to make her feel whole again. She needed him to protect her from people who would hurt her.

'Do you have everything you need?' he asked, interrupting her reverie.

'Yes, for now. But I would like to do more research.' She smiled up at him. 'I've become very interested in archaeology recently. I want to learn more.'

'Then I expect you will. You were always a quick study. Not to mention very determined.' She felt him kiss her hair. 'You will be careful tomorrow, Kate?' he asked in a concerned voice.

Kate looked up and smiled slyly. 'You mean you won't be spying on me all day?'

Edwin sighed. 'Much as I would love to spend every minute of every day with you, I can't.'

Kate shifted onto her knees so that her eyes were level with his. 'Where do you go?' she asked curiously. 'When you're not with me?'

Edwin looked vague. 'I don't know,' he answered, but Kate noticed that he avoided her gaze. She wanted to ask if he knew what would happen to them in the future, but she was scared of the answer.

'I wish we could be together again,' she blurted. 'I wish we could go back…'

Edwin shook his head. 'You would hate it,' he told her bitterly. 'Just as you did then.'

Kate stared, shocked. 'That's not true!' she protested. 'How can you say that?'

He sighed. 'Kate, you only remember snippets of that life. I remember all of it! You may have loved me, but you were desperately unfulfilled by your role as my wife.'

'No, Edwin -'

'Don't interrupt, Kate. You must listen!' The intensity of his gaze made her fall silent. 'Before we married, you wanted to be free, to travel, to experience the world. Remember? Those desires didn't disappear just because we fell in love. Oh, you tried hard to be a good wife. You efficiently ran our household. You dutifully called on family and friends and received callers to our home. You hosted dinners and acted with decorum whenever we were out in public. But you grew to resent it. It wasn't enough for you. It was as though you had been born in the wrong time.

'You believe we had an idyllic marriage. We didn't.' He paused as Kate's lips began to tremble, then pressed on. 'My work took me from you far more frequently than I would have liked. I often worked in the evenings, in the museum or in my study. I had to travel, too. In fact, we spent precious little time together.

'You hardly ever complained, but I knew you were unhappy. I knew you wanted to have a baby, but every month we were disappointed. We both feared you were barren, yet we did not share our concern with each other. I hid in my work, and you became increasingly withdrawn.

'John and Sarah married about a year after us, and Sarah became pregnant almost immediately. You were devastated, although you hid it well. No one ever guessed how bereft you felt, but you could never hide anything from me. You stopped seeing people, feigning illness or some other excuse. But really you simply wished to avoid facing Sarah's pregnancy. It was around that time I was offered the Amarna expedition. I didn't want to leave you alone in Edinburgh, given your frame of mind. At the same time, I didn't want you to live in a dirty camp for weeks on end. I didn't know what to do for the best. Thankfully, you wanted to travel to Egypt with me.

'Things took a turn for the better, for as soon as you boarded the train to Liverpool, you began to return to your old self.' His lips curved into a sad half-smile. 'The journey to Egypt was like our second honeymoon, and you know the result of our rekindled passion.' Edwin stopped and raked his hands through his hair. Kate was crying quietly. He had crushed her with the truth of their difficult marriage. 'But the truth is, if we had returned to Edinburgh, if we had raised a child, you would still have known no peace. You would still have felt trapped and suffocated, like a beautiful bird in an ornate cage. Like the golden eagle…'

Kate shook her head slowly, her wide eyes begging him to stop. 'Please, Edwin, don't -'

'Kate, you have to accept the truth so that you can move forward. Think about your life with the lawyer. How did you feel throughout your marriage?'

She stared at him as realisation dawned. 'I felt…stifled.' He nodded, encouraging her chain of thought. 'All my life I've felt stifled, even by my family.' Her mind raced. History had repeated itself. She had bowed to convention, and put other people's happiness before her own. It had only caused her frustration. And now she was alone. She looked uncertainly at Edwin, dreading more of his hurtful revelations. 'If I had been unable to conceive, would you have left me?'

Edwin shook his head. 'No, darling. Never. I loved you. How could I hurt you?'

'When you were away from home, were you ever unfaithful?'

He smiled tenderly. 'Kate, you were not my first lover. But you were my last.'

Kate's gaze dropped to the floor. 'I'm sorry,' she murmured.

'No, Kate. I'm sorry I've hurt you, but please understand my aim is to help you.' She looked exhausted, as she tried to assimilate this new and unexpected information. Edwin stroked her cheek, his touch feather-light. 'It's late, love, and you need to rest...'

Kate passed her hand wearily across her reddened eyes. When she looked up, he had gone. With her mind still reeling, she prepared for bed.

Later, when she burrowed under the duvet, she felt a chaste kiss on her cheek. Edwin's voice was soft and husky as he whispered in her ear. 'You're so beautiful, Kate. Sleep well, my love.' His mission for that day was accomplished: he had planted the seed of change.

CHAPTER 9

Kate woke in a pensive mood, Edwin's words still fresh in her mind. He had effectively dispelled her illusions of a perfect past life, but he had done so to prevent her from repeating her mistakes. She felt grateful for his brutal honesty, and now strove to change her preconceptions. She no longer had to behave according to the rigid parameters set by family and spouse. It was time to explore the world as a single, independent woman. And that meant she would definitely have to stop always choosing the safe option. Going riding with David felt like a good first step.

When she opened her front door to him, David couldn't help noticing that Kate looked very trim in black jodhpurs, long black riding boots and a fitted green top. Kate had stored them in the back of her wardrobe for years, but they were still in good condition. Her contemplative expression was replaced with a warm smile as David took her black gilet and riding hat from her, and put them in the back seat of his car. He held open the passenger door of the car as Kate climbed in, and solicitously checked she was comfortable before they set off for the East Coast.

At first they were both a little nervous, having never spent much time alone in each other's company. They made polite small talk about work and the weather. But Kate was curious about the man who looked like a male model, and had a reputation for being anti-social. Kate's instincts told her he was just reserved, possibly shy. She wondered how old he was, as he looked too young to merit the title 'professor'.

'Where did you go to school?' she asked eventually, hoping an inoffensive question might encourage him to open up.

David looked almost embarrassed. 'Near Cambridge,' he replied quickly and sensed her curious glance. Keeping his eyes on the busy

157

Edinburgh roads, he continued, 'My parents were both in the Foreign Service, so I was sent to boarding school when I was five.'

Kate glanced at him sympathetically, imagining a small blond boy clutching a suitcase and feeling all alone in the world, in a strange place without his parents.

'Did you always want to be an archaeologist?' she asked, in case talking about boarding school was a difficult topic. Sure enough, she saw his lips curl into a boyish smile.

'I was always interested in art and history, especially ancient Egypt.' He gave a derisory laugh. 'I suspect the "Indiana Jones" films had an influence! Mind you, those films make archaeology seem a lot more glamorous and adventurous than it actually is. I studied archaeology at Edinburgh University, then specialised in Egyptology.' Kate smiled at his animated expression. 'We still have so much to learn. It's fascinating!'

The atmosphere lightened, and conversation flowed easily as they left Edinburgh and took the picturesque road along the coast, passing the small towns of Musselburgh, Port Seton, Aberlady and Gullane. It was a clear day, so the Firth of Forth looked blue and inviting. The green hills of Fife were clearly visible on the other side of the estuary. David was a good driver, confident and considerate. Kate observed his easy grip on the steering wheel, his fingers long and slim like Edwin's. His posture in the driving seat was relaxed, and Kate felt completely safe.

Somewhere between Dirleton and North Berwick, David turned off the main road onto a single-track road and headed in the direction of the sea. After a few minutes, they arrived at a rambling stone farmhouse. A woman appeared from the house, wearing a padded jacket, muddy trousers and wellington boots. She was around sixty years of age, her short hair almost white. Her kind face was weathered, evidence of a lifetime spent outdoors.

'Good morning, David!' the woman called in a broad Scots accent. 'Good morning, Kate!'

Kate looked up at David in surprise.

'I phoned ahead to say I was bringing a friend,' he explained.

Kate held out her right hand to the grey-haired woman, who shook it and cheerfully introduced herself as Annie Paterson.

'Right then, we'll get you mounted up,' Annie said briskly. 'Kate, tell me about your riding experience.'

As Kate and Annie talked, they walked around the side of the farmhouse and past a huge barn. Since David found it difficult to drive while wearing riding boots, he took his riding gear out of the car and slipped into the farmhouse to change. Several chickens sauntered about the yard, pecking at the dirt. At length, they came to a stable block for six horses. Kate gave a small cry of childlike joy when she saw the pair of horses tied to a rail. One was a tall chestnut hunter, with a gleaming coat and silky mane and tail. The mare turned her head to look at them with huge, soulful brown eyes. She pawed the ground impatiently when she saw David striding towards them. The second horse was a smaller stallion, dark as midnight except for one white sock and a white star between his mischievous dark eyes. His mane and tail were coarse, and his black forelock fell like a badly-cut fringe between his twitching ears. He stood quietly resting one hoof and eyed Kate speculatively.

'They're beautiful!' Kate sighed. 'How many horses do you have, Annie?'

'Och, these two aren't mine,' Annie replied with a wave of her hand. 'They're David's.'

Kate tried not to show her surprise; it wasn't obvious to anyone at work that David was wealthy, but Kate knew livery was very expensive. David approached the horses from the front.

'They're both rescue horses,' he muttered, embarrassed. He untied the black stallion and led him into the middle of the yard. Kate watched as he checked the horse's feet, then the bridle and finally the saddle. Annie looked on, shaking her head in amusement. David practiced this routine every time he rode, even though he knew Annie was meticulous. Finally, he looked up and beckoned Kate over to meet her mount.

'This is Zack,' he said, his voice low so as not to startle the horse. 'He's quite placid. Mount up, and you can do a few warm-up rounds of the paddock before we set off.'

Kate was immensely relieved that she managed to bounce up into the saddle without looking like a sack of potatoes. David handed her the reins, solicitously checked the girth and helped Kate adjust the stirrups. Meanwhile, Annie opened the gate to the paddock next to the stable block and stood waiting for them. David stepped back and critically observed Kate as she gathered her reins and gave Zack a gentle kick. The horse immediately walked forward towards the paddock.

Kate was elated - she already felt transported to a better place, where Mark and misery did not exist. She was delighted to discover her riding skills had not deserted her. Annie handed her a riding crop as she passed through the paddock gate, smiling at Kate's joyful expression. David led his own horse towards the paddock. He gave Annie a questioning glance and Annie nodded to assure him that Kate would be able to ride on the quiet bridle path. They watched as Kate walked Zack around the grassy field a couple of times, before coaxing him into a gentle trot. Annie saw David tense and his fingers tighten on the fence. She patted his hand, smiling at his unwarranted concern. Kate had a good seat and looked very calm and confident in the saddle. Zack reacted well to Kate's energy and trotted along happily. At last, Kate rode Zack towards them, grinning ecstatically while Zack bobbed his head impatiently. David swung gracefully into the saddle of his mare, and Annie opened the gate again to let him through. He led the way to the top of the paddock, where a second gate led out to the bridle path.

They rode quietly along the lush country lanes, ducking occasionally under low branches. Kate watched David's back swaying gently with his horse's movements. He looked at one with the horse, as if riding was second nature to him. Occasionally he twisted around in his saddle to check on Kate, but otherwise they rode in comfortable silence. Tension left their bodies; Kate felt lighter and more at ease than she had in weeks. The morning sun warmed their backs, and the birds sang in the trees and scented hedgerows.

After a while, the lane opened up, and they emerged onto an expanse of grassland. Kate could see the beach beyond. It was cooler here, and the breeze brought the salty tang of the sea to her nostrils. She drew level with David.

'Shall we trot along the beach?' he asked, his eyes dancing. His horse pranced eagerly, anticipating a faster pace.

'I would love that!' Kate replied eagerly.

They urged the horses into a fast walk and traversed the grass, riding down a shallow slope to the deserted beach. Kate tightened the reins and adjusted her seat. With the gentlest of aids, Zack bounced into a trot. Kate felt so happy she giggled spontaneously. David looked across at her and smiled to see her girlish dimples and sparkling eyes.

Kate slid from the saddle, ran up the stirrups and loosened the girth. Pulling the reins over Zack's head, she kissed his soft nose and scratched his ears. The horse was hot, so Kate walked him slowly around the yard to cool him down. Zack took the opportunity to nuzzle Kate's pocket in the hope of finding a treat. David walked his horse at the other end of the yard while he talked quietly with Annie. When the horses were cool enough to return to their stables, David and Kate led them to their stalls. As Kate secured a blanket over Zack's back, she heard David crooning softly to his horse. Kate smiled, idly wondering if he spoke to his lovers that way, too. She removed Zack's bridle, listening to David singing quietly to his beloved mare. Kate stifled a giggle. David always appeared so aloof at work - who would guess he was such a softie?

Annie gave Kate a hug as they stood by the car. 'We'll see you again?' she asked.

Kate smiled noncommittally, not wishing to presume David would bring her again. 'Thanks for everything, Annie,' she said, evading the question. She climbed into the car, and David closed the door. He slid into the driver's seat and looked across at Kate, admiring her rosy cheeks and bright eyes. He was glad he had brought her.

'Thank you so much, David!' Kate said sincerely. 'I had a wonderful time!'

David gave her a gentle smile. 'I can see that,' he replied. He looked out of the windscreen into the distance, where North Berwick Law rose like a grass-covered pyramid on the horizon. 'North Berwick is just a few minutes from here. We could get a bite to eat...'

Kate smiled at his elegant profile, his bashfulness warming her heart. 'I could buy you an ice cream,' she suggested. He glanced at her, looking surprised at the notion. Then he nodded and started the engine.

David and Kate sat on the beach wall, looking across the sea to Fife as they ate ice cream in the warm sun. Kate's eyes were locked on the outcrop of large rocks on the far side of the beach. Memories threatened to overwhelm her. She felt them intensely even though they had not been part of her own life. She could still feel the icy water lapping around her ankles. More powerful were the memories of being pulled into Edwin's arms, his hungry and insistent kisses, and the desire blossoming in her innocent body. Kate's breath caught in her chest.

David looked down at her. She looked miles away and wore a faint look of distress. 'Penny for them,' he said, nudging her gently with his elbow. Startled out of her reverie, she looked up at him in surprise and quickly shook her head dismissively. But David could tell she had been fretting about something.

'What are you up to for the rest of the weekend?' he asked lightly, in an attempt to draw her thoughts away from her anxieties.

Kate shrugged. 'I'll finish the story for the schoolchildren tonight, hopefully. Tomorrow I have to do mundane stuff like housework and supermarket shopping. I'm having Sunday lunch at my brother's house...'

David saw Kate grimace. 'Is that not a good thing?' he asked, bemused by her lack of enthusiasm.

Kate ate some more of her chocolate ice cream, pondering her reply. 'I love my family,' she began. 'But I get fed up with my Mum and Ben

161

always trying to protect me from life. I know they mean well, but they make me feel so helpless and inadequate.' She looked up at him, surprised at her candour. What was it about him that made her readily confide in him? Perhaps it was his stillness, or his air of calm self-assurance.

David set his empty ice cream cup on the wall beside him. 'Kate, you're neither,' he assured her firmly. 'I'm sure they act the way they do because they love you.'

'I know. But now more than ever I need to prove I can be strong and stand on my own two feet.' Kate smiled wryly. 'At least if it's a nice day my niece and nephew will drag me out to the garden to play with them. My brother will probably make some remark about the three of us being at the same level!'

Kate finished her ice cream and took the two cups to the nearby litter bin. She returned to sit next to David on the wall. 'What about you?' she asked. 'Do you see family at the weekend? Or do you go clubbing until the wee hours?'

David snorted. 'I don't go clubbing. And I don't have family in Edinburgh.' Kate recognised another ambiguous reply but did not pry further. 'I'll probably go for a run this evening. Tomorrow I'm going to Ratho to the indoor climbing centre.'

'Goodness me!' Kate gave a mock gasp. 'Are you an adrenaline junkie, then?'

David tilted his head slightly, considering. 'I suppose I am, sometimes,' he replied slowly. 'But I like to keep fit in preparation for trips to Egypt, because you need a lot of stamina to cope with the conditions on a dig.' His words caused Kate's mind to flash back to her time in Egypt with Edwin. 'Besides,' David continued ruefully. 'If I keep busy, I won't have time to mope.'

Kate glanced up at him, but he was looking out to sea. She wanted to touch his arm in a gesture of consolation, but refrained. The breeze had strengthened, blowing wisps of hair across her cheek. The sun hid behind a passing cloud. Kate shivered and hugged herself. David slipped off his jacket and placed it around her shoulders, careful not to touch her in case the gesture was misconstrued as a prelude to something more intimate.

'You didn't have to do that,' Kate told him gently but snuggled gratefully into the soft moleskin. The jacket was warm and held a pleasant masculine scent. 'But thank you.' In recent years, Mark had forgotten the concept of chivalry when it came to his wife; Kate savoured David's kindness.

'Shall we go back to the car?' he asked reluctantly.

'Yes,' she sighed. 'It's time I went home and did some more writing and research.' She handed David his jacket as they approached the car. He dug into one of the pockets and brought out a slightly bent business card, which he passed to Kate.

'If you need help with your work, my numbers and email address are on there,' he told her, as he opened the car door for her. 'Or if you need to talk...' His voice drifted off.

Kate looked into David's eyes, searching warily but seeing only compassion. Despite his reputation, David was quite amiable and a real gentleman, too. How could somebody hurt him the way they obviously had recently? She smiled at him as she took her seat, wondering if she should offer the same favour in return. But David seemed all business as he fastened his seatbelt and started the car, intent on reversing out of the parking space. North Berwick had narrow roads, and it took them some time to negotiate the busy Saturday traffic and find the main road back to Edinburgh. Once clear of the town, David switched on the iPod docked between the front seats, and Kate discovered to her surprise that they shared the same eclectic taste in music.

It took them an hour to reach Kate's house. Once again, David left his seat to hold open the car door for her and retrieved her belongings from the boot. The pair stood self-consciously on the pavement. David wanted to invite Kate to dinner, as he had enjoyed her company. She had allowed him to be himself and demanded nothing in return. He was reluctant to lose the feeling of contentment her presence had brought him. Kate wondered if she should invite him in for coffee, or offer to cook something for their dinner. The gesture felt too forward, though, and David might feel obliged to accept against his will because he was such a gentleman.

David broke the silence. 'I won't be in the museum on Monday,' he told her, pushing his hands in his pockets. 'I'm teaching at the university.' He felt stupid as he realised she was probably already aware of which days he taught at the university.

Kate was suddenly reminded of a scene from 'Raiders of the Lost Ark', during which the ruggedly handsome Indiana Jones addressed a class of students. As Jones had glanced at one of the girls, she closed her eyes to reveal the words 'I love you' written on her eyelids. She wondered if David provoked such a reaction among his students.

'If you finish your piece on your Egyptologist,' David continued. 'You can email it to me.'

Kate nodded. 'I'll do that.' She held her riding hat against her chest as she drew out her keys from her gilet pocket. When she looked up into David's green eyes, she saw sadness lurking in their depths, or maybe it was loneliness. In that moment, David looked isolated. 'And thank you for a really wonderful day.'

David smiled diffidently. 'I enjoyed it too, Kate. Perhaps we could do it again?'

Kate lowered her eyes. 'I would like that...'

'Good luck tomorrow.' He grinned at her. Kate chuckled and walked up the short garden path to the front door. David waited until she had stepped over the threshold before climbing back into the car. Kate watched him drive away, then sighed contentedly and closed her front door.

Kate sat on the chair in the hall to remove her riding boots. The answering machine on the hall table blinked wildly, announcing several messages. Kate hadn't taken her mobile out with her; she found it intrusive and felt it was rude to answer calls when she was out with someone. She took a deep breath, and was about to play the messages when the doorbell rang. For a split second, she wondered if David had come back and resolved to invite him in for coffee. Pulling open the door, she was dismayed to see Mark standing on the doorstep. He looked angry, his eyes narrowed and his mouth compressed into a grim line. Instinctively, Kate placed her body in the doorway to deny him entry. Determined to hide her anxiety, she adopted a calm expression and waited for him to speak.

'Didn't take you long to find a replacement!' he snarled, nodding in the direction David had taken. 'Is he the one you've been having the hot dreams about?'

'He's a friend from work,' Kate said curtly, flushing because she had not realised that Mark had witnessed and interpreted her vivid dreams of Edwin.

'Perhaps someone should tell him he's wasting his time with the Ice Maiden,' Mark sneered.

Kate winced as his cruel words cut at her heart, but she refused to let him see her pain. 'What do you want, Mark?' she asked wearily.

'You have paintings on your walls, which belong to me. I want them.'

Mark had spent thousands of pounds on paintings while they were married, using money accrued from bonus payments. Kate despised them, as she had no love for modern art, but she was not allowing Mark through her front door.

'You can have them,' she replied. 'But we'll do it properly through our lawyers -'

Mark's expression darkened further. 'Oh, yes! We have to do everything *properly.*' His tone was acidic and dripped sarcasm. 'Like the way you had divorce papers served!'

'What do you mean?' Kate asked, a feeling of dread creeping up her spine.

'*What do I mean?*' he mimicked, his face puce. 'I mean the divorce papers were served to me when I was in a meeting with a new client - a very famous client, and therefore very rich. Winning their case would have helped me make a name for myself, as well as a lot of money. I would have been a step closer to becoming a partner. But when the papers were served, and it became common knowledge that you had cited infidelity as the reason for divorce, the client took their business elsewhere. I've been left in the shit! My boss is *enraged.* I might lose my job, you stupid bitch!'

Kate resisted the urge to back away from his fury. She gripped the door, her knuckles turning white. 'I'm sorry,' she said evenly. 'I didn't know they would serve you the papers at work. But the reason cited for our divorce is the truth. You were unfaithful -'

'And you were fucking frigid!' he shouted, taking a step towards her. Kate could smell alcohol on his breath. 'Should I tell everyone that? Or shall I tell them you're a whore who already has another man in her bed?' He grasped the door and tried to push past her. Suddenly, Kate felt herself pulled backwards into the house. She felt a forceful rush of air and suddenly Mark was propelled back along the path as if something had pushed him with force. He doubled up, clutching his stomach. Kate saw him stare at her with eyes full of fear, before the front door slammed shut.

Running upstairs to her bedroom, Kate looked out of the window onto the street. She saw Mark running up the street to his car, continually looking behind him as if in fear of pursuit. He dropped his car keys on the road twice before finally gaining entry to the BMW and driving erratically down the street. Kate wondered fleetingly how much alcohol Mark had imbibed and if he had exceeded the legal limit. She wondered if she should call Gemma and alert her to her lover's rash decision to drive while under the influence. Before she could make a decision, she felt a familiar presence in the room and rounded on Edwin angrily.

'You didn't need to do that!' she shouted at him. 'Is it not bad enough that my friends think I'm insane? Now my ex-husband will think I can summon vindictive ghosts!'

Panting from his exertions, Edwin seemed vexed by Kate's ungracious response. 'You were afraid!' he explained angrily. 'I was worried he was going to hurt you. And I didn't like the way he spoke to you!'

'It's none of your business!' she raged. 'I can take care of myself! Why does everybody treat me like a child?'

'Perhaps because you're prone to making rash decisions!' he shouted back.

'What the hell do you mean by *that*?'

He walked towards her as she reflexively backed against the wall, suddenly fearful of the fury in his black eyes. His tone softened a little. 'You took the wrong path, Kate,' he murmured sadly.

'When did I do that?' she demanded impatiently. 'When did I take "the wrong path"?'

'Had you taken the right course of action at the right time, everything would have been different.' Edwin's voice became strained as he battled with his anger. 'We wouldn't be here! We could have had a second chance!'

'That doesn't explain anything!' Kate wanted to slap him for his inability to give a clear-cut answer. *'Tell me what you mean!'*

'You wouldn't understand…'

His patronising remark riled Kate even further. 'I'm not a bloody teenager, Edwin!'

His eyes flashed dark as obsidian, and Bastet started to rattle on the bedside table. Edwin stepped in front of her and placed his hands on the wall either side of her shoulders, as if attempting to cut off her escape. Kate could feel his energy pressing against her; her whole body tingled as she flattened herself against the wall, fearful of the abilities he may possess.

'No, you're the older and wiser Kate who rushed into marriage with an adulterous, conniving swine instead of waiting for the *right* man.' Edwin closed his eyes, his jaw rigid and his brow furrowed. Finally, Bastet stopped trembling.

Stung by his sarcasm, Kate was frantically trying to decipher his words. Did he mean she had somehow manipulated events and changed her destiny? Obviously, she had married the wrong man. Had the right man been there all along, already in her life somehow? Had she already met the corporeal Edwin Ford and thrown away their second chance at happiness?

'Where is he then, this man who was meant for me? How did I mess up meeting him? *Tell me what I did wrong!'*

Edwin lowered his head, avoiding her angry stare. 'What does it matter now?' he muttered. When he looked at her again, his face was full of sorrow. 'Were you in love with Mark when you married?'

166

Kate looked down at the carpet, her vision blurring with tears. She finally conceded that she had deceived herself into believing she loved Mark. Why she had done it, she could not be sure. Perhaps it had been a rebellious act against her family. Perhaps it was because she had met Mark at a time when she was vulnerable, lonely and naïve; she had been dazzled by Mark's glamorous lifestyle and his extravagant courtship. She had become dubious about a career in hard-nosed journalism but had been too cowardly to voice her reservations, and marriage had seemed like a reasonable alternative. She lived in fear of disappointing her family. She loved Ben, but her clever and successful brother was a hard act to follow. *I've been so stupid! I've wasted so much time!*

Kate took a deep breath and looked into Edwin's eyes. 'I thought I was until I started to dream of you,' she told him. 'When I started to remember my life with you I realised my marriage in this life was a sham.' She looked away, grief-stricken at the loss of the last few years. Her life felt futile. 'But now I know that *our* marriage wasn't perfect, either...'

'You could be so stubborn and impulsive at times!' Edwin sounded irritated, his voice rough. Kate hung her head, awaiting further harsh judgements against her character. 'When I agreed to go on the expedition to Egypt, I tried to persuade you to stay safely in Edinburgh with your parents,' he continued. 'But you used every womanly trick at your disposal to get your own way.'

Kate looked up to see a small, exasperated smile appear on his handsome face. 'You said you didn't want to leave me behind,' she reminded him.

'I couldn't bear to be without you, despite our marital problems. I realised that you were desperate to get away from Edinburgh. And you needed something to take your mind off our inability to conceive. Even so, we knew that a pregnancy at that time would be inconvenient and perhaps dangerous. We agreed to take precautions.' He stroked her cheek, his fingers tracing the line of her jaw. His expression and voice softened. 'I tried to keep my distance, but you could seduce me with a glance. And when we stopped in Naples...' Edwin gave her a lopsided grin, his expression downright goofy.

'That's when it happened,' Kate said quietly. 'I remember.'

Edwin shook his head, as though the memory amazed him. 'In hindsight, I'm not at all surprised.' He drew his fingers through her thick dark hair and she shivered. 'Your feminine charms were considerable indeed. You were irresistible - and insatiable.'

Kate looked away sadly, remembering Mark's cruel barbs about her lack of passion as a lover. A virgin until her marriage, Kate had tried to learn how to please Mark but had been plagued with feelings of inadequacy, especially when she frequently caught Mark eyeing more sophisticated women. She had faked her cries of pleasure in order to speed the conclusion of the act, sure that Mark would be too intent on his own satisfaction to notice. At first, Kate had been content with the emotional and physical connection. But as time passed she tried to avoid sex altogether, and eventually Mark made excuses, too. He spent more time working, either in the office or in the study at home, and nurtured his own separate social life. Perhaps he had been seeing other women for years, which would explain his indifference. Even when she had tried to initiate lovemaking, he had remained unmoved. Except for that last time, when her need had been fuelled by dreams of Edwin's touch. Kate recoiled in disgust from the memory of having sex with Mark when he was already sleeping with Gemma. Had he spent their encounter comparing her to his more voluptuous and experienced lover? She folded her arms across her body defensively, feeling how thin she had grown in the last few weeks. She no longer felt feminine or desirable. Her eyes felt hot as she struggled to contain the sob which rose in her throat.

'Mark called me a frigid ice maiden,' Kate's voice was little more than a miserable whisper. 'And he's right.' She held herself tighter, feeling utterly broken.

'He was the wrong man, Kate. You can't give yourself to someone you don't really love, or trust. You acted as you did to protect yourself.' He reached for her hands, and touched her forehead with his own. 'But my fiery Kate is still here, simmering under the surface. You have to let her out, love, for you are more stifled now than you ever were when we were married.'

Kate's hands and forehead tingled as he shared his loving energy with her. 'I was raised to act with decorum...' she murmured helplessly, then lifted her head sharply as Edwin started to laugh.

'Not this again!' he groaned. He laid his palm on her tear-stained cheek. 'Do you remember torturing yourself with the rules of propriety while I was frantically chasing you?'

'I remember you deliberately making it difficult for me to obey them.' She smiled at last, as she recalled their budding romance.

'And when were you happiest?'

Kate reflected. 'When I could be myself?' Edwin nodded, smiling. 'And when I was with you,' she continued. 'Will we ever be together again, Edwin?'

Edwin stroked her back tenderly, sending shivers up her spine. 'You were mine before. You'll be mine again. I promise.'

Kate looked up at him archly, starting to feel a little better. 'A woman is no longer considered property, Edwin Ford!' Her expression became solemn. 'Will we be together again in *this* lifetime?' Or will I have to wait until I'm dead? She shoved the shocking thought out of her head.

Edwin sighed. 'Sweetheart, I'm too tired to answer difficult questions. What's important is that I'm here now, and I'm going to help you get on the right path in the time that I have. But you have to find your strength again, and you have to heal your wounded heart.' Edwin closed his eyes, his energy fading. He fought the sensation, desperate to stay with Kate for as long as he was able. 'Darling, I can't stay much longer,' he warned. 'Tell me about your day. Did you enjoy your ride?'

'It was perfect,' she replied happily, sitting on the edge of the bed. 'I had a lovely time, on a lovely horse. And we went to North Berwick.'

Edwin was silent for a while, as though remembering the day he had spent in the seaside town. 'And how was the Egyptologist?'

Kate looked up at him coyly. 'Professor Young was the perfect gentleman. He didn't try to tempt me to behave inappropriately - unlike *some* men I could mention.'

Edwin grunted in response, but a mischievous smile played on his lips. 'I couldn't help my behaviour,' he said defensively, as he sat next to her. 'You were too tempting.' He tugged a lock of her hair. 'You're still too tempting.' When Kate shook her head dismissively, he cupped her chin with his hand. 'I mean it. You are a beautiful woman. I can say that categorically.' He grinned at his own blunder.

Kate's face showed indignation. 'Have you been spying on me in an inappropriate fashion?' she demanded, realising she wasn't as angry as she was making out.

Edwin's eyes flashed wickedly, and he chuckled. 'Not spying, exactly. I wanted to see how you were. I didn't see anything I hadn't seen before. We were married, after all! I will say one thing, though.' He kissed her upturned nose, making her smile at the tickly sensation. 'Modern undergarments are delightfully flimsy!'

CHAPTER 10

Kate finished Edwin's biography and emailed it to David on Monday morning. Even though he was rushed off his feet, David took the time to read Kate's work in his lunch break. He was impressed by her talented writing skills and surprised by the depth of her knowledge, which proved she had done her research. Of course, David couldn't have guessed that some of the information had been gleaned from an interview with the subject himself.

Jess was setting out Norse artefacts for the afternoon workshop on Vikings when Kate came into the room like a tornado, her eyes wide in panic.

'Jess!' Kate squeaked, sounding out of breath.

'Kate!' Jess squeaked in reply, mimicking Kate's startled expression.

'I just got an email from David!'

'And it was obviously hugely exciting!'

'He wants me to present my story on Thursday.' Kate wrung her hands. 'What shall I do? I've never spoken in front of a group before!'

Jess laughed at her friend's misplaced anxiety. 'Kate, David already emailed me about this. He asked me to help you prepare. You've nothing to worry about, because you'll be fine. David obviously has confidence in your abilities.' She gave Kate a meaningful stare, but Kate still looked fretful. 'You know your subject, don't you?' Jess grinned. 'In fact, I would say you know your subject *very* well!'

Kate walked in tight circles as she read over her cue cards again, oblivious to the work going on around her. The room was being prepared for the ancient Egypt presentation which was due to start in fifteen minutes. Kate had already downloaded illustrations onto the computer and checked they would appear on the screen behind her. Jess had rehearsed the presentation with Kate several times; Kate was now word perfect and would easily deliver her narrative within her allotted fifteen-minute time slot. Still, Kate fretted that once she started talking about Edwin, she could easily overrun and that would cause problems for David and his team.

David stood in the doorway, watching Kate's lips moving silently as she read. He beckoned to Jess to join him in the hallway.

'Are they here?' Jess asked, for the group of children were due to arrive at any minute.

'Not yet,' David replied. 'The reception desk will radio when the children arrive. I wanted to talk to you about Kate.' Jess remained silent, waiting for David to continue. 'I'd like Kate to take over some of my assistant's duties. I wondered if you and I could get together and agree on a new work schedule and training programme for her.'

Jess's eyes narrowed suspiciously; David was clearly showing her professional courtesy, as he did not have to consult her at all. The archaeologist was a valuable member of the museum staff, who had published many articles in archaeological periodicals. Although his main area of expertise was ancient Egypt, he held a wealth of knowledge on other ancient civilizations. Jess recalled that David had acted as a consultant when the museum acquired some Japanese armour and weaponry a couple of years before. He was held in high esteem and as a result, usually got what he wanted. He also had a reputation for being a hard taskmaster, with exacting standards. Jess had heard that a lot of David's students quit his classes, unable to cope with the pressure he put them under to work diligently and without respite. Those who remained to complete the course did so with excellent results, and most of them found success in their chosen field.

David watched Jess consider his proposal, realising he had a less than stellar reputation with his colleagues. Jess folded her arms. 'Have you spoken to Kate about this?' she asked. 'Or discussed it with Gray?'

'I didn't want to mention it to Kate until I had spoken to you. If we can work out a schedule, I'll take it to Gray. If he approves it, then I'll speak to Kate.'

'That's very considerate,' Jess said grudgingly and gave him a direct look. 'Kate has been going through some difficult stuff, lately. I won't condone a punishing schedule for her.'

'I'm not planning one,' David said hastily. 'Kate wants to learn about Egypt, and I'd like to teach her.' He glanced up, as if he could see Kate through the wall. 'She has so much potential, and I just want to help her reach it. I admit that some of her duties could be considered mundane, but she'll also have to attend workshops and lectures, and

171

possibly accompany me on field trips. Over the summer, I'll be involved in some restoration work and Kate could help. Don't you think she would enjoy that?'

Jess smiled. 'I think she would love it. But she's a valuable member of the Events team, too. She has a real way with people, especially kids...' Jess sighed. 'Okay, let's put our heads together and see what we can work out.'

David's radio squawked into life, announcing the arrival of the schoolchildren. David left to meet his class, and Jess called out to her team to prepare for battle. Kate was standing at the side of the screen, testing her headset and microphone. Jess had laughingly suggested Kate dress like Indiana Jones, but Kate had decided on a white shirt, beige trousers and her tatty brown lace-up boots.

Once the class were seated and quiet, David stood before them and outlined their activities for the morning. He exuded his usual quiet confidence, his perceptive gaze sweeping the eager young faces before him. He smiled at Kate encouragingly as he introduced her to the children, and then took a seat in the corner of the room.

'Good morning, boys and girls!' Kate smiled warmly as the children politely returned her greeting. 'Take a look at the screen behind me.' Using the remote control in her hand, Kate displayed photos of Egyptian relics. She had used the Ancient Egypt Exhibition catalogue to find Edwin's artefacts, and had photographed the few which were on display. 'These objects are on display in the museum - see if you can find them when you walk around the Egyptian gallery later. They were brought here in 1890 by a young man called Edwin Ford.' She paused briefly to survey the room and ensure the children were still listening. 'He's one of my ancestors.' Kate saw some of their eyes widen in surprise, David's among them. 'I'd like to tell you the story of how Edwin brought these beautiful things to us.'

Kate began a brief account of Edwin's birthplace and education before moving onto his expedition to Egypt. She told the story of Edwin's team finding the queen's tomb, supporting her words with illustrations of the desert, and a picture of a cleverly-concealed tomb entrance situated in a cliff-face. Nick dimmed the lights as Kate told the group about a dusty narrow tunnel, lit only by the lanterns of the brave expedition team. Her audience were captivated by the tale Kate wove of booby-traps and treasure. They listened in awe as she described the dashing hero who survived the arduous mission to Egypt and brought his treasure to Edinburgh, so that people could marvel at its beauty and learn about the magnificent civilization which had ruled northern Africa so long ago.

Kate ended her presentation by mentioning Edwin's expedition with Flinders Petrie, which resulted in the acquisition of the Qurneh burial display. The mention of Petrie allowed David to step in beside her and seamlessly continue his own presentation; Flinders Petrie claimed the exalted title 'father of modern archaeology' and David planned to show the children some of Petrie's methods at work.

And so Kate's presentation was done. David explained that they were going to move to one of the workrooms used by his team, but first they should thank Kate for her enthralling presentation. He smiled at Kate and led the loud applause. Kate blushed and looked up at Jess, who was sitting at the back of the room. Standing next to her, his face beaming with pride, was Edwin.

While David and some of his colleagues showed the children how to write their names using Egyptian hieroglyphs, Kate quickly quartered a tray of apples. The class were going to 'mummify' apple slices by placing them in sealable food bags with a mixture of baking soda and salt, to emulate the way Egyptians used the natural desiccant natron to mummify corpses. The children would be instructed to take the bags home and put them on a sunny windowsill for a week.

As Kate carried the tray of apples to the worktables, she watched David laughing with the children as they tried to draw hieroglyphic symbols. Despite his somewhat serious disposition, David was clearly enjoying himself. As Kate set the tray down beside the other equipment needed for apple mummification, David clapped his hands and swiftly moved onto the next activity. His enthusiasm was infectious, as the children gleefully mixed up their homemade 'natron' and added the fruit. Surprisingly, David encouraged the children to email his team with their findings once seven days had passed.

The children were allowed a short break before their tour of the Egyptian gallery. As the teachers and staff escorted the pupils to the toilets, Kate cleared up the messy tables so the children could eat their snacks without them being seasoned with salty baking soda.

'Your presentation was excellent,' David said from behind her. She glanced up at him and smiled appreciatively. 'Nice touch, to say he was your ancestor.'

Kate dropped her eyes to her work, offering no response, as the room filled up with children once again.

For the next part of the workshop, David led the group to the sarcophagus Iufenamun. The priest lay sedately in his wrappings, apparently indifferent to his exposure. Kate stood at the back of the group, offering silent support to the children who were visibly nervous

173

about being so close to a dead Egyptian. She was surprised when one little girl moved closer to her, almost hiding her face behind Kate's arm. Most of the children crowded round David, who was crouched before the display case pointing out different hieroglyphs and the stories they told. Intuitively, Kate turned and walked to a bench a short distance from the mummy. Within moments, the little girl and one of her companions had joined her. One of the teachers looked up, perturbed, but Kate smiled at her reassuringly.

'We don't like looking at that mummy,' the little girl explained in a timid voice.

'I'll let you in on a little secret,' Kate said softly, tucking a stray wisp of hair behind the girl's ear. 'I don't like looking at him, either. But we have to remember that it's only the remains of a person in the case. His soul - the special part of him which made him who he was - is gone. Do you know what I mean?' The girls looked at Kate uncertainly. 'Think of it this way. You open a really good present. It has a lot of fancy wrapping. The present inside is the best, most wonderful thing you can imagine. But, the wrapping -'

'It's just wrapping,' the second girl interrupted.

'Yes, it is!' Kate grinned.

'And we recycle it!' the first girl chimed in, and the three of them giggled.

David had finished talking about Iufenamun and was looking pointedly in their direction. The teachers gathered up their pupils as David approached Kate. 'Was I boring you?' he asked curtly.

Kate was offended by his tone, but stood firm. 'The girls were a little frightened by the dead man in the display case. I thought it wise to allow them an escape. Surely you don't want them to have nightmares?' Kate flinched as the Millennium Clock started to chime, but kept her defiant gaze fixed on David.

David's expression was grim. 'They're not going to like what's waiting for them in the workroom, then...'

Kate's eyes filled with dread. 'What?'

'An unwrapped mummy I managed to borrow from the university. He's in a glass case, but he's remarkably well-preserved. And there's a short video on the unwrapping process.'

Kate groaned. 'You need a Plan B. And you need to let these kids choose whether or not they want to see this...thing. They're not like us; they haven't learned to swallow their fears and put on a brave face.' She saw David wince at her remark and immediately regretted it. 'I can take them to another room and tell them a story or something...'

David grimaced. 'What kind of story?'

The idea came to Kate instantly. 'I'll tell them about Amarna. If I can access the internet I can show them pictures, too. It's on topic, and it's of current archaeological interest.'

David nodded reluctantly. 'Okay. There's a small office next to the workroom. Use that.'

'Thank you,' Kate said, irritated by his attitude. She walked over to the group of children. The two girls each took one of her hands, and they made their way to the first floor.

'Do you have children?' one of the girls asked. Kate noticed from their name tags that they were called Alice and Hayley. She was also aware that David was right behind her and could hear their conversation.

Kate shook her head, and for a moment her smile disappeared. 'No, I don't,' she replied, trying to sound nonchalant.

'Are you married?' Hayley asked and Kate shook her head again.

'Do you have a boyfriend?' Alice inquired.

Kate chuckled and looked down at the girl. 'What's that got to do with ancient Egypt?'

Alice lowered her voice, but she could still be heard clearly. 'Is the professor your boyfriend?'

Kate heard David cough as her own ears turned red. 'No!' she said emphatically. 'Now, here we are in ancient Egypt. Can you see any of the artefacts I told you about?'

Four of the children decided against examining the unwrapped mummy, electing instead to sit around the computer with Kate in the office next door. She accessed pictures of present-day Amarna - avoiding photographs of recently excavated burial plots - and showed the children a reconstruction of the great city. There were also photos of jewellery and household items which had been found less than a metre under the sand.

'Have you been there?' asked the only boy in her group. Kate thought he looked very sweet, with silky dark hair and big brown eyes framed by long eyelashes.

'No,' Kate replied, feeling strange as she denied a version of the truth. A gentle breeze on the back of her neck announced Edwin's presence in the room. 'But Edwin Ford was there.'

'Tell us about it!' Alice pleaded.

Kate hesitated, wondering how Edwin would feel if she discussed the ill-fated expedition. She reasoned that his aim in life had been to educate people about ancient Egypt, and she could do that for him now. So she told the children as much as she remembered about the trip to

Akhetaten in 1891, how Edwin had lived in a canvas tent as he supervised the building of mud-brick huts. She told them about the food and the sandstorms and the water pumps used to clear out excavated areas before they were inspected for artefacts. To make the pumps work, they had tied the machinery to a camel or donkey which was then led in wide circles by one of the local boys. The picture Kate painted of this procedure made her audience giggle. Lastly, she told them of a stone tablet, a love letter to a beautiful queen. As she haltingly spoke the words inscribed on the tablet, Kate could feel her eyes sting with unshed tears. She was relieved when the door opened, and one of the teachers bustled into the room to collect her pupils.

The children noisily thanked Kate, then left to join their classmates. The room felt suddenly empty and silent. But Kate knew she wasn't alone, and when she turned around Edwin was behind her.

'I'm sorry if I've upset you,' Kate said softly, looking into his sad eyes. 'It wasn't my intention. I just want people to know about you.'

'Well, you did a good job of that today!' Edwin replied, and sighed. 'That little boy -'

'I know.' Kate felt as if a weight had been placed on her heart. 'Our own child could have looked just like that.'

Edwin touched her face, and Kate closed her eyes, imagining she could feel his fingers. 'You will be a wonderful mother one day.'

'Kate -' David called as he stepped into the room. Kate spun round, Edwin fading behind her. David looked stern and unsmiling.

'Did your group enjoy ogling your unwrapped mummy?' Kate asked. *Oh hell, that didn't come out right!* Kate heard a faint snigger behind her and coughed to hide the sound, as well as her own embarrassment. David was staring at her, not quite sure how to respond. He wasn't speechless for long.

'They enjoyed it, actually, and learned a lot. How were your sensitive souls in here?'

Kate's chin lifted a fraction, and her eyes flashed. 'They learned something, too. I told them about Amarna, including the expedition of 1891 and more recent projects -'

'And thankfully saved them from a sleepless night,' David added sardonically.

They faced one another across the room, unaware of Jess hovering in the doorway. She could hear the exchange and did not want to disturb them, curious to see if the high-and-mighty professor was about to meet his match.

'If I have, then I'm glad!' Kate retorted, a new self-confidence rising within her.

'Children come here to learn,' David reminded her. 'Not to help you hone your maternal instincts.'

Kate clenched her fist and inhaled sharply at his stinging remark. She wondered fleetingly about the recent collapse of his relationship and who had been to blame, instinctively feeling sorry for David's ex-partner. 'I suggest you rethink the things you show ten year-olds. Or at least inform the teachers beforehand. Perhaps the dead bodies would be more suited to workshops for teenagers.'

David knew she had a point, but was not about to concede. He was also destabilised by the sudden awareness that she was getting under his skin. 'I think I'm best qualified to make that decision, don't you? And I would prefer it, in future, if you didn't encourage people to walk away from me when I'm talking.'

Kate was furious but kept her voice level. She discovered she was not intimidated. 'We can't all have a stiff upper lip, Professor. I used my intuition and helped those children, and I would do it again! I'm not some dumb blonde who can't think for herself!' Kate became acutely aware of David's hair colour. She heard Edwin snort with mirth. Outside the room, Jess covered her mouth to hide her laughter.

'No,' David snapped. 'You're acting more like a redhead right at this moment!'

As Kate wondered how David knew she had strands of coppery-red in her hair, Jess decided it was time to intervene. She walked purposefully into the room. 'Children!' she said firmly. 'If you're *quite* finished -'

David was saved by his radio. One of his team informed him that an urgent phone call had been transferred from reception, and the caller was currently on hold. David barked his reply, before turning back to Kate. 'We'll finish this later.'

Kate glowered at him. 'I'll be waiting.'

As he passed her, Jess saw the startled look on David's face. She was astonished to see his lips twitching, as if he wanted to laugh. She looked at Kate, and saw her giggling behind her hand. Jess shook her head, flummoxed by what she had just witnessed.

'I'm going to grab some lunch before the next workshop,' she told Kate. 'Are you coming?'

Oddly exhilarated by the altercation with David, Kate gave Jess a wide smile. 'I'll catch up in a minute, okay?'

When Jess left the room, Kate looked behind her. Edwin was grinning at her with admiration in his eyes.

'I told you feisty Kate was still in there,' he reminded her. 'I'm very pleased to see her again, though I feel sorry for Professor Young...'

Kate frowned. 'Why?'

Edwin brushed her hand, his energy tickling her palm. 'Why? Because he's been burned by your fiery temper, but won't reap the reward of reconciliation. Sometimes I used to irritate you on purpose...' He smiled as she blushed shyly. 'Be gentle with him, Kate. I like him. He reminds me of...well, me.'

Kate was indignant. 'He's nothing like you!'

Edwin stroked her cheek, and Kate felt as if a butterfly had brushed against her skin. 'Sweetheart, you only knew me for a very short time. And I was completely different with you. When things were good between us, you brought out the very best in me.' He looked into her lovely eyes, as he felt himself being pulled away. He hated the thought of leaving her. 'I have to let you go for lunch. I just wanted to do this -' He kissed her forehead. 'And I wanted to tell you that I'm very, very proud of you - although, of course I deserve some of the credit!'

Kate's day improved even further that afternoon, when she received an email from her solicitor. Mark would not contest the divorce, nor did he want a share of Kate's house. Their joint assets would be split equally. Mark had decided to sell the paintings which were now stacked in Kate's hallway, and he planned to give his wife half the money.

Kate was euphoric. Within a few weeks, she would be Kate Grahame again.

The second week of May heralded Kate's final week on probation at the museum, and her fourth week of living alone. She was becoming stronger, and her newfound vigour motivated her to make changes to her home. With Ben's help, Kate had spent the weekend repainting her bedroom, which was now a soft rose colour and indulgently feminine. Ben had been amused at his sister's uncharacteristic display of girlishness, but he was also relieved that she was attempting to rebuild her life.

The dreams of her past life had ceased. Kate felt a strange mixture of relief and regret, but assumed she had been given all the information she needed. She began to highlight the changes she needed to make in order to move forward. Regretfully, she realised that she had hurt both Edwin and Mark with her indifference. Kate could not forgive Mark's infidelity, but she dearly wished she could apologise to Edwin. She had not seen or felt him since the day of the Egyptian workshop.

She had avidly read the books on Egypt which David had lent her, soaking up the information like a sponge. Kate wanted to ask the archaeologist what she should read next, but she had not seen him since their argument. Although David had been arrogant and overbearing, Kate could not help smiling every time she thought about trading insults with him. Jess had warned her that offending David might be detrimental to her career, but Kate remained unrepentant. She was curious as to his whereabouts, but had to wait until the middle of the week before their next interaction. It came in the form of an email which arrived as she was amending the worksheet on Romans.

The email was originally from Adam Gray, who had sent it on to David. David had forwarded it to Kate, hoping it would act as an olive branch. It had been composed by one of the teachers who had accompanied the class to David's Egyptian workshop. The teacher praised the professor and his team for a well-organised and informative event. She asked Gray to pass on her gratitude to Kate, for noticing the discomfort of some of the children and providing an alternative activity.

'Ha!' Kate cried out in triumph, causing Nick to look up in surprise. She considered sending a reply to David, but decided to let him wait. She was enjoying the opportunity to use her writing skills and did not want to interrupt her creative flow.

In his small office in the university, David was pacing the floor impatiently. It was exam time, and David liked to be available to answer questions and offer advice. To this end he spent some time in the office every day so that his students could drop by if they needed help. At this precise moment, however, he was distracted by Kate's lack of communication. Half an hour had gone by since his initial email, but she had still not sent a reply. He drummed his long fingers impatiently on the desk, wondering if he should tell Kate that Gray had agreed to allow her to assist David at his discretion. Then David remembered that he was not supposed to broach the subject with Kate until he and Jess had established a work schedule.

He also wanted to tell her that the urgent phone call he had received last Thursday had been from the parents of his close friend, Ethan. The fellow archaeologist was in the Royal Infirmary, suffering from a serious head injury which had been caused in a climbing accident in the Highlands six weeks before. Ethan now lay in a coma while those around him could only wait and hope. David was dismayed that he had not been informed of his friend's accident sooner, but now visited the hospital as often as he could and ensured Ethan's parents had everything they needed. In order to be near their son, they had been forced to leave their home near Carlisle and rent a flat in Edinburgh. Unfamiliar with the city, they had quickly come to rely on David.

David sighed, willing an email to appear from Kate. His lips twitched into a smile as he reminded himself how infuriating she was, and he chuckled as he recalled their heated battle of words. Far from angering him, her hot-headed insolence had filled him with a perverse delight. Then he frowned, as he wondered if perhaps she had been insulted by his remarks.

When Kate discovered that David had emailed her again, she felt unaccountably gratified.

'Kate,' it began. (David had wanted to begin with 'How's my favourite redhead?' but thought better of it.) 'I just wanted to make sure you received my forwarded email from Adam Gray, as my laptop has been misbehaving.'

Kate's fingers hovered over the keyboard as she pondered her reply. She gave the screen a wicked grin, and swiftly typed a short reply: 'Yes, thank you.'

In his lonely office, David ground his teeth in irritation as he read the three measly words. He checked his watch, desperate to return to the museum.

As soon as Kate walked into the Egyptian gallery on Wednesday afternoon, she could sense Edwin's presence in the stillness. The silence was punctured by the group of children who preceded Kate and Jess. The Egyptian workshop was led today by a member of David's department, who steered them to the row of sarcophagi.

Kate stopped in front of the Qurneh display, and quietly watched Edwin crouching beside the sarcophagi within. The display exhibited two coffins: one belonging to a woman, the other a female child. Items found in the burial site indicated they had been wealthy, possibly of royal blood. Edwin gently stroked the surface of the rectangular wooden coffin belonging to the unknown child, his expression pensive.

'How are you?' Jess asked abruptly, watching her friend gaze at the display with misty eyes. 'I feel like we haven't had a gossip for ages!'

Kate looked up and gave Jess a small smile. 'I'm okay. Why don't we go for something to eat after work?'

'I'd like that - as long as we don't talk about work.' Kate's eyes had drifted back to the exhibit. 'Have you seen your mystery man again?'

Kate nodded slowly without looking at Jess. 'Several times,' she admitted. 'Not enough.'

'That sounds intriguing - and hopeful. Might you and he be starting something?'

Kate miserably shook her head. 'It's impossible...' She looked into Edwin's solemn eyes.

'Why?' Jess's quiet tone was full of concern.

Edwin had moved to the collection of burial goods situated near the sarcophagi. He crouched down carefully. 'Tell her to watch,' he murmured to Kate.

Kate glanced at the children and saw that their attention was still focused on the sarcophagi. She turned to Jess, who had apparently not heard Edwin's voice. 'Watch the pot down there, Jess.'

As Jess looked down at the ancient pot, she saw it lift a few inches from its pedestal then gently return to its resting place. She stared, struggling to understand what she had just seen. Dumbly, she gaped at Kate. 'Please don't tell me that he's...'

Kate looked completely despondent as she nodded. 'He's the original Edwin Ford. Not flesh and blood.' She heard the group of children moving and tried to compose herself, blinking to stem the tears which always seemed eager to fall. 'Can I have a minute, Jess?'

'Tell her she's left her communication device in the staffroom,' Edwin said as he appeared beside Kate. 'And it's been making a noise.'

Kate smiled weakly; the whole situation felt ludicrous. 'He says you've left your mobile in the staffroom, and it's been ringing.'

Jess still looked stunned, her eyes huge. 'Thank you,' she stuttered uncertainly to the display case, before walking off to join the group.

Kate turned to Edwin, taking care to appear as if she were merely looking at a display. 'I haven't seen you for a while,' she murmured, adding, 'I missed you.'

'I've been spending some time with Professor Young,' he explained.

Kate looked surprised. 'Why were you with David?'

Edwin shrugged and smoothly deflected her question. 'He's very good at his job. More importantly, he's a good man.' Edwin rested his hands on Kate's upper arms. 'People have the wrong idea about him, Kate. He protects his heart.' He touched her cheek. 'He is the key.'

As Kate tilted her cheek towards his palm, she felt his energy waning. She looked up at his face, noticing a new translucency. 'The key to what?'

'He can help you. Stick with him, and treat him kindly. He's in pain.'

'I will, Edwin,' Kate promised. She looked up to see him smirk. 'What?' she questioned.

'Agreement without heated negotiation,' he grinned impishly. 'I'm not used to such obedience!'

181

Kate looked over her shoulder, noticing that the group were now at the opposite side of the gallery and would be leaving soon. The thought of parting from Edwin again made her heart sink. 'Edwin,' she began urgently. 'I'm so sorry I hurt you when we were married. I loved you so much. I'm sorry if I made you miserable.'

He gave her that heartbreakingly sad smile. 'I wasn't miserable, my love. I understood. I should have done more to help you...' He shrugged helplessly. 'Our life turned out as it was supposed to. We must accept it. But you have a chance to shape your future.' He stopped talking and looked into the middle distance, before gazing at her woefully. 'Kate, sweetheart, I will have to leave you soon.' Edwin winced at the look on her face, which conveyed the anguish she felt. 'You must prepare yourself.'

Adam Gray made Kate wait anxiously until Friday afternoon before summoning her to his office to discuss her probation. She knocked on the half-open door then hesitantly stepped over the threshold, surprised to see both Jess and David sitting with Gray at a round table in the corner. Jess gave her a reassuring smile which told her not to worry. David's gaze was impassive, his ego still slightly dented by Kate's vexatious email. He rose from his seat to pull out a chair for her. She sat down carefully, her eyes on Gray, who was watching her intently.

'Kate,' Gray began, feeling it would be inappropriate to call her 'Mrs Forrester'. 'We are very pleased with your work. Even though you hold none of the qualifications normally required to work in the Education and Events department, you have excelled yourself.'

David's jaw tightened a fraction as he heard Gray casually throw out an insult swathed in a compliment, but Kate's gaze remained unflinching.

Gray tapped a manila folder in front of him. 'I have your appraisal, which Miss Mortimer will discuss with you later. There are many positive comments, as well as constructive criticism. In short, it seems you have become a valuable member of our staff, and I would like to congratulate you on your success.' He paused for effect, giving Kate the opportunity to smile politely and voice her thanks. 'We have been considering a permanent role for you, and have decided on a work schedule.'

'*If* you agree,' Jess added, glancing sidelong at Gray. Kate raised an eyebrow, avoiding David's intense gaze. 'Miss Mortimer would like you to stay with the Events team, and has a training plan in mind to enhance your abilities. However,' Gray narrowed his eyes slightly in anticipation of Kate's reaction. 'It seems you have also impressed

Professor Young with your efficiency. He would like you to act as his assistant on a part-time basis, until he can find a replacement more suitably qualified for the role. He has drawn up a work schedule with Miss Mortimer.'

Kate's eyes flashed with momentary anger, before she brought herself swiftly under control. David had organised a schedule without consulting her. Were men always going to manipulate her into doing their bidding?

Jess recognised the signs of her friend's annoyance. She reached across to touch Kate's arm. 'It's just a rough schedule at the moment, Kate. We'll sit down and look at it together, and make sure it's going to work.' She looked pointedly across the table at David. 'We're not going to work you like a packhorse.'

'But you will have an opportunity to learn,' David added quietly. 'And add to your talents.'

Kate looked at Jess, then at Gray. 'I know I have a lot to learn. I'll continue to do my best.'

As Gray continued to talk about scheduling and expectations, Kate's mind drifted for a few seconds. Her eyes focused on the bookcase against the wall behind him. She remembered a similar bookcase in James Grahame's office, and a copy of 'Jane Eyre'. She could almost see James sitting at his huge leather-topped desk, placed in the same spot as Gray's smaller desk. The table she was sitting at today was in the same area as the desk she had occupied while writing the exhibition catalogue. She recalled Edwin perching on the desk, offering her a taste of Arabic coffee. She also remembered him sitting with his long legs resting on the desk of his tiny office along the corridor. Where he had sketched her likeness, where she had brought his lunch in the early days of their short marriage. Where they had bickered about insignificant things and where he had kissed her so lovingly...

Kate snapped back to the present, sitting up straight in her chair. Gray was bringing the meeting to a close. He stood up and offered Kate his hand. Thanking him, Kate smiled and shook his hand. Gray then ushered Kate and Jess out of the office, as he had words to exchange with David Young.

Kate contemplated her new work programme as she washed her dinner dishes. Jess wanted her to be more involved with workshops and their participants, rather than playing a supporting role behind the scenes. The museum was used as a venue for many corporate events and social functions, and Kate would be trained to liaise with these clients. They had recently been asked to arrange a wedding reception in December, which would demand a huge amount of work and co-ordination. Kate was eager to begin her new role.

The prospect of working for David filled her with uncertainty. She had seen a different side to his character lately, a rigidity and arrogance she mistrusted. And yet Edwin seemed to identify with him.

The doorbell rang. Kate dried her hands and padded to the door, looking through the spyhole first. She was surprised to see David standing there. Kate looked down horrified at her baggy jumper, leggings and slipper socks. The doorbell rang again, sounding impatient. Kate took a deep breath and opened the door. David's expression was grave, as if he knew she had contemplated not opening the door.

The speech he'd rehearsed in the car evaporated from his head, and he wondered suddenly if he'd overstepped a boundary in calling at her house uninvited. But at work she had proved elusive all week.

'Hi,' he stuttered, feeling her gaze burning a chink in his armour.

'Hi,' she replied, folding her arms across her chest defensively.

David eyed her casual appearance, thinking she looked sweet in her oversized grey sweater and wondering if it had belonged to her husband. He took a breath and made an effort to speak coherently, at the same time feeling aggravated because she could unsettle him with a mere look. 'I get the feeling you're angry with me...' Kate did not respond, but continued to gaze at him steadily, unnerving him further. 'I wanted to try and explain -'

'You could have called,' Kate observed. 'Or sent an email.'

David brought his hands from behind his back. He held up a large tub of chocolate ice cream. 'I think it's better to do these things face-to-face, don't you?' His confidence grew as he saw a reluctant smile tug at the corners of her mouth.

Kate tried to frown at him; he wasn't playing fair, but her angry heart began to melt along with the ice cream. With a theatrical sigh, she stepped back and ushered him into her home. David followed Kate to the spacious kitchen and accepted her invitation to sit at a large oak table surrounded by leather-clad chairs. The kitchen walls and units were a dazzling white, the uncluttered work surface a glittering blue granite. An archway cut into another wall led to the living room, where French windows provided a view to the garden beyond. Kate deftly scooped ice cream into glass dessert bowls and sat down across from David. He watched her lift a spoonful of ice cream to her lips, her eyes closing in appreciation.

'How did you know you could bribe me with ice cream?' she asked, her eyes twinkling.

'I took a risk,' he confessed and gave her a mischievous grin. 'What else works?'

Kate shook her head. 'You'll have to find out for yourself, Professor.'

They enjoyed their dessert in silence for a while, David trying to organise his thoughts, Kate relishing the taste of good quality chocolate ice cream. After a few mouthfuls, she looked up at David and tilted her head. 'I thought you had some explaining to do?'

David looked perturbed. 'I do. I just don't know where to start…'
Damn it, I've got a PhD and she makes me as tongue-tied as an awkward teenager!

'Start with this new schedule you've cooked up for me.'

David detected a tone of resentment; perhaps he should have warned her about his idea, after all. 'Jess and I worked on it together,' he said defensively. 'She's adamant that it should allow you to develop your skills without overwhelming or overtaxing you.'

'I'm not a delicate flower, David. And I'm not afraid of hard work.'

'I know.' He looked uncomfortable. 'It's just…well, I have a bit of a reputation for being…demanding and difficult to work with.' He lowered his eyes to his bowl, unwilling to reveal his flaws to her.

Kate smiled wryly. 'Really?' she said innocently, sucking her spoon. 'Imagine that!'

David looked up as he realised she was teasing him, and relaxed. She couldn't be *that* angry with him, after all. 'A lot of the tasks I'll give you will be administrative. I'll need you to attend Monday night lectures, but you'll be responsible for setting up the meeting room. Once the exams are over, I'll be running a class at the museum on Friday mornings, so you'll be helping with that.'

'Well, at least I'm qualified to do those things,' Kate observed, a hint of reproof in her tone.

David let the remark pass. 'I might have to go on a couple of local field trips, and I would like you to accompany me. I'll also be overseeing the conservation of some of our artefacts, and any work carried out needs to be recorded.' He looked at her earnestly with his startling green eyes. 'I thought I could help further your education. But I've also discovered how valuable you are, especially with your people skills. I sometimes find people…difficult.'

Kate delighted in his praise, but kept her face serious. 'You're better with dead people?'

David shrugged. 'They don't make unreasonable demands, question my authority, or insult me.' Now it was Kate's turn to hear a note of reproof, but she remained unabashed.

185

'And how will you expect me to behave, while I'm working under your command?' She raised another spoonful of melting ice cream to her lips, feeling slightly unnerved because David was watching her.

'I expect you to behave as you always do, with decorum and efficiency. You'll be much more involved in classes, now. If you see anything in a workshop itinerary which you think may be unsuitable for an age group, I want you to tell me. Then we can have alternative arrangements in place.'

'You mean so we don't end up arguing in public?' Kate was frowning, stung by the word 'decorum'.

David glanced away, remorseful. 'I'm sorry,' he murmured. 'I acted badly that day. I'm not used to…But I shouldn't have insulted your intelligence.'

'So you're not looking for a dumb blonde?' *Why do I keep needling him?* Kate silently scolded herself. *Why can't I shut up?*

David looked directly into her eyes, throwing her off-balance. 'I like the secret redhead.'

Kate gave him a sidelong glance as she collected his empty bowl and put it in the sink with her own. She wondered briefly if Edwin were watching them. If so, he must approve of her visitor, for there was no evidence of ghostly displeasure.

'I might have to lean on you a little in the next week or so,' David said apologetically. 'My students are sitting their exams so I'll be at the university a lot. And a friend of mine is in the Royal Infirmary. I'd like to visit him when I can.'

David gave Kate the sketchy details he had about his friend's accident, and was touched by Kate's compassion when she offered to help him in any way she could.

'Come riding with me tomorrow, then,' David replied quickly.

'How is that going to be helpful?' Kate asked, laughing.

'I have purely selfish motives,' he told her. 'I need to unwind. If I'm on my own, I'll spend the time in my own head. If I'm with you, I won't have time to brood.' *And with you, I can just be me.*

'Why? Do I keep you on your toes?'

David rose from his seat, pulling his jacket from the back of the chair. His eyes narrowed as he looked at her. 'You can be quite infuriating, do you know that?' Kate giggled and nodded in agreement. 'I see I'm going to have to raise my game.'

David woke abruptly from his dream and sat up in bed, his heart pounding. Running his fingers through his tousled hair, he tried to compose himself, but the dream had unsettled him. Switching on the lamp beside his bed, he tried to recall the hazy details.

He had been standing beside a tall stone obelisk, presumably in Egypt. There was a hot breeze, and sand was blowing lightly around his legs. Two saddled Arab horses stood nearby, nuzzling each other's necks. A woman was approaching, and in his dream David had felt a rush of pleasure at the sight of her. As she stopped before him, he realised it was Kate. She reached up and lovingly stroked her hand down his cheek. In the next moment, he had pulled her into his arms and they were kissing, his hands roaming over her body as she clung to him. And then he woke up.

David was confused, disturbed, and annoyed that he had been pulled from his dream at such an inconvenient moment.

Kate was drifting between sleep and wakefulness, her body feeling almost liquid against the mattress. She became aware of voices speaking softly around her, and she could feel Edwin in the room.

'It's time to go, Edwin,' a man's voice said, in a strong Scots accent Kate had heard before.

'No,' Edwin replied vehemently. 'I can't leave her. Not yet. I have to be sure -'

'Laddie, if you don't leave soon it will be too late, and none of this will matter.'

'Then I'll stay here and be damned! I'd rather be with her like this than lose her again!' His voice was full of emotion.

'Edwin, son,' the other man said gently. 'You're not so selfish that you would sacrifice another soul to satisfy your own desires. She's not our Katie, laddie. You have to let her live her own life. You've done everything you can to help her. Now it's time to go.'

Even in her semi-conscious state, Kate could feel Edwin's torment. 'I can't leave without saying goodbye to her. Please give me a little more time...' He sounded broken and lost.

The other man sighed. 'Do it now, son. Then you must go. You have no more time.'

'I understand.'

Kate sat bolt upright in bed, her conscious mind resuming control. 'Father?' she called into the darkness, for she knew that James Grahame had been in the room with Edwin; her bedroom was filled with the familiar smell of cigars and whisky, her Victorian father's only extravagance.

'No, darling, it's only me.' Edwin was sitting on her bed, stroking her hair, smiling the tender smile he reserved for his beloved Kate. The bedside light glowed dimly, but there was enough light for her to see his smile slip and be replaced with a heartbroken expression.

Kate couldn't bear to part with him. The thought of his imminent abandonment filled her with panic. 'Don't go, Edwin!' she begged. 'Please don't leave me alone!'

Edwin felt like screaming; he was leaving her again, as he had done in Cairo. And once again, she was pleading for him to stay. To him, the intervening years between that event and this moment did not exist. He relived that moment in Cairo over and over, he relived Kate's death again and again. But this time he was forced to witness her despair without being able to soothe her with his touch. Desertion was his only option, but she would live on and hopefully be happy, with or without him.

'You're not alone,' he told her earnestly. 'There are many people who care about you, both in this world and the next. We'll be together again, in time.'

A frightening thought occurred to Kate. 'Am I going to die? Is that how we'll be together again?'

Edwin flinched. 'No, you're going to live the life you're supposed to. And you'll be happy -'

'I want to live with you!'

'Sweetheart, *this*,' he gestured to his body. 'This is not living. We can't be together this way, you know that. You have to carry on with your life.'

Great, racking sobs shook Kate's body. 'Edwin, I need you to stay...'

'Kate, you don't need anyone. You're more than capable of walking your path alone. And remember what you've always told me: you are not my wife. I will always love you for the Kate you are now, just as I loved the Kate I was married to. You will carry that love in your heart always, so I'll be with you always. But I can't give you what you need, what you deserve. Not like this.' He tried to smile. 'Do you remember the tablet you found in Akhenaten when we were together? The love letter you made Jackson translate, which made me seethe with inane jealousy?' Kate nodded. 'It's in the Cairo museum. After my Kate passed away, Jackson held onto it so the Italian team wouldn't take it. The kind lad gave it to me, but I couldn't accept it and told him to keep it. He donated it to the museum.' He stroked her face. 'You should go and see it.'

'If I go to Egypt, will we be together again? Edwin, how will I know if I'm on the right path?'

188

Edwin's expression was unreadable. 'You might find what you're looking for in Egypt, that's all I can say. And I believe you have already started down a better path. But I would ask one more favour of you...'

'I'll do anything.' Kate started to cry again, knowing she only had a few more precious moments with him.

'My Kate,' Edwin whispered. He paused, closing his eyes to ward off the pain and the sight of Kate's devastation. 'Please, would you take her some flowers?'

Still sobbing, Kate nodded. 'She liked violets,' she stammered.

'Yes,' Edwin murmured. 'Yes she did. And so do you.' He lifted his head, listening to a voice only he could hear, then looked sadly back at Kate. 'Darling, it's time.'

'Edwin,' Kate whispered, watching in horror as he started to become transparent. 'Where will you go?'

He shook his head, unable or unwilling to answer her question.

Kate looked into his beloved face for the last time. 'I will always, always love you, Edwin Ford.'

'And I'll always love you, Katie Grahame. For eternity.' He stroked her hair, but Kate barely felt his fading energy. 'Now close your eyes, my love.'

As she obeyed, the tears flowed beneath her lashes, and she felt Edwin kiss her lips. She tilted her head back and reached up for him. Her fingers closed on air.

CHAPTER 11

David eyed Kate's pale face with concern as she walked down the path towards him, offering a feeble smile in greeting as she climbed into the car. She looked tearful, her eyes red and ringed with shadows. When he slid into the driver's seat she was staring at her hands, her fingers linked together tightly in the hope that their discomfort would stem her tears.

'What's the matter?' he asked gently. She continued to stare at her hands a moment longer before glancing up at him. David gave her a kind smile, wondering if he should offer her a hug. Kate wished he would hold her so that she could take comfort from a warm embrace.

Kate shook her head and smiled weakly. 'Nothing,' she replied quietly. 'It's nothing.' Her voice caught in her throat. 'I'm like you today, David. I need to be with someone so I don't brood.'

With an understanding nod, David started the engine and headed towards the town centre, and a whole new set of road works and diversions.

'How's your friend?' Kate asked, looking out of the window. It seemed to her that the streets were full of couples, holding hands, kissing, looking into one another's eyes. David had the same thought, his dream of Kate still playing out in his head.

'There's no change, I'm afraid,' David replied with a sigh.

'Does he have family?'

'His parents have come up from Carlisle. They've been staying in a flat for the last few weeks, so they can be here when Ethan wakes up. I'm taking them out to dinner tonight - they don't know anybody else in Edinburgh.'

Kate looked at David's profile, his brow furrowed in concentration. Perhaps Edwin had been right about him. He was clearly worried about his friend; perhaps their relationship was more than a simple friendship. 'That's kind of you,' she told him.

'Why don't you come out with us?' David asked suddenly.

Kate wondered if he had issued the invitation out of pity; she hated the idea that he felt sorry for her. She smiled graciously and shook her head. 'No thanks. I'm going to visit my mother tonight, and I have things to do at home.' *Like cry my eyes out.*

'Another time then,' he said lightly, pretending he wasn't disappointed.

As David negotiated the quickest route out of Edinburgh, he told Kate amusing anecdotes about his students and colleagues. She was lulled by his warm, soothing voice, but still noted that he refrained from talking about anything too personal. By the time they pulled into the farmyard, David was relieved to see Kate looking more like her usual self. He was also glad that when Kate climbed out of the car, Annie enveloped her in a motherly embrace and walked with her to the stables while David went to change into his riding gear. Although they talked mainly about horses, Kate was heartened by Annie's warmth and kindness. Zack was already tacked up and waiting, passing the time by playfully nudging the rump of David's haughty mare. Kate checked the girth and prepared to mount up.

'Best wait until David carries out all his pre-ride checks,' Annie advised her, rolling her eyes. 'He does it every time. I think he maybe had a bad fall at one time, and now he's taking no chances.'

'Has he ever brought anybody else riding?' Kate asked suddenly. *Why do I need to know that?*

Annie gave her a knowing look and shook her head. 'Not for a very long time.' She patted Kate's arm. 'I'm glad he's found you.' David walked towards them from the farmhouse. 'Now we'll just stand back and let him check your horse like the gentleman he is.'

Moving to stand in front of Zack, Kate stroked his velvety nose and allowed him to nuzzle her hair. She watched David check everything but the horse's teeth, while the chestnut mare whinnied impatiently.

'What's your horse called?' she asked, as David stroked his hand over Zack's rump.

'Ginger,' he replied absently.

Kate was expecting a beautiful, exotic name, perhaps something in Arabic. 'Ginger?' she repeated, incredulous.

David gave her a resigned look as he realised she would use this information to tease him. 'She's light on her feet.'

Kate snorted with laughter as she mounted Zack and set off for the paddock, where Annie stood holding the gate open for them. Once in the lane, Kate took the lead, enjoying the warmth of the May sunshine on her tense back. David watched as she leaned down in the saddle and patted Zack's ebony neck, planting a kiss on his scruffy mane. The ring of his mobile phone pulled David roughly from his contemplation.

Kate rode on a short distance then stopped to wait for David. She saw him frown as he listened to his caller.

'Right,' he said decisively. 'Remove it from display and take it to the workroom. I'll look at it on Monday, and we'll see what can be done. And be careful with it! Yes, it's strange, but these things happen. Yes, you too. Bye.' He put his phone back in his jacket pocket, but Kate could see he was perturbed.

'Alright?' she asked, as he caught up with her.

'Odd.' David chewed his lip. 'One of the artefacts in the Egyptian gallery just cracked while it was on display. A visitor was looking at it, and it just...cracked.'

Kate suddenly felt uneasy. 'Which artefact was it?'

'It was a little alabaster pot which was brought to the museum around 1890, I think.'

'By Edwin Ford,' Kate murmured, and David saw her expression change. She suddenly looked completely woebegone.

'We'll look at it on Monday,' he said, in an attempt to console her. *Why is she so upset about an Egyptian pot?* 'We may be able to repair it - you can come and help.'

'Will that fit in with my new schedule?'

'Ah,' David smiled at her. 'You're mine on Mondays. And Fridays.'

Kate drew herself up straight in the saddle, indignant but smiling again. 'You may want to rephrase that, Professor Young!'

He tittered at her annoyance, enjoying the spark in her eyes. 'You will be working *within my department* on Mondays. Is that better?'

'Humph!' she grunted and urged Zack into a fast walk towards the beach.

David would not allow her to canter on the beach, citing her lack of recent riding experience as the reason. She tried pouting and grumbling about his unnecessary judiciousness, but he would not be swayed. So she had to content herself with trotting along the deserted beach at the water's edge instead. Kate felt invigorated as her tension and misery left on the sea breeze, at least for a little while.

Her happiness was short-lived. Once they had returned the horses to the stables, and Kate realised she would soon be returning to an empty house, her heart felt heavy once again. As she settled Zack in his stall, she felt her eyes sting with tears and wearily struggled to keep them at bay. She dug a Polo mint from her pocket and held it out to Zack, stroking his neck as he nuzzled her palm. When David looked over the stall door, he found her leaning her cheek against Zack's shoulder and whispering to him while the horse munched food from a bucket.

'They say it's good to talk,' David rested his arms on the stall door. 'To people, as well as horses.'

Kate forlornly shook her head. 'I don't need to,' she replied, failing in her attempt to sound strong and self-reliant.

David sighed and opened the stall door to let her out. 'Kate, it's fine to let your guard down now and again.'

Kate left Zack with a final pat, closing the stall door behind her and sliding the bolt home. 'Not in my experience,' she disagreed. 'Besides, *you* don't.'

David shrugged. 'I'm different.'

Kate rounded on him angrily. 'Why? Because you're a big tough man? Because you're not a weak, whiny woman?'

Instead of giving her an argument, David impulsively slipped his arms around her and held her gently. At first, her body was rigid, her arms held up defensively between his chest and hers. He thought she made a soft noise, almost like a squeak.

'I've always had to keep my feelings to myself, Kate,' David tried to explain. 'Even a friendly hug is a major effort for me. So you should be a bit more appreciative.' He chuckled when he heard her giggle weakly against his jacket. Both of them wondered how their new, tentative friendship had developed so quickly. They had been relative strangers just a few weeks before, and now here they were flaunting their innermost feelings. Almost.

She looked up at him uncertainly. 'How are you, David?' she asked. 'It's been a few weeks since you broke up with your partner.'

'Actually,' he replied warily. 'I'm relieved. Things hadn't been going well for a while. I'm disappointed in myself, for being unable to keep a relationship going. Maybe I'm better on my own...' He took a deep breath. 'How are you after *your* break-up?'

Kate looked down at his jacket. 'I'm relieved, too,' she admitted. 'I'm also hurt, ashamed, humiliated...and a bit lonely.' *And, by the way, I've lost my soulmate. I feel like a part of me has gone and might never come back.*

'Why should you feel ashamed?'

Kate was silent for a long moment. 'I couldn't keep my husband happy. I wasn't enough.'

David's arms tightened around her, and Kate took solace from his warmth. 'Did he cheat on you?' David asked softly, his jaw tightening at the thought. She felt fragile in his arms. Recent events had taken their toll on her, physically as well as emotionally.

Kate nodded. 'He had an affair with one of my friends.'

David swore under his breath. 'Then he's the one who should feel ashamed.' He tilted her chin up with one finger. 'And it's his loss, right?' She looked up at him, unconvinced. 'At least we're both free to do as we please. You should do things which make you happy.'

'What do *you* plan to do?'

David grunted. 'There's a possibility I might be going to Egypt at the end of the year.' He didn't see the flicker of disappointment in Kate's eyes. 'I haven't decided, yet. But the thought of being away at Christmas is appealing...'

'Why? Do you have issues with Christmas?'

'Yes.' He didn't elaborate.

'You'd rather spend Christmas day in some musty old tomb? Or with ancient dead bodies?'

'Is that worse than spending the day with difficult people and putting on a happy face? Or having to field a million nosy questions about your life, career and apparent unwillingness to procreate?'

'Touché.'

'I think Gray would like to see the back of me for a while,' David surmised with a wry smile. 'He's given me a little shove by supplying me with an intern.'

Kate leaned back and looked into his face with apprehension. 'So you won't need me?'

'On the contrary,' he told her firmly, making no effort to release her from his embrace. 'I have a lot of work lined up for you. Our intern is one of my best students. He's just submitted his thesis and needs work over the summer. I'm quite happy to provide some work experience for him, and hopefully I can help him find a permanent job once he gets his PhD.

'Gray's hoping that, if I have a qualified archaeologist to assist me, I might be more inclined to spend a few weeks in Egypt. I have almost the whole summer to make my decision, so I'm going to let him stew. Besides, in the past I've worked in Egypt with Ethan. I'm not sure I want to go without him.'

'I see.' Kate's curiosity about David's relationship with Ethan increased.

David gave her a boyish grin. 'There. I let my guard down for five minutes, just for you. Happy now?' *Should I also tell you I had a dream about you and you feel almost exactly as I imagined?*

They were interrupted by David's phone, and Kate walked out into the yard to give him some privacy. When he joined her a few moments later, a wide smile brightened his handsome face.

'Ethan's awake!' David announced with obvious relief.

After bidding Annie a hasty farewell, they headed back to Edinburgh. Kate felt guilty that David would have to take her home before he could visit Ethan, especially when she noticed he was driving faster than usual.

'David, you could just drive to the hospital,' she suggested. 'I can easily get a bus home from there.'

He shook his head. 'No, I'll take you home first. Besides, I'm starving. I'll grab something to eat and then go to the hospital. His parents will want to spend time with him, anyway.'

An idea formed in Kate's head. She thought it through, and then spoke up. 'Why don't I make you something to eat? You know, to say thank you. Then you can go to the hospital.'

He glanced at her, unsure. 'You don't have to thank me for anything. And you said you had things to do.'

'I also have homemade pasta sauce in the fridge,' she smiled.

'Kate,' David sighed between mouthfuls of pasta. 'This is really, really good.'

'My sister-in-law is Italian,' Kate explained. 'She's passed on a few recipes. I can now make a mean lasagne, among other things.'

David grinned. 'I make a mean baked potato.'

Kate watched in amusement as he mopped up his pasta sauce with a piece of crusty bread. It made her feel good to see him enjoying her cooking. She had shooed him out to the garden while she prepared their meal, but after five minutes he had returned to the kitchen with an offer to help. It had not felt awkward at all, Kate realised, to have him slicing bread and setting the table. Away from work, David was relaxed and playful, and he made her feel completely at ease. She knew, however, that his solemn and detached demeanour would return on Monday.

'You have a nice house,' David commented. 'The garden's lovely.'

Kate's aunt had landscaped the garden with plants which needed little attention, including an apple tree, and some beautiful rose bushes. It occurred to Kate that, with Mark gone, she would now be solely responsible for the maintenance of the garden.

'I'm very lucky,' Kate agreed. 'My aunt left it to me in her will.' She felt embarrassed as she saw David's surprise. 'But I feel like I'm rattling around in here on my own.' Kate looked down at her empty plate and sighed. 'I don't want to sell it, though. I'm the third generation of my family to live here.'

'Make it yours,' David advised. 'You may fill it up again.'

Kate flushed uncomfortably. 'What's your house like?' she asked, steering the conversation away from her own situation.

David grunted. 'I live in a rental flat. Not as much privacy as I would like. But it's just a place to rest my head. Maybe one day I'll put down roots somewhere...' He looked wistful. 'But not quite yet.'

David insisted on helping with the dishes before leaving for the hospital. Kate balked at the thought of her impending solitude, but she gave David a confident smile as she walked with him to the gate.

'Thank you for today, David.' She folded her arms in front of her chest, hugging herself. 'I'm glad your friend is awake.'

'Thanks for feeding me,' he replied, not sure whether he should hug her again. 'I'll see you on Monday.' He seemed to hesitate, his gaze inquisitive, before finally climbing into his car. Kate kept her arms wrapped firmly around her body as she watched David drive away.

On Sunday, the sky was grey and full of dark clouds. Undaunted by the threat of rain, Kate left her silent house mid-morning and bought some flowers at the supermarket. She then walked to Dean Cemetery, her heart heavy as lead. She entered the vast burial ground through the gate behind the Gallery of Modern Art, overwhelmed by the countless graves and unsure where to start looking for the headstones belonging to Kate and Edwin. Closing her eyes, she tried to connect in some way with her surroundings, in the hope that her intuition or something more spiritual might guide her. After a few minutes, Kate started walking.

She found them in a corner, under a Rowan tree. Two matching slabs of granite marked their final resting place. Kate Ford's was engraved with her name, the dates of her birth and death, and the word 'beloved'. Edwin's gave the same information, with the inscription 'beloved husband of Katherine'. Kate was overcome with feelings of grief, pity and loss.

Kneeling before the graves, Kate placed pink roses in the rusting little vases which sat in front of each stone. 'I'm sorry they're not violets,' she whispered. Rising from the damp grass, she stepped carefully between the graves and stooped to kiss the top of each headstone. But she felt unable to leave, and stood helplessly before them as the rain started to fall.

She jumped violently as her phone rang. Swallowing the cleansing sobs which welled up in her throat, she murmured tremulously, 'Hello?'

'Katherine, it's Mum.' Elizabeth knew by the sound of Kate's voice that something was wrong. 'Where are you?'

Kate paused before replying, remembering Eleanor's love. Perhaps it was time to build bridges with her mother. 'I'm walking in Dean Cemetery,' Kate replied, then started to cry. 'Mum -'

'Stay there, dear,' Elizabeth told her. 'I'm coming to get you.'

Kate strode into the museum on Monday morning with a new sense of purpose. She had spent Sunday with her mother, and for the first time the two women had really talked and listened to one another. Kate had divulged the details she had discovered about her past life, but not about her encounters with Edwin. Elizabeth had been fascinated, but agreed that Kate should now put it to rest and concentrate on her own life. They had discussed Kate's new work schedule, her desire to learn more about archaeology and ancient Egypt and how David was helping her. Elizabeth had provided advice, encouragement and succour, regaling her daughter with tales of the difficulties she had encountered as a young woman working in a male-dominated industry, and how she had overcome them. Kate started to look upon her sometimes aloof mother as an inspiration, and found their new openness therapeutic.

Before she started work, Kate gathered up James Grahame's portfolio and the Qurneh file, and returned them to the archives. Lewis was already working at the desk, and he beamed up at Kate as she set the boxes before him.

'Good morning, Lewis,' she smiled. 'These can be returned to the archives.'

'Of course,' he replied, blushing. 'You didn't have to bring them all the way here - I could have picked them up. Did you find what you were looking for?'

Kate nodded. 'Yes, thanks. I understand there will be an archive clear-out over the summer?'

'Yeah, a lot of the really old stuff will be going, to make room for more recent information.'

Kate took a deep breath. 'Lewis, if the portfolio of James Grahame is to be disposed of, could you let me know?' Kate flushed under his curious gaze. 'James Grahame was my great-great-great grandfather, and he was director of the museum.' She assured herself that her interest was in acquiring information on her ancestry, which could then be passed to future generations.

Lewis whistled under his breath and made a note on a piece of paper. 'I'll keep an eye out for you,' he told her, impressed by her family connection to the museum. Kate gave him a wide smile in gratitude, and went off to begin the first day of her new work schedule.

David had sent Kate a very business-like email to inform her that he would not be available until later that morning, and asked her to proceed with the arrangements for that evening's lecture on the engineering of the pyramids. He had attached the accompanying handout to be proof-read and printed, along with the list of attendees and the items he would require from storage. Kate methodically set to work, first checking the seminar room was booked for them that evening, then arranging for the artefacts to be removed from storage. Once she had completed the paperwork, she went down to collect the storage items. By the time she returned, David was in the office. Without preamble, Kate reported that she had completed the arrangements for the presentation as he had requested.

'You're all business today,' he commented dryly. Kate thought he looked worn and tired, but did not comment.

'What would you like me to do next?' she inquired.

'We have to look at that cracked pot,' he told her, mirroring her professional attitude even though he had hardly slept.

Ethan had woken from his coma in some distress. Even after the doctor had sedated him, Ethan had been disoriented and agitated. He had babbled constantly about having to return to a place he was unable to name. His parents had been upset and at a loss as to how to help him, so David had remained at his friend's bedside on Saturday evening until Ethan had eventually fallen asleep. David had then taken Ethan's parents for a late supper before driving them home. After a few hours of restless sleep, David had returned to the hospital on Sunday morning to find a much calmer Ethan. He had spent most of the day with his friend, helping him piece together the events which had caused his accident, and attempting to raise his spirits. This morning, however, David's own spirits were low; as soon as he had closed his eyes on Sunday night he had dreamed of Kate. Now, as he looked at her, he could feel himself blushing.

'This afternoon, I have to visit two people who want to donate items to the museum. I'll need you to come and take notes and photographs of the pieces, so take your lunch break between twelve and one. Have a look at our archives - I need to know what we currently hold in samurai swords and scarab beads. Okay?'

Kate nodded, and followed him to the workroom where Edwin's pot awaited them. As Kate entered the white room, she recognised it immediately. She had visited this room in her past life, on the day she

198

had come to see the artefacts for the exhibition before they went on display. Kate felt her chest grow tight as her eyes fell on the table where the alabaster pot once numbered 52a lay nestled in a box, surrounded by soft cotton. David pulled on protective gloves, gesturing for Kate to follow suit. They sat down at the table, and David carefully lifted the little pot, cradling it in his palm. There was a desk lamp next to him, fixed with a large magnifying glass. He held the pot under the glass, examining it in the light, then nodded thoughtfully. Carefully, he handed the pot to Kate and directed her to examine it for herself.

Kate peered through the magnifying glass at the pot in her hands, remembering the last time she had held it. She could see a small crack in its smooth surface. David watched a tendril of dark hair fall over her face, and resisted the urge to tuck it behind her ear. Kate lovingly placed the pot back in its box and turned to David with hope in her dark eyes. 'Can you fix it?'

David nodded confidently. 'A little epoxy should do it.' He stood and walked over to another table in the far corner of the room, where a man and a woman in white coats were repairing another artefact. David returned with a small amount of epoxy and a tool which looked like a large toothpick. He set them before Kate. 'Use the pin tool to paint the epoxy down the line of the crack.'

'You want me to do it?' Kate squeaked.

'I'm sure you have a delicate enough touch,' he teased, but gave her an encouraging smile.

Kate took a deep breath and picked up the pin tool, the pot held gently in her other hand. Then she turned back to David and shook her head. 'I can't,' she insisted. 'It's too precious. You do it.' She offered him the tool, but he refused to take it from her.

'Don't you think Edwin Ford would want his champion to fix the pot he brought us?'

It was a strange thing to say, but it was enough to make Kate return her attention to the artefact. Biting her lip in concentration, Kate carefully applied the epoxy to the hairline crack. Her hands shook at first, but with David's gentle reassurance, Kate relaxed and in the end made an excellent job of repairing the little pot. Satisfied with her work, David set it back in its nest of cotton to set. He instructed Kate to write a short report on the repair and add it to the notes on file for the artefact. She smiled at him for the first time that morning and returned to their office to find the information David needed on swords and scarab beads.

Kate enjoyed a quick lunch with Jess before joining David for a walk to the south side of Edinburgh, where Kate had shared a flat with Gemma in their student days. As they walked briskly across the Meadows, she briefed David on her findings: the museum had a large collection of scarab beads in storage, but few were on display. As David was aware, having been involved in its acquisition, the museum currently displayed a full set of samurai armour.

The owner of the scarab beads was an elderly man called Peter Jenkins, who lived in a small flat on Argyle Place. He ushered Kate and David into his cosy sitting room and urged them to sit on an old leather sofa. Once introductions had been made and they had discussed the unusually warm weather, Mister Jenkins handed David a canvas pouch. Kate watched in silence as David took the beads from the pouch. Some of them had been strung together, while others were loose. He fingered them carefully, looking for any markings which would identify them as having been purchased at a modern-day market stall by an unsuspecting tourist. After a while, David concluded that the little scarabs of carnelian and blue faience were indeed of ancient Egyptian origin.

'Do you know anything of their provenance, Mister Jenkins?' David asked.

'They were brought back from Egypt by my uncle in around 1908,' the old man replied. His eyes twinkled like shiny buttons, and he smiled wistfully. 'He was an archaeologist. He found them on a dig near Luxor, I believe. I'm afraid that's all I know.'

David nodded and turned to Kate, who was writing down the facts. 'I would concur,' he murmured. He looked over the beads once again, before returning them to their pouch. 'They're very beautiful,' he told the old man kindly, and Kate could hear a 'but' coming.

'I was hoping they might be worth something...' Mister Jenkins sighed. Kate looked up, but masked her surprise; she had thought the beads were to be donated, and had not realised that people expected payment for their gifts to the museum. David, however, was unfazed by the man's revelation.

'I'm afraid the museum can't make an offer for them, as we have quite a lot of these already and more are being dug up all the time.' David saw the disappointment in the old man's face. 'If it would help, I could write you a letter of authenticity, which you could take to an auction house. You may be able to sell them privately. But it would help if you could find anything of your uncle's to back up their provenance, such as letters or some other paperwork.'

Peter Jenkins smiled at David's kindness. 'I'd be very grateful for a letter of authenticity, Professor Young. And I'll have a look for my uncle's paperwork.'

'He may have kept a small diary,' Kate offered. 'Archaeologists used to write everything in notebooks.'

David grinned as he stood and prepared to leave. 'These days we have iPads. But I sometimes think notebooks would be easier.' He extended his hand. 'I'm sorry we couldn't be more helpful, Mister Jenkins. I'll send you that letter by the end of the week.'

Their second visit was to a large house not far away in the affluent area known as the Grange. This time the door was answered by a tall woman in her fifties who seemed to look down her nose at them even before she ushered them into her elegant living room. David's eyes fell instantly on the long box lying on a glass coffee table. He quickly glanced up at their hostess. 'May I, Mrs Adams?'

She nodded curtly as she sat on the faded chintz sofa opposite. David opened the box and revealed a curved samurai sword inside an ornate sheath. Kate saw blatant admiration on his face and a covetous gleam in his eye as he lifted the sword from its quilt of thick black velvet and unsheathed it.

'Katana sword from the Edo period,' he murmured reverently, while Kate scribbled quickly in longhand. 'Forged in the early nineteenth century.' Kate saw him execute a short lunge and another manoeuvre which made her wonder if fencing might be another of his interests. 'Excellent balance.' He sat down to examine the weapon, taking a magnifying glass from his jacket pocket and passing it up and down the blade and hilt. 'No damage to the steel, a little acceptable wear to the hilt.' He looked up at Mrs Adams. 'This is in very good condition, Mrs Adams. What can you tell me about its history?'

'It was my grandfather's,' she said. Her voice was sharp and cold. 'A trophy from the war.'

David nodded thoughtfully as he ran his fingertip carefully along the edge of the blade. Finally, he looked up and smiled at the dour-faced woman. 'I'll submit my report to the museum today, Mrs Adams. You should hear from us by the end of the week.'

'How much can I expect to be paid for it?'

Kate thought the woman was extremely rude, and a little callous; she couldn't imagine selling any of her family heirlooms, but this woman was obviously keen to make some money on what may have been one of her father's prized possessions. Once again, David remained calm and unruffled. He answered her question while using his phone to take photos of the sword.

'I'm afraid I couldn't say. We were sent to examine the sword and make our recommendations. As I said, you should hear from our acquisitions team very soon.' He stood and extended his hand. The woman gave his fingers a limp squeeze, as if she really didn't want to touch them, and ushered them out of her house.

Kate was aggravated by the woman's discourtesy. 'Do you have to deal with many people who are rude to you?' she asked, as they walked back to the museum.

David shrugged, unconcerned. 'They don't bother me. I accept that I'm the messenger, and if they don't like what I have to say, they'll want to shoot me. The sword is a nice piece, though. I'll recommend it to the acquisitions team, and they'll take it from there. My job is done. Your job is to write up the notes and email them to acquisitions as soon as you can.' David stopped as they passed a small shop. 'Since you've been so efficient today, why don't I buy you an ice cream?'

Kate dragged herself wearily to her locker that night, wishing she could just curl up on one of the long sofas in the museum and go to sleep. She had worked steadily all day, completing every task David had allocated and helping with his evening presentation. Thankfully the visitors had not lingered, so Kate had been able to clear up the room while David answered some emails. Now, she was looking forward to a hot bath and a soft bed.

'Here you are!' David exclaimed, as she shrugged into her jacket. 'I thought you'd gone. I'll drive you home.'

Kate hesitated. 'Aren't you going to the hospital?'

'It's too late. I'll go tomorrow.' He looked at her speculatively. 'Are you hungry?'

Kate thought about it and shrugged. 'Not ravenously so. Why?'

'Can I buy you dinner?' he blurted. They looked at each other awkwardly, before David broke the uneasy silence. 'You've done such a good job today…'

Kate gave a dry chuckle. 'David, if you feel you have to buy me dinner every time I work hard, you'll soon be out of pocket.' She gave him a tired smile. 'Thanks for the offer, but I think I should just go home. Hot bath, early night, you know the drill.' She saw his disappointment and felt sorry for him; perhaps he was lonely, too. 'But I would definitely appreciate a lift home.'

When she arrived at the office on Tuesday morning, Kate was surprised and a little peeved to see a young man sitting at her desk and using her computer. She coughed pointedly, and the man immediately looked up through a long, floppy fringe. He hastily vacated her chair and offered his hand.

'Hi - I'm Steven Brodie,' he announced, as Kate shook his hand. 'I'm Professor Young's new intern.'

She eyed the tall young man with black hair, sparkling blue eyes and an open, honest face. He looked to be in his mid-twenties, and was rakishly handsome. *Are there any ugly archaeologists out there?* Kate wondered wryly. She kept her expression unreadable, thinking that he had a cheek using her desk.

'I'm Kate,' she told him. 'Where's Professor Young?'

'I'm here,' murmured a familiar, velvety voice from behind her. She saw Steven's face light up with obvious admiration. 'Sorry I'm a bit late, Steven.' He started to unpack his laptop bag.

'You must be the Professor's Girl Friday,' Steven said to Kate, then immediately regretted the careless remark. Kate's eyes flashed, and her feeling of pique increased as she heard David snort in amusement behind her.

'Actually, I work for the Professor on Mondays, too,' she replied tartly, with a sardonic smile. She turned to David haughtily, just as Jess entered the room. 'I trust you will provide your intern with a desk of his own?'

'I'm working on it...' he replied, green eyes glinting. David eyed Jess with regret, knowing she had come to take Kate away. Had Jess not appeared he and Kate might have indulged in another verbal sparring match.

Jess could not believe she had to intervene again. 'Kate, let's get a coffee then we can start preparing for the first workshop. You won't need your desk much today.'

As she passed him, Kate threw David an insolent glance. David's eyes sparkled with amusement, and his lips twitched as he tried to hide his smile.

'Is working with him not going well?' Jess asked with concern as they made their way to the seminar rooms.

Kate gave her friend a wide smile. 'On the contrary, it's going very well, I think!'

Jess chuckled. 'I have some good news for you, by the way. The head of Events wants your piece on Edwin Ford to be added to the itinerary for the workshops on ancient Egypt.'

Kate turned to Jess, her face aglow with pride. At last, people would know his name and what he did for the museum. 'That's fantastic!'

'We need you to alter the language slightly, so that anyone on the team can deliver it. At the moment, it's very...personal to you. As it should be...'

Kate could see Jess was worried about her reaction to these instructions. 'That's okay, Jess,' she assured her. 'I can adapt it. It's not a problem. I'm glad the material will be used again.'

Jess smiled a little sadly, feeling sympathy for her friend. 'I thought you would be.'

Between workshops, Jess proceeded with Kate's training. Kate was expected to learn the content of all the workshops, so that she would be able to lead groups and deliver presentations. By Wednesday of that week, Kate's head was full of new information, and threatening to overload. Luckily, she was able to spend the latter part of the afternoon at her desk, catching up with correspondence and learning about the workshop on Victorians.

As she was reading, an email arrived from her solicitor, informing her that the divorce papers needed to be signed. Kate arranged an appointment for Friday lunchtime, hoping that it would not disrupt whatever plans David had for her. Her concentration was hampered further when she received an email from Mark. She hesitated before opening it, fearing further vindictiveness, but Mark merely asked if he could meet her after work on Friday. He wanted to deliver the cheque for her share of the money earned from the paintings, but did not want to visit her at home. Kate smiled ruefully at the memory of him being assailed by her over-protective phantom soulmate. Strengthened by the perception that her life was finally changing for the better, she agreed to meet Mark at a bar near the museum. She then attempted to return to her studies for the last half hour of her shift.

Within the space of five minutes, Kate became aware of a pair of chino-clad legs standing before her desk. Steven was holding two large ring binders and wearing a pensive expression on his youthful face. She decided not to be confrontational, because they would both be working for David and she did not wish to cause her friend any complications.

'What can I do for you?' Kate inquired amicably. Steven grinned in relief and pulled up a chair.

'Actually,' he began. 'I thought *I* might be able to help *you*. Professor Young tells me that you're keen to learn about archaeology - Egyptology, in particular.' Kate nodded. Steven tapped the ring binders on his lap. 'I thought you might like to have a look at my notes from university. I've brought the course notes for the first year, and all I have on ancient Egypt. You'll probably want to scan-read a lot of it, as the first year of the course covers evolution and early civilizations. When you're finished, I can give you my notes from year two, which covers Scottish prehistory and archaeological techniques. But there's no rush to read them - you can keep them for as long as you like.'

'Assuming you can decipher his scrawl,' David drawled, as he came into the room.

Kate scrutinised Steven's expression, not sure whether he was being helpful or patronising.

Steven lowered his voice so David could not overhear. 'We didn't get off to a very good start, Kate,' he said, apologetically. 'I want to make a good impression on you - so can we start again?'

He looked at her hopefully, like a little boy. Kate put him out of his misery. 'Yes, of course, Steven. Thanks for being so thoughtful. I'll take your notes home tonight and start reading.' She glanced at David. 'And I'm sure your writing is just fine.'

Benedict Grahame brought his wife and children to the museum on Thursday, and invited his sister to join them for lunch in the brasserie. He studied Kate with his doctor's eye as she descended the staircase to meet him. She had grown thinner, her face was pale and her eyes still wore a slightly haunted look. When he reached down to embrace her he heard her sigh wearily against his chest, but when she stepped back Kate gave him a bright smile.

Daniela and the children were still in the Imagine gallery, so Ben and Kate secured a table and ordered coffee while they waited. They chatted about Ben's work at the Sick Children's Hospital, and Kate hesitantly revealed that she would be signing her divorce papers the following day. She wisely chose not to tell Ben about her planned meeting with Mark, as she knew this would incur her brother's disapproval.

Kate stopped talking as David approached their table, holding a pack of sandwiches. She smiled at him and then turned to her brother, who was gazing speculatively at the other man.

'Ben, this is one of my supervisors,' she told him. 'Professor David Young, our Egyptologist.' She turned to David. 'Professor Young, this is my brother, Doctor Ben Grahame.' She smiled inwardly; men loved to parade their important titles.

Ben invited David to sit down, and David took the chair next to Kate. 'So my sister is your assistant?' Ben asked, his eyes clearly sizing

205

up the archaeologist and immediately recognising the look David bestowed on Kate.

'Yes,' David replied, untroubled by Ben's obvious scrutiny. 'And she's learning about archaeology at the same time.'

'Have you been to Egypt recently?'

'I was on an expedition last winter, excavating cemeteries. Some would say it's a gruesome task, but it's a way to find out about the lives of ancient Egyptians. We uncovered some graves belonging to men who had helped build the pyramids, and used the bones to discern long-term injuries consistent with spending hours hauling slabs of stone. It was fascinating! We can also get an idea of what afflictions and illnesses the people suffered, as well as mortality rates.'

Kate smiled affectionately at David as his eyes sparkled with enthusiasm. His hand slid across the table to Kate's mug of coffee. As his fingers curled around the handle, she smacked his hand playfully but allowed him a sip of her drink.

'I understand that polio is still rife in parts of Egypt,' Ben began. 'Did you find any evidence of polio in the bones you unearthed?'

Kate stopped listening as she spied Daniela and her two children approaching the brasserie. She waved, and within moments was surrounded by her noisy niece and nephew. Her four-year-old niece, Rebecca, showered her with kisses as she clambered onto Kate's lap. Seven-year-old Luca was more sedate, only allowing his aunt to put her arm around his shoulders and squeeze him. Kate made more introductions and Daniela took her seat, giving Kate a meaningful glance. She was obviously impressed with Kate's new friend, and immediately involved David in small talk which verged on the intrusive.

Luca held a plastic dinosaur which he had purchased in the gift shop with his pocket money. He showed it to Kate, roaring to illustrate the fierceness of the Tyrannosaurus Rex. Kate let out a little roar of her own.

'You might want to try a more menacing tone,' David suggested playfully, rising from his seat. 'You know, like the one you use with me.' He grinned disarmingly.

Kate attempted another roar, this time looking at David and showing her teeth. 'Better?' she asked, mischievously.

'Hmm...' he responded. He looked around the table. 'I'll leave you to your lunch. I've got a conference call to take.' David smiled at the children. 'Enjoy your visit - and make sure you visit ancient Egypt!' He touched Kate's shoulder lightly, said goodbye to the group and strolled back to work.

Daniela's eyes were alight. 'Who is *that*?' she breathed to Kate in admiration. Ben rolled his eyes, aware that his wife had been too busy ogling the archaeologist to listen to Kate's introduction. He was unperturbed; their relationship was solid and intensely passionate. 'Tell us *everything*!'

Kate rolled her eyes, looking just like her brother. 'He's my boss. That's it. Now are we eating, or what?'

On Friday morning, David, Kate and Steven discussed the Open Studies course on Egyptology. This would take place every Friday morning, starting the following week and continuing for ten weeks. David had already written the first three lectures but now had to plan the practical work which would take place during each seminar. Steven was assigned the task of sourcing the artefacts and excavated material needed to demonstrate the practical work of archaeologists. He would also provide suitable illustrations to go with each lecture.

Kate was responsible for arranging the venue and liaising with those who had been allocated a place on the course. David asked her to inspect his lecture notes and the accompanying handouts and provide feedback. The course had been made available to members of the public, as well as those with pertinent qualifications.

Thankfully, they broke for lunch in time for Kate to rush to the solicitor's office and sign the divorce papers. It felt oddly anti-climactic, and when Kate returned to work she felt too restless to settle down and read the large file of lecture notes. After two hours, her befuddled brain refused to digest any more information on archaeological processes, so she decided to take a break and make a hot drink. She was surprised to see David and Steven standing in the staffroom, chatting and drinking coffee. With a quick smile, she greeted them, filled her mug then returned to her desk. She reluctantly admitted to herself that she felt a little jealous, but tried to feel pleased that David was obviously happy with his intern. Steven would be more useful to David than she could be; perhaps David would send her back to the Events team because he did not need her after all.

Just before the end of Kate's shift, David decided to check on Kate's progress. He immediately noticed Kate's grim expression, her hair tousled as if she had spent the afternoon running her fingers through it. When she glanced at him, her wide brown eyes showed signs of fatigue. David wheeled his chair over to her desk and sat next to her, leaning an elbow on her desk.

'How are you getting on?' His voice was tentative, as if he feared her response.

Kate tried to appear alert as she sat up in her chair and willed her voice to sound cheerful. 'I have a suggestion,'

'Go on,'

'The people on the course are not professional archaeologists and may know very little about Egyptology. I think it's important that the handouts reflect this. They should be easy to understand - not patronising, but written in layman's terms.' She took a deep breath and continued carefully. 'Some of the notes are a bit...highbrow.'

It struck her then that she had been part of a similar discussion with Edwin in her past life, when she had been asked to help write the exhibition catalogue. Kate wondered if David would share Edwin's reaction to her suggestions, and was surprised when he nodded in agreement.

'Can you rewrite the parts which are too complicated, or boring?'

'I'll need you or Steven to check I've kept the facts right, but I'll try.'

'Good. I'll bear your observation in mind when I'm writing the other lectures.' He watched her stare blankly at the computer screen. 'You look tired,' he observed.

'Just one of those days,' Kate murmured, not looking at him. 'At least it's Friday...' David continued to sit beside her, his fingers absently rubbing at a smudge on his trousers. Kate turned to face him. 'I need to leave sharp, tonight.'

'No problem - I didn't expect you to do all this work today. Do you need a lift somewhere?'

'No, thank you. I'm meeting someone at the bar across the street.'

'And why does that make you look so apprehensive?'

Kate inhaled deeply. 'I'm meeting Mark, my now ex-husband.' She looked down at her lap, feeling self-conscious about revealing the sordid details of her life to a man she barely knew. 'I signed my divorce papers at lunchtime.'

'Why didn't you tell me?' He sounded exasperated. 'How do you expect to concentrate on your work after doing that?'

'I've done my best!' she cried indignantly. 'And it's nobody's business but mine!'

'My issue is not with your work,' he explained, lowering his voice to a more conciliatory tone. 'My issue is with you dealing with such a difficult thing on your own.'

Kate ground her teeth, her jaw twitching. She was growing tired of people treating her like a delicate child; it was time she proved that she was strong enough to fight her own battles. She turned slowly to David, forcing herself to appear calm. 'David,' she said, quietly. 'I already have an over-protective big brother. One is more than enough.'

David did not flinch from her fiery gaze. 'I have no intention of stepping in for your brother.'

Oh, God! Kate cried to herself. *I've had this conversation, too!*

Checking her watch, Kate noticed with relief that it was nearly five o'clock. 'I have to go,' she told him, and began to shut down her computer.

David stood up and returned his chair to his desk. She could be so prickly and defensive sometimes that he didn't know what to say to her. He wanted to offer to accompany her, to make sure she would be safe, but he knew such a suggestion would be met with derision. So he merely said goodnight and left the room.

Kate spent ten minutes in the ladies' toilets ensuring she looked smart, refusing to give Mark the impression that she had fallen apart in his absence. With her head held high, she strode from the sanctuary of the museum and crossed the road to the bar next to Greyfriars Church.

Mark was waiting for her, looking immaculate in a navy suit and polished shoes. When he saw her cross Candlemaker Row he offered up a small smile, tinged with shame and remorse. Kate was stunned when he leaned down and lightly kissed her cheek. Taking her by the elbow, he led her into the bar and found them a relatively quiet table in a corner. The bar was already filling up with the post-work crowd, who jostled for space among the tourists. Mark left to buy drinks and returned with a whisky for himself and a white wine spritzer for Kate. She watched him hang his jacket on the back of the chair and adjust the cuffs of his white shirt, which were fastened with the understated cufflinks she had bought him for his last birthday. Kate was unexpectedly filled with sorrow and regret. She may not have loved him passionately, but she realised she had cared for him and was partly to blame for their divorce. She had kept part of herself hidden from him, had not completely committed herself to him or their marriage.

'Quite a lot of your workmates are here,' Mark informed her with a wry smile. 'Are they keeping an eye on you?'

'I don't need anyone to keep an eye on me,' she replied, and Mark detected a new note of assertiveness in her voice. But despite the tough exterior she was projecting, Mark could see the sadness in her expressive eyes. It was the gaze of a woman who had lost her innocence, and Mark knew he was to blame for that.

'How are you?' he asked.

Kate was not going to turn the meeting into a revenge attack. 'I'm fine,' she said, with a vague shrug. 'How are you?' When Mark also shrugged, Kate asked, 'Why did you want to see me, Mark? We could have done this through our lawyers.'

Mark had laid his hand on the table, inches from Kate's. Stretching out his fingers, he touched the edges of hers, but she moved her hand out of reach. 'I wanted to say goodbye.'

'Why?' she asked, surprised. 'Where are you going?'

'I'm going to work in our New York office. I'm flying out tomorrow.'

'Are you happy about that?' Kate already knew the answer.

'Yes. But I wish the circumstances surrounding my departure could have been different. Kate, I'm so sorry...' He looked into her eyes and Kate could see that, at that moment, he meant it. 'And I'm sorry about the way I behaved the last time I was at the house. It was unforgiveable. I'd been drinking, and I don't think I knew what was going on...'

Kate shook her head dismissively, a lump rising in her throat. 'Mark, please let's just put it behind us. It's in the past now. We both have to move on.'

'I've been an idiot.'

Kate gave him a weak, rueful smile. 'Yes, you have. But our marriage may not have worked out in the long run. I want to have children, Mark. And you don't. I won't compromise on that.'

Mark wished he had never announced his desire to remain unburdened by offspring, for he was no longer sure it was the truth. But he could tell from her face, and the conviction in her lovely eyes, that it was too late for them. He took a sip of his Glenmorangie and fished an envelope from his jacket pocket. He slid it discreetly over to Kate and smiled. 'I told you those paintings were an investment!'

Kate dropped the envelope into her handbag without opening it, embarrassed to be accepting money from him. 'Is Gemma going to New York with you?' she asked abruptly.

Mark sighed. 'Gemma was not pleased at being named as a co-respondent. And she had no patience for my "mood swings" during the divorce proceedings. She dumped me - and she's already found a replacement.'

'I'm sorry,' Kate murmured, but even she wasn't convinced by the sentiment. She wanted to leave, as she felt unbalanced by this whole meeting. Mark had not acted in the way she had expected; he had been more like the man she had dated, before ambition and work had hardened him.

Kate rose from her chair, her expression composed. 'I need to go, Mark,' she explained but did not elaborate. Reluctantly, he stood up and followed her out into the street. In another corner of the bar, David rose from the table he shared with some of his colleagues and prepared to leave.

Kate and Mark faced each other in front of the statue of Greyfriars Bobby. By mutual consent, they embraced. It was a once-familiar act which now felt unnatural.

'Please take care, Kate,' Mark said earnestly. 'If you ever need anything -'

'I hope you find what you're looking for in New York.' Kate interrupted him. And she realised she meant it.

Kate stepped out of his embrace, pulling herself up straight. Mark cupped her cheek with his hand and leaned down to kiss her forehead. There was no false promise to keep in touch from either of them. With a final, wistful glance, Mark crossed the road and walked along Chambers Street. Kate watched him walk out of her life, cursing the lump in her throat and the heavy feeling in her heart. She had watched two men leave her in the space of a week. *How many more?* A tear threatened to fall from between her lashes and she swallowed hard. *Damn it! I promised myself I wouldn't do this anymore!* She turned away from Mark's receding figure - and her eyes fell on David as he crossed Candlemaker Row and walked towards her.

Remembering Mark's comments about her colleagues keeping an eye on her, Kate guessed he had seen David in the bar. Kate gazed at her part-time supervisor suspiciously, her whole demeanour warning David to be on his guard.

'Were you in the bar?' Kate asked indifferently.

David tried to think of an equally off-hand reply, but her steady gaze was mildly disconcerting. 'Did everything go okay?'

Kate felt herself raise an invisible shield around her to safeguard her emotions and make her resilient. David seemed to have an unsettling quality which made her want to confide in him and ask for his support. But she did not want to continually confess her troubles to David, and risk appearing fragile.

'Yes,' Kate lied.

'Do you need anything?' David could see she was drawing herself up to deliver a strong reprimand, having correctly deduced that he had only gone to the bar to assure himself of her safety. He sensed this was not going to be as enjoyable as their previous skirmishes.

'David,' she began, pushing her hair back out of her face. She moved to the side of the pavement to let a group of noisy Italian tourists take photographs of the statue of Greyfriars Bobby. David moved to stand beside her, shielding her from the jostling tourists. 'You told me not long ago you had no agenda where I was concerned. What's this all about? I'm confused.'

David stood very still while he composed his answer. 'I thought we were friends...'

'Friends don't spy on one another!'

'I wasn't spying. I was having a drink with Steven,' he told her, trying to sound innocent.

'And where is Steven now?'

David gestured back towards the bar. 'Still there, getting to know some of his new colleagues.'

'So there was a whole gang of you watching me?'

'No, of course not!' *It was just me.* 'They probably didn't even see you.'

In a fury, Kate stamped her foot on the pavement. 'David, I don't need looking after, or protected! In future, please respect the boundaries of our so-called friendship. In fact, perhaps it would be better if we didn't spend too much time together. You have Steven now, so you don't need an additional assistant. Am I not surplus to your requirements?'

Before he could reply, Kate's phone began to ring, and she removed it from her handbag, grateful for an excuse to leave him.

'Kate,' he began, reluctantly. 'I have to go and see Ethan -'

'Then go!' she snapped. 'I don't need baby-sitting!' At that, Kate turned and walked towards the bus stop on George IV Bridge. When she answered her phone, she was glad to hear Jess's cheerful voice inviting her to dinner on Saturday evening. When Jess heard the anger in Kate's voice, she asked what was wrong.

'You won't believe what David bloody Young has just done!'

CHAPTER 12

David walked into Ethan's hospital room to find his friend grinning at the young nurse who was leaning over him, her ample bosom very close to her patient's face. With a twinkle in his brown eyes, Ethan murmured something to her. Giggling, she straightened and sashayed from the room.

'Ethan, for God's sake!' David spat in disgust, slumping wearily on a hard plastic chair. 'You're in hospital - don't you ever stop?'

'Have to make sure everything's still in working order,' Ethan joked, scrutinising his friend's disgruntled face. 'What's up with you, Grumpy? Students late with their homework again?'

'Belt up!' David muttered. He heaved a sigh. 'How are you? You seem to be making a miraculous recovery.'

'I'm getting out tomorrow,' Ethan looked sidelong at David. 'But Mum and Dad have to go home on Sunday.'

'So where are you staying?' David asked distractedly. Part of him was still standing on the pavement beside the statue of Greyfriars Bobby. He wondered how he could have handled the situation differently, and what he could do to make amends. He doubted ice-cream would work, this time.

'Actually,' Ethan raised his voice slightly to harness David's full attention. 'I was hoping you could put me up, just for a couple of weeks. The doctors want me back for check-ups. Once they're happy that I've still got all my marbles, I can go home and recuperate for a while.'

'*Have* you still got all your marbles?' David leaned back in his chair, a sardonic smirk on his face.

Ethan looked grim. 'I hope so,' he murmured. 'Though I still feel as though I'm missing something...'

213

'Do you have memories from when you were in the coma?' David recalled how distraught Ethan had been upon waking.

'It's more like a memory of a dream. I was somewhere. I was happy. I didn't want to leave.'

'Were you alone?'

'I don't remember...' Ethan shook his head and put a smile on his pale face. 'But enough about me. What's eating you today?' He waited patiently as David got up and walked to the window, which overlooked the car park.

David leaned against the window frame, arms folded. 'My assistant,' he muttered.

'Don't tell me you're unhappy with yet another intern?'

'No, I have a good intern who shows real potential. My assistant, however, has the ability to drive me insane.'

'Wait - you have an intern *and* an assistant? How did you swing that?' David did not reply. Ethan sighed impatiently. 'As usual, getting personal information from you is like pulling teeth. What's the problem with your assistant?'

David leaned his head against the cool glass. 'She's very good at her job. But sometimes she can be so infuriating!' He pushed himself off the window frame and commenced pacing the length of the private room. 'She's prickly, defensive, impertinent and determinedly independent. And yet, at other times, she's kind, intuitive, playful...'

'Oh dear,' Ethan murmured. David threw him a questioning glance. 'You've got a thing for your assistant, haven't you? Don't you ever learn? Haven't you just finished a relationship?'

'I don't have a "thing"!' David spat derisively. 'We seem to butt heads regularly at the museum, but when I take her riding, she's completely different. She baffles me and intrigues me at the same time.'

'So she's a woman with schizophrenic tendencies!' Ethan scoffed. 'What a surprise! And you've taken her riding?'

'We're just friends. Or so I thought, until today. I think I crossed a line unintentionally, and she went ballistic. I don't know how to fix it.'

'Don't,' Ethan advised. 'You don't need an assistant if you've got an intern. Break personal contact with the woman and escape the conflict.'

David passed a hand wearily over his eyes. 'I can be myself with her, Ethan.'

Ethan watched his friend for a moment, having never seen him look distraught before. 'Why don't you take some time off, Dave? Clear your head a bit. And come to Egypt with me this year.'

David looked up in surprise. 'You're going back?'

'As soon as I'm able, I'm off.' Ethan hoped the feeling of loss which plagued him constantly would lessen once he returned to the Nile Valley. He always felt more at peace with himself in Egypt.

David looked down at the floor, mentally flicking through the pages of his diary. 'Perhaps I *could* take a few days off...'

'He's just so exasperating!' Kate fumed, balling her fists as she paced the carpet of Jess's living room. Then her face softened. 'And at other times, he's so sweet...'

Kate had arrived at Jess's flat in desperate need of a rest. She had worked all day in the Imagine Gallery, helping young children with arts and crafts. Some of the youngsters had been rude and badly-behaved. Many of the parents had not intervened, obviously believing that it was the staff's job to control their unruly offspring. For the final hour of her shift, Kate had sought refuge in the office, where she worked on the handouts for the Open Studies course. But her head ached, and she couldn't stop glancing at David's tidy desk and wondering what he was doing. At the end of her shift, she marched at a punishing pace to Jess's top-floor flat on Gillespie Place and sank thankfully into Jess's comfortable sofa with a glass of wine and a mushroom pizza.

Jess and Erin had spent their day shopping for Erin's wedding dress. Erin was engaged to Jason Macmillan, an osteopath she had met at a life coaching seminar. The pair were to be married in Saint Lucia at the start of August, with Jess attending as chief bridesmaid. Kate listened avidly to the wedding plans, which sounded wonderfully romantic while still remaining tasteful and understated.

As women do, they covered many subjects throughout the evening. Their discussions ranged from the latest gaffe of the local government, to the latest trends in fashion and what they found annoying about the men in their lives. Kate relayed the details of her meeting with Mark, and David's audacious presumption that he could follow her to a bar and spy on her.

'Are you still going riding with him?' Jess asked. She was beginning to suspect that the rumours about David were completely unfounded.

'I've been twice,' Kate admitted. 'But I've signed up for extra Saturday shifts at the museum to earn some extra money. I'm thinking of going to Egypt in December, so I need to start saving.'

'You don't think that you argue because there's an attraction between you?' Erin asked carefully. Kate snorted and shook her head unconvincingly. Any attraction would have to be on her side, if the rumours about him were true. Kate wasn't about to confess to a foolish, unrequited crush.

'You know, Kate,' Jess began. 'You haven't taken any holidays this year. Given the difficult few weeks you've had, maybe it would be a good time to take a week off.' She watched Kate consider the idea. 'Do it before the school holidays and there shouldn't be any objections. What about the week after next? It's a quiet one for the Events team, if I remember rightly.'

Kate chewed her lip, contemplating a week by herself. She would be left alone to reflect on the past, and perhaps plan for the future. She wouldn't have to pretend to be strong when she actually felt broken and vulnerable. 'I don't know,' she murmured. She had deliberately kept busy so that she would not have time to dwell on her losses. The thought of having to face them was daunting. 'It's very short notice, isn't it?'

'It'll be fine if I approve it,' Jess told her, detecting a stalling tactic. 'Think of all the nice things you could do for yourself.'

'I was thinking of joining a Tai Bo class which starts on Tuesday,' Kate admitted, her expression thoughtful. Then she bit her lip. 'I'll have to ask David.'

'Send him an email,' Jess suggested. She opened her laptop. 'Write it now before you talk yourself out of the idea. And don't you dare apologise for shouting at him - he needs to be put in his place!'

Feeling like a sulky teenager, Kate accessed her email account and then pondered the wording of the email. 'I don't want to hurt his feelings,' she said softly.

Jess chuckled. 'You're entitled to ask for time off!'

Kate didn't want David to think she had gone over his head or that she and Jess were ganging up on him, so she sent her request to both Jess and David, seeking permission to take a week's holiday at the end of the month. She frowned as she sent it, worried about what conclusions David would draw when he received the message so soon after their disagreement.

'You're being very diplomatic, given his behaviour,' Jess noted.

Kate closed the lid of the laptop. 'I was told to be kind to him,' she said quietly.

'Who told you that?'

Kate looked at Jess and Erin, loath to bring up a subject which was still painful, despite her attempts to put it behind her. 'Edwin.' Kate's voice was barely more than a whisper.

Erin sat up, the inquisitive therapist coming to the fore. 'Jess told me about her experience in the Egyptian gallery,' she began. 'Has something else happened?'

216

Kate was determined to control her emotions, but her voice was uneven as she answered Erin. 'He's gone. For good.' Briefly, she relayed the details of her final meeting with Edwin, unwilling to put the whole thing under a microscope again and pick it apart. Erin, ever intuitive, realised Kate's reluctance to discuss the matter, but wanted to ensure that Kate was able to move on.

'What do you think you've learned, Kate?' she asked gently.

Kate was silent for a while as she tried to vocalise her thoughts. 'I think the whole past life experience was meant to wake me up to something,' she began slowly. 'Perhaps to the fact that I haven't been true to myself.' Erin nodded encouragingly as Jess refilled Kate's wine glass. 'Victorian Kate was strong, she knew her own mind. Her father encouraged her to have opinions, and she had a thirst for knowledge. She flouted convention sometimes but never courted scandal.

'Kate found it difficult to live within the confines of Victorian society, and she felt held back because she was a woman. Had she not met Edwin, she may have pulled free of society's constraints and lived the remarkable life she wanted. And yet, when she married she tried to adopt the role of a good Victorian wife, and she wanted to be a mother. But, even though she married her soulmate, she felt unfulfilled and suffocated by her life.

'Even Edwin wanted to control Kate to a degree, and he wanted her to be content with her lot in life. He could become exasperated by her occasional lack of decorum. Like when she wore trousers and no corset in Egypt.' Kate chuckled at the memory. 'Had they been married for longer, I wonder if Kate would have conformed? Given what I've learned about their marriage problems, would they have stayed together?'

Kate stared wistfully out the tall living room windows, which overlooked Barclay Church. She could see the Meadows beyond, the trees bright with new leaves which fluttered in the breeze. 'All my life I've tried to do the "right" thing in order to win approval. I've allowed myself to be manipulated so that I could make people happy. I've stifled my own desires. I'd like to discover what would please *me*, as Kate would have done had she been able. I may not live in an age where women are coddled, but I have the right to pursue my own dreams and desires.'

'And yet you're planning to go to Egypt in the hope of finding today's Edwin?' Erin asked. 'Supposing you don't find him? What if you do find him and he's not what you expect? Finding her soulmate didn't make Kate Ford's life complete.'

217

Kate sighed. 'To be honest, Erin, I've tried not to think about that too much, as I find it difficult to rationalise. I'll go to Egypt and hopefully visit the places Edwin and Kate visited. I want to see the tablet Kate found in Amarna. As to hunting down the reincarnation of Edwin Ford, I have no earthly idea how I would do that. Perhaps I should just leave it to Fate; if we're meant to be together, something will bring us together. If I don't meet him in Egypt, then once again I've "taken the wrong path". But I want to live my life. For me. Is that selfish?'

'You're looking for approval again,' Erin pointed out with a smile. 'But it sounds to me as though you're heading in the right direction.'

'I don't want any more regression therapy,' Kate decided. 'I don't want to be consumed by the past. I don't want the future to be about finding Edwin. I feel love for him, but I never really knew him. I don't think even his wife knew him that well. I base my feelings on a handful of memories from a past life, and the knowledge that we share a soul connection. It's not a love which *I* nurtured in *my* heart. I feel like I miss him, and sometimes I long for him so intensely it hurts. But it would be more rational to miss Mark, not Edwin. My marriage has collapsed, and I'm living alone for the first time in my life. I admit that I'm lonely, and I'm finding it hard to adjust. But I want to stop pining for Edwin and put myself back together. Surely walking the "right path" is about improving myself and enjoying my life?'

'It's not about living like a nun, though,' Jess pointed out.

Kate shrugged. 'I'm not ready for another relationship, Jess. The prospect of dating and trusting another man is scary right now. I want some time to myself. I'm going to start evening classes. I'm learning about Egyptology. And I'm going to hold a barbecue on the weekend of the Diamond Jubilee, so make sure you're free!'

Kate stopped in the doorway of the empty office as her eyes fell on the small pot plant in the centre of her desk. She caught her breath when she realised it was an African violet, with dark purple flowers and velvety leaves. There was no message to reveal the identity of the person who had left it, but on the desk in front of the pot was a new name badge: Katherine Grahame.

Kate looked around the room, finding no evidence to suggest any of her colleagues had arrived before her and left the gift. She sat down, thoughtfully stroking the leaves of the little plant. Fastening the name badge to her sweater, Kate ran her finger across the gold lettering. She was Katie Grahame again, and that felt good. Like a second chance.

Once she switched on her computer, Kate discovered two emails from David. The first was addressed to her and simply said 'holidays approved'. The second had been sent to a number of people on a mailing list and announced David's intention to take the week off. There was no explanation for the sudden vacation, only instructions for the work which needed to be done in his absence. He was not to be disturbed except in an emergency, and only by email. Steven and Kate were to continue with the tasks already allotted to them, under the supervision of Doctor Callum Rankin. Doctor Rankin would preside over Friday's class, and Steven and Kate were to ensure the venue was prepared accordingly.

The note was concise, almost curt in its delivery. Kate stared at the message, stunned. Steven was surprised at David's impulsiveness, as the professor was a stickler for careful planning and not usually prone to spontaneous acts. The pair commenced the day's work in subdued silence. Kate spent several hours reading and editing the lecture notes for Friday's course. She emailed them to Doctor Rankin, and then started work on the handouts. She checked her alterations with Steven to make sure she had not inadvertently altered any relevant facts, before sending them to Rankin for approval. Rankin was satisfied with her efforts and confirmed she could print off the handout for Friday's group. By the end of the day, Steven and Kate had completed all the preparations for that week's lecture. Both of them went home that night wondering if they should call David and make sure he was okay, but neither of them was brave enough. Kate placed the mysterious African violet on her bedroom windowsill as a reminder of Kate Ford's strength of will, in the hope that she could learn to emulate it.

On Tuesday evening, Kate attended her first Tai Bo class in a church hall near her home. Her classmates were a mixture of ages and levels of fitness, but the male instructor was patient and encouraging. Although Kate found some of the routine difficult to follow, she enjoyed the session and felt energised as she marched home.

Kate spent another three hectic days with the Events team, participating in workshops and processing bookings. Nick helped her familiarise herself with the contents of the many handling boxes, which were filled with a mixture of genuine artefacts and replicated items, as well as specimens from the natural world. There were boxes on a variety of subjects, such as Vikings, early Scots, animals and meteorites. She also spent some time studying Catherine the Great, in preparation for the museum's imminent exhibition.

By Friday, Kate had issued invitations to her barbecue the following weekend. David had not contacted either Kate or Steven, which Kate felt was inconsiderate at best. She still felt angry with him, but a part of her was worried that something was amiss. Even so, she was too proud to call him. The Egyptology class was a success; Doctor Rankin was an excellent speaker and teacher, who had the ability to hold the attention of everyone in the room. The attendees left the workshop satisfied and looking forward to the next. Rankin praised Kate and Steven on their excellent organisational skills, before leaving them to clear up. After tidying the room, the pair went for a pub lunch and moaned about their errant boss. In the afternoon, Steven went to work with Doctor Rankin, and Kate commenced work on the notes for next Friday's class. The thought of working the following day was disheartening, but hopefully she would not be assigned to the Imagine gallery.

David tried to forget about work, but felt guilty about taking time off when a new course was about to start. He brought Ethan home to his flat and unpacked the large holdall of belongings which Ethan's mother had brought from Carlisle. He tried to make sure his friend rested, but Ethan was like a caged animal. He was restless and irritable and could not stand to be confined to David's small and sparsely furnished flat. After two days, Ethan insisted they do *something*, so David took him for a very unsatisfactory walk around the Botanic Gardens and Inverleith Park. After a hospital check-up confirmed Ethan was on the mend and could increase his activity levels, Ethan badgered David to take him indoor rock climbing. David reluctantly agreed to this outing, but conversely refused to take Ethan to the museum to meet his colleagues and have lunch.

David tried hard not to think about one particular colleague. The more he tried to push Kate from his mind, the more intensely he dreamed about her. Several times during the week, he nearly surrendered to his inexplicable desire to call her. But whenever he spotted David's fingers hovering over the keypad of his phone or laptop, Ethan reminded him that he was on holiday. David consoled himself by calling Steven on the Saturday before his return to work, to ask how the week had gone. Steven's report on the week's activities was tediously detailed, and he pointedly told David that Kate had sought him out every day to make sure he was managing without his supervisor. It was clear to David that Steven and Kate had formed a friendship, which would no doubt become a united front when the pair disagreed with him. Steven also informed David that Kate was working that day, as she had the previous Saturday, and that he was meeting her for a drink after work. The young intern hesitantly asked if David would like to join them. David wanted nothing more than to see Kate, but politely declined; Ethan had already demanded a night out in the town centre, hopefully with 'benefits'. Ethan's charm and good looks ensured he got exactly what he wanted.

David woke in the early hours of Sunday morning in a stranger's bed. Silently, he dressed and left the New Town flat, filled with shame and self-disgust. At home, he stood under the shower for a long time and tried to piece together the details of his drunken night out with Ethan. In vain, he tried to scrub himself clean.

Kate spent the first half of her week's holiday behaving like one of Edinburgh's myriad tourists. She wandered round her city admiring the architecture, and took a bus tour to learn more about the capital's dramatic history. The weather stayed dry, allowing her to stroll in Princes Street Gardens, the Botanic Gardens and along the beach at Silverknowes. She booked a cruise on the 'Maid of the Forth' and indulged in an afternoon's sailing under the June sun.

Still bristling at the recurrent recollection of her argument with David, she spent some time trawling the internet for information on the arrogant Professor Young. Through the university website, she discovered he had studied in Edinburgh and graduated top of his class. He had an MA with honours and a PhD in archaeology. Academically, he was brilliant and was the youngest professor in his field in this country. His successful teaching career was interspersed with numerous trips to Egypt, Asia and Europe. He had written many articles which had been published in archaeological periodicals, some of which were now used as teaching aids in universities across the country. Kate read a couple of David's essays, and grudgingly admired his eloquent style of writing.

His university profile mentioned his enthusiasm for horse riding and numerous sports. He had also won several fencing tournaments, and currently helped run the university fencing club. Kate was impressed to discover that David held a brown belt in judo. She could find nothing about his personal life, however. There were a couple of fuzzy photographs of David at university functions, but no mention of a partner. Not surprisingly, he did not subscribe to any social networking sites. Kate ended her search feeling a little frustrated by the lack of information on David's character. She also felt a little like a stalker, so she furtively shut down her computer and occupied her mind with something else.

Kate met her mother for dinner on Monday night and went out for pizza with Jess on Tuesday after Tai Bo. Since she was in the city centre on Wednesday, she met Steven for coffee in the art gallery on the Mound but he deliberately refrained from talking about work. Apart from these meetings, Kate enjoyed her own company and kept her mobile phone switched off for most of each day.

On Thursday morning, she visited Dean Cemetery to lay flowers on the graves of Kate and Edwin. She felt glad to see the sun shining on Kate's headstone, remembering how Edwin's wife had wanted to rest in a sunny place. She still felt something akin to grief, but Kate also felt a sense of purpose emerging from the darkness. She had not forgotten Edwin, but she no longer pined for him. Admittedly, being away from the museum had helped. Kate hoped she would not weaken once she returned to work, where she would be surrounded by reminders of Edwin and her past life.

The visit made her subdued and pensive, so she returned home and commenced an activity she found both relaxing and rewarding: she made lasagne. As the meat sauce simmered gently, Kate began to make a shopping list of the food she would need for Saturday's barbeque. Kate was excited by the prospect of feeding and entertaining her friends, having never hosted such an event on her own before. Her sister-in-law had offered to help with the cooking, but Kate knew that once Daniela took over Kate's kitchen, she would take over the whole party. Kate felt her own culinary skills were more than adequate. As she contemplated how wonderful her party would be - even if it rained - the kitchen phone rang. She answered it cheerfully and was delighted to hear David's voice. The anger she had nursed for nearly two weeks evaporated. Even so, she kept the pleasure from her voice and adopted a neutral tone.

'How are you?' she asked lightly. 'Are you glad to be back at work?'

'It's very quiet,' he replied, and she could tell he was smiling. 'And very tranquil. Everybody's doing what's asked of them.'

Kate heard a familiar snigger at the other end of the line. 'Is Steven with you?'

'Yes, he is.'

'Tell him I enjoyed our chat over coffee yesterday.'

She heard David convey the message, along with a slightly tetchy enquiry about Steven's rendezvous with Kate. When he returned to the phone, his voice had a somewhat peeved edge to it.

'We're heading down to the Collections Centre at Granton,' he explained to her, his voice deceptively casual. 'I wondered if you'd like to join us. I'm going to change some of the displays in the Egyptian gallery, and you previously complained that we didn't show enough

222

jewellery.' He could sense her hesitation, so ploughed on. 'We're going to look at some of the jewellery from the 1890 exhibition.'

Kate bit her lip. *Oh, he's such a devious pig!* David knew she would jump at the chance to visit the Collections Centre; the hangar-like building was a veritable treasure trove. She could almost see David's calculating expression as he waited for her to acquiesce to his request. She determined not to give in to his demands.

'I'm on holiday, David,' she told him airily. 'Take some photographs and I can look at them next week, if you like. But I'm sure you two can manage on your own.'

'We could do with a feminine perspective,' David pressed, annoyed that she was making him plead.

'I'm busy,' she said, firmly. 'And I'm making lasagne.' She heard him sigh, and realised that she had missed him. 'Why don't you come for dinner after you've been to Granton? I can look at the photos then.'

His voice perked up. 'Okay. I'll dump Steve at a bus stop or something.'

'Hoi!' Steven sounded indignant. 'I'm standing right here!'

Kate laughed. 'Steven is invited, too, David. Assuming he likes lasagne.'

'He'll eat anything,' David declared. 'What time do you want us?'

Kate looked at her watch. 'About six?' *That way I can tidy up and make myself look nice.*

'Shall I bring ice cream?'

'Ice cream, chocolate and the current Caped Crusader always welcome,' she teased, suddenly shocked by the realisation that she was trying to irk him with her comment. 'I'll see you later. Be hungry.'

Kate answered the door wearing jeans and a blue printed blouse. Smiling warmly, she ushered Steven through the front door, reaching up to kiss his cheek in welcome. David presented her with her favourite chocolate ice cream, and favoured her with a look which told her he hadn't appreciated being toyed with over the phone. Nevertheless, he tilted his cheek towards her to receive a quick, self-conscious kiss.

Kate eyed the men surreptitiously as they ate, anxiously awaiting their reaction. She saw Steven's eyes close as he slowly chewed his food, his pleasure obvious.

'Kate,' Steven breathed. 'You cook better than my mum!'

Kate smiled appreciatively, her satisfaction increasing when the men eagerly accepted second helpings. Kate felt completely content as she watched David and Steven enjoy her cooking; Mark had always complained that her lasagne was too rich.

Once they had finished eating, David handed Kate his phone so she could look at the photos he had taken of the artefacts in the collections store. While she perused them, he cleared the plates from the table then sat down across from her. Her expression was contemplative, and a little wistful. David could not know that Kate was reliving the first time she had seen some of the pieces he had photographed. He thought he saw a flicker of pain cross her face.

Kate came across a picture of the heavy jewelled collar she had imagined on the neck of the spoiled Louisa Ramsay, along with the hefty ornate earrings which matched them. David had selected some of the little golden charms, and the beautiful scarab brooch of blue faience. He had also found the stone tablet engraved with the story of Osiris and Isis. Kate smiled at the beautiful figure of Isis spreading her elegant wings.

'She's so beautiful...' Kate breathed.

'Yes,' David murmured, admiring Kate's faraway expression.

'There's not a lot of information regarding their provenance,' Steven complained.

Kate did not look up from the images. 'They were found by a team in 1889 in a tomb which may have belonged to a queen or other female member of the royal family, but no concrete evidence was ever found. Many of the hieroglyphs in the tomb had been defaced, suggesting the owner may have fallen out of favour. Like Akhenaten. You should read the catalogue for the 1890 Ancient Egypt Exhibition.'

Steven's jaw dropped. 'How d'you know that?' he asked in amazement, frantically trying to recall if these facts were contained in the university notes he had lent her.

Kate glanced up. 'Oh, I've been doing some research,' she answered evasively.

'Edwin Ford,' David guessed, but Kate did not respond. Instead, she left the table and busied herself with spoons and dessert bowls. 'Those pieces all look great,' she told them with a forced smile. 'I'm sure people will find them interesting.'

Steven stood, and looked apologetic. 'Kate, I'm sorry, but I'm meeting some friends at the West End.' He looked at his watch. 'In like, ten minutes!' Pulling on his jacket, he hurried to the front door. Kate followed, shaking her head good-naturedly.

'By the way, I've finished reading your first year notes,' she told him, feeling pleased with herself.

'Already?'

'Well, I only had to read them and make some notes. I didn't have to write the essays or sit the exams.'

'D'you have any questions?'

'I've emailed them to you, but don't rush to reply if you're busy. Can I borrow your second year notes?'

Steven leaned down to kiss her cheek affectionately. 'Of course you can, you wee swot! See you on Saturday!'

When Kate returned to the kitchen, David was still sitting at the table. He looked up from playing with his phone. 'So Steven has taken charge of your education?' he asked, sounding a bit put out by the concept.

Kate sat down in her chair. 'You were away,' she reminded him. *You left us without any explanation.*

'What's happening on Saturday?' he asked curiously, attempting to deflect her obvious need to scold him about the sudden abandonment of his duties.

'I'm having a Jubilee barbecue,' she announced. Kate had not yet invited David, as she had wanted to issue the invitation personally rather than wirelessly. Whenever she was with him, an alarm bell seemed to ring from far away, warning her not to let him get too close. In spite of this, she felt drawn to him and enjoyed his company. And the urge to tease him was irresistible.

'And is it an interns and assistants-only barbecue?'

Kate flashed him an impertinent grin. 'No, it's an interns and assistants and their grumpy boss-type barbecue.' She grimaced at her terrible English, and giggled as she saw his eyes narrow. 'I've also invited my family and some friends.' She gave in to the tantalising impulse to wind him up. 'Would you like to come?'

Kate watched David pretend to think about her offer as she set a bowl of ice cream in front of him. He made a show of checking the calendar on his phone. 'You can bring someone, if you like.' As she sat down, it suddenly occurred to her that she would be happier if he came alone. The thought unnerved her a little.

David raised his head and looked at her intently. *'Bring someone?'*

Kate savoured her first spoonful of ice cream. 'Yes. I've told everyone they can bring someone. Nick's bringing his girlfriend, and Erin's bringing her fiancé. Not sure about Jess, or Steven...'

'And you?' David was suddenly alert.

'What about me?'

'Who are you bringing?'

Kate gave him a sly look and tried not to laugh at her own impudence. 'Me? I'm not *bringing* anyone. I live here.' David exhaled in exasperation, and Kate smirked into her bowl. She watched him play with his dessert. 'You could bring Ethan,' she suggested.

'No,' David said, sounding adamant. *I'm not letting him anywhere near you.*

'Bring someone else, then.' Kate wondered why David was so opposed to her meeting Ethan, but she was also curious to discover if he had met someone worth bringing to a party.

David looked up at her and experienced a moment of panic, but her expression assured him she was ignorant of his moment of alcohol-induced weakness the week before. 'Stop fishing.'

She grinned, abashed. 'Don't you have to be getting home to Ethan?'

'Ethan has a date with a nurse.' *So we probably won't see him until Sunday.*

Kate resisted the temptation to smooth his furrowed brow. 'Why don't you stay for a while, then? It's a beautiful evening. We could sit in the garden.'

'I'll help you with the dishes, first.'

'Naturally. I expect nothing less.'

Kate's garden, in fact her whole house, was like an oasis of tranquillity to David. Settling into a garden chair, he stretched out his legs and basked in the evening sun. He breathed in the smell of freshly-cut grass, mingled with the heady scent of roses and lilies. After setting a cup of coffee on the little table beside him, Kate sat quietly in the chair next to David. They rested in companionable silence, listening to the birds singing their evening song.

Kate sat behind her dark sunglasses, feeling the last of the sun's warmth on her face. She fancied she could feel new freckles bursting out onto her nose and idly wondered if she should have used sunscreen. It occurred to her that a sunscreen-white nose was not an attractive look, and then she wondered why she would want to look attractive for a man she tentatively considered a friend, and sometimes a major pain in the backside. *Why would he care how I look, if he prefers men to women?*

Glancing sideways, she saw David had his eyes closed and was resting his head on the back of the chair. He had allowed his hair to grow a little; the ends curled over the collar of his shirt. Dark blond strands fell becomingly over one eye, and Kate watched as he raised a hand to run his fingers through his hair, pushing it off his face.

At last he sat up to drink his coffee, his whole body feeling relaxed. He didn't want to return to his gloomy bachelor flat in Stockbridge, which was currently cluttered with Ethan's belongings. It was entirely possible that Ethan would bring his date back to spend the night at the

226

flat, and David dreaded the thought of walking in on them. It had happened several times in the past.

Kate watched his expression change from calm to troubled, but left him to his thoughts. As she sipped her own coffee, she looked around her beautiful garden. She had been teaching herself how to look after the plants; their healthy growth gave her a glow of satisfaction and she never tired of admiring the roses.

'I have to go home,' David announced reluctantly. He did not move from his seat.

'Yes,' Kate replied, dryly. 'You look as if you're keen to go.'

'I have to do the Open Studies class tomorrow...' he moaned. 'I'll have to deal with people...'

Including giggly girls, Kate thought. 'You have Steven to help you,' she reminded him, amused by his petulant tone.

David shook his head, his eyes downcast. He looked down at the grass. 'It's easier when you're there.'

'Why? Because I frighten off all the women who would like to chase the pair of you through the galleries?'

David groaned, and Kate laughed. 'In case you're hoping I'll take pity on you, please remember I'm on holiday tomorrow. I have to go shopping for food and start the preparations for Saturday.'

David looked up at her, wishing she would take off her sunglasses so he could read her expression. 'I could help,' he offered, and then realising what she would say added, 'Oh, let me guess - you don't need help. You can do it all by yourself.'

Kate pouted and gave him the reproachful look he had come to know well. 'Actually,' she began, reining in the urge to throw something at him. 'I *do* need help. Mum's helping me with the shopping and Ben will be handling the barbecue like a fire-loving caveman. My sister-in-law will be providing some of the food - probably the best food - and everyone will just pitch in when they get here.'

'Why do you think your sister-in-law's food will be better than yours?'

Kate sighed. 'Remember, she's Italian. Her cooking and organisational skills are far superior to mine.'

'Well, your lasagne beats any lasagne I've ever tasted. In Britain and Italy. Actually, I had something similar to lasagne in Hong Kong once. It was vile!' David was pleased to hear her laugh again; he hated to hear her self-deprecation.

Against his will, David forced himself to stand up. He stretched, then stepped back to allow Kate to walk between the glass patio doors ahead of him. As he followed her along the hall, he stopped in front of a photograph on the wall. It showed a young Kate in her graduation gown, her expression one of innocence tainted with sadness. David admired the long pre-Raphaelite hair which fell over one slender shoulder. He felt as though he had seen this girl before, a long time ago. He turned to Kate as she waited by the open front door; he liked her shorter hair, and the curling tresses which often fell over her face and irritated her.

'What time shall I come over on Saturday?' he asked, as he stepped onto the sandstone path. A glorious sunset streaked the reddened sky with tones of pink and orange. The air was balmy and soft.

'If you're bringing a guest, come over at about two.' She saw him roll his eyes. 'If you're not, and would like to make the salad, you can come earlier. But remember, my family will probably be here.' *And they will ask all sorts of tactless questions.*

'Okay,' David tried to sound non-committal. Carefully, he leaned down and gently kissed her cheek. Her skin felt soft against his lips, and he inhaled the faint scent of her perfume. 'Thank you for a delicious dinner.' *And for providing sanctuary, again.* 'You cook better than my mum, too.'

'Dad! Look what I've found!' The little boy squinted through the glare of the hot sun, looking for his father. He knelt beside a hole he had dug, about half a metre square and ten centimetres deep. He held a small trowel in one hand, his treasure clutched carefully in the other. Behind him, a tall obelisk stood sentinel over the ruins of a city. A village shaded by palm trees could be seen in the distance.

David crouched beside him, his hand caressing the blond head. He smiled affectionately into the boy's big brown eyes, his heart filled with love and pride. 'What have you found, my intrepid explorer?' he asked his eight-year-old son.

Slowly, his eyes on his father, the boy uncurled his fingers. In his palm, he held a small scarab brooch. It was encrusted with dirt, but they could plainly see the bright blue faience of its curved back. David's eyes widened, and he pulled the boy into his arms in a rough embrace.

'That's *amazing*!' David cried. 'I haven't found anything yet!' David stood up and hoisted his son over his shoulder, as the boy wriggled and laughed. 'Let's go and show your beautiful mother. Where is she?'

'Kate!' David called in his sleep. '*Kate!*'

CHAPTER 13

Kate spent most of Friday preparing food for her party, concocting tasty dishes such as tiramisu, ice cream and homemade burgers. By the time she had cleaned the house, moved some of her furniture around and brought extra chairs downstairs, she was exhausted and fell gratefully into bed. Waking early, she was relieved to see the sun shining in a cloudless blue sky. Hopping out of bed like an excited child, she prepared bread and pizza dough and pottered around the kitchen for a while before taking a long shower and spending an inordinate amount of time dressing and styling her hair. After changing her outfit several times, Kate decided on a chic summer dress in French navy with white polka dots, along with dainty summer shoes.

The phone rang at about eleven o'clock, and Kate answered it with one hand while she whipped a bowl of cream with the other.

'It's me,' David's voice was low, as if he did not want to be overheard. 'Have you made the salad yet?'

Kate chuckled. 'No. Are you volunteering?'

'Yes, if you don't mind having me under your feet?'

'I take it you're coming alone, then?'

David grunted in response. 'Ethan has a guest in my house.' His voice dropped even further. 'Actually, he has a guest in my bed.'

'In your bed?' Kate was shocked; what kind of friends *were* they?

'I gave him my bed when he moved in. It's a double. The one in the spare room is a single. I'm cringing - do I have to go on?'

'Please don't!' Kate blushed. 'You're welcome to come here. But be warned, my family are due in an hour or so. You may find yourself cringing again.'

David looked Kate up and down approvingly, making her blush and squirm with embarrassment. He had only seen her in a dress once before, on the night of her anniversary dinner, and he hadn't really paid much attention to the figure of another man's wife. Remembering his manners, he pushed his eyes up from her slim bare legs to her eyes. His own cheeks flushed as he recalled the features of their son. He held out a bottle of champagne.

'This is for you,' he stuttered. 'And so are these.' In his other hand, he held a box of violet creams.

Kate looked momentarily taken aback. 'What made you buy me violet creams?' she asked softly.

'I wasn't sure which chocolates you liked, and these miraculously fell off the shelf into my hands. Don't you like them?'

She gave him a wide smile. 'They're one of my favourites.' Taking his arm, she led him inside. 'Come in. We have lots to do.'

Elizabeth Grahame used her own key to let herself into Kate's house, and was intrigued to hear a man's laughter coming from her daughter's kitchen. She was very surprised to see Kate standing next to the young professor from the museum, supervising him as he arranged toppings on a pizza. When Kate turned and saw her mother, she immediately looked guilty under Elizabeth's questioning stare. Kate introduced David again, her eyes begging Elizabeth not to say anything controversial. Thankfully, Elizabeth was cordial and conveniently decided to string up some Union Jack bunting she had brought with her. Kate grimaced, but let Elizabeth take her little flags into the garden. Amused, David continued to position the pizza toppings.

'Who are you most like?' he asked Kate. 'Your mother or your father?'

In which lifetime? 'I don't know. Neither. I'm an enigma.'

The sound of loud voices in the hall announced the arrival of Ben and his family. Daniela swept into the kitchen, her two children rushing past their mother in order to greet their aunt. Kate knelt down to accept a fierce embrace from her precocious niece. Rebecca was dressed in a blue satin Cinderella gown, complete with satin slippers and a tiara. She stepped back to kiss Kate on the lips.

'We've been to Italian class!' she told Kate excitedly. 'Come ti chiami?'

Kate kissed Rebecca's button nose. 'Mi chiamo Katerina. Tu sei una bella principessa oggi!'

Rebecca twirled in her gown. 'Grazie, Zia Katerina!' She turned to David, not at all shy. 'My name is Katerina, too!' She danced around her aunt. 'Rebecca Katerina Grahame!' The little girl stood behind Kate and wrapped her arms around her aunt's neck. Kate held out her arms to her more dignified nephew. Luca gave a heavy sigh and rolled his eyes, before hugging his aunt and quickly stepping back.

'Let me look at you, Luca!' Kate beamed, taking his chubby face in her hands. Her eyes sparkled. 'So handsome!' she told him, giggling as the boy blushed.

She looked up to see Daniela eyeing David curiously. David hadn't noticed; he was too busy watching Kate with two children who shared her colouring, his dream vividly coming back to him.

'Remember my friend David from the museum?'

David smiled kindly at them, but Rebecca and Luca were more interested in their aunt.

'Auntie Katie,' Luca began. 'Did you make any treats?'

Kate chuckled. 'I've made lots of treats! But you have to eat some healthy stuff first, okay? Then you can have treats, if Mum and Dad say it's alright.' She looked at Daniela and received a smile of approval.

Elizabeth bustled into the room to look for string in the kitchen drawers. She glanced down at Kate, who was still held in Rebecca's tight embrace. 'You could have some yourself if you'd just hurry up,' she muttered, giving her daughter a sideways glance.

Kate flushed as she stood up, watching the children run out to the garden. 'I'm in no hurry,' she murmured, acutely embarrassed.

'You don't want to leave it too long!' Daniela piped up, with a simpering smile. 'It's better to have children when you're young.'

'Well, in case you hadn't noticed, I'm on my own, and these things generally take two.' She saw Daniela open her mouth to speak again. 'And actually, I'm enjoying being on my own right now.' Shrugging, Daniela retreated and left to join her children.

Ben wandered into the kitchen, his eyes narrowing when he spied David leaning against the counter, obviously right at home. He nodded to David in greeting. 'The trestle tables are in the hall, Katie,' he announced, noticing his sister's tight-lipped expression. He looked at the plates of food lined up on the dining room table. 'This looks great!' he enthused. 'Katie's for Christmas dinner this year?'

Kate was taking fresh bread from the oven. She placed the baking tray on the counter and turned to her brother, who had moved to stand opposite David. 'Actually, I probably won't be here this Christmas.' Elizabeth stopped rummaging and stared at her daughter in surprise. 'I'm going to Egypt.'

'On your own?' David and Ben said at the same time.

Kate looked from one to the other, her expression determined. 'Why not?'

'It's not safe, Katie,' Ben advised. 'Western women don't get treated with respect in some of these places. I don't think you should go.'

'Women don't always get treated with respect here, either!' she retorted, and Ben saw he had scratched at a healing wound with his remark.

'Even so, I'm not happy with the idea of you going out there alone.'

Kate angrily pushed a lock of hair from her eyes as she threw trays of pizza into the oven. 'You're not my father, Ben, and even if you were, I'm old enough to make my own decisions. Besides, I won't be alone all the time.' She glanced at David. 'Steven said that if he's working out there, he'll spend some time with me. We've already discussed it.'

'So this is what happens when I go away for a week...' David muttered grimly.

Kate turned to him. 'Don't you start!' she warned him, brandishing a teaspoon threateningly. 'You, and - and your BBC voice!'

'Who's Steven?' Ben asked, his expression ominous.

His over-protective attitude needled Kate. 'He's my toy boy!' she snapped. 'We've been having an affair for ages! We have an illicit rendezvous in one of the museum cleaning cupboards several times a week! It's my aim to work my way through all the male employees by the end of the year.'

'*Katherine!*' Elizabeth scolded.

'Not ladylike...' Ben shook his head but smiled inwardly at her uncharacteristic show of spirit.

It was Ben's turn to be threatened with a teaspoon. 'Does Daniela know about all the things you got up to at medical school? What about that time in the pharmacy with the -'

'Alright!' Ben cried in surrender. 'Forgive me for showing concern! But can't you join a tour group or something?'

'Like a special tour for single people?' she asked disdainfully. 'An 18-30 holiday, perhaps?'

'Absolutely not!' He frowned in frustration. 'When did you get so...feisty?'

'You mean she wasn't always like this?' David asked, giving Kate a mischievous smile.

'No,' Ben shook his head. 'She used to be much more -'

'Pliable,' Kate spat.

'Much more co-operative and eager to please,' Ben corrected.

'Pliable and easy to manipulate,' Kate maintained. Taking a deep breath, she tried not to let Ben rile her further. 'I want to go to specific places in Egypt,' she explained, calming down. 'And Steven can help me. We're friends.'

'Has this got something to do with the past life stuff?' Ben asked, and then remembered he wasn't supposed to know about Kate's regression therapy.

Kate glared at her mother; did Elizabeth have to tell her beloved son everything? She was relieved to hear the doorbell ring. 'Ben, please set up the tables in the living room between the kitchen archway and the French doors to the garden. I want to put the food inside the house, so that it doesn't get covered in bugs. Then could you please do your job and light the barbecue?'

Jess, Erin and Jason stood at the half-open door brandishing wine, cheesecake and trifle. They were closely followed by more members of the Events team, including Nick and his girlfriend, Lucy. Having stopped working to argue with her brother, Kate was now behind schedule. After settling her guests, she raced back to the kitchen to remove the pizza from the oven. David was still in the kitchen, processing the exchange he had just witnessed. Kate handed him a bread knife and indicated he should start slicing bread.

'I didn't know you could speak Italian,' David remarked as he deftly cut the bread.

'Oh, I only know a few words,' Kate answered. 'The children go to classes and then they teach me.' *And Edwin taught me some words which I can only use in private, with someone special.*

'What did your brother mean about "past life stuff"?'

'It's a private matter, and I don't want to talk about it.'

David could tell from her hesitant tone that the topic disturbed her, so he changed the subject. 'Can I ask, are you and Steven -'

'Don't be daft! We're friends. And in any case, he's a bit younger than me.'

David gave her a sly glance. 'You like older men?'

Kate kept her gaze averted. 'Contrary to the wishes of my family, I'm in no hurry to tether myself to *any* type of man in the near future.' *I'm going to wait for my soulmate, this time. Hopefully, he'll be wearing a badge.*

'And you don't like my voice?'

Kate gave him an apologetic smile and looked away shyly. 'I like your voice very much. It's very…soothing.'

'Is that a polite way of saying it's boring?'

Kate giggled. 'I don't have time for this right now! Help me get this food on the table!'

With the help of her friends, Kate soon had the food and drinks laid out on three tables in her lounge. She had invited some of her neighbours, thinking that they could not complain about noise if they were at the barbecue themselves. Kate made lots of introductions and ensured everyone had a drink. Daniela sashayed around the assembly of people, her curvaceous body advantageously displayed in a white dress reminiscent of Marilyn Monroe's in 'The Seven Year Itch'. The dress also drew attention to her long black hair, which she occasionally tossed artfully off her face. As Kate took a plate of sausages and burgers to Ben for cooking, she noticed her brother eyeing his voluptuous wife covetously. Even though Daniela sometimes irritated Kate, she was glad her brother was happy. She deposited the plate of raw meat at the side of the barbecue and then fetched Ben a bottle of beer.

Elizabeth joined her children. 'I hope you don't mind, Katie, but I invited the Spencers. I saw them the other day and Tom was asking how you were getting on. They haven't seen you for such a long time.'

Kate glanced at her brother in trepidation. Tom Spencer was a doctor who had known their father. Throughout her teens, he had taken every opportunity to touch Kate 'accidentally', or to kiss or embrace her. Her parents had never noticed her discomfort. Tom's wife, Helen, had also been oblivious to his lecherous advances. Ben, however, had once observed his sixteen-year-old sister squirming out of Tom's grasp in the garden of their family home. He had ensured Kate was never left alone with the frisky medic again.

As fate would have it, the Spencers walked into the garden right at that moment. Ben squeezed Kate's hand and put down his barbecue fork. Helen was a tall, willowy woman who had always dressed plainly and walked quietly in the shadow of her loud and pompous husband. Kate hugged her in welcome. She turned to Tom, her body tense. Although he was around sixty, Tom tried hard to look and dress like a much younger man. He held out his arms for a hug, but Ben casually stepped in front of Kate. He shook the man's hand and drew him into a conversation about medicine.

Steven was last to arrive. He walked into the garden carrying a bouquet of flowers. Relieved to have escaped Tom's grasping hands, Kate hugged Steven tightly.

'I was going to say sorry for being late,' Steven laughed. 'But if it means I get such a nice welcome, I'll be late more often!' He kissed Kate's cheek and handed her the flowers. David passed the pair, holding his ringing mobile. He gave Steven a pointed look, which made the younger man grin mischievously. Kate watched David walk into the living room, curious as to the identity of his caller.

'That will be his master's voice,' Steven muttered sarcastically.

'Who do you mean?'

'Ethan. He's badgering David to go to Egypt with him this winter.'

'Will he go, do you think?' Kate tried to sound blasé.

Steven shrugged. 'He seems to be oddly ambivalent. When I was at university, he went to Egypt every year. This year, he seems unsure. But I'm sure Ethan will wear him down.'

'Are they very close, then?'

'You know the professor, Kate. He keeps everything close to his chest. It seems like they've been friends for a long time - that's all I can tell you. By the way, I left my second and third year notes on your hall table. Once you've waded through them, you'll only have my final dissertation to read. Now, I'm starving! Feed me!'

As planned, Kate's guests helped themselves to food and drink. Kate watched as Daniela took her husband a plate of food and proceeded to feed him morsels in a very seductive manner, glancing up at him from beneath her lashes. She felt envious of her sister-in-law's ability to be effortlessly and overtly sensual. Kate had never so much as held Mark's hand in front of her family. An image suddenly flashed into her mind, a memory of being fed slices of juicy peaches by long fingers, which she had nipped with her teeth. Edwin had cultivated Kate Ford's sensuality. Wistfully, Kate wondered if she would ever enjoy such experiences in this lifetime.

Kate mingled with her guests, joining a group of friends from the museum and regaling them with tales of her week as a tourist. They laughed as she told them about her climb to the top of the Walter Scott Monument. The worn stone stairs were too narrow to allow people to pass on them, so Kate had been forced to reverse to the landings several times in order to let others come down the stairs. By the time she reached the top terrace, she felt as if she had made the ascent three times. She also described her wonderful trip on the 'Maid of the Forth', recommending it as a possible staff excursion.

'It's such a shame you have to do all these things on your own!' Daniela smiled winsomely as she joined them.

Kate remained calm, although the remark stung. She smiled brightly at Daniela. 'Actually, it's lovely to be able to do things on my own. I have nobody to answer to, and nobody to please but me. I highly recommend it!' She excused herself, and wandered over to the rose bushes. David and Steven stood nearby, talking with some of Kate's neighbours. She walked over to join them, but was intercepted by Tom Spencer.

'Ah, the prettiest rose of them all!' he cried, putting his arm around her shoulder. David turned in time to see apprehension flit across Kate's face, before it was replaced with a mask of geniality. He listened to her converse politely with the older man, whose gaze wandered lasciviously over her body. At length, Kate claimed she had to go and take something out of the oven. She couldn't stop herself from tugging her skirt down as she walked away, knowing Tom would be watching her rear view. *If Edwin were here, Tom would be in trouble,* Kate thought, remembering what he had done to Stan.

'I'd like to put something in her oven...' Tom murmured as he watched her go.

'Steady on, mate!' Steven protested, eyeing the man with disdain.

David's eyes were threatening as he scowled at Tom. 'That's not a polite way to speak about a lady,' he said brusquely, overcome with an urge to punch him.

Tom gave a short, derisory laugh. '*Is* she a lady? She's divorced, isn't she?'

'Her divorce is none of our business.' David's voice was ominously quiet. 'Please don't cast aspersions on Kate's character.' He nodded towards Helen standing alone in a corner of the garden. 'Is that your wife standing on her own over there? Perhaps you should see if she needs anything.'

In the kitchen, Kate bent over to pick up a knife which had been carelessly dropped on the floor, and was shocked to feel a hand stroke her backside. Standing abruptly, she whirled to see Tom leering at her. Without thinking, she slapped him hard across the face with her free hand, the other still clutching the knife. Stupefied, Tom covered his stinging cheek with his hand. The lust in his eyes was replaced with outrage.

'Out of respect for your wife,' she hissed, 'I won't kick you out of my house.' Kate raised the knife slightly to make her point. 'But if you come near me again, I'll go straight to my brother.' The implication was clear; Ben could make life difficult for Tom if his colleagues found out about his unseemly behaviour.

'Well, perhaps you shouldn't be giving off the wrong signals!' he spat in disgust. 'Every man out there can tell you're gagging for it!'

He marched out of the kitchen, just as Jess came in the other door. She saw Kate's look of defiance change into a look of apprehension. 'What's happened?' she asked, and was outraged when Kate explained.

'Am I giving off those signals?' Kate asked anxiously.

Jess snorted as she started running hot water into the sink. 'The only signal you're giving off at the moment is that you're not to be messed with!' She squirted washing-up liquid into the water. 'And no, you don't give off any of the signals he's suggesting. He only said that to be spiteful.'

'Do people think I'm a loser because I like doing things on my own?' Kate picked up the dish towel to dry the dishes Jess had washed. Tom had shaken her confidence.

'Don't be daft! It's great that you're so independent and aren't afraid to be by yourself. I can't be bothered with people who always have to have company, or have to have a radio or telly on in every room when they're on their own. It's as if they're too scared to be alone with their thoughts.' She glanced at Kate. 'Mind you, it's nice to have the company of the right person, now and again. Don't you think?'

David strolled into the kitchen carrying another pile of dirty plates. Kate playfully threw the dish towel at him, and moved away from the sink to bring desserts from the fridge.

'While I've got you two together,' Jess began, 'I need to bring up a work issue.' Kate placed a large dish of tiramisu on the kitchen table. 'It's about the December wedding at the museum. The bride and her mother are coming in for a tour tomorrow, and we'll be discussing the arrangements. I'd like you to attend the meeting, Kate.'

Jess and Kate looked at David, who rolled his eyes and sighed. 'Fine. But only this once.'

Kate dipped a spoon into the corner of the tiramisu and fed it to David. 'Nice?'

David licked his lips. 'Delicious. What else have you got?'

'Well, tiramisu is Ben's favourite. Chocolate cake is Luca's favourite and Rebecca loves chocolate mousse. I've made fruit salad, Jess brought cheesecake, and Erin brought trifle. What's *your* favourite dessert?'

David sucked the rest of the tiramisu from the spoon and gazed at Kate with a roguish gleam in his eye. 'Not on your menu,' he murmured enigmatically. He picked up the tiramisu and carried it to the table in the living room, leaving a speechless Kate behind him.

'What did he mean by *that*?' Kate mused.

Jess shook her head. 'Now *that's* a mixed signal!'

Kate looked at her and frowned. 'What d'you mean?'

'You two,' she said dryly. 'You're either fighting or flirting!'

'We don't flirt,' Kate said slowly. *Do we?* 'We just...tease one another.'

'Aye,' Jess chortled. 'That's one way of putting it!'

As everyone over-indulged on dessert, Kate returned to the kitchen to make coffee. It was now early evening, and she knew that her party would be breaking up soon. The children had slumped on the sofa and were quietly watching cartoons. David followed her into the kitchen to help. 'Have you eaten anything today?' he inquired, as he spooned coffee into the coffee machine.

Kate shrugged. 'I've been too busy to eat much. I'm not very hungry, anyway.' In fact, she had been too nervous about being a good hostess to eat. During their marriage, Mark had enjoyed entertaining his friends but had never helped with the cooking. Kate had, therefore, spent most social gatherings in the kitchen.

'I could get you a plate of something now,' David offered.

She patted his forearm. 'That's kind, but I'm fine. I can always eat later, when everyone's gone, and I've cleared up.'

David sighed. 'I wanted to help you with that, but I'm going to have to leave you earlier than I planned.'

'Oh? Why's that?' Kate kept the disappointment from her voice.

'Ethan has decided to go home tomorrow, so he wants us to go out for a drink tonight. I'll be driving him down to Carlisle in the morning. So Ethan will be drinking, and I'll be watching.' *And staying out of trouble, this time.*

Kate felt unaccountably protective of David; it seemed that Ethan snapped his fingers and David danced to his tune. 'I thought you said Ethan was in a relationship with a nurse?' she asked. 'Now he's just going to leave?'

'I said that Ethan had a *date* with a nurse,' David corrected.

'Which evolved into a sleepover at your flat.' Kate pointed out.

David smiled at Kate's naivety. 'Ethan doesn't do serious relationships, Kate. He has a sailor's attitude to romance - a warm bed and a willing partner in every port.'

Kate frowned. 'Are all archaeologists like that?' *Was Edwin like that, before he married?*

David reached out to touch Kate's elbow. He gave her a look which made Kate's cheeks feel hot. 'No, we're not.' He paused, still gazing at her intently. 'At least I'll get my bed back.'

Kate was acutely aware that they were standing very close to one another. David's breath smelled faintly of the single beer he had nursed all afternoon. When she looked up into his eyes, she saw there were gold flecks in the green irises, and he had a tiny scar on his right cheekbone. Mark was a fair-skinned blond who burned easily in the sun, but David's skin had a healthy golden tone. Kate forgot her home was full of guests who might be feeling neglected by her absence.

238

'Drive safely, tomorrow,' she said softly. Kate was perplexed by the almost seductive look in his eyes, and by the effect he was beginning to have on her. *Pull yourself together,* she told herself firmly. *You're just lonely and sex-starved! And you can't be making eyes at him! You've only just divorced Mark, you desperate hussy!*

'I always do,' he assured her, making no move to step out of her personal space. 'What are you doing tomorrow?'

'Domestic stuff in the morning, massage in the afternoon, early night.'

David dismissed the image of someone's hands massaging Kate's warm skin. 'You've enjoyed your week off, then?' Kate nodded, wondering how it would feel to rest her head on his chest. David tentatively pushed an errant curl from her cheek. 'Zack misses you,' he declared, out of the blue. 'And his illicit Polo mints. So I hope you're not working next Saturday?'

'I'm not,' she answered weakly.

'I'll pick you up at the usual time, then.'

'Yes, Professor…'

'Kate, people are going home,' Elizabeth interrupted them.

Reluctantly, Kate moved her gaze from David's hypnotic stare to her mother. 'I'm coming,' she squeaked.

Daniela and Ben were first to leave. Ben picked up his weary daughter and turned to his sister. 'If you go ahead with your trip to Egypt, you'll need vaccinations. I can look into it for you, if you like.'

Kate relented, realising that Ben only wanted to keep her safe. 'Alright, Ben. Thanks for helping out today.'

'You did great, Katie. It's been a really good day.'

Elizabeth wanted to stay and help Kate clean up, but the Spencers offered to drive her home and Kate encouraged her to go. She embraced Helen Spencer at the door, but Tom gave Kate a wide berth, cautioned by her steely gaze. After a while, only Jess, Steven and David remained. Jess went out into the garden to collect crockery, while Steven and Kate walked to the door with David.

'I'm sorry I can't stay,' David told Kate as he stood on the path.

'It's alright, she's got me!' Steven said brightly and put his arm around Kate's shoulders. David eyed him suspiciously while Steven stared brazenly back. Sometimes, Steven thought, his boss could be incredibly witless.

'Then make sure you do the heavy lifting,' David commanded his intern. As he walked away, Kate felt as though the sparkle had just gone out of her day.

On Sunday, Kate waited until late afternoon before texting David to ask if he was safely home in Edinburgh. It had rained all day, and Kate was worried about David driving on wet country roads.

'All in one piece,' he replied, almost immediately. 'And I have clean sheets!'

Kate smiled in relief. Now she could enjoy her massage.

CHAPTER 14

The Events manager had asked Jess and Kate to dress smartly for Monday's meeting with the future bride. Kate turned up for work cowering under an umbrella to protect her carefully styled hair from a Scottish summer downpour. As she hung her trench coat in her locker, David appeared with a mug of coffee.

'Good morning,' he murmured, eyeing her appearance. She usually wore trousers to work, but her outfit today was a welcome change. Kate had opted for a black pencil skirt and an open-necked blouse of turquoise silk. Her legs were lengthened by high-heeled black courts, which she hoped would not torture her.

Kate looked up from smoothing one leg of her sheer black tights and automatically flushed under his piercing gaze. 'Good morning,' she said shyly, gratefully accepting the mug and warming her cold hands on its smooth surface. She suddenly wished she had brought a cardigan; the room was freezing, and she found she was shivering.

'How was your massage?' he asked.

'Bliss!' she sighed, remembering the wonderfully relaxing Slavic Massage. Even though she had been required to strip completely, she had basked in the sensation of having hot massage oil dribbled down her back. With a towel strategically placed to maintain a little modesty, the talented female therapist had deeply kneaded and stroked Kate's tired flesh until it felt like jelly. Kate had gone to bed almost as soon as she got home, and slept deeply for nine hours straight. 'I will definitely be doing that again!' she breathed. 'How was your drive?'

'Long,' he replied grimly. 'And the weather was terrible.' He took the mug from her and drank a mouthful of coffee. Faking indignation, Kate snatched it back. 'Still, at least I've got my house back.'

'Let me guess, you're not good at sharing, either?' Kate's lips twitched as she sipped the warm drink.

David raised an eyebrow. 'I'm sharing my coffee…'

Kate swallowed, embarrassed at her presumption. She handed the mug back. 'Sorry,' she muttered. 'I'll go and get my own.'

She moved towards the kitchen area, but David caught her wrist. 'Kate, I was joking!' He smiled apologetically, holding out the mug of coffee. 'This is yours. Drink it before it gets cold.' His thumb stroked the smooth skin of her wrist. Kate gently disengaged herself from his grasp and reclaimed the now tepid coffee, still feeling the silky stroke of his fingers on her skin.

'You're mean!' she pouted, finishing the drink and washing the mug before checking there was fresh coffee for her colleagues. She and David walked together along the quiet corridor to their office.

'You have the meeting with the bride today,' he stated.

'Yes,' Kate replied, feeling apprehensive about her new assignment. 'I have no idea what to expect.' She sat down and switched on the computer.

David perched on her desk. 'I expect you'll be dealing with a woman who is trying to plan the perfect wedding,' he said helpfully. 'Whatever that is.'

'Indeed,' Kate murmured, taking her notebook and pens from her desk drawer. Not wishing to discuss weddings with David, she changed the subject. 'What's on your agenda today?'

Nick wandered in, looking half asleep. He grunted at them and walked over to his desk in the far corner of the room.

'I have lots of gruelling meetings this week,' David continued, grimacing as he anticipated difficult conversations with Adam Gray and the head of his department at the university.

'Gruelling how?'

'I want to do something that certain people are not going to like.'

Kate looked up from her keyboard and tried to interpret the strange look he was giving her. 'Best sharpen up your negotiating skills, then,' she suggested. 'And use your famous charm!'

Steven strode into the room with a cheerful good morning and proceeded to unpack his bag. Jess followed him, and the pair continued a conversation they had started in the corridor.

'You think I'm charming?' David asked, lowering his voice.

Kate met his mischievous gaze. 'David,' she began, her eyes dancing at the prospect of teasing him. 'I have a whole list of adjectives to describe you!' Kate started to laugh.

David shook his head sadly and folded his arms. 'And just when I was going to let you canter…'

Unfortunately, their bantering was interrupted by Jess. 'Kate, we have to meet Audrey in the entrance hall. Are you ready?' Kate stood up, gathering her notepad and pen. Jess eyed Kate's smart outfit. 'You look nice today.' Jess was smartly dressed in a tailored black trouser suit and crisp white blouse. 'You should dress like that more often.'

'On Mondays and Fridays,' David said under his breath as he walked to his desk. He turned to Kate, his expression serious. 'I'll want that list, later.'

Kate walked past him and then looked over her shoulder in a very alluring manner. 'Not even for a canter, Professor Young!' She followed Jess from the room.

'Well, what is it today?' Jess asked as they walked towards the entrance hall. 'Flirting or fighting? As if I need to ask!'

Audrey Rutherford ran the Events and Education department with the proverbial iron fist in a velvet glove. She had worked for the museum for seventeen years, rising to her current position through hard work and dogged determination. A tall, strong woman, she carried herself erect like a sergeant major. Always immaculately dressed in a dark suit, Audrey kept her dark hair in a neat chignon and her make-up flawless; Jess once remarked that Audrey's lipstick was too scared to stray over her lip line. Audrey demanded dedication and competence from her staff, but always offered praise where it was due as well as constructive criticism. As a result, Audrey was highly respected by her colleagues. Every event was organised like a military campaign, and all of them were successful.

This morning, however, Jess and Kate were slightly disconcerted to see a look of apprehension on Audrey's face. She stood in front of the long reception desk, a clipboard held against her chest. Spotting her two assistants, she walked towards one of the leather-clad benches and invited them to sit. They had twenty minutes before the arrival of their client, and Audrey wanted to brief her staff on her plan for the meeting.

'The bride, Juliette Michaels, has a fair idea of what she wants,' Audrey told them diplomatically. 'I've already had a long conversation with her on the phone. She's coming today to put her ideas in place on the floor, so to speak. We'll be catering for one hundred and fifty guests. If Miss Michaels already has a caterer in mind, we'll liaise with them. She has already chosen a DJ to supply the music; we'll liaise with him directly, possibly set up a meeting so we can agree the best area for him to set up his equipment. We'll need to organise extra security for the night, and arrange for some of the exhibits to be moved or receive extra protection. No doubt we'll have to arrange flowers and table decorations. I'll delegate tasks once we've met with the bride-to-be. Any questions so far?' Jess and Kate shook their heads, so Audrey continued. 'The groom is an army captain, based here in Edinburgh. That means many of the guests will be soldiers.' Audrey grimaced as she contemplated the damage drunken military personnel might cause to her beloved museum. 'Both families are wealthy, so I'm guessing money is not a problem. Even so, we should provide a competitive quote for the reception.'

They glanced up as they heard loud female voices from the direction of the revolving doors. Kate's feeling of foreboding increased as she saw three tall, elegant women striding purposefully towards the cowering receptionist.

'Right,' Audrey said briskly, standing up and straightening her jacket. 'Let's do our very best to make them happy. But remember, this is our museum and its well-being is our first priority. We can't give in to any unreasonable demands.'

The bride-to-be had the deportment of a woman who knew she was beautiful. Her long black hair cascaded over her shoulders and back, brown eyes flashing under long curling eyelashes. Kate and Jess looked enviously at her perfect figure and long legs. She resembled her mother in looks, but the older woman's features had softened becomingly with age. Her salt-and-pepper hair was neatly styled in a shoulder-length cut. The third woman appeared to be the youngest, and Kate guessed she was the younger daughter, possibly the maid-of-honour. She was more homely than her breathtaking sister and clearly did not share Juliette's confidence. Kate immediately warmed to a kindred spirit.

Introductions were made, coats were hung in the cloakroom, and Audrey and Juliette led the way up to the Grand Gallery. From the outset, Juliette bombarded them with her grand plans for the perfect wedding reception. Kate hastily scribbled the concepts in her notebook in neat shorthand. As Juliette strolled around the Grand Gallery as if she owned it, she pointed to where she felt the dance floor should be and where the disc jockey should set up his sound system, overriding Audrey's suggestions. Her manner was offhand, at best; she spoke to Audrey as if to a mere lackey, and looked at Jess and Kate with disdain. She also never missed a chance to needle her little sister, Tara. More than once, Kate caught Tara rolling her eyes at her sister's overbearing attitude and grandiose ideas. When Juliette asked if a red carpet could be put on the staircase to the gallery, Tara spluttered with laughter, which she quickly hid from her mother and sister. Mrs Michaels made a weak attempt to rein in her eldest daughter, but Juliette reminded her that 'daddy said she could have whatever she wanted'.

Juliette indicated the exhibits which would have to be moved out of the way, including Iufenamun, whom she said was 'gross'. Kate suddenly felt protective of the Egyptian priest. It was bad enough that the poor man was exposed to gawping visitors every day, without being insulted into the bargain. At that moment, she realised that this haughty, spoiled young woman was almost a replica of Louisa Ramsay, in character as well as appearance.

Audrey did her best to be accommodating, but Kate was gratified to hear her refuse any demands which would be detrimental to the museum or its exhibits. At length, Audrey took them to one of the offices, where she had refreshments brought for their guests. Audrey brought out a portfolio which showed photographs of past receptions, in the hope of giving the bride more tasteful ideas regarding layout and decoration. Juliette had already decided on gold table linen, which made her mother grimace. Audrey tactfully suggested that white table linen would look striking in the Grand Gallery and that perhaps the gold could be subtly displayed in the centrepieces.

Juliette wanted large floral displays everywhere, preferably in golden urns. Kate finally spoke up.

'If you place floral displays along the wall which is lined with exhibits, they'll create more of a conflict than an impact. Perhaps it would be best to limit them in the Grand Gallery. You could put displays at the foot of the staircases, for example, or in the doorways to the other galleries. The lighting here might make golden urns look garish, so why not consider glass or crystal vases, perhaps on plinths?' Kate glanced at Audrey, who nodded imperceptibly for her to continue. 'Also, the museum looks beautiful in candlelight. How do you feel about tea lights on the tables? Candlelight would also reflect off the glass vases and give the gallery a softer glow.'

Juliette pouted at this seeming opposition to her wishes, but Mrs Michaels nodded in agreement.

'That sounds very tasteful, dear.' She smiled kindly at Kate.

'What sort of flowers did you have in mind?' Jess asked the bride.

'Oh, white lilies. I adore them!'

'They will be very costly in December,' Jess warned her. 'And you'd have to be careful about the pollen, in case it stained your dress.' Jess was treated to another pout, but carried on anyway. 'Do you have any ideas about the design of floral arrangements?'

Juliette pulled some thick bridal magazines from her large designer handbag and handed them to Jess. 'I've marked the ones I like.'

Mrs Michaels looked at Kate and Jess. 'We would be happy to consider any other designs you come up with.'

Audrey took up the thread then, drawing their attention to the florists used by the museum and photographs of floral arrangements they had provided in the past. The women pointed out the ones which pleased them, which in Juliette's case tended to be the most ostentatious, and therefore the most expensive. Catering was the next topic of discussion. Juliette's plans for a royal banquet had to be tempered to what could realistically be served at the museum. Again, examples of past catering services were shown but the bride was not drawn to any specific menu. Eventually, Audrey brought the meeting to an end, promising that quotes and menus would be sent to them within a week. She left Kate and Jess in the office while she escorted the Michaels women to the cloakroom, and fairly slumped in her chair on her return. She then delegated the tasks she knew Jess and Kate could handle and sent them on their way so that she could take off her shoes and enjoy a well-earned cup of tea by herself.

David found Kate slouching glumly in her chair leafing through a magazine, her shoe-less feet resting on the chair she had borrowed from behind his desk. A pile of thick magazines sat on the desk beside her, along with a large ring binder, her notebook, some paper and coloured pencils. She seemed oblivious to his presence, so David moved quietly to her desk, lifted her feet from his seat and sat down with her ankles still in his hands and her feet on his lap.

'Lunch break?' he asked.

In Kate's opinion, it was inappropriate to allow David to massage her feet. She lifted her feet from his knees and put them on the ground. Sitting up in her chair, she tossed the wedding magazine crossly on the desk. 'Research,' she grumbled.

David looked at the magazine, which displayed a resplendent bride on the front cover. He noticed the other magazines appeared to be in the same vein.

'You look like you want to run away,' Kate commented, amused that the sight of wedding dresses seemed to unnerve him.

David ignored her sarcasm. 'How was the meeting?'

'It was an enlightening experience.'

'Oh, really?' David was sceptical. 'And how was the bride-to-be?'

'She has a lot of ideas. But I suppose that's only natural.' *We only ever plan to marry once in a lifetime.* Kate sighed. 'I've been given the task of designing floral arrangements. She wants grand displays everywhere, but…'

'Her demands are unreasonable and not to your taste.'

Kate frowned at him. 'Oh, so you read minds now?'

'Have you had an actual lunch break?'

'No, I need to have something to show for my efforts by the end of today.' Kate laid her head on her desk, frustrated. Helping to plan someone's wedding was harder than she had anticipated.

'I don't know why they've put you on this assignment,' David muttered.

Kate jerked upright and she glowered at him. 'Why?' she snapped. 'You think because I couldn't make my own marriage work I shouldn't be involved in planning someone else's? In case I'm cursed?'

'No, Miss Snappy! Because reading bridal magazines on someone else's behalf is a waste of your talents. Why don't we go and do something more interesting? I could easily get you off this assignment.'

'Certainly not!' Kate was indignant.

David swivelled his chair so that they were sitting side-by-side. 'Show me what you've got.'

'I'll manage,' she replied, testily. 'Go and do your own work.'

He smiled at her uncharacteristic display of ill-temper, realising that this assignment would be difficult for her, but she would hide behind her mask of stoicism.

'Show me,' he insisted.

Sighing impatiently, Kate picked up one of the magazines and turned to a page with the corner turned down. The illustration showed a large, Roman-style urn painted in a garish gold colour. It sat on a plinth carved in the shape of a Corinthian column. The urn was filled mainly with white lilies, with smaller white flowers used as fillers. Much of the foliage had been spray-painted gold.

'This is what she wants,' Kate told him matter-of-factly.

David tried to think of a tactful response. 'Yuck!' he blurted. Kate made a sound of agreement. 'What's your idea?'

'Well, I haven't found anything I liked in her magazines. The Events portfolio has some lovely displays which suit the museum.' She hesitated. 'I made some sketches of my own ideas...'

David held out his hand for the drawings which lay on her desk, hidden by the ring binder. He looked at them with a critical eye, discovering she was quite a talented artist.

'The wedding is on the first of December,' Kate explained. 'I thought we could use flowers which are in season.'

The vases she had drawn were of cut crystal - she had scribbled 'Edinburgh Crystal' under the design. They sat on simple plinths and were filled with lilies, but Kate had used foliage in different shades of green. Eucalyptus provided a softer, silvery hue. Ivy trailed over the vases.

'I assume she won't be having lilies in her bouquet,' David mused. 'The pollen's lethal on clothing, especially white...'

Kate let out an involuntary giggle at this unexpected comment. 'I assume not,' she replied. 'Her colour theme is white and gold, which must be carried over onto the table settings.' She giggled again as she caught his grimace of distaste. 'I suggested candles on the table, perhaps tea lights, or floating candles. The Grand Gallery would look beautiful if the lights were dimmed and the room was lit by candlelight, don't you think?'

'That's very romantic, although you would have to check with Health and Safety about the candles. And I'm not sure how Security would feel about us creating more darkened recesses for people to misbehave in.' David coughed, embarrassed, and returned his attention to Kate's drawings for table centrepieces. She had designed delicate arrangements; small glass bowls holding a tea light and ringed with ivy and Gypsophila, and larger shallow bowls with golden floating candles. A chunkier version showed a thick, gold pillar candle sitting in a posy of white flowers.

'What does the bride suggest for the tables?'

'Audrey has persuaded her to opt for white table linen, but this is the sort of thing she likes.' Kate opened another magazine and pointed at an illustration of a large floral arrangement sitting in the centre of a table, in the preferred colours of gold and white.

'Too large and ostentatious,' David declared. 'The guests won't be able to converse across the table - it's not intimate at all. And lilies, again! At least Edinburgh's dry cleaners will benefit. The scent of so many lilies will be overpowering. Add to that the scent of lots of women's perfumes mixed together...serious headache.'

'I think you've missed your calling!' Kate smiled, watching him leaf through the magazine for more ideas.

David gave her a reproachful look. 'I like your designs, except for the one with the chunky gold candle. Something simple, delicate and tasteful would be best. And I prefer white roses to lilies. If she wants displays everywhere, tell her she can't have them against the display wall - they'll clash with the exhibits. If she wants to have her reception in a museum, she should be prepared to embrace what we stand for.'

'That's just what I said!' Kate exclaimed.

'Good.'

'Except,' Kate bit her lip. 'She wants us to move Iufenamun - I believe she referred to him as "gross".'

David stared at her, askance. 'You've agreed to that?'

'Audrey said we would look into the options available. So what are they? I don't want him being used as a drinks table.'

'I thought you didn't like him?'

'I believe he should be resting in peace, not be put on display for tourists. And certainly not to be gawped at by rowdy soldiers!'

'It's a military wedding?' David looked grim, his mind quickly travelling the museum galleries in search of other items which might need extra protection.

Kate nodded. 'The groom is a captain, so I would imagine most of the military guests would be quite high-ranking and able to behave. How can we protect Iufenamun?'

'We can build a kind of crate to go over the top of the exhibit, or screens to go around the glass case. We're not wheeling him into a cupboard.'

'Thank you. I'll pass that along.'

Steven walked in, his black hair tousled. He smiled tiredly at Kate and David.

'All finished?' David asked briskly.

Steven nodded and turned to Kate. 'I've been building a plate-shaped jigsaw where all the pieces look the same. What are you doing?'

Kate explained her new assignment as Steven pulled his chair to the other side of Kate's desk and picked up a magazine. He began flicking through the pages, muttering as he glanced at the photographs of women modelling expensive wedding dresses. 'Yuck, yuck, ooh, she's hot, yuck, not bad...'

'Airbrushed, airbrushed, airbrushed...' Jess said, looking over Steven's shoulder. She grinned at Kate and tossed her friend a Mars Bar and a bottle of water. 'How goes it?'

Kate gleefully tore the wrapper off the much-needed chocolate bar and took a bite. She closed her eyes, leaning back and relishing the taste of melting chocolate and caramel on her tongue.

'Kate!' Steven chided. 'You make eating chocolate look almost pornographic!' He laughed as she immediately sat up, and Jess playfully cuffed his ear.

'I've drawn some ideas,' Kate told Jess. She glanced at David, who had his eyes on her chocolate. 'David has been very helpful.' She turned to David. 'I'm not sharing my chocolate,' she told him firmly.

David gave her a wolfish grin, before grasping her wrist and biting off a piece of Mars Bar. She squealed in protest and pulled her arm from his grasp, glaring at him as he chewed while making appreciative noises. The phone on Jess's desk rang, and she left them to answer it.

'Do you want a lift home tonight?' he asked suddenly. 'Your feet will be aching after a day in those shoes. I'll wait for you in the entrance hall at half past five.'

'That was Audrey on the phone,' Jess called from her desk at the other side of the room. 'Miss Michaels is coming back on Friday to see how we're progressing. Apparently she has more ideas to discuss. Audrey wants us both at the meeting.'

'You can't have Kate on Friday,' David said, adamantly shaking his head. 'I have work for her to do, and we have a workshop. She's worked for you all day today, as it is!'

'The meeting will be during lunchtime,' Jess replied with a frustrated sigh.

'Then you'll have to make it between one and two.'

'Excuse me,' Kate piped up. 'I *am* in the room!'

Jess turned her attention to Kate. 'The meeting is at one on Friday. If your slave-driving supervisor allows it, we can grab a quick lunch beforehand.' She tilted her head towards David.

'I can clear up after the workshop,' Steven offered. 'That would give you half an hour for lunch.'

David put the magazine down and stood up. 'Fine, as long as Kate is back for two o'clock. Right, I've got a meeting with Adam Gray. Steve, write up the report on your morning's work and add it to the records.' His eyes softened as he looked down at Kate. 'I'll see you later.'

Kate watched David stride from the room, thinking how solid and strong he looked. He was the image of masculine virility, and yet his opinions about flower arrangements seemed distinctly…feminine. Kate could not fathom him out; he had more hidden depths than the ocean. She sighed wistfully and returned to the task in hand.

Kate's fingers caressed the sharp angles of the large amethyst crystal 'cave' she was in the process of buying from the museum gift shop. She had seen it that morning and thought it would make a lovely wedding present for Erin. The shop assistant placed the large crystal into a box and processed the purchase. Hefting the heavy box in its carrier bag, Kate walked over to one of her favourite exhibits while she waited for David in the entrance hall.

The striking limestone coffin lid of Paamunnesutawy stood about two metres high and over half a metre wide at the shoulders. The imposing piece belonged to an anthropoid coffin from the time of the early Ptolemies, and was thought to originate from Upper Egypt. Blank eyes looked down at Kate as her gaze meandered over the black-painted hieroglyphs which decorated the front. The coffin lid had been purchased by the museum in 1908. *Near the end of Edwin's life,* Kate thought sadly. She wondered if he had facilitated the purchase, if his hands had caressed the now pitted limestone and deciphered the messages depicted in a rectangular panel down the length of the body. She still remembered those hands, slightly rough from work, the fingers long and tapered. A small sound escaped from her lips as a lump caught in her throat. *Every time I think I'm moving forward, I remember something which takes me back.*

'Are you ready?'

Kate jumped at the sound of David's voice behind her. When she turned to him, David saw an inexplicable look of sorrow in her dark eyes. She quickly harnessed her emotions and forced a smile, picking up the carrier bag which she had set on the ground between her feet.

'Hey there, Professor! Haven't seen you at CC Blooms for a while!' They both looked up as Stan swaggered up to them, his eyes greedily homing in on Kate's chest even as he addressed David. 'Looked like you were well in there, last time I saw you!'

'I don't know what you mean,' David replied curtly, with a feeling of impending doom.

'I was there with the wife a couple of weeks ago, after a show at the Playhouse. I saw you in the bar with that wild lad who worked here for a while. You were quite wrapped up in a very tasty piece!' He nudged David and gave him a salacious grin. Kate stared at David, watching alarm flit across his face, followed by anger. He gave Stan a weak smile which did not reach his eyes and bid the tactless man a hasty goodnight. As David strode out of the museum, Kate had to almost run in her high heels to keep up with him.

The journey home was silent and uncomfortable. David was already remorseful of his actions on that night. Now he was mortified that Kate had been apprised of them, however vaguely. She would draw her own conclusions and would no doubt think less of him. Kate's feelings were in disarray. She knew she shouldn't care what David did in his spare time, as she had no claim on him whatsoever. And yet, the thought of David with a new partner was disturbing. Stan had not specified whether the 'tasty piece' had been male or female. Surely he would not describe a man in such a way? And yet, Kate knew that CC Blooms was ostensibly a gay bar. She flicked a discreet glance at David, whose concentration was focused on the busy road ahead. Kate had limited experience of men, and she struggled to interpret the mixed signals David had been sending out. *Perhaps I should just ask him,* she mused, but she knew she didn't have the audacity to ask such a personal question. Weakly, she reminded herself of Edwin's insinuation that her soulmate awaited her in Egypt. David's romantic interludes were not her concern.

Once he had parked in front of her house, David nodded to the bag which Kate clutched tightly on her lap. 'What have you been buying?' he asked awkwardly, waiting for her to ask the inevitable question.

'It's a wedding present for Erin,' Kate explained, trying not to sound as dispirited as she felt.

'Are you going to the wedding?'

Kate forced a laugh. 'No. They're getting married in Saint Lucia. But I wanted to get them something because Erin has been very kind to me. She's helped me a lot recently.'

'She's a hypnotherapist, isn't she?' David asked with interest. Kate nodded, knowing what the next question would be and wondering how best to answer it. 'At your barbecue she told me that she specialises in past life regression.'

Kate turned to him, and he saw her jaw tighten. 'You probably think that's a load of rubbish,' she surmised.

'I have an open mind,' he replied, and noted her look of surprise. 'There seems to be evidence to support the notion that we've all lived numerous lifetimes.' David suddenly remembered a heated exchange between Ben and Kate in her kitchen. 'Did you discover a previous lifetime?'

'Do you often frequent CC Blooms?'

David got the message: she wasn't going to answer his question and he certainly didn't want to answer hers. He got out of the car to open her door for her, taking the heavy bag so that she could get out of her seat. Kate thanked him politely for the lift as she took the bag from him. He held open her gate to let her pass, but she continued walking up the path, her keys already in her hand and her eyes on her front door.

Another week passed swiftly and Kate worked diligently as always, absorbing every new experience. Some of her time was spent helping Nick with museum tours. The museum ran several free tours throughout the week, each with a different theme. Kate accompanied Nick on the 'Taster' tour, which showed visitors around the numerous galleries, providing a little information on each. Another tour offered visitors an insight into the supernatural aspects of Scotland's history and, of course, there was a specific tour of ancient Egyptian exhibits. Kate was impressed by the wealth of information Nick imparted to his tour groups, but she worried about how she would remember all the facts if she ever had to lead a tour herself. Although Nick was seen by his colleagues as an exuberant character who seldom took life seriously, he was an inspiring tour guide who knew how to keep his listeners enthralled and could answer all their questions with confidence and an air of good-humoured authority.

Kate and Jess made progress with their arrangements for Juliette Michael's wedding reception. Kate was surprised when Mrs Michael decided she preferred Kate's idea for floral decorations, overruled her daughter and asked Kate to ascertain the cost. Kate then liaised with the florist who had been selected to manage the floral arrangements for the wedding and soon had a comprehensive estimate to pass on to Audrey.

By Friday, Kate was apprehensive about seeing David again, as they had not spoken or seen one another since Monday evening. Throughout the morning, they focused on their separate roles. Kate used the Friday workshops as an opportunity to learn, and usually sat at the back of the room making her own notes. Since she was responsible for editing and typing up the handouts, she was reasonably conversant with the subject material.

In the afternoon, David announced that he had to attend yet another meeting. He instructed Kate and Steven to create a new display for the Egyptian gallery using the jewellery from the collections store. As Steven searched for the jewellery photographs he had downloaded, David took Kate to the corner of the room, out of earshot.

David's eyes searched her face for some indication of her feelings towards him at that moment, but he could read nothing in her pokerfaced expression. 'Are you still coming riding tomorrow?' he asked falteringly.

Kate gave him what she hoped was a forthright look. 'Actually, I was going to tell you I can't.' She saw disappointment in his eyes. 'I'm going out tonight, and it looks like it might be a late night. I've been asked out tomorrow, too. I'm sorry.' In fact, she was going to the supermarket after work and planned a pampering evening at home on her own, culminating in a movie starring her favourite actor. On Saturday evening, Ben had asked her to babysit so he could take Daniela out for an anniversary dinner. For reasons she couldn't quite explain, Kate wanted David to believe there were people in her life who wanted to spend time with her. She didn't want him to think she was a lonely divorcee who desperately snatched every little crumb of affection tossed her way. Although she was horrified at the notion, she also suspected she had an urge to make him a little jealous.

'I see,' he said tightly, denying his impulse to ask where she was going and who would be accompanying her. 'Well, have a good weekend.' He raised his voice so that Steven could hear him. 'Please continue working on your new display on Monday, and make sure all the preparations are made for next Friday's workshop. I may be late on Monday morning.'

By the time David appeared on Monday, it was nearly lunchtime. Kate and Steven had conscientiously continued to create a new exhibit for the Egyptian gallery, which at the moment consisted of a large rough sketch with accompanying notes on the pieces they planned to use. Kate had also prepared the paperwork required for Friday's class. Steven was busy gathering the items required for practical work, so David decided that the intern should remain at the museum to complete his task. Kate would accompany David to the Collection Centre to make a final decision on the jewellery they would need for the display.

Kate went out on her own at lunchtime and sat in Bristo Square with a sandwich, enjoying the June sunshine. Groups of tourists stood admiring the architecturally stunning McEwan Hall, named after the founder of the famous Edinburgh brewing firm. Sir William McEwan had been a Member of Parliament in his time, as well as an art lover and philanthropist. Designed in the late nineteenth century by Sir Robert Rowand Anderson, the circular building was originally planned as part of the adjacent medical school, but was instead used for examinations, graduations, lectures and concerts. Seating two thousand people, the hall was still a popular venue.

Kate idly watched people passing through the square, her mind wandering. Jess was going on holiday on Wednesday and would be flying out to Saint Lucia for Erin's wedding on Friday. Nick would be her supervisor until Jess returned, and they would work together on the events planned for the last three weeks of the school term. Nick had suggested that Kate might like to speak at some of the workshops, rather than simply assist the pupils. As a result, Kate would be talking about Edwin's career three times in the next fortnight. She sighed wearily as she contemplated the presentations which would refresh her past life memories.

The thought of David's continued presence in her life made Kate decidedly uneasy. Her feelings for him were complex, inappropriate and unwelcome. He shielded himself behind an invisible barricade which prevented anyone from getting too close, so how could he nurture a friendship with anyone? And yet, he would know every little detail of Kate's life, familiarise himself with all her emotions, delve into the depths of her soul. She resolved to keep David at arm's length. She would be polite, professional but detached. At least, she would try...

Her phone proclaimed the arrival of a text: 'Prof's looking for you. He wants to leave for the collections store in half an hour. Warning - he's grumpy. Just tore a strip off me for "unsatisfactory performance".' Kate shook her head, feeling sorry for Steven. She fervently hoped the young man wouldn't go the same way as David's last intern, as Steven showed real promise as an archaeologist; that much was obvious from his work at the museum and the contents of the many essays Kate had read from his course notes. Checking her watch, Kate saw she still had fifteen minutes left of her lunch hour. David had no right to be checking up on her whereabouts. As she strode purposefully back to work, she prepared for battle.

Every time he had to stop at traffic lights, David's fingers drummed an irritated rhythm on the steering wheel. More than once, the Land Rover's tyres shrieked as David crossly pulled past a vehicle which impeded his progress to the collections store at Granton. Kate ignored his fit of pique, her attention fixed on the scenery outside the window. She knew he had been forced to attend more meetings than usual recently, many with Adam Gray, who had no love for the difficult professor. Kate also remembered that Gray was trying to persuade him to go to Egypt in the winter and had given David the summer to make his decision. Perhaps the time had come for David to make up his mind. Whatever the issue, Kate made no attempt to soothe him. When he parked in the car park at Granton, she immediately climbed out of the car and headed for the door of the vast warehouse.

They were greeted by a woman wearing a white lab coat, and shown into a stark white room with a table, a computer and two chairs. The items they had come to see were spread on a thick white cloth on the table, and a box of latex gloves sat next to them.

'These are the items you requested,' the woman addressed David briskly. 'Once you've confirmed your selection we'll arrange to have them delivered to Chambers Street. Let me know if you'd like to see anything else.'

'Thanks, Doctor Brownlee,' David replied, taking off his jacket and placing it on the back of a chair.

Kate turned to the woman, whose business-like attitude was somewhat intimidating. 'Doctor Brownlee,' she began hesitantly. 'Do you store many of the exhibits from the 1890 Ancient Egypt Exhibition? Very few are displayed in the museum...'

The doctor looked surprised by the question but gave Kate a warm smile. 'We don't have all of them. Some have been sold over the years, or damaged beyond repair. You're welcome to peruse our database.'

She moved to the computer, her fingers tapping the keys efficiently. Once she had accessed the database, the doctor left the room.

Kate removed her jacket and pulled on a pair of gloves, her attention drawn to the items on the table before her. The most striking piece was the heavy jewelled collar Kate remembered so well.

'Can I touch them?' she asked David, not looking up from the necklace.

'You can touch whatever you like,' he replied, his voice low. Kate wondered if the double entendre had been deliberate, but chose to ignore it. She had no patience for male ambiguity, a trait David seemed to share with Edwin.

As she stroked the beads of lapis lazuli, an image of Edwin's smiling face swam into her memory. Swallowing hard, she brought her focus back to the table. Smaller beaded collars had been laid out, along with a row of delicate bracelets. Kate picked up a pair of tooled gold earrings and was amazed by their weight, which must surely have caused discomfort to the wearer. There were other earrings and charms of animals and hieroglyphs. Small alabaster cosmetic pots sat next to little tools for applying kohl. Her eyes fell on a small hand mirror with a decorative handle, its circular reflective surface now tarnished with age. Still fighting memories of Edwin, Kate's eyes filled with tears of frustration. She carefully picked up the mirror and held it in her hands, wishing only to look into the silver and see his face smiling lovingly back. Kate felt utter despair at her inability to control her feelings, and wished she could slap her own pathetic face.

David watched her examine the items on the table, admiring the tenderness with which she handled each piece. He wondered why Kate had such an interest in the 1890 exhibition. In fact, he had many questions for Kate which would no doubt anger her and so he refrained from asking them. Had Erin Mortimer regressed Kate, and if so, what was the connection between Kate, Edwin Ford and the 1890 exhibition? Kate knew more about the museum from that time than could be gleaned from research alone. Her presentation on Ford had been subjective, not borne from historical study and suffused with conjecture. She had given the impression to all in the room that she had known the Victorian archaeologist. David had assumed Kate was simply a good writer and narrator, but perhaps there was more to the story than met the eye...

He saw her remove a glove and wipe her eye; was that a teardrop on her finger? David frowned, but knew he must pretend not to notice.

'Shall we arrange to have these pieces delivered, then?' he asked.

Kate sniffed, squeezing her eyes closed to fight the tears. She nodded, and then turned towards him, her mask in place. 'Can I search the database for something?'

David pulled out the chair in front of the computer so that she could sit down and begin her search. A few minutes later, she sat back with a triumphant smile and pointed at the image on the screen. The black marble statuette of Bastet looked haughtily back at her.

'I have one just like it at home,' she commented.

'Was this brought in for the 1890 exhibition?'

'Yes,' Kate tried to sound offhand.

'Did Edwin Ford bring it from the tomb of the unknown royal woman?'

'Yes.' In spite of her efforts, Kate's voice caught in her throat. She was thrown back to the museum workroom, where she had stroked the black cat under the chin.

David saw an inner struggle taking place within her. Those expressive brown eyes gave her away even when she pasted on an expression she wanted the world to see. 'And you got this information from research?' he inquired, and Kate nodded. David gazed at her steadily, and Kate knew he didn't fully believe her. Nevertheless, he ceased his questioning and walked towards the door. 'I'll go and ask them about the statuette and organise the delivery. You can look through the database, if you like. I'll come back and get you.'

Kate discovered that the warehouse stored the statue of Anubis, one of the papyrus scrolls, and the sarcophagus which had never been unsealed. As expected, typing Edwin's name into the search window produced no results. But he was in the room with her, his essence fused with the items on the table. He whispered to her through the mirror, his words of love caressing her ears. Kate fought the urge to weep, to cry out his name with unbearable longing. She wished Erin had used hypnotherapy to make her forget Edwin and her past life. The memories seemed set to cripple her emotionally.

She stumbled from her seat and pulled on her jacket. Gathering up her bag, she left the room, bumping into David at the door. He looked at her stricken face with concern and lightly touched her arm. As he expected, she moved out of his reach.

'Can we go?' she asked.

David nodded and led the way to the car park. 'It's nearly five o'clock. I'll take you home.'

Kate shook her head. 'I can get a bus across the street.'

David looked perturbed. 'Kate, this isn't the best neighbourhood -'

Kate spotted a number thirty-eight bus in the distance. 'The bus is just coming. I'll see you at work.' She walked quickly out of the car park to the bus stop and caught the bus, once again leaving a speechless David in her wake.

CHAPTER 15

Kate gave her presentation on Edwin Ford twice that week, which proved to be a poignant experience. Her audience, however, was unaware of Kate's inner turmoil. She was inundated with questions about the hero who was passionate in his tireless quest for knowledge of an ancient civilisation, and who had strived to spread that knowledge throughout Scottish society. Each night Kate returned to her empty house with a heart which felt as if it had been wrung out.

By Friday, Kate felt drained and battered. She arrived at the museum earlier than usual but found no solace in the building which, despite its facelift, still reminded her of that other life. Her head aching, Kate tried to concentrate on preparing the seminar room for the morning's workshop. When he arrived to help, Steven sensed her subdued mood and did not engage Kate in their usual cheerful repartee. By the time David turned up with his notes and laptop, his assistants were sitting quietly in the back row of seats. In a hushed voice, Steven was giving Kate the answers to questions she had posed a few days before, having read more of his course notes. Kate was taking brief notes, but David noticed the absence of the affectionate smile she always bestowed on Steven. She was sitting in a tightly closed, defensive position, her hair falling over her face as she wrote.

They looked up as David crossed the room and placed his laptop on the table set at right angles to the wall which supported the projection screen. He greeted them briefly, noting Kate's weary expression. His radio crackled, and a voice advised him that the Egyptian artefacts from the collections store would be delivered at around one o'clock. David informed his assistants they would spend the afternoon mounting the pieces for their display, and should aim to place them in the Egyptian gallery by the end of the day.

David lectured his class on the work of Sir William Matthew Flinders Petrie, the first archaeologist to carry out a triangulation survey on the Pyramids of Giza. He had been a pioneer of systematic methodology and the preservation of artefacts. Petrie had developed the method of seriation for dating fragments of pottery, which David illustrated in the practical assignment. Throughout the morning, David glanced frequently at Kate, and more than once he saw her staring vacantly into space, her thoughts elsewhere. But then, he surmised, she probably knew the course material back to front.

Once the workshop ended, Kate and Steven cleared up the room, and Kate accepted Steven's offer of a coffee and a slice of cake in the first floor café. David was sacrificing his lunch hour to participate in a conference call with Egypt and London. After sitting in the café for half an hour with Steven, Kate took a short, refreshing walk. On her return, she was crossing the Grand Gallery when her eyes fell upon a little girl standing on her own in the middle of the polished floor. As she neared the child, Kate could see tears running down her round face.

Kate crouched down so she was at the girl's eye level. 'Are you alright, sweetheart?' she asked kindly.

'Sono perso!' the child hiccupped in Italian. 'Voglio Mama!'

Understanding that the girl was lost and looking for her mother, Kate took her hand. 'Mi chiamo Katerina,' she told the girl, and pointed to her identity badge. Standing, she led the girl to a bench in the centre of the gallery, and gestured for her to sit. Taking a seat next to her, Kate activated her radio. 'This is Kate Grahame,' she began. 'Urgent message to all floor staff: I've found a small Italian girl, looks to be about five. She has lost her mother. We're sitting in the centre of the Grand Gallery. I'll wait with her until her mother is located. Out.'

Kate smiled reassuringly at the little girl, gave her a tissue from her handbag and asked in Italian for her name and age. The girl's name was Rosa and, as Kate had guessed, was five years old. Comforted by Kate's presence, the girl dried her eyes and began to speak in rapid Italian. Kate understood that she was on holiday from Rome with her parents and older sister.

After ten minutes, a small woman with black hair ran up to them, her arms outstretched towards Rosa. A member of the security team accompanied her. Rosa jumped from her seat and ran into her mother's arms, where she received a fierce embrace and several kisses all over her face. The woman looked gratefully at Kate. 'Thank you so much!' she exclaimed in heavily-accented English. The next moment, Kate was pulled into the woman's arms.

'It was my pleasure,' Kate smiled kindly, as the woman released her and vigorously shook her hand as was the custom in Italy. She looked down at Rosa. 'Ciao, Rosa!'

As Kate walked towards the Millennium Clock and the offices beyond, she saw David standing at the bottom of the escalator, having witnessed the emotional reunion between mother and daughter.

'What was that about?' he asked.

'The little girl wandered away from her mother. I saw her standing in the middle of the gallery and kept her company until security brought her mum. They're Italian, hence the dramatics.' She passed her hand across her forehead, feeling her headache returning.

'Kate,' David began cautiously. 'Are you quite well today?'

Looking up at him, Kate could see his concern. She tried to give him a reassuring smile. 'Yes, I'm just tired. And I have a headache.'

He paused before speaking again. 'Do you have plans for this weekend?' Kate shrugged as she began to walk towards their office. David kept pace with her as they passed Iufenamun. 'I'm going riding tomorrow. Why don't you come with me? The sea air would put some colour in your cheeks.' He quickly back-pedalled. 'Not that there's anything wrong with your cheeks -' David rolled his eyes at his own ineptitude. 'Once I start preparing for the new term, I won't be able to go riding as often...'

Kate turned to see consternation on his face; she had never seen him tongue-tied before. 'Can I let you know later?' she asked. David nodded. 'Are you coming to supervise us this afternoon?'

'I can't,' he replied. 'Besides, I want to see what you two can achieve.'

'So it's a test?'

'No, it's a learning experience. Let me know when you've finished.'

A knock on the half-open door made David look up from his work. Lewis stepped cautiously into the room carrying a file box.

'I was looking for Ms Grahame,' he announced sheepishly, intimidated by the professor's stern gaze.

David guessed that Kate had enlisted Lewis's help with more of her research, and noted the young man's disappointment at her absence. He had 'crush' written all over him. 'She's out,' David told him curtly, and then relented. 'I can give her a message, if you like.'

Lewis put the file box on the edge of Kate's cluttered desk. 'Tell her she can keep this file,' Lewis said, with a proud grin. 'It was about to be thrown out, but I rescued it for her. I know she wouldn't want it to get lost, even though the museum has no use for it.'

David was intrigued. 'Why would Kate want it?' he asked the blushing youth.

'It's James Grahame's portfolio,' Lewis explained, feeling gratified that he knew something the esteemed archaeologist did not. David still looked nonplussed. 'He was the director of the museum, and Kate's great-great-great grandfather.'

David was stunned by this revelation. 'I had no idea...' He looked up at Kate's champion of the archives. 'I'll let her know you brought the file. I'm sure she'll be in touch to thank you.' He watched Lewis's eyes light up with delight at the prospect. The young man fairly bounded from the room.

David gazed at the box speculatively for a while; another piece of the puzzle. He kicked himself for not making the connection. He remembered Kate studying the portfolio a few weeks before, but she had claimed it was to help her with some research and had not divulged any family connection. At that time, she was still Kate Forrester.

Sighing, David returned to the onerous task of writing lecture notes. He was finding it difficult to compose his next presentation, which was to be an outline of the very complicated Egyptian religion. Idly, he wondered if Kate could do a better job of writing the notes. David felt weary, having spent the last few weeks battling with the bureaucracy of both museum and university in order to bring his plans to fruition. He was no diplomat, and the process exhausted his patience. He longed to travel somewhere far away to enjoy a peaceful holiday in the sun, but he fervently wished he could take someone with him. A particular someone who sat at the messy desk across the room...

David jumped in his seat at the sound of a loud thump. Glancing over the top of his screen, he saw that the box had fallen off Kate's desk, its contents strewn in a wide arc across the floor. David rose from his seat, chiding the absent Lewis with a mild oath for placing the box so precariously on the desk. Crouching down beside the papers, he picked up an old catalogue from the 1890 Egyptian exhibition. Leafing through it, he found descriptions of the exhibits and recognised some which were currently on display. He turned to the first page of the catalogue and stared in disbelief at the words printed there: Written by Mister Edwin Ford and Miss Katherine Grahame.

Putting the catalogue back in the musty box, he gathered up some more papers from the carpet. There were newspaper clippings reporting the success of the exhibition and praising those involved in such a commendable enterprise. There were notes written in James Grahame's own hand, although David knew that the director's official correspondence would be stored in one of the massive ledgers of directors' letters, which were held in the archives. He wondered if Kate was aware of their existence.

David put the papers in the box, and then reached across the carpet for the remaining two items. They were sepia photographs, and as David's eyes scanned the faces he became completely still. The first photograph showed a group of four people. From their dress, David knew the photo had been taken near the end of the nineteenth century. An older couple smiled at the camera, the man standing proudly behind the woman. Next to him stood a tall young man, dark curly hair falling over mischievous eyes. Seated in front of the young man was…Kate. David reached up for the magnifying glass on Kate's desk and peered at the photo. The young woman smiling back at him was the image of Kate. Some of the puzzle pieces started to fall into place in David's head, although the emerging picture was incomprehensible.

His fingers trembling slightly, David balked at the remaining photo. It was a wedding photo, showing a couple who were clearly very much in love. The radiant bride was Kate. Her husband…

David choked at the scene before him. *This can't be right!*

'David, what are you doing?'

Startled, David looked up to see Kate standing over him, her face white. She could see shock in his expression, as if he'd seen a ghost. He dropped to his knees on the carpet, a photo in each hand.

'I'm sorry, Kate,' he stuttered distractedly. 'Lewis brought this for you. It was going to be disposed of and he thought you might like to keep it. You have to thank him, by the way, and I think he has a crush on you. He must have put the box on the edge of your desk, because it fell off and everything fell out. I was just picking it up and I saw…these. Kate, what's this all about?'

Kate gazed at him, seeing incredulity in his widened eyes. She felt sympathetic but wary; did she know him well enough to trust him with her secret? David could see her hesitation, the guarded look which indicated she was contemplating her next course of action.

'Lewis said that James Grahame was your great-great-great grandfather,' he began, hoping he could encourage her to explain further. She nodded reluctantly. David held up the family photograph. 'Is the older gentleman James Grahame?' She nodded again. 'Do you know who the other people are?'

Kate knelt beside him and David could feel her trembling slightly as her arm grazed his. She took the photograph from him and held it reverently, her finger pointing to beautiful, smiling Eleanor. 'His wife, Eleanor,' Kate explained, her voice barely audible. Her finger moved to the young man. 'This is their son, John, a lawyer and my great-great

263

grandfather.' Her voice caught, and she closed her eyes briefly. 'And this is their daughter, Katherine.'

'The same Katherine who co-wrote the exhibition catalogue?' he asked, gazing at her intently as he struggled to rationalise the evidence before him. Kate nodded again, her heart sinking as David held up the wedding photo. 'She was a beautiful bride,' he commented, his voice low.

'She was young and in love,' Kate whispered.

David forced himself to ask the question, even though he dreaded the answer. 'With Edwin Ford?'

'Yes. She loved Edwin Ford.' *More than life itself.* 'She was only twenty when they married.'

David rubbed his hand across his face. 'Kate, do I need to state the obvious?'

'It's a family resemblance, David. Genetics. That's all.' Kate took the photograph from him and returned it to the box. Standing, she closed the portfolio and put it on her desk. She couldn't look at him, and she was afraid to reveal anything else.

David stood and went to close the office door to give them privacy. He returned to stand in front of Kate, forcing her to meet his gaze. 'I wish you'd talk to me,' he entreated.

'I can't,' she muttered. 'I don't know how to talk about this. And I don't want you to think I'm mad.'

'Why do you feel the need to deal with everything on your own?' David sounded exasperated.

Kate's eyes flashed. 'Because I have issues with trust!'

He held her gaze with his own. 'You can trust me.' The look she fired him suggested otherwise. 'Have you discussed this with anyone? Who do you talk to, when you need someone to listen and provide support?'

'Jess and Erin know some things. My mother knows a little, and obviously she will have discussed it all with my brother. That's it. I'm not the sort of person who whines about her problems to all and sundry.'

'That must be hard, given the last few months. You've had to watch something end which you hoped would last forever. And now this,' He gestured towards the portfolio. 'Whatever it is. It must be hard to understand.'

Kate looked away, hiding her distress from him. 'I can't talk about it. Not to you.'

'Kate, please let me help.' In a final attempt to breach her defences, David took her hand. 'I won't judge you, whatever you say to me. All

I'm offering is an ear and a shoulder - as a friend.' He glanced away in case his eyes betrayed his true feelings. 'The only benefit I require is to see you content -' He stopped as he found her staring at him, her eyes hunting for signs of his sincerity even though he was laying himself bare before her.

'Why?' she asked quietly.

'Because I care about you,' he blurted.

Kate frowned, troubled. In her mind, his often flirtatious behaviour was not consistent with his rumoured homosexuality. She felt as if he were toying with her affections while she toiled to find balance in her life. 'David, you send out a bewildering array of signals! One day we're "friends", and the next day you're distant. You want to know all about me but reveal very little about yourself. I don't know how to act with you other than to keep my defences up. I won't be hurt again.'

David lowered his head. 'I'm sorry. I'm not great at opening up.' He glanced up with a wry smile. 'Perhaps you could teach me?'

The sound of Kate's radio made them both jump. 'I'm still standing in the Egyptian gallery, Katie Grahame. Where are you?'

Kate's eyes widened; she had forgotten all about Steven. 'Sorry, we're just coming.'

'I should think so, too!' he chided impatiently. 'It *is* Friday night, you know!'

Kate looked up at David, once again pushing her quandary to the back of her mind. 'I came to tell you we've finished the new display. Will you come and look?'

'In a minute,' he told her firmly. 'You said you had a statuette of Bastet in your house. Did you buy it?'

Kate looked puzzled and a little startled at the sudden shift in topic. 'It belonged to my aunt. She said it was a family heirloom, but I don't know its provenance. Why do you ask?'

'Would you let me look at it? I could probably date it for you. It might have belonged to James Grahame's time, or it might even be an original Egyptian artefact.'

'I'll think about it,' Kate replied evasively. She headed for the door, eager to escape another troubling encounter with David Young.

Steven and Kate had created an eye-catching display. The necklaces were arranged on a board at the rear of the display case. Small platforms of varying heights exhibited jewellery, earrings and charms. Tools and pots were arranged on the floor of the case, flanked by the statuettes. The dimmed lighting bounced off Bastet's sleek curved back, making the black marble gleam. Interesting information was displayed for each artefact. David nodded his approval, and Kate and Steven exchanged a grin of triumph. It was not in David's nature to gush with praise, however, and he led them over to a display case at the other end of the gallery which showed examples of shabtis.

'From Monday onwards, we'll examine the artefacts on display for signs of damage. Those which require conservation will be removed to the workroom. We'll start with the shabtis. Thank you for your good work on the jewellery exhibit. Steven, you can go and start your weekend.'

Steven put an arm around Kate's shoulders and gave her a quick squeeze, before trotting out of the gallery. He had a date, and didn't want to make a bad impression by being late.

Kate smiled as she watched her friend's hasty departure. 'He has a date,' she commented. 'He must be keen on this one.' She turned to see David looking at her awkwardly, and suddenly she felt dispirited again. 'What?'

'I wondered if you would like a lift home.'

Kate contemplated carrying the bulky portfolio home on the busy bus. 'I would appreciate a lift home. Thank you.'

David took a convoluted route home in an attempt to avoid rush-hour traffic, but the drive still took half an hour. He asked Kate to select a CD and she chose a collection of classical music, before sitting back and closing her eyes. By the time David pulled up in front of her house, Kate was feeling much more relaxed and amenable.

'Would you like to look at my statue of Bastet?' she asked him, making no attempt to leave the comfort of the leather car seat. She yawned.

'I have the makings of a beef stir fry in the boot,' he informed her. 'I went shopping at lunchtime and stuck my stuff in the fridge in the staffroom. Why don't I cook some dinner while you relax?'

'I thought you couldn't cook?' she asked, her eyes teasing.

'Even *I* can manage a stir fry.'

Kate was tired; she acquiesced without a fight. 'Okay. I'll help you chop stuff.'

David laughed ruefully. 'Actually, I bought it already chopped.'

Kate laughed in disbelief. 'Lazy besom!' she rebuked as she climbed out of the car.

Once David had been shown where the cooking utensils were kept, he set to work, chasing Kate from the kitchen. Kate decided to take a quick shower and sneaked into her en-suite bathroom, locking the door behind her. By the time David summoned her, she had changed into her favourite leggings and oversized jumper. As Kate took her seat at the neatly-laid table, he thought she looked like a teenager. He set her plate before her and watched for her reaction. Kate inhaled the lovely smell of fried steak and a variety of vegetables in some kind of sauce. He had cooked noodles, too, and bathed them in soy sauce. Kate picked up her fork and started to eat. As she chewed, she made a noise of appreciation which made David beam with pleasure and start eating his own dinner.

They deliberately kept the conversation in neutral territory to prevent possible antagonism. David made Kate laugh by relating Steven's dismay at being asked to restore another broken plate, while Kate described the antics of some children who had attended a Vikings workshop that week. Nick had made Kate dress up and pretend to be a Norse warrior's wife, complete with blonde plaited wig and helmet. Once they had finished their meal, Kate automatically rose to clear the plates and wash up, but David stopped her.

'I made the mess, I'll wash up. Go and get your cat.'

Kate reluctantly left him in the kitchen and climbed the stairs to her room. Sitting on her bed, she picked up the little black cat and stroked it thoughtfully. Finally, she made her decision; Kate went to her wardrobe and took a box from the shelf. She then opened the small safe hidden at the bottom of the wardrobe and took out a small, velvet-lined jewellery box. Completely disregarding her reservations, she took the three items downstairs and placed them on the kitchen table.

David had finished washing the dishes; they lay neatly stacked on the draining board. Drying his hands on the towel, he sat down opposite Kate. He could see she was troubled and knew she was questioning her decision to trust him with something she felt deeply about. David picked up the little cat, his fingers gliding over the smooth curves. He looked closely at the engraving on Bastet's carved collar, and then looked under the plinth the cat rested on. There were some Egyptian characters engraved in one corner, but they were not ancient hieroglyphs. David's brows drew together, and he frowned. He recognised the pottery mark.

Looking up into Kate's anxious eyes, David smiled gently. 'It's Egyptian,' he told her. 'But not ancient. By the pottery mark on the underside I can tell you it was made in the mid-to-late nineteenth century. There were a lot of these statues made for Victorian tourists. This particular piece was made near Alexandria. If you want it valued, we could ask someone from the museum to help.'

Stunned, Kate remembered that Edwin had kept a statue of the goddess on his desk in Abercromby Place. *It can't possibly be the same one - can it?* She got up from the table and absently started to dry the dishes.

'Have I said something wrong?' David asked, concerned that he had aggravated her again.

'No,' Kate answered quickly. 'Like I said, it's an heirloom. I don't need to have it valued - it has sentimental value.' She saw David eyeing the other two boxes and gestured for him to go ahead and open them. Kate's heart tightened as he opened the jewellery box and gently drew out the gold locket. Holding the locket in his palm, he opened it and gazed upon the two locks of hair twisted together, careful to keep his expression blank. The wedding photo from Grahame's portfolio was seared into his brain, so he knew the darker hair was Ford's and the other strands belonged to his wife. He closed the locket without touching the hair, his thumb lightly caressing the initials etched into the gold.

'Edwin gave it to his wife on her twenty-first birthday,' Kate murmured.

Without looking at her, David nodded slightly and put the necklace back in its box. He picked up the diamond ring. Kate had obviously cleaned it, for the stone twinkled in the light. 'Katherine's engagement ring?' he asked softly. 'Yes,' Kate replied, remembering North Berwick beach and Edwin's fingers in her hair. 'He proposed first in the museum, and properly on North Berwick beach after he had bought the ring.' She watched David replace the ring and close the box, failing to notice his jaw tighten as he resolved never to take Kate back to North Berwick. His face remained impassive as he opened the final box, a shoe box lined with layers of tissue paper. He brought out the scroll first, the family tree tied with red ribbon. Kate watched him peruse her ancestry, thinking he looked the consummate professional, and grateful that he was handling her precious possessions with care and respect. Her defences started to slip a little.

David retied the scroll and placed it on the table. He brought out some old photos next, of the Grahame family. *A close and loving family,* David thought enviously. There was another wedding photograph, but David could not bring himself to look at it. Kate did not notice David lay it face down on the table and pick another item from the box. Placing it on the table, David carefully peeled away several layers of tissue paper to reveal a delicate lace veil. He recognised it immediately from the wedding photo as Kate Ford's bridal veil. He wrapped it up again and turned to the last item in the box. It was a small, leather-bound notebook wrapped in a piece of ageing silk. As he carefully opened the worn pages, a folded piece of

268

paper fell out. Kate turned away as David unfolded Edwin's sketch of Kate, so she didn't see the tortured look which passed across his face. Biting the inside of his cheek, David folded the paper again and leafed through Edwin's diary. Details of the man's expeditions were crammed into the pages in neat handwriting. There were rough sketches and hand-drawn maps. Turning the pages, David's eyes caught a mention of Kate. He read Edwin's words silently to himself.

'I confess I have an almost sadistic desire to rile her at times. I find the outbursts of my Kate's fiery temper glorious to behold. Having roused her passions, I can anticipate the bounteous rewards of a ceasefire.'

David couldn't help but smile. Glancing at Kate, he wondered if she shared her namesake's temperament. He flicked to pages which recorded the ill-fated expedition to Amarna and Edwin's thoughts on the location of Akhenaten's tomb.

'Have you read this?' David asked.

'Not all of it,' Kate answered. *I couldn't bear it.*

'He wasn't far off, you know,' David mused, finally looking squarely at Kate. Sensing her unease, he gave her a smile which did not dispel the sadness in his eyes. 'Akhenaten's tomb. He was close to finding it. But there are no more diary entries after December 1891.'

Kate was unconsciously twisting the dish towel tightly between her fingers. *He would have found the tomb if he'd gone to Egypt alone.* 'Kate Ford died in January 1892.'

David looked surprised. 'In Egypt?'

Kate nodded sadly. 'She travelled with him to Amarna but fell pregnant on the journey.' Inexplicably, she blushed. When she continued, her voice was sad and expressionless. 'They spent Christmas in Cairo, and that's when she told Edwin she was carrying their child. He refused to let her return to camp, and decided it would be safer to leave her with some friends in Cairo. He returned to Amarna to await a replacement team leader. While he was away, she slipped getting out of the bath. She fell, miscarried and became gravely ill. Edwin was summoned - against her wishes - and made it to her bedside just a few hours before she passed away.

'He brought her back to Edinburgh, as she requested. She's buried in Dean Cemetery. They both are. Edwin never recovered from her death, although he kept working at the museum. His last expedition was to the Qurneh burial site. He contracted an illness while he was in Egypt and died shortly afterwards.'

269

David's eyes had darkened with anger. 'So your hero left his young wife with strangers in Cairo - pregnant, alone and probably scared - while he went back to work?'

Kate became defensive. 'It was a different time. She understood that his work was important, and he had no choice but to return to the dig site. He promised he would return to Cairo as soon as he was able and that they would come home. He had only been gone for a week when she became ill.'

'He shouldn't have taken her out there in the first place!' David argued. 'Conditions in those days were terrible for the men, let alone a pregnant woman!'

'She loved him, David! She insisted on going with him. They had only been married for sixteen months. Edwin didn't know she was pregnant - she kept her suspicions to herself until she saw the doctor in Cairo.' Kate couldn't bear to tell David that the Fords' marriage was in peril because of Kate's dissatisfaction with her life.

'How do you know?' he snapped, angry that she should defend Edwin Ford for behaviour he himself would never consider.

'Because I remember it,' Kate whispered, and sat down heavily in her chair. She leaned her head in her hands, and waited for him to laugh at her apparent insanity. Instead, David sat down opposite, gently pulling her hands from her face and placing them on the table. He placed his hands over hers and gazed into her face, but Kate could see no sign of censure in his kind eyes.

'You've had regression therapy?' he asked gently.

'Yes.' She sounded resigned; once she told him about her past life he would undoubtedly run for the hills.

'What made you do it?' He patted her hand. 'You don't have to tell me if you don't want to. But it might help you to talk about it.'

'I started having dreams.'

'When?'

'Not long after I started working at the museum.'

'Was your marriage already in trouble at that time?' He heard her inhale sharply at the question. 'I'm sorry if I've overstepped. You don't have to answer that.'

Kate looked sheepishly at the grained surface of her grandmother's kitchen table. 'I suppose it probably was, though I was too stupid to notice.'

David squeezed her hand. 'What did you dream about?'

Kate blushed at the memories which came flooding back. 'Edwin Ford...'

'Go on,'

'I dreamt about a life in Victorian Edinburgh as the daughter of James Grahame. I met Edwin when he started working on the exhibition here. The dreams were so vivid they disturbed me, so I discussed them with Jess and she suggested I visit Erin. Regression provided more information. Edwin and I - or rather, the other Kate - fell in love and got married. They went to Egypt and she died. The end.'

'So, one could hypothesise that you are the reincarnation of that Katherine Grahame?'

'Is this where you tell me I'm crazy?'

'No. I'm trying to understand, so help me out.'

'Then yes, that's one theory.'

'It would follow, then, that you believe Edwin Ford may also be reincarnated.' He scrutinised her expression. 'I suppose that Edwin and Kate would be considered soulmates. So it would be only natural for you to try and reconnect.' He inhaled deeply. 'Are you looking for your soulmate, Kate?'

Kate looked at their hands for a moment, and then looked him squarely in the eyes. 'Do you think we only have one soulmate to choose from?'

'I don't know. Is he the reason you want to go to Egypt?'

'I want to go to Egypt to see the country,' she answered, side-stepping the question. 'My aunt visited Egypt many times, and I was raised on tales of ancient Egypt. I want to visit Amarna because Kate Ford was there. While she was at the dig site, she unearthed a stone tablet which was believed to be a letter or poem to Nefertiti. It's in the Cairo museum. As for finding my soulmate - if it's my destiny to be with him, then I'll be with him. Whoever he is.' From somewhere deep inside her, Kate heard a tiny voice shriek in protest, and she felt suddenly laden with guilt at the thought of forsaking her duty to Edwin.

David felt a twinge of hope; perhaps she wasn't hell-bent on finding her modern-day Edwin Ford, after all. 'What do you think triggered your dreams in the first place?'

Kate shrugged. 'I don't know. Perhaps I was…lonely.'

'Perhaps it was because you returned to the museum,' David suggested. 'You have a strong connection to that place. Some say that buildings retain energy from people and events. Perhaps you can sense it somehow.'

'You believe that?' Kate was incredulous.

'Kate, I visited the temple at Karnak a few years ago. The place has a powerful energy I can't describe. There's a definite atmosphere which demands reverence.'

'Then I'm never going to be able to forget,' Kate murmured despondently. Edwin would haunt her forever.

'Would you consider leaving the museum?' he asked, keeping the fear from his voice.

'No,' Kate answered firmly. 'I love my job. And I love the museum - although I liked the old one better.'

'Understandable. I have to admit I preferred it myself, especially the rotunda and the grand staircase at the back.'

Kate grasped his hand and grinned in delight. 'Me, too!' Her expression became serious once more. 'But I want to put all of this behind me. I have a chance to make a life for myself, but every day I'm reminded of the past - my past and her past. I don't know what to do.'

'Why do you want to forget your past life? Did your regression involve reliving the moment of your death?'

'No,' Kate would never tell David she had met Edwin's spirit. 'But the memories fill me with a longing for something I can't have, and that hurts.' She struggled to explain. 'Life was a lot simpler for girls back then, even though they were restricted. They didn't have to worry about paying the gas bill, or climbing the career ladder -'

David chuckled. 'No, they just had to decide what dress to wear and who would dance with them at the ball...'

Kate smiled ruefully. 'Don't get me wrong, I like being independent and in charge of my own life. But when I'm having a bad day...I yearn to go back there. I suppose that makes me sound like a weak bimbo...'

'I think I understand,' David said kindly. 'You've had a difficult year so far. Your soul must be screaming out for respite. And I gather you've been taking a crash course in archaeology on your own time.' He was referring to Steven's course material, and the informal tutorials he held in order to answer Kate's questions.

'I want to learn!' Kate felt defensive; was he implying that she was a weak woman who couldn't cope?

'And that's commendable, but it also implies you're spending a lot of time at home. What are you doing for fun?'

She tried to look nonchalant. 'Stuff...'

'Specifically?'

'I hope you're not going to do that man thing where you try to fix everything?'

'I'm in no position to fix you when I can't fix myself. Answer the question.'

'I go to Tai Bo once a week, and I often go out with Jess. Occasionally, I swim at the sports club nearby. And I'm thinking about starting some other evening classes.'

272

'But you're home on your own a lot?'

'What's your point?' she snapped, testily. 'That I'm a sad old spinster? Are you going to suggest I get a cat?'

David smiled at her grumpy retort. 'I'm suggesting that you should create new memories of your own. It seems you keep returning to happy memories from a past life. Don't you have happy memories of *this* life?'

Kate thought about it. 'Some, from childhood. Mostly of time spent with my aunt, but they're spoiled by the memories of her illness, and her death. My parents travelled a lot when I was growing up, so Ben and I stayed with Aunt Margaret a lot. Mum and Dad pushed us to work hard at school. Obviously they were delighted with Ben's achievements, but I think my father was rather disappointed in me. Dad was very different from James Grahame, who encouraged his daughter to think for herself and speak her mind. Behind closed doors, of course.'

'If she was anything like you, she'd have done that whether her parents approved or not!'

Kate giggled, knowing he was right. She smiled at him, amazed at how good it felt to talk to him and relieved beyond belief that he was still sitting at the table, listening and allowing her to talk.

'My upbringing was similar to yours,' he informed her. 'My parents pushed me academically, making me ambitious and oblivious to anything but my own aspirations. Unfortunately, they're not entirely happy with my choice of career. I think they see it as "airy-fairy".'

'I'm sorry,' Kate said, sympathetically. 'I think the work you do is wonderful.'

David saw from her flushed cheeks that the comment had been inadvertent. 'Thank you,' he murmured, savouring her praise.

'Do you want some coffee?'

'Only if I've made you feel a little better,' he smiled. David knew she had not revealed every detail of her past life experiences. Undoubtedly, there would be memories of Edwin Ford she would cherish in her heart for ever. But he was content that she had trusted him enough to confide in him a little.

'Do you think I'm a nut job?' she asked tentatively.

'No. But I wish you would remember that you're loved in this lifetime, too.' His sincerity made Kate avert her eyes. *Just not by my husband,* she said to herself. *But perhaps Mark could say the same about me.*

'I think remembering a past life is a gift, of sorts,' David continued, changing tack. 'Don't repress it. Learn to accept it, but don't be held prisoner by it. At least you remembered a life where you were loved. Clearly, Ford adored his wife, although I disagree emphatically with his decision to drag her off to the desert and then abandon her while she was carrying his child. Had it been me, I would have acted differently. I would have stayed with my wife - to hell with the job!'

Kate had never considered this point of view. If he had loved her as much as he claimed, why had Edwin not chosen David's option? Still, she continued to defend his actions. 'It wasn't all his fault. She was very persuasive and knew how to get round him. They had agreed not to…' Kate's face flushed scarlet, and she cleared her throat.

'Succumb to their passion?' David supplied, charmed by her discomfort. 'But they couldn't keep their hands off one another?' Kate rose from the table and filled the kettle to hide her acute embarrassment. David laughed, but his laughter was edged with bitterness. 'I'm sorry - I won't say any more. Kate, when you're in the museum - in fact, wherever you are in Edinburgh - remember that you walk in the footsteps of the people who loved you. You walk in the places where you once felt joy. Let it comfort you and strengthen you. I don't have that solace. Not in Edinburgh, at any rate.'

Kate dropped a chamomile tea bag into her mug and a teaspoon of coffee into David's. 'You're not happy in Edinburgh?' she asked, her eyes watching steam rising from the kettle spout.

'I've tried to put down roots here, but so far it hasn't worked.' He sighed. 'Let's just say that I have more unhappy memories than happy ones.'

'So where were you happy?'

David was quiet as Kate filled their mugs and placed David's coffee in front of him. She squeezed out her tea bag and returned to the table. He looked thoughtful. 'My grandparents had a cottage in the Cambridgeshire countryside. I spent most of the holidays there, and it was idyllic.' He shrugged off whatever memory had held his attention and looked up at Kate with a wistful smile. 'I guess we both need to create some new memories.'

As he sipped his coffee, David looked thoughtfully towards the garden, which was bathed in a dusky pink light. Following his gaze, Kate stood up and walked towards the patio doors with her mug of tea. She opened the doors and stepped outside, finding the air thick with the scent of roses and lilies. David followed her, breathing deeply of the fragrant garden. Kate glanced at her watch, surprised to discover it was nearly nine o'clock.

'I didn't realise it was so late!' she exclaimed. 'I'm sorry - I've taken up your Friday night.'

'You make it sound like a bad thing,' he chided gently. 'I was only going home to work.'

Kate tutted. 'And you've got the cheek to criticise me!' She leaned down to smell a pale pink rose, deeply inhaling the luscious scent.

'Let's stay out all weekend,' David suggested impulsively.

Kate frowned dubiously. *So much for keeping him at arm's length.* 'How do you propose we do that?'

'We could go camping,' he quipped.

Kate glowered. 'Get knotted! Living in a tent may have been fine for Victorian Kate, but it's absolutely not for me!' *Not unless I had Edwin with me, or a close substitute.* Kate gazed defiantly at David, who chuckled.

'I see - you're a girly girl, after all. Well, we'll start with riding in the morning.' He saw Kate tilt her head expectantly, so continued with his proposition. 'I have two tickets to a concert at the Usher Hall tomorrow night, which I bought - well, a while ago. We can go out for an early dinner, then on to the concert.'

The idea of spending the whole day with David outside of work filled Kate with an irrational fear, as if she were crossing a boundary. There was an air of impropriety about it, as if they were arranging an illicit rendezvous. But she couldn't argue with David's logic. She needed to get out and create new memories, and she always felt safe with him. 'What's the concert?' she asked hesitantly.

'Royal Scottish National Orchestra playing a selection of classics,' David replied, fully expecting her to decline his offer. She had been taking small steps to change her life, and he realised he was asking her to take a leap. He continued to admire the plants so she wouldn't be intimidated by a direct stare.

'That sounds nice,' she commented, still uncertain. 'I've never been to the Usher Hall...'

'It starts at seven thirty,' he informed her. 'We could eat at around five thirty. Where would you like to go?'

'There's a nice Italian restaurant in Shandwick Place,' she offered, absently wringing her hands. 'But I'll pay for dinner.'

David gave her a grave look. 'No, you won't.'

Kate pouted. 'I'll pay half, then. Or I'm not going. Friends usually split the bill, after all.'

David sighed as he pulled his mobile from his pocket and quickly searched for the number of the restaurant. Before Kate could change her mind, he called and reserved a table. He could see her jaw tighten and her eyes flash; his assertiveness was like a challenge to her independence. David relished the now familiar expression, and the way

275

she drew herself up to her full height, even though she was much shorter than him.

'I see you've returned to Bossy Professor mode,' she snapped grouchily.

He grinned at her, his green eyes twinkling with mischief. 'I only do it to irritate you.' He strolled past her, heading towards the house. She stuck out her tongue at his broad back and followed him inside. David knew it was time to go, but was reluctant to leave her.

'Shall I take these things back upstairs for you?' he offered, pointing at the heirlooms on the table.

'No, I'll manage,' Kate assured him, unwilling to let him see her bedroom.

David stepped into the hall, once again stopping before Kate's graduation photograph. He gazed into those innocent brown eyes, and then turned to the more worldly eyes of the Kate he knew. 'I'll pick you up at nine,' he told her. 'And I'll bring you back after riding so you can do whatever women do before a night out. Will three hours be enough time for you to get ready?'

Indignant, Kate playfully slapped his arm as she reached to open the front door. She looked up at him with an earnest expression on her face. 'Thank you, David. For all you've done tonight.'

'Hush!' he exclaimed with a grin. 'You'll give the neighbours the wrong idea!' David grimaced as she hit his arm again, and then smiled at Kate. 'I'm glad I could help,' he said softly. 'Make sure you lock up. I'll see you in the morning.' He took a last look at her, standing in her baggy jumper and leggings. With a wave, he closed the gate, got into his car, and returned to his silent flat.

CHAPTER 16

David frowned as Kate settled herself into the passenger seat, radiating an air of tension both in her expression and body language.

'Didn't you sleep?' he asked, noting the shadows under her eyes.

Turning to face him, Kate managed a thin smile and shook her head. She had been plagued by nightmares so horrific she had turned on the bedside light in the hope it would chase the demons away. Lying in the silence of her room, Kate feared she was being punished for confiding in David and allowing him into her life. Now she felt jittery through lack of sleep, even after two mugs of herbal tea.

Sleep had also eluded David, who had been tormented by visions of Edwin Ford grinning smugly at him while embracing a Katherine Grahame who changed in appearance from Victorian Kate to the Kate who was now sitting next to him. David had finally given up trying to sleep and gone out for an early morning run.

'Hopefully, the sea breeze will chase away the cobwebs,' David said kindly as he started the car. Kate nodded, hoping they would chase away angry ghosts, too. David was playing Chris Isaak's 'Wicked Game' album. Kate leaned back and closed her eyes, letting the sultry music wash over her as David drove them out of the already bustling city. But some of the tracks were sad, the talented singer despondent over a lost love, and Kate's mood darkened further. David was also thoughtful on the journey as he mulled over an email he had read that morning. The universe - and David's superiors - had seen fit to grant his wish, but instead of elation he now had mixed feelings about the whole matter.

'I need a holiday,' David sighed wearily.

Kate turned her head, nestling into the seat. *Oh, I love this car!* 'You've just had a holiday,' she reminded him.

David snorted. 'That wasn't a holiday,' he disagreed, but didn't elaborate. 'I mean a holiday away from here.'

'Where would you go?' Kate looked out at the widening expanse of the Firth of Forth, deep blue in the sunshine.

Somewhere warm, and near the sea. Where there's no mobile phone reception and no Wi-Fi.'

Kate smiled, warming to the concept of tranquil isolation. 'And who would you go with?' she inquired. 'Or would you just pick up a companion along the way?'

David gave her an enigmatic smile, aware that she was fishing again but wondering if the comment was also a dig at him for the night at CC Blooms. She had obviously been thinking about Stan's tactless revelation, and David wondered what her feelings were. He remained silent for the remaining ten minutes of the journey to Annie's farm as he rehearsed in his head how to tell Kate his important news.

'Kate, there's something I have to tell you,' he began, as he parked the car in Annie's yard. He glanced at her uncertainly. 'I'm going to Egypt.'

Kate felt as if she had been punched in the stomach. *First Mark, then Edwin, now David,* she thought to herself miserably. She felt suddenly abandoned but hid her feelings from David. She had planned to go to Egypt for a week in December, but had not arranged it yet. She knew the archaeological season started around October and ended in January. Would David be in Egypt all that time? Was this the reason he wanted to spend the weekend with her, because he was leaving soon? 'How wonderful!' she enthused. 'When will you be going? Where will you be working?' *And how long will I be left without you?*

Before David could reply, Annie knocked on his window and bid them good morning. After exchanging pleasantries, she led them to the horses. As usual, David checked over their mounts while Kate waited with Annie. Annie glanced sideways at Kate, seeing tears in the younger woman's eyes. Instinctively, she slipped her arm around Kate's shoulders and gave them a squeeze. The gesture made Kate want to cry, but she bit her lip and forced her face into a wide smile as David called her over to Zack. Once mounted, she followed David and his beautiful horse into the paddock towards the far gate. But Kate was tense and distracted, and this unsettled Zack. When a rabbit ran out under his hooves, the horse whinnied in fright and reared. Unprepared, Kate fell to the hard ground. She had the presence of mind to roll away from Zack's flailing hooves, curling into a tight ball on the ground. Within seconds, David was on his knees beside her, scooping her into his arms and holding her against him.

278

'Are you alright?' he asked, panic etched on his handsome face. Kate muttered incoherently against his sweater. 'Kate, does anything hurt?'

Kate mentally probed her body to identify any painful areas. The fall had momentarily forced the air from her lungs, but otherwise she seemed to have escaped with merely wounded pride and a sore backside. She reached up to unfasten her riding hat. David laid it beside him on the ground but continued to hold her. She sat on the damp ground, huddled into his warm chest. Sighing, she closed her eyes and breathed in his scent. He smelled divine; minty and citrusy with an undertone of alpha male.

'Only my backside,' she mumbled. 'I'm alright. Just give me a minute...' She drew up her knees and leaned against him, wishing she could stay in this position all day. David looked down at her, relieved she was unhurt, but also acknowledging how good she felt in his arms. Opening her eyes to glance up at him, Kate was disconcerted to see him looking at her lips. Slowly, Kate sat up and David helped her to her feet. Annie was watching them shrewdly, having tied the calmed horses to the fence.

David looked at Kate self-consciously. 'Well, I'm glad you're okay,' he blustered. 'Can't have my assistant injuring herself before an expedition.'

Kate became instantly alert. She looked at David, scrutinising his face. 'What did you say?' she asked stupidly.

David finally looked into her eyes and held her gaze. 'I want you to come to Egypt with me - as my assistant. If you think you might like that job?'

David nearly fell back to the ground as Kate threw herself at him, wrapping her arms tightly around his neck. '*Yes!*' she exclaimed ecstatically. 'Yes! I accept! Thank you so much!'

Annie watched the pair, and wondered why David looked as if his heart might break. He was unable to resist sliding his arms around Kate's back and inhaling the sweet scent of her hair. Kate pulled back a little, her hands sliding down to rest on his chest. David saw concern in her lovely eyes.

'What about Steven?' she asked.

David smiled; it was typical of Kate to think of another's welfare before her own. 'He'll be going, too.'

'Are you sure you need us both? Where are we going?'

'You'll both have plenty of work to do. And we're going to Amarna.'

'Amarna...'

David saw her eyes grow distant, and felt a pang of jealousy as he guessed she was reminiscing about her time in Amarna with Edwin Ford. 'We can discuss the details at dinner. Are you okay to ride?'

Kate returned to the present, her body suddenly feeling cold as his arms dropped from her shoulders. 'Yes, but I have lots of questions -'

'They can wait,' he interrupted, picking up her riding hat and refastening it under her chin. 'Get back on your horse.'

Kate walked slowly towards Zack, her thoughts tumbling haphazardly in her head. *Is this why he's been stuck in meetings and conference calls for weeks? How long has he been planning this and why didn't he ask me first?* It seemed unlikely that David would be allowed to take two assistants on an expedition. *How can I be useful on an archaeological dig? Why would he want to take me with him?* Avoiding further speculation, Kate untied Zack's reins from the fence and stroked the horse's nose. Zack lowered his head and nudged her shoulder as if in repentance.

'It's alright, sweetheart,' she crooned softly. 'I'm sorry I scared you.' She kissed the horse's nose, whispering softly as Zack's ears twitched. Kate pulled her packet of Polo mints from her pocket and gave one to Zack, ignoring David's disapproving look and his muttered comment that the horse should not be rewarded for bad behaviour.

'Are you going to stand there kissing him all day?' David asked.

'We all need to be kissed sometimes...' she told him, arching her eyebrows. She was surprised to see him blush, and hid a smile as she hoisted herself back into the saddle. Annie insisted Kate walk around the paddock to make sure both horse and rider were calm enough to take to the bridle path. She then allowed them to continue their ride.

Zack walked along the path dejectedly, as if ashamed of unseating his rider. Ginger, however, was jumpy and eager to move at a faster pace. Once they reached the beach, the magnificent chestnut mare pranced impatiently on the sand.

'She wants to gallop,' David observed, reining in Ginger once again. He looked along the deserted beach. 'Can you wait here while I let her stretch her legs?'

'Can't we come, too?' Kate asked, already knowing what his answer would be.

'I don't want you to gallop, especially out here in the open. Keep Zack on a tight rein - his instinct will be to follow Ginger.'

Kate patted Zack's neck and sighed in disappointment. She adjusted her position in the saddle in order to hold Zack in place, while David headed towards the calm water's edge. He urged Ginger into a trot, then into a canter and finally, when he was halfway down the long stretch of

280

sand, Ginger sprung into a gallop. Zack pawed at the sand, but Kate kept him still as she watched David lean lower over Ginger's burnished neck. The surf splashed around the horse's pounding hooves, her mane flying free in the breeze. They slowed at the end of the beach and turned, accelerating into a gallop for the return journey. Kate watched in awe, holding her breath at the impressive spectacle of horse and rider in perfect harmony. Gradually, they slowed to a controlled canter, then a fast trot. When they had almost reached Kate and Zack, Kate urged Zack forward into a trot.

'Show off!' Kate called to David, as she and Zack trotted past with their respective heads in the air. Kate followed the line of the surf, David cantering to catch up. He saw Kate shortening the reins and sitting deeper in the saddle.

'Don't you dare!' he warned her.

Kate glanced at him, a challenge in her eyes. 'Dare what?' she asked innocently, and kicked Zack lightly into a graceful canter. As they cantered along the empty beach, Kate experienced a wondrous sense of freedom which made her want to shout triumphantly into the breeze. Zack's canter was fast and smooth; clearly he was enjoying the pace as much as Kate. She laughed with pure joy, aware that David and Ginger were closing the distance between them. Zack pulled at the bit, wanting to outrun the other horse, but Kate would not let him speed up. As they neared the bridle path which led onto the beach, she gradually slowed the horse. Patting Zack's neck, she leaned over to kiss his thick mane. 'Well done, darling,' she murmured to him. 'Thank you so much!'

David's irritation faded when he saw Kate's face flushed with happiness, her euphoric smile displaying her captivating dimples. Her eyes sparkled with exhilaration and she breathed deeply of the fresh sea air, standing up in the stirrups to stretch her back; keeping Zack back from a full gallop had taken all her strength. She glanced at David coyly, before guiding Zack back up the bridle path.

Annie was in the stable yard when they returned. She smiled at Kate's joyful face and chuckled at David's perturbed expression. 'Good ride?' she asked Kate, holding Zack's reins while Kate slid from the saddle.

'Oh, it was wonderful, Annie!' Kate enthused. 'We cantered!' She glanced sidelong at David, who had dismounted and was leading Ginger to the middle of the yard for a cool-down walk. She giggled like a naughty schoolchild, and Annie raised a bemused eyebrow. 'David's not pleased. He told me not to canter, but I didn't listen.'

Annie snorted derisively. 'Since when did men always know what was best for us women?' She patted Kate's cheek. 'You look much better now, dear.'

Kate smiled affectionately at Annie as she led Zack to join David and Ginger. After a few circuits of the yard, they led the tired horses to their stalls and removed their tack. Kate fed Zack two more mints while she stroked his neck and kissed his cheek. 'I love you, Zack,' she murmured, scratching his nose. 'You're my sweet boy.' She was unaware that David was watching her over the stall door.

'You're spoiling him,' he pointed out, but his voice held the same warmth she saw in his gaze. Kate smiled lovingly at Zack as the horse gazed at her adoringly with liquid brown eyes.

'He deserves it,' she declared, kissing Zack one final time before leaving his stall. David remained where he was, forcing Kate to brush against him. Looking up at him, Kate saw a stern look on his sun-warmed face. She put on a look of repentance. 'I'm sorry if I made you cross.' Despite her efforts, her lips twitched.

'No, you're not. You took an unnecessary risk, especially after falling off. I would have preferred you to have cantered in the paddock, to begin with.'

'David, I've played it safe all my life,' she told him quietly. 'But thank you for looking out for me.' She smiled at him. 'I've always wanted to canter along a beach, near the water's edge. You've made one of my wishes come true.'

'You cantered well,' he said grudgingly. 'You have a very good seat.'

Kate chuckled as she saw him flush at his comment. 'Oh, do I really?'

David sighed in exasperation. 'You can be *so* irritating!' He walked out of the stable, Kate laughing as she followed him into the yard. There, she embraced Annie and obediently got in the car as David held her door open. Annie walked round to the driver's side with him.

'Don't waste time, laddie,' she advised him quietly. 'Snap her up before someone beats you to it.'

'Even if that were a possibility,' David replied, his voice low. 'It's too late. She has already been snapped up. Kate and I can only be friends.' Uncharacteristically, David caught Annie in a quick hug before climbing into the car and starting the engine.

'No more maudlin music,' he told Kate. 'Find something else.'

They enjoyed a relaxed journey back to Edinburgh, the sea sparkling on their right and a clear blue sky overhead. Kate was desperate for information on the expedition to Amarna, but David insisted she wait until dinner and stop distracting him with her persistent questions. He drove her home, studiously ignoring her pouting lips as he retrieved her riding gear from the boot, and informed her he would return at five o'clock.

Too distracted to do anything constructive, Kate wandered aimlessly around the garden. She wished she could speak to Jess, but calling her friend on Erin's wedding day would be completely unacceptable. Kate hoped their day was going well and looked forward to seeing the wedding photos. She thought about phoning Ben, or her mother, but decided it would be best to wait until she had all the details of the expedition before breaking the news. David had asked her not to contact Steven, as the intern had not yet been briefed about his new assignment. The prospect of returning to Amarna filled Kate with excitement but also trepidation. Regardless of what she might encounter in Egypt, Kate resolved to perform her duties to the best of her abilities, for David's sake. Naturally, her mind wandered to the handsome, complicated archaeologist. He had looked stunning on the back of a galloping horse, completely in control of the powerful animal. Kate quivered involuntarily and decided to occupy herself with some housework before sinking into a hot, scented bath to ease her aching backside.

David rang the doorbell at exactly five o'clock, and when Kate opened the door he gawped like an idiot. She was wearing a simply-cut dress of peacock blue satin. The sweetheart neckline exposed a modest expanse of smooth, creamy-coloured skin. Capped sleeves hid the tops of her shoulders and the hemline rested just above her stocking-clad knees. The dress elegantly skimmed curves which had diminished in the stress of the last few months. Her dark hair shone, the waves curling around her face and caressing her neck. Small Ceylon sapphire studs twinkled in her ear lobes, a matching gold necklace hung around her throat. Her make-up accentuated her dark eyes and long lashes, and David noticed she was wearing lipstick in a very flattering shade of red.

David stood on the path, his lips parted as his brain fumbled for words. His open stare made Kate blush; only Edwin had looked at her with such intensity, as if he could see into her soul. To break the spell, Kate reached for her bag and the velvet jacket which matched her dress. Leaving the hall light on, she locked her front door. David held the car door open for her.

'You don't have to do that, you know,' she told him with a smile.

'My grandfather taught me to treat women with respect,' he replied hoarsely. He cleared his throat as he closed Kate's door. She watched him walk in front of the car, thinking how handsome he looked in a blue-grey suit with a pale blue, striped shirt. It was David's turn to blush, when he caught her look of appraisal.

'That colour suits you,' he murmured self-consciously as he fastened his seatbelt.

Kate smiled graciously. 'Ditto.'

David parked in Melville Street, and they walked the short distance to the restaurant. Crossing Shandwick Place was reminiscent of crossing a bomb site; the road was scarred by a wide trench which ran the length of the street, another casualty of the interminable tram works. Ugly metal fencing surrounded the site and pedestrians crossed the street using narrow metal gangways. The restaurant was an oasis of calm by comparison, the interior softly lit by wall lamps. Kate traversed the polished marble floor carefully, petrified of slipping in her high heels. The handsome young waiter showed them to a secluded corner table, gallantly helping Kate with her jacket and pulling out her chair under David's unappreciative gaze. Once they had ordered, Kate leaned forward and gazed at David eagerly.

'Please, David, tell me about the expedition!' she pleaded. 'You've made me wait long enough!'

David's expression and tone were business-like. 'For us, it will be a teaching expedition,' he began. 'The university offers the trip to second and third year students. Amarna is looked after by a charitable trust, which is trying to conserve the area and restore some of the monuments. They're fighting an on-going battle with a nearby village, which is expanding towards the old city. The village's own cemetery is in danger of encroaching on the edge of the city, but the villagers seem unconcerned. The trust has set up a new scheme where interested parties can donate towards the rebuilding of the temple.' He stopped to sip from his glass. 'This year, our group will be excavating graves in the southern cemetery. As you know, we can learn a lot about the Egyptian way of life from forensically examining bones.' He observed Kate's grimace of distaste. 'There will be other groups from other countries, but we'll all have our own areas to excavate. Unlike the old days, when archaeologists vied for prime sites.' He grinned ruefully.

Placing the starters on the table, the waiter opened Kate's napkin and placed it delicately on her lap, unaware of David's narrowed eyes.

'What do you need me to do?' she asked, once the waiter had gone. 'I'm not an archaeologist - how can I be of use?'

'I want you to be the student liaison. In my experience, many of them need a bit of reassurance before embarking on their first expedition. You can help prepare them, so you'll need to learn all about

Amarna and the conditions they can expect to face when they're out there. You'll probably have to supervise their travel arrangements and make sure they have the necessary vaccinations. Out there, you'll be their support -'

Kate frowned. 'You want me to mother them? I thought you didn't like me to hone my maternal instincts?'

David shrugged, looking shifty. 'Well, it's not something *I'm* good at, is it?' he retorted. 'You'll be responsible for organising the work groups and collecting their reports each day for collation. On the archaeological side, you'll be doing some excavating and cataloguing.'

'Been there, done that,' Kate muttered carelessly as she speared a cube of melon.

David tilted his head. 'You remember being there before?' he asked in amazement. 'What do you remember?'

Kate looked at her plate, wary of discussing her past life any further. 'I don't remember my past life in its entirety, David,' she said, her voice low so she could not be overheard. 'Just images, scenes, feelings.'

'Of what kind?' he persisted.

Kate looked at him meaningfully. 'Many are of a personal nature.'

'Oh,' he muttered, playing with his salad. 'Well, can you tell me what you remember of Amarna?'

Kate shrugged. 'I lived in a tent, then a claustrophobic mud-brick hut. I think work-wise I was confined to the cataloguing tent. Edwin was intent on keeping me safe.' She flushed at the memory of him. 'I must have badgered him, because I recall a day when I was allowed to dig in an area surrounded by walls. I had to descend a ladder to get there, and I used small tools. That's when I found the tablet etched with the love letter for Nefertiti.'

'Which is now in the Cairo museum.' David curbed his natural instinct to interrogate her further. His curiosity was tempered by his jealousy of Edwin Ford, and the hold he still had over Kate.

'I believe so,' Kate smiled, her eyes distant. 'I remember Edwin being angry because his wife shunned corsets and ladylike clothing in favour of breeches and a shirt. But Victorian Kate knew how to use her womanly wiles to get round him. He gave me my first taste of Arabic coffee…'

'I wonder if you'll like it this time,' David mused, reaching out to touch her clenched fist as it rested on the table.

David's touch brought Kate back to the present. 'Where will we be staying?' she inquired.

'We can spend a few nights out in a tent if you want to,' he teased. 'But Amarna has a fairly modern centre with dormitories, shower rooms and intermittent Wi-Fi. We'll be based there. You and I will fly out a couple of days before the training expedition starts on the eleventh of December. The students will be out in the field for ten days. I'll be there for a fortnight, but you can come home with the students if you wish.'

David paused to finish his salad, aware that the waiter was hovering nearby. Sure enough, as soon as David placed his cutlery on his empty plate, the waiter swooped in to clear the plates. A second waiter arrived to place their main course before them, generously sprinkling each plate with parmesan and black pepper.

'How much will the trip cost?' Kate asked tentatively.

David took a mouthful of hot lasagne to give him time to formulate an answer, wincing as the food burnt his tongue. Kate was so sharp and inquisitive, she would spot any ambiguity he was careless enough to reveal. 'Well,' he began carefully. 'You should understand that Adam Gray was not pleased with my request to take you, initially. I had to elucidate the advantages in order to bring him round to the idea. As a result, he has a few tasks for you to perform while you are in Egypt. He wants to meet with us on Monday. He insists, however, that you use your paid holiday allowance to go on the expedition. The museum will provide a little of the funding. Since I'm permitted to take one assistant, the university will also provide funding. We'll have to pay for our flights to London, and for our vaccinations, if necessary. Obviously, you'll need some spending money. I'm sorry, Kate, it's the best deal I could negotiate.'

Kate reached over to touch his arm in reassurance. 'David, you did brilliantly! It's more than I deserve, given my lack of qualifications. But what about Steven?'

David looked pleased with himself. 'He'll be helping us to an extent - I intend to send him out with the students and oversee their orientation. They'll be flying out a couple of days before us, you see. But I've managed to arrange for him to assist an archaeologist who is currently working in Amarna for the Egypt Exploration Fund, and so they'll pay Steven's expenses.'

'Who will he be working for?'

'Ethan,' David murmured, looking at his food. 'Hopefully, Steven won't pick up too many bad habits.'

'Is Steven happy with this arrangement?'

'I called him this afternoon. He seemed pleased - even more so when I told him you would be coming, too.'

Kate grinned. 'He's such a sweetie!'

David raised an eyebrow. 'As I recall, that wasn't your first impression.' He smiled as she giggled. 'Can we eat now, or are you still channelling your nosey journalist?'

Kate smiled her way through their meal, her eyes alight with excitement at the prospect of a trip to Egypt with David and Steven. Her joy was infectious, lightening David's own heart. He stole pasta from her plate and allowed her to taste his lasagne. They abstained from dessert, finishing the meal with coffee instead. Kate then battled with David's masculine pride over payment of the bill. She unashamedly donned a wide-eyed, hurt and pouting expression which forced him to surrender and let her pay half. Her expression changed to one of wicked satisfaction as soon as the bill was paid. She deliberately irked David further by smiling coquettishly at the waiter as he helped her with her jacket. David felt an overwhelming urge to smack her curvaceous backside as she passed him in the restaurant doorway. Instead, he looked down at her high-heeled suede shoes.

'Can you walk in those shoes, or shall I get the car?'

'I can walk, thank you very much!' she replied tartly, but took the arm he offered in case she caught her heel in a crack in the uneven pavement. The temperature had dropped, and a breeze played with Kate's curls as they walked up bustling Lothian Road to the Usher Hall. The reddening sky hinted at another beautiful day for Sunday, although dark clouds were rolling in from Fife.

Their seats were in the stalls and offered a good view and plenty of legroom for David's long legs. Kate found his attentiveness endearing; he had bought her a programme, offered to take her jacket to the cloakroom, asked if she desired a drink and ensured she was comfortably seated. Kate wistfully acknowledged that she had not been treated so considerately for quite some time.

The first half of the concert was superb; their seats offered an unparalleled quality of sound, and Kate was captivated. As the temperature in the theatre increased, David became aware of Kate's perfume. A faint, intoxicating scent. Glancing at her, he couldn't help noticing the way her lips were parted, the rise and fall of her chest as she watched the orchestra, entranced. Sensing his eyes on her, Kate turned to him. David smiled sheepishly and returned his attention to the orchestra.

During the interval, David bought them each a soft drink at the bar while Kate waited in a corner of the crowded room. She watched David weave his way through groups of people with two glasses in his hands.

A trio of older women stood in his path. They all wore inappropriately revealing dresses, and watched David with predatory eyes. One of the women deliberately stepped in front of David, and he blushed as he accidentally brushed the woman's ample bosom with the back of his hand.

'Oh, you naughty boy!' the woman simpered, as her friends giggled girlishly. Kate pressed her lips together as she fumed silently.

'I'm so sorry!' David spluttered.

'That's quite alright, darling,' she purred, stroking David's arm and squeezing his bicep. With a tight, apologetic smile, David kept moving towards Kate.

'Perhaps you should start wearing a badge with your preferences on it,' Kate commented, throwing the woman an icy look as she took her drink from David. 'It would save you a lot of embarrassment.'

David took a gulp of his drink. 'My taste in women shall remain private,' he grumbled.

Kate stared at him, the huddling cougars forgotten. *There. He's said it. At last I know for certain.*

'What?' David asked, discomfited by her look of astonishment. 'What did I say?'

'Nothing...' Kate murmured and concentrated on her glass of lemonade.

David slipped his arm around Kate and drew her towards him, out of the way of a large group of people who walked past them. He noticed she avoided his gaze. 'Kate, have you been listening to idle gossip about me?' When she didn't answer he cupped her chin and lifted her face so she would look at him. Her cheeks were pink with embarrassment. 'Kate?'

'It was way back when I started working at the museum. I didn't know anybody - how was I supposed to know what was gossip and what was the truth?'

'And what did you hear?'

'It doesn't matter...'

'Tell me anyway.' His eyes darkened.

Kate sighed. 'Someone said you were gay,' she muttered quickly. 'But it wouldn't matter to me if you were, as long as it made you happy.'

'You could've just asked me.' *You should have asked me weeks ago.*

She looked almost taken aback by the notion. 'No, I couldn't! It's none of my business!'

David looked crestfallen. 'Oh, Kate...'

The bell rang to announce the start of the second half of the concert, and David and Kate followed the tide of people returning to their seats. David's hand rested on the small of Kate's back protectively. Dismayed by this latest revelation, his thoughts churned chaotically throughout the rest of the concert. He could hardly focus on the music, which began to sound almost dissonant. When he started drumming his fingers on his leg, Kate reached over and squeezed his hand to stop him fidgeting.

It was drizzling when they emerged from the Usher Hall, and much cooler. David surveyed the wet pavement, concerned that Kate might slip. 'Wait here and I'll bring up the car,' he told Kate as they stood on the steps.

Kate buttoned her jacket and turned up the collar to keep out the cold. 'I'd rather get some fresh air,' she decided and slipped her arm through his. 'But you can stop me from falling on my behind. Again.'

As they walked down Lothian Road, Kate sensed the change in David's mood and knew she was to blame. 'I'm sorry if I've upset you, David,' she said earnestly. 'Don't let it spoil a lovely day.'

David stroked the hand which rested in the crook of his elbow. 'I'm disappointed that you listened to spiteful gossip,' he explained, making Kate feel worse. 'You have to realise that I've ruffled a few feathers in the time I've worked at the museum. I'm very protective of my privacy, and this irritates those who like to know every detail of other people's lives, probably because they have nothing better to do. It seems that people will just make things up to be malicious.' *And why the hell would you think I was gay, given the way I behave towards you?*

Kate refrained from pointing out that David liked to know every detail of *her* life. 'So when Sleazy Stan was talking about seeing you at CC Blooms, he was just being malicious?' Kate saw a nerve twitch in David's jaw.

'No, I was there.' David prepared himself for an interrogation and knew he would have to provide answers, given Kate's openness about her past life regression.

'With a woman?' Kate's voice was strained.

'I went with Ethan. He's a bad influence on me, but that's no excuse.'

'So you met her in the bar,' Kate probed. David winced as he felt her hand drop from her arm. 'Have you seen her again?'

David suddenly felt wretched, walking beside this woman who was so innocent. 'No, Kate. It wasn't like that.' He took a deep breath. 'It was a drunken one night stand.'

Kate scowled at him accusingly. 'Did *she* know that? Or is she currently torturing herself waiting for you to call her?'

'She knew what was going on. She didn't even ask for my number, which led me to believe it was acceptable behaviour for her. It wasn't acceptable for me, however. I left her flat in the middle of the night and spent an hour in the shower. It wasn't my finest moment - I'm not proud of myself. I don't make a habit of behaving that way and I don't plan to do it again anytime soon. And, as far as I'm aware, I'm the only one who was hurt by my actions.' He glared at her angrily. 'There! Is that enough information for you? You would have made a really good journalist, you know!'

They had reached Shandwick Place, but instead of walking towards Melville Street, Kate headed for the bus stop on Queensferry Street.

'Where are you going?' David called impatiently.

'I'll get the bus,' she replied, wounded by his outburst.

David caught her hand and stopped her in her tracks. 'You will not get the bus,' he told her firmly. 'I'm taking you home -'

'I'll get the bus,' she repeated, firing him a look of defensive anger.

'No, I'll take you home,' he insisted. Aware that they were being watched by a group of sneering teenagers waiting at the bus stop, David pulled Kate into the dingy privacy of Queensferry Street Lane. Gently, he took her face in his hands and looked into her eyes. 'I'm sorry, Kate,' he said. 'I'm sorry. I don't want to discuss that night with you - I'm too ashamed. I don't want you to think badly of me.'

'I don't,' she whispered hoarsely.

'I don't want anything to change between us,' he told her adamantly. 'I value our relationship. A lot. I want things to stay the way they were before you found out about me.'

In the dim light, Kate saw an intensity in his green eyes she hadn't witnessed before. He was being completely honest with her, but it seemed he was also trying to tell her that he didn't want their relationship to advance. She wished she could ask him what sort of relationship he really wanted. She wished she could decide what sort of relationship *she* wanted with *him*.

'I don't want you to treat me differently just because you now know I'm straight.' David wanted desperately to kiss her.

He's right, Kate thought. She would be instinctively wary around a heterosexual man because she had been hurt by one. The vague notion that David might be gay had offered a kind of security for her; they could tease and flirt with one another and not worry about anyone having an agenda. Now everything was different, and she would have to modify her behaviour accordingly. But she still wanted his company, his friendship, and the solace he offered. She asked herself if that would be enough, and at the same time cursed her lack of fidelity to her soulmate.

Floundering for the right words to say, Kate leaned against him. She felt David exhale as his arms encircled her, his cheek resting on the top of her head.

They drove home in silence, both aware that their relationship had altered. The light rain had turned into a downpour which lashed the windscreen. When they parked at Kate's gate, David unfastened his seatbelt in order to get out and open Kate's door. Kate touched his sleeve and shook her head. 'Don't get out,' she told him. 'It's wet.'

David remained silent as Kate left the car and ran up her path. The security light above her door blinked on, illuminating her in a pool of golden light as she slid her key into the lock. Stepping into the safety and warmth of her home, she closed the door on him.

Kate laid her mug of chamomile tea on her bedside table and climbed into bed. Even though she had donned pyjamas and socks, she felt cold. She picked up Bastet and held the cat against her heart, unable to stem the flow of tears.

So much for making new memories...

CHAPTER 17

Adam Gray's secretary announced Kate's arrival before ushering her into the deputy director's office. Gray sat behind his oversized desk, his hands clasped under his narrow chin. Steven and David were seated before him on the other side of the desk. Studiously avoiding David's quizzical stare, Kate took the empty seat next to Steven. Despite her nervousness, she could feel a comforting presence in the familiar room, as if someone were watching over her. She raised her eyes to look directly at Gray.

'Well, Miss Grahame,' he began, in his clipped voice. 'I understand you've agreed to travel to Egypt as Professor Young's assistant. He has been working tirelessly to secure your position.'

Out of the corner of her eye, she saw David shift restlessly in his seat. 'I'm very grateful,' she said to Gray.

'You realise, of course, that your lack of appropriate qualifications makes this whole situation highly irregular?' His eyes locked with hers meaningfully.

Horrified, Kate realised that Gray was implying that she and David shared a personal attachment. She sat up straight and stared at the pompous little man, her eyes flashing. 'I intend to work hard while I'm in Egypt, Deputy Director,' she said tersely. 'And I'll undertake whatever training is necessary for me to do my job.'

Gray snorted. 'I hardly think you can become a qualified archaeologist in four months, Miss Grahame!' Kate heard Steven's sharp intake of breath. 'And I hope you will apply the same zealous attitude to your work here.'

'Kate has been reading my course notes, Deputy Director,' Steven interjected. 'She's currently working on year two, and studies in her own time.' He bravely held Gray's steely gaze.

David sighed, barely concealing his exasperation and contempt. 'For the purpose of this trip, Kate will only have to learn about Amarna and be acquainted with current excavations. For the most part, she will be acting as my student liaison. I'm sure you will agree that she already possesses the skills needed for that role.' He gazed at Gray, his mouth set in a grim line. They had already discussed Kate's responsibilities at great length, so there was no need to raise the matter again. David rankled at Gray's time-wasting, as well as his apparent need to bully Kate.

Gray cast the subject aside with a wave of his hand and turned his attention back to Kate. 'While you are in Egypt, I want you to provide us with regular reports of the work undertaken. In addition, it would be useful for you to prepare a daily blog for the museum website, so that people can see how our money is being spent.' Kate nodded compliantly. Gray took a deep breath, and his eyes narrowed meanly as he continued. 'As you will be aware, we require extra holiday cover at this time of year. You should consider volunteering for extra weekend shifts, aiming to work at least one extra weekend every month.' He surveyed the group before him; Kate looked acquiescent, as expected, while the two men were staring at him with impotently truculent expressions. 'Right, I have another meeting, so you can go. Have a good day.' He stood up, the signal for them to leave his office. The three of them filed out past the secretary. Steven touched Kate's arm in a gesture of consolation as he strode past her and hastened along the corridor.

'Kate,' David called.

Kate rolled her eyes, too disheartened to deal with David. She stopped and turned, assessing his mood. He wasn't happy, that much was obvious from the brooding eyes and set jaw. She inhaled deeply, tired from another sleepless night and impatient to get through the day so she could go home again and think. 'I have a lot of work to do this morning, Professor Young,' she told him impassively.

David winced at the sound of his title. 'I'm sorry,' he began. 'I didn't realise he was going to treat you that way. Making you work weekends is unfair.'

Kate shrugged, glancing in the direction of Gray's office to make sure they were not being overheard. 'I already work the occasional Saturday, so it's not a big deal. I want to go to Egypt, and this is a way for me to do it. I'll adapt. As I've said before, I'm grateful for the opportunity.' She turned to proceed along the corridor, but David took her arm.

'I tried to call you several times yesterday.'

David saw her eyes flash defiantly as she looked up at him. 'Sunday is a no-phones day for me. Besides, I was out for most of the day, and I left my phone at home.' It was a slightly twisted version of the truth; Kate had gone to the supermarket with her mother in the morning and had spent the afternoon at home, alone.

'And you just ignored the "missed calls" message, and your answering machine?'

Kate floundered. 'My mobile was off -'

'No, it wasn't.'

Kate gave an exasperated sigh. 'Professor,' she hissed. 'I don't have the time or inclination to discuss this right now.'

Riled by her intractability, David opened the door of the office behind her and guided her inside the room. Closing the door, he leaned against it. 'Well, I do,' he growled. 'So please explain why you avoided my calls. I only wanted to make sure you were alright.'

Kate felt anger rise within her, and clenched her fist. 'My welfare is not your responsibility. Now let me out! If we're discovered in here, the gossips will have a field day. Gray already suspects that there's something inappropriate going on, and I would like to keep my job.'

'I don't care about gossips,' he asserted, folding his arms. 'You should know that by now.'

'Well, I do! As a divorcee, I already have a questionable reputation in some quarters.'

'People who think that way are not worthy of your concern. You know the truth behind your divorce and that's all that matters. Why didn't you call me back yesterday?'

Kate averted her eyes. 'I think it would be best if we kept our relationship professional,' she murmured, aware she sounded unconvincing. 'There's too much at stake...'

David straightened, his expression indignant. 'Women! You're all the bloody same!' he spat. 'I have never judged you, not once. Can't you afford me the same courtesy? This is all because of one stupid slip-up, isn't it?'

'Don't you swear at me!' she hissed back. 'I don't care about your promiscuity! It's you who's getting all dramatic about it!' Kate *did* care, but it was time to ease her emotional burdens, not take on more. 'You are a complete enigma, David Young, and I'm tired of trying to work you out. I need to fix myself - I can't fix you as well. Now bloody well let me out, before we set tongues wagging!' She walked purposefully towards him.

David couldn't help himself; Kate was even more beautiful when she was angry. Edwin Ford had been right. 'Maybe we should give them something to talk about...'

Kate stopped, stunned by his remark. She wagged an admonitory finger at him. 'See! Prime example! You claim you just want us to be "friends" and then you come out with something like that!' She stamped her foot, and David bit his lip to prevent a snigger. 'Stop flirting with me!'

'Oh, of course,' David's voice dripped sarcasm. 'I have to back off because you're waiting for the great Edwin Ford to come back and sweep you off your feet! What man could possibly match him?'

Kate became aware of a sudden heaviness in the room, as though a black cloud hovered over them in the small office. Realising where she stood, she looked around the room, an almost fearful expression on her face. She remembered the wooden desk littered with papers which were held in place by the rock paperweight. And she vividly recalled being soundly kissed while her husband leaned against the closed door.

'Oh God, what is it now?' David asked in exasperation. 'What idyllic memory have you recalled this time? Is the perfect man here in the room with us?'

The light blinked out, leaving them in complete darkness in the windowless room. Kate squealed and in her haste to leave the room she walked into David, who put his arms around her to calm her. He could feel her trembling as she clutched his shirt.

'It's only a blown light bulb,' he soothed her. 'What's the matter with you? Are we in *his* office?'

'Yes! Please open the door!' Kate begged, feeling guilty and frightened at the same time.

'Forgive me, first.'

Kate squirmed in his grasp, but his arms tightened around her. 'Forgive you for what, you idiot?'

'For whatever I did to hurt your feelings. For my flaws, and my failures. Stop wriggling - you're standing on my foot!'

'Stop sending me mixed messages, David.'

'I'm not the only one who sends out mixed messages, Kate...'

Kate knew he was right - she was guilty of flirting with him, too. 'Well, I'm sorry,' she murmured. 'We both need to stop it. It's not fair.'

David hesitated. 'Then can I try and explain my real feelings? Since we're in the dark?'

'No,' Kate replied emphatically. 'We have to work together, and I want to focus on my job. I don't want to complicate my life any further. I want our relationship to be...platonic, but it might be better to limit the time we spend together to working hours only. We both have issues to deal with.'

David lowered his head to touch the top of hers. At that moment, he felt he could be happy being a poor substitute for Edwin Ford, if only for a few weeks. 'Are you sure that's how you really feel?'

'Yes,' she lied.

'Then perhaps you could explain to me why you're holding me so tightly...'

Kate hadn't realised that she had slipped her arms around his waist, and pressed her cheek against his chest. She'd been breathing in Eau-de-David, enveloped in the safety of his embrace. She pulled back, cross with him again and equally angry at her own lack of restraint.

'I'm scared of the dark,' she muttered.

David snorted in disbelief. 'Unlikely.'

'Please, David,' she implored. 'You said you didn't want our relationship to change.'

In the darkness, he stroked her thick, wavy hair. 'The only thing which has changed is your perception of me. My feelings remain the same -'

'Don't,' she begged. *I'll only hurt you.* She lifted her face and realised that he had lowered his head towards her. She could feel his breath on her lips.

'You're saving yourself, aren't you?' he asked, sounding utterly deflated. 'You're waiting for the 2012 version of Edwin Ford. How can you be sure you'll find him? Or that you'll like him, if you do?'

'I don't expect you to understand,' Kate murmured, her voice hoarse with the tangle of emotions she felt. 'I don't fully understand it myself.'

'Try me.'

Kate vowed this would be the last time she confided in David Young. He was getting too close to her heart. 'I remember being with him,' she breathed. 'So intensely. And now I'm without him. I feel as if I'm missing a part of myself, and it hurts.'

David sighed in resignation. 'Now *that*, I understand.' He groped for the door handle and opened the door. As he blinked against the harsh light of the white-walled corridor, he came face to face with Gray's snooty secretary. She stared, appalled, as David and a mortified Kate emerged from the dark room. David pointedly tucked in his shirt as he gave the woman a disarming smile. 'The light bulb needs changing in there,' he commented, smirking at her scandalised expression. He glanced at Kate, who glowered at him and strode along the corridor, her face scarlet.

David and Steven spent the rest of the morning in one of the workrooms, while Kate prepared the worksheets for Friday's class. Steven returned to their office at lunchtime and sat down at his desk, scooting his chair across to Kate's desk and leaning his elbows on the table top.

'I'm glad you're coming to Egypt,' he announced.

Kate smiled as she continued to type. 'Are you looking forward to going?' she asked him, and was surprised to see him frown.

'I suppose so. I'm just not sure about Ethan.'

Kate's fingers hovered over the keyboard. 'Why?' She tried to sound offhand. 'Have you met him?'

'I met him a couple of times when I was a student. He's not at all like Professor Young, and he's got a reputation for being a bit of a maverick.'

Kate gave Steven an affectionate smile and resumed her swift typing. 'I'm sure you'll be fine, Steven. Besides, Professor Young and I will be there with you.' Steven grunted. 'How was your date on Friday night?'

'Good, I think,' he replied, his handsome young face brightening at the memory. 'At least this one hadn't heard of Professor David Young.'

Kate glanced up again, puzzled. 'What do you mean?'

Steven rolled his eyes at Kate's lack of understanding. 'When I date girls with connections to the university or the museum, it seems some of them go out with me in order to try and get to him.'

'Get away!' Kate exclaimed, horrified. 'That's terrible!'

'I know -' Steven stopped talking as Nick entered the room and sat down to check his emails. He was followed a few minutes later by David. Kate and Steven looked up as Nick triumphantly punched the air.

'I've got permission to organise a ghost tour in the museum for Halloween!' he explained, doing a little victory dance in his seat. He looked hopefully at Kate. 'I'll need ideas, ghost stories, and maybe volunteers to dress up like they do on the Edinburgh city ghost tours. Kate, can you help with some research if you've got time?'

'Sure, Nick. Whatever I can do to help.'

'You should definitely include the filing room near Gray's office, Nick,' David advised, his eyes on Kate. 'I've just been in there and the light went out.' David watched Kate's face turn pink and felt a sadistic delight in her discomfiture. 'There was a decided fluctuation in the temperature of the room, and a heady - sorry, *heavy* atmosphere.'

'I'll see what I can dig up,' Nick decided. 'Thanks, Professor Young.'

'You're welcome. I'm sure Kate could discover some background information on that room.' He sauntered over to Kate's desk, wearing a deadpan expression. 'I'll be doing tomorrow's ancient Egypt workshop,' he informed her. Kate's heart sank, but she kept working. 'I understand you'll be presenting your piece on the estimable Mister Ford?' Kate nodded once, her expression stony. 'Could you ensure the seminar room is set up properly and ensure we have all the equipment we'll need?'

Kate glanced at him disdainfully. 'Nick is my Events team supervisor this week. You'll have to check with him.'

Steven, caught in the middle, cringed. He felt the relationship between Kate and David was constantly fraught with tension, but didn't understand the cause. Sometimes their exchanges were hilarious, but at other times they seemed ready to explode. Then there were those occasions where he felt as though he were playing gooseberry and wanted to shout at them to get a room.

'Kate will be preparing the room for the workshop, Professor,' Nick called from his corner, flashing Kate a cheeky grin. 'With her usual efficiency and attention to detail.'

Kate looked at David as if she would stick her tongue out at him. Steven decided to intervene before the pair resumed their verbal tussle. 'Are you nearly finished, Katie? We could go for lunch.' He looked up at David inquiringly. 'Do you want to come?'

'I wouldn't want to intrude,' David replied, his tone mildly sarcastic. 'Besides, I've got to run into town to buy a birthday present for my mother - I'm going to spend the weekend with her in London. I had hoped to get the job done yesterday, but my plans were thwarted.' The last sentence was for Kate's benefit, as David had originally hoped to take Kate out on Sunday. He had envisaged a walk in the Gardens, a wander round the Art Gallery, and lunch. He had then hoped to enlist Kate's help to buy his mother's gift. But she had been unreachable, in more ways than one. 'Unfortunately, I'm clueless when it comes to buying presents.'

Kate ignored the wheedling tone which had crept into his voice, but became aware of three pairs of eyes watching her expectantly. She ground her teeth in exasperation. 'Swarovski,' she muttered, not looking up.

'Still clueless,' David said mildly, knowing he was goading her and loving every minute.

Sighing, Kate dropped her hands from the keyboard and addressed him as if he were a child. 'The Swarovski shop is on Princes Street, between Frederick Street and Castle Street. They sell beautiful things for all tastes, and most budgets. The sales assistants are very helpful.' She threw him a scathing look. 'And very pretty.'

Nick chortled behind his computer screen, enjoying the altercation immensely. David's eyes narrowed. 'I don't suppose you could spare half an hour to come and help me choose something?'

'No, I have errands to run. We can look at their website, if you like.'

'That's hardly the same.'

'I'm sure you'll do just fine, Professor. If you're stuck, go for something delicate and subtle.' She smiled brightly at Steven. 'Give me five minutes, and I'll come out with you. I could murder a smoothie!'

Steven clenched his fist to stop his gloved hand trembling as he reached into the display case for the wooden box of Egyptian shabtis. The miniature sarcophagus-shaped people had been recovered from a tomb, the dormant servants of a pharaoh, destined for reanimation in the afterlife and an eternity of servitude. Kate gave him an encouraging smile, but Steven was aware of David's critical stare from behind him. His supervisor was perched on a folding chair he had taken from a hook on a nearby wall, having already reminded his assistants to heed the handling protocols for these artefacts. Carefully, Steven lifted the box of shabtis and placed them in a plastic crate lined with packing material. They would be taken back to the workroom for close examination to ascertain whether they needed any conservation work.

They had erected small barriers around the area to redirect visitors. Steven placed the crate safely beside David's seat and turned back to the display case to gather more of the little slave-people. His confidence growing, he selected a larger figure which had its own individual sarcophagus and put it in the box Kate held up for him.

'Can I ask your advice about something?' he asked quietly.

'Sure,' Kate replied, making sure the shabti was properly protected in its temporary abode.

'When should I call Megan?'

'Megan?'

'My date from Friday.'

'You haven't called her yet?' She gave him a disapproving look as he placed a second figure in the box. Although their voices were low, David could hear their conversation.

'I invited her for coffee on Sunday,' he said defensively, and Kate saw his blue eyes soften. 'I think I really like her, Kate.'

'Where did you meet her?'

'At judo practice.'

Kate snorted. 'So you're dating someone who can beat you up?'

Steven grinned. 'I like quick-witted girls who can defend themselves. And besides, she's really nice. And gorgeous. She has shiny, strawberry-blonde hair, and eyes the colour of cornflowers. She's not tall, but she has a stunning figure -'

'I think I get the picture!' Kate chuckled at the dreamy look in his twinkling eyes.

'So when should I call her? I feel I should play it cool - I don't want her to think I'm desperate. But I don't want to miss the boat, either.'

'Tuesday,' Kate suggested.

'Tuesday? That's *ages* away!'

'It's tomorrow. As you say, you don't want her to think you're a creepy stalker.' Kate threw a mischievous, sidelong glance at David. 'Call her. If she doesn't answer the phone, leave a message. Make sure she hears your voice. Text as a last resort, as the written word can be misconstrued. The personal touch is always better.' She saw by his expression that Steven was slightly puzzled by her advice.

'Of course, she may be the type of awkward wench who won't phone you back,' David growled from behind them. Steven sensed tension and appealed to Kate with a pleading look.

'Don't listen to him,' she advised. 'You're so cute she won't be able to resist you!' Kate laughed as Steven blushed.

David stood. 'Are you two quite finished?' he asked tersely.

'Do we have enough of these?' Kate asked Steven, nodding at the box she held and ignoring her petulant supervisor.

'Yes. We'll take them to the workroom and start examining them.' He placed a card in the display case, apologising to visitors for the missing items. Then he lifted the barriers and took them to the storage cupboard next to the public toilets.

'Doesn't he have sisters of his own?' David asked, locking the display case.

'He was your student for six years,' Kate told him curtly. 'Didn't you ever bother to find out?'

'I teach my students. I don't adopt them.'

'He has a younger brother. No sisters.'

'So he's adopted you as his older sister?'

Kate glared at him, hearing him stress the word 'older'. Before she could spit out a retort, Steven had returned and picked up the crate of shabtis. He led the way to the conservation workroom, where they set the boxes on a table. Kate sat down at the computer to access the records for each piece; they needed to know what damage was already recorded, and update the records accordingly. With David's patient supervision, Steven and Kate examined each shabti under the magnifier to ascertain its condition. Only one of the little figures needed a minor repair, which Steven carried out while Kate updated the database. By the end of the day, they had examined all the shabtis on display and carried out a small amount of conservation work. David informed them that they would be working on the pottery display on Friday afternoon.

Kate slipped out of the museum at the end of her shift and swiftly caught the bus home, relieved that she had escaped without being detained by David. She pushed persistent thoughts of him from her mind as she closed her front door on the world and climbed the stairs to the sanctuary of her bedroom. Stripping off her clothes, Kate poured a warm bath and sank gratefully into the violet-scented water. Still she battled to get David out of her head, to stop speculating on what he had wanted to say in the darkness of Edwin's office. She could not allow herself to get side-tracked by the gorgeous archaeologist whose hypnotic green eyes pulled at her with an almost magnetic force. Her mind returned to the darkened office, and how strong David's chest and arms had felt as he embraced her. Kate reflected that David was very similar to Edwin in build. Like Edwin, David possessed beautiful hands with long, tapering fingers. Her breath caught in her throat as she remembered how skilled Edwin's hands had been at bringing her body to life. Idly, she wondered if David's hands possessed the same dexterity. Growling with frustration and blushing at her thoughts, Kate abandoned her bath and made some dinner.

Afterwards, she sat at the kitchen table to read more of Steven's notes, her laptop beside her so she could search for additional information. The essay she selected was a biography of the female pharaoh Hatshepsut, the daughter of Queen Ahmose and Tuthmosis the First. Ahmose's failure to provide a male heir induced her husband to select a suitable substitute from the royal harem. Prince Tuthmosis, the son of a secondary queen, was married to Princess Hatshepsut. He eventually succeeded his father, but after only three years on the throne Tuthmosis the Second died in mysterious circumstances. The royal couple had only one daughter, Neferure, and so once again an heir was chosen from the harem. Since the new pharaoh was only an infant, Hatshepsut was appointed regent and ran the country efficiently for the next two years. Then, inexplicably, Hatshepsut was crowned king. She ruled Egypt for over twenty years, building magnificent temples, protecting Egypt's borders and masterminding trade agreements with other nations. Her reign was peaceful and prosperous and should have been lauded by historians. Instead, after her death in 1457BC, her monuments were destroyed and her images and titles defaced. No trace of her remained, and it was implied that these acts had been authorised by her vengeful stepson, Tuthmosis the Third.

The essay was eloquent and comprehensive; Steven speculated on her reasons for ascending the throne. He suggested that she had not been an immoral stepmother whose goal had been to seize power. Instead of fearing her stepson and possibly having him murdered, she had groomed him to be her successor.

Far from languishing impotently in the background, Tuthmosis the Third had been well-educated and became the Commander in Chief of the army. For reasons which were unclear, Tuthmosis removed his father's body from the tomb he shared with Hatshepsut in the Valley of the Kings and reburied him elsewhere. Yet Steven pointed out that there was no evidence to support the belief that the pharaoh was responsible for the attacks on his stepmother's monuments.

During the female pharaoh's reign, a rumour surfaced that Hatshepsut had fallen in love with her stepson's tutor, and Steven proposed that this scandal could have been the reason that her people tried to erase her from history. Had the powerful, determined ruler been undone by human frailty, a victim of her own desire to connect with another soul?

The essay concluded with an account of how Egyptologists were now restoring damaged inscriptions. Eventually, Hatshepsut would be reinstated to her rightful place in the history of Egypt's eighteenth dynasty.

Enchanted by the story of the formidable female king, Kate searched online to see what else she could discover about the unorthodox Egyptian powerhouse. She discovered that Hatshepsut had charged her masons to depict her as a male pharaoh, complete with masculine figure and a false beard. Her name meant 'Foremost of Noble Ladies'. Many websites displayed pictures of the temples built and restored by the Hatshepsut, which strengthened Kate's resolve to visit Egypt. She could walk in the footsteps of so many compelling characters.

As Kate was reading, an email arrived with a jarring 'ping', inciting her to take a break from her studies. David had sent an email with the names and contact details of the students who would be going on the excursion to Amarna. Although the university would issue information packs to the students, David had advised them to direct any queries about the trip to Kate. Kate would then act as liaison between the students and their professor. David hoped that she would field the largely inconsequential enquiries from apprehensive students preparing for their first expedition.

In a second email, Kate found the aforementioned information pack. She groaned as she realised she would have to become well-acquainted with the extensive document.

Kate exhaled impatiently when a third email arrived from David - couldn't he leave her in peace? This one gave the contact details of a female archaeologist currently working in Amarna, should Kate wish to contact her for information on the project. He also provided the website address for the Amarna Project so she could read about the work which was currently underway. David pointed out that some of the Amarna team provided updates on their work via social media, and suggested she subscribe to their posts. He also asserted that Kate should increase her fitness levels, in preparation for working in the heat of an Egyptian winter. He offered to provide a training programme, which made Kate raise her eyebrows in indignation; she was hardly a couch potato. She typed a brief message to confirm she had received his emails.

Within seconds, he sent a reply. 'You realise you have just contacted me outside working hours?'

Kate tapped her chin with a finger, weighing up the consequences of engaging in a cyberspace bickering session with him.

'You started it. I was just being polite.' She sent the email before common sense prevailed.

'I assumed you would open the email at work tomorrow. It's very late - why are you not tucked up in bed yet?'

'I'm reading. And who says I'm not tucked up in bed already?'

'It's a scientific fact that using electronic devices before bedtime is detrimental to a good night's sleep.'

Kate frowned, wondering if he was being suggestive. In her mind's eye, she saw him sitting in front of the screen with that sly look in his eyes which made a shiver run up her spine.

Another email arrived. 'Do you have Skype?'

Kate started to giggle, realising he was being slightly risqué. 'Yes,' she typed.

'Want to have a video chat?'

Kate could almost feel him leering at her. Hadn't he listened to anything she had said in Edwin's office? 'No. I've seen enough of you for one day.'

'What are you reading?'

Kate hoped she hadn't bruised his ego with her comment. 'I've just read a wonderful essay about Hatshepsut called "Evil Stepmother?" Steven writes with such fervour about her. It's almost a thing of beauty. I loved it.'

'Steven's coursework is excellent, but that's not one of his essays. It's one of mine.'

'Oh...' Kate said aloud.

Steven looked down at the long-stemmed pink rose which had been carefully placed on Kate's desk. He was considering whether he should put it in a mug of water when its intended recipient came through the door. Seeing the puzzlement on Steven's face as he stood behind her desk, Kate gave him a questioning glance. He pointed at the perfect bloom.

'It wasn't me,' he said hastily. 'It was here when I came in. Honest.'

'Again?' Kate picked up the rose and held it delicately to her nose just as David entered the room. He raised an eyebrow at his intern.

'It wasn't me!' Steven repeated, blushing at David's unspoken accusation. He glanced at Kate, whose eyes were inexplicably sad. 'And what d'you mean, again? Does this happen often?'

Kate hadn't noticed David's arrival. She held the rose in her palm, admiring the way dew still clung between the petals. 'A few weeks ago, I found an African violet on my desk...'

'Who's giving you flowers?' Steven asked, intrigued.

Kate shrugged, unable to speculate. She turned towards the door, intending to fetch a mug of water from the kitchen. Seeing David at his desk, she flushed.

'Looks like you have an admirer,' he commented, his face unsmiling. He was surprised when she continued on course for the kitchen without offering a rejoinder. She returned moments later with the mug of water, silently placed the rose in the mug and set it on her desk. Without looking at either of them, Kate left to prepare for that morning's workshop on ancient Egypt.

Kate delivered her presentation on Edwin Ford with the now familiar feeling of a stone weight around her heart. Her ardour for Edwin Ford was all too evident to David, who noticed tears in her eyes as she finished her talk and nodded to him to continue the workshop. As he took up the presentation, he was aware that she left the room for a few moments. Kate stood outside the room, leaning against the cool wall of the corridor, forcing back her tears. Taking a tissue from the pocket of her trousers, she blew her nose and gathered her strength, mentally donning the armour which would protect her. Kate took a deep breath, and returned to the workshop to help the primary five children mummify apples and tour the Egyptian gallery.

David delegated the interpretation of Iufenamun's sarcophagus to Steven while he moved to stand beside Kate. All the children were entranced by the inscriptions on the coffin and crowded around a crouching Steven, listening to his lively chatter. None of the children were daunted by the mummy lying in the case. David nudged Kate gently with his elbow. 'Are you alright?' he asked softly. 'Your presentation was great, but you looked like you were finding it difficult.'

Kate glanced up at him before turning back to watch Steven with the children. 'Was it obvious to everyone in the room?'

'No, just to me. They probably just assumed you were passionate about your subject. You seem unable to hide it.'

Kate rubbed her forehead wearily. 'David, please don't start on me again.'

One of the teachers joined them. She was a kindly woman of about fifty, with curly grey hair and blue eyes which twinkled behind large glasses. 'Your Mister Ford was quite the iconic figure,' she commented to Kate. 'You painted a rather splendid picture of him.'

'Yes,' David added, a hint of bitterness in his tone. 'He puts the rest of us poor archaeologists to shame.' He walked off to lead the group to the Egyptian gallery.

David had taken Kate's advice and excluded the unwrapped mummy from the workshop. Instead, he described how mummies were now examined digitally, using non-invasive scanning techniques. He showed them the scans of Iufenamun, explaining how they had been able to determine that the priest had been around forty when he died. The precise cause of death had not been established, but no trauma had been discovered on the body. His limbs had been individually wrapped, and packing had been placed beneath his skin. Four packages of embalming material could be seen nestling within the chest cavity, and David told his captivated group that these probably contained internal organs. They could also see where scarabs and charms had been placed between the layers of bandages. David went on to describe how a medical artist had used the CT scans to create a plaster model of Iufenamun's skull. Clay was then applied to the model to reconstruct the facial muscles and skin. The completed model of Iufenamun's head was cast in bronze and put on display beside his body.

At the end of the session, David asked for questions and was surprised to see a number of small hands shoot into the air. He beckoned for Steven to join him, and the two men answered all the questions clearly and humorously. Kate felt immensely proud of the pair of them, especially when she saw them both blush at the cheers which accompanied the applause they received from the class.

'And let's not forget Kate,' David called over the noise. 'Please thank her for her inspiring presentation on Edwin Ford. If it weren't for him, the Egyptian gallery would be a lot less interesting.' He led the applause himself, his mouth smiling, and his eyes wistful.

Kate was thankful that she was not required to wear a costume for the afternoon workshop; Nick and a male colleague enacted the fight scene between the Roman soldier and the Caledonian warrior, which drew gales of laughter from the audience. Afterwards, Kate tidied the room and returned to the office in time to hear the phone ringing on Jess's desk. She ran across the room and picked up the receiver.

'Kate Grahame speaking, how may I help you?' she asked. There was a hesitant pause at the other end.

'Is this the Kate Grahame who has just been given a place on the Amarna expedition?' The male caller's voice was deep and slightly distorted, as if he were calling from another country.

'Yes,' Kate replied hesitantly. 'Can I help you?'

'Well, let me see...' the caller drawled. 'My best friend has bent over backwards to secure your position on this trip, even though you are patently unqualified. Perhaps you could tell me *exactly* what role you will be playing, and what your intentions are towards my friend?'

Kate's face reddened. 'My intention is to do my job,' she replied sharply. She looked up as David strolled into the office, his attention on his iPad. 'Now, could you please give me your name and tell me why you're calling?'

Hearing the strain in Kate's voice, David looked up.

'This is Ethan,' the caller announced. 'And I'm looking for Professor David Young. Your boss.'

'Professor Young has just arrived in the office. I'll hand you over to him.'

'Oh, Kate?'

'Yes?'

'I look forward to meeting you in December, so I can see what all the fuss is about.'

Too stunned to comment, Kate passed the phone to David and marched back to her desk. David turned his back to her, but Kate could hear his side of the conversation.

'I wish you'd behave yourself!' she heard David hiss down the phone. 'No! Mind your own bloody business!' There was a pause while he listened to his alleged friend, then Kate heard David sigh. 'Brunette,' he said, avoiding her quizzical glance. 'No, brown.' Now he looked embarrassed. 'No. I don't know! No, I won't ask! Did you want something important?'

Her shift at an end, Kate locked her desk and switched off her computer. She was thinking about that evening's Tai Bo class and her body already buzzed with anticipation. David caught her eye and gave her an apologetic smile. He mouthed the word 'sorry' as he tried to listen to Ethan. Kate responded with a small smile and a dismissive shake of her head; it wasn't David's fault that his friend was an ignorant prat.

Kate forgot all about her tribulations during the Tao Bo class. She enjoyed the upbeat music and the way her body felt as she worked. The movements were becoming easier, and she was able to stretch further and kick higher. By the end of the class, Kate felt like a warrior woman and bounded up the hill which led from Roseburn to her house. Her mobile rang when she was halfway up the hill, and she answered it cheerfully.

'You sound out of breath,' David's warm voice sounded bemused.

'I'm walking home from Tao Bo,' she explained.

'D'you need a lift? I could pick you up.'

'I'm not *that* unfit!' she laughed. 'I'm nearly home. Did you want something?'

'I wanted to apologise on behalf of Ethan. I gather he was less than polite to you this afternoon. I'm sorry.'

'It's not your fault. Besides, I'm more than capable of dealing with a difficult phone call.' Unconsciously, Kate squared her shoulders as she marched along the pavement. 'And I can deal with idiotic, smart-mouthed archaeologists, too. I'm learning Tao Bo.'

Kate could hear a smile in David's voice. 'I'd better watch my step, then.'

Kate had reached her house. 'David, I'm home, and I have to rummage in my bag for my keys. I'll see you at work, okay?'

'Yes, you will. Sweet dreams, Kate.'

David kept his distance for the rest of the week, and refrained from sending Kate suggestive emails. When they met briefly at work he was friendly, but Kate perceived a growing detachment. It was as though he had forgotten all the inferences he had made about his feelings towards her. She didn't realise that David was struggling to regain his aloof demeanour, and harness his emotions. His brittle composure threatened to slip when he walked through the Egyptian gallery on Friday afternoon and found Steven and Kate leaning over the railing, guffawing like children.

'Not funny, Grahame!' he heard Steven admonish. 'Anyway, what have you got planned for the weekend that's more exciting? Heavy date?'

'Ooh, yes!' Kate said mysteriously, her voice breathy. She was unaware of David's silent approach from behind her. 'As a matter of fact, I have!' Kate and Steven turned in unison as they heard David clear his throat. He strove to remain poised and not let them see the devastation he felt. *She lets me believe she's waiting for her soulmate, and now she has a date?*

'I'm heading off to the airport,' he announced, focusing his gaze on Steven. 'You two have a good weekend.' He turned on his heel and left the gallery.

'You, too, Professor,' Steven called to David's retreating back.

'He's been very preoccupied this week,' Kate commented, piqued that he had all but ignored her.

'He doesn't like London,' Steven replied. 'So, what about this heavy date, then?' He poked Kate in the ribs, making her laugh.

'Steven, I have a hot date with a pizza, a glass of wine and an old movie. I might have a big bar of chocolate, too. I'm going out with Jess on Saturday, though. Working on Sunday.' Kate grimaced at the thought, but brightened again as she anticipated spending time with Jess, who had called her earlier in the day to arrange their outing.

'Well,' Steven began, grinning. 'Remember to take precautions. Take lots of exercise over the weekend or that chocolate will do terrible things to your backside.'

Kate's fit of giggles was drowned out by the chiming of the Millennium Clock.

Kate and Jess spent most of the day talking. Over morning coffee, Jess showed Kate beautiful photos of Erin's wedding and idyllic Saint Lucia. While they browsed the shops in Princes Street, Kate updated Jess on events in her own life. As they sat in the Gardens with a lunchtime ice cream, they discussed work at the museum and the Michaels wedding. Eventually, they bought some food at a supermarket and went back to Kate's house, where they prepared dinner and ate al fresco in the verdant garden. At dusk, Kate walked Jess to the bus stop and waited with her until her bus arrived before strolling home.

Kate walked around the ground floor of her silent house, a little lost now that she was alone again. She locked the doors and windows, tidied up and went for a bath which she hoped would have a soporific effect. As she lay in the tub up to her neck in sweet-smelling bubbles, her mobile phone rang. She sat up and stretched over to the little stool which stood near the bath. With slippery damp fingers, she accepted the call.

'Hello?' she said, blowing bubbles from her nose.

'It's me,' David murmured, his voice low. 'Am I disturbing you?'

You disturb me all the time, David Young. 'Well, I'm at home,' she replied evasively. 'Why are you calling? I thought you were spending the weekend with your parents?'

'I am,' he muttered. There was a long pause. Kate waited patiently, curious and at the same time circumspect. 'I just needed to hear a friendly voice.'

'So you called me? Why not Ethan? Or someone else?' She kept her voice level, as she had no wish to irritate him and start another squabble.

'Talking to Ethan never helps. And you know there's nobody else.'

'I know nothing of the sort!' Kate changed position, causing the water to shift around her.

'Kate, are you in the bath?' David asked, sounding delighted.

'None of your business!' she said primly, smiling as she heard him chuckle.

'Talk to me,' he urged, throatily. 'Is the water nice and hot?'

Kate gasped at his audacity. *He's impossible!* 'If your mind is in the gutter, I suggest you relocate it. Or I'll hang up.'

He laughed. 'I'm sorry - I couldn't help it.' He sighed. 'Why don't you tell me about your day? And try to stop splashing, because the sound just puts pictures in my head.'

'Well,' Kate began, resting her toes on the faucet. 'You'll be pleased to hear I started the day with an early morning swim.'

'How many lengths did you manage?'

'I didn't count,' she fibbed, because she had got bored after twenty lengths.

Kate recounted the details of Erin's wedding, gushing about the bride's simple silk dress, Jess's dress, the flowers, the food, the beautiful location. She also regaled him with an account of her day with Jess.

'Did you buy anything nice?' David asked

'I bought a new CD, called "Between the Minds". Have you heard of Jack Savoretti? His music is so beautiful it almost reduces me to tears.'

'I'll be sure to check it out.'

'So what's going on with you?'

David groaned. 'I didn't call you so I could moan about my issues.'

Why did you call me, then? 'I know, but I'm offering to listen.' Kate heard him sigh heavily.

'It's just as I suspected. I got a dressing-down for breaking up with Diane. It seems I'm too fussy.' Kate suppressed a snigger. 'I could have been perfectly happy with her if only I had been less picky and more open to making a commitment. She and I were perfectly matched, apparently.'

'Surely you are in a better position to judge than your parents?' Kate asked gently, realising the effort it cost him to divulge details of his private life. 'Wouldn't they prefer you to be happily single than in a relationship which makes you miserable?'

'They seem to think I'm a miserable beggar, whether I'm single or not.' He paused. 'The thing is, I'm beginning to think they're right. I definitely did not want to commit to Diane, but perhaps I'm not able to take that step with anyone. On the other hand, going home to an empty house every night is starting to lose its appeal.'

Kate empathised, but also wondered if he was surreptitiously warning her about another of his flaws. Who was she to offer relationship advice, or extol the virtues of living alone? She tried to steer him onto a less difficult subject. 'Where are you, right now?'

'I'm in a spare room in my parents' house.' Kate noticed that he didn't say he was in *his* bedroom, in *his* home.

'Did you spend your childhood in that house?'

'Some of it…'

'Don't you feel any comfort from being home?'

'I'm not home…'

'What's it like? The house, I mean.'

'Large and ostentatious.'

Kate could hear the distaste in his voice and smiled. 'You'd rather be in a tent in the desert?'

Another heavy sigh. 'I'm not sure about that anymore, either.'

He sounded so miserable, Kate felt he would return to Edinburgh immediately if she gave him an excuse. 'I thought you liked your job?'

'I do, but every part of it is contaminated by politics. I'm no good at playing that game. I want to teach archaeology, but I'm disgusted that the university accepts more foreign students than it does Scottish kids simply because it needs to make money. Free tuition is supposed to help Scottish youngsters, but it's more like a hindrance.

'I want to work in the field and discover things which advance our knowledge of past civilisations, but we constantly have to beg for money and battle against bureaucracy. I wish we could just all work together and share our knowledge with the world.'

Kate chuckled, but she felt a familiar twinge of nostalgia. 'You sound like someone I used to know,' she murmured.

David was silent for a few seconds. 'Then at least I have something in common with the venerable Edwin Ford.'

'Actually, you share a number of traits,' she said quickly. He didn't inquire further. 'David, can I ask you something?'

'It depends if we're going to end up arguing.'

Kate took a deep breath. 'I understand you've gone to a lot of bother to take me to Egypt. I don't want you to get into trouble over this, and it seems your decision hasn't been met with approval. Why do you want me to go?'

Rather than seeking validation, Kate was worried that she would be more of a burden than an asset. There was a faint crackling on the line as she waited for David to answer.

'Kate,' he began. 'You *know* why.'

An uncomfortable silence hung in the air as Kate struggled to form a response.

'How was your date?' David asked warily.

Kate was baffled. 'My what?'

'Someone's been leaving you flowers. And I heard you telling Steven you had a date.'

Kate couldn't decide if she was amused, or angry. 'Yes, with Cary Grant.' She heard him exhale, no doubt irked by his own stupidity. 'I had a night in, you fool, and watched an old film. As for the flowers, it's probably some twit playing a practical joke.' She decided she was offended by his supposition. 'David, how could you think I would go out on a date? It's the furthest thing from my mind.' *As I keep trying to tell you!* She drew her knees up to her chest protectively, her voice dropping even lower. 'I'm still smarting from humiliation. How can I be sure history won't repeat itself?'

'Your ex was the one who was unfaithful. He was to blame for your divorce, not you! But don't give up on us, Kate. We're not all bad. I know you're waiting for "the one", but he might not be perfect either.'

Kate suddenly felt miserable. 'Mark wasn't entirely to blame for the collapse of our marriage, David. I was also at fault. And it seems that I made Edwin suffer, too.'

'Do you want to talk about it?' he asked softly.

'No,' she murmured. *Damn it, I've confided in him again, and this time I've revealed one of my many flaws.* 'David, I'm cold.'

'I'm sorry, angel.' David bit his lip as he realised he had inadvertently uttered a term of endearment. 'I didn't mean to make you sad again. Forgive me.'

'I do,' she stuttered, slightly shaken by his almost loving tone. 'I'm just...cold.'

'Get out of the bath and warm up, then. Go and listen to your new CD. I'll see you on Monday.'

David stretched out on out on the lonely single bed in the room he had used as a child. The walls were bare, all evidence of his boyhood removed. Lonely and tense, he had been unable to resist calling Kate. Hearing her voice had made him realise that he couldn't make his feelings disappear, after all. Now he desperately wanted to return to Edinburgh and make her listen.

He contemplated their discussion, smiling fondly at Kate's description of Erin's wedding. He knew some women would be envious of a wedding in an exotic place, but Kate was thrilled that her friend's nuptials had gone to plan. David idly wondered if Kate would like to be married in foreign climes...

As for her concerns about the assignment in Amarna, David knew she genuinely did not want to cause him professional difficulties. But was she really oblivious to his motives, or was she just going to pretend there was no connection between them?

Sighing, he closed his eyes in a vain attempt to stop his mind from constructing images of Kate in the bath. But his brain was intent on enhancing its artistic abilities.

Rising from the bed, David switched on his laptop and downloaded the album she had mentioned. His consolation would be to listen to the same music as Kate, three hundred and fifty miles away.

Kate was bathed in sweat, her breath coming in short gasps. She wanted only to sleep, to escape the exertion of her labour.

'That's it, Katie! Well done!'

Kate looked down between her raised knees and saw a man in doctor's scrubs wearing a surgical mask over his face. She was in a stark white room, lying on a hard bed. The lights above her were painfully bright. There was movement off to the side somewhere, and then she heard an almighty wail. A baby's cry. Eyes wide, Kate looked at the doctor at the foot of the bed. He pulled off his mask, and Ben grinned at her with obvious relief.

Kate frantically scanned the room for the source of the heart-wrenching cry. Another figure in scrubs and mask approached her bed, carrying a swaddled bundle as if it were the most precious thing in the world. He held it close to his chest as he leaned down towards her and kissed her damp hair. His gold wedding band glinted as it caught the harsh light.

Kate, you're so clever!' he said earnestly, his voice full of emotion. 'I love you so much!' She reached up to take the little bundle in the blue blanket. 'We have a son, Kate! A perfectly beautiful little boy.' With his arm still around his son's tiny body, he pulled down the white mask. David's green eyes swam with joyful tears.

Kate woke with a start. She remained motionless, the better to recall the details of her dream. When she had gone to bed that night, she had wished for a dream from her past, which might provide guidance. Instead, she had been granted a glimpse of a possible future. She had given birth to a son, and he was David's child. Kate smiled into the darkness.

CHAPTER 18

'Right, it's the last week of term. We're choc-a-block with workshops and school visits so we can't go to Gray's Monday morning meeting. We also have to go over arrangements for holiday activities and make sure we haven't missed anything. Can we have our handover meeting now, before the first workshop?' Jess was talking *at* Nick, rather than *to* him.

Nick, more laid back than his supervisor, scratched his beard. 'I take it you had a good rest, then? Yes, I can talk now. Give me ten minutes so I can gather the paperwork.'

'Hurry up, then! The first workshop is in an hour.' Jess turned to greet Kate, who had just arrived in their office, her eyes distant and her lips curved in a mysterious smile. 'Well, good morning, dreamy!'

Jess saw Kate blush as David followed Steven into the office. Steven asked Jess about her holiday, but Kate didn't hear Jess's reply; she was held captive by David's penetrating stare, and the memory of him tenderly holding their son.

'Well, Katie, did you take my advice?' Steven chattered, stepping into her line of sight. Kate looked at him blankly. 'Did you get lots of exercise at the weekend?' he asked, facetiously enunciating each word as if Kate were deaf.

Understanding dawned. 'Yes! I went swimming and did some yoga. And Jess and I walked for miles on Saturday.' She grinned at Jess. 'Didn't we?'

'Yes,' Jess concurred. 'We were very virtuous.' They both burst out laughing, remembering the amount of unhealthy food they had consumed.

'You realise we have to get fit before we go to Egypt?' Steven told Kate sternly. 'Working in the heat requires stamina.' Kate thought he sounded just like David, who had approached Kate's desk with a sheet of paper. He handed it to her, holding her gaze with his own.

'Suggested physical activities which provide the best results,' he murmured, wondering if their phone conversation would have repercussions.

Kate read the list with Jess looking over her shoulder. They both grimaced at David's suggestions: running, indoor rock climbing, swimming, sessions at the gym. Kate looked at Jess in horror.

'You realise our Kate is just a wee woman, not a hulking brute?' Jess asked David, who was clearly unmoved by their obvious distaste.

'Four weeks before we go to Egypt, I usually arrange gym sessions for the students. Two sessions a week in the university gym.' He looked directly at Kate. 'Mandatory.' His look dared her to object. Kate looked at Steven disconsolately; he nodded balefully, confirming David's declaration.

Jess patted Kate's arm. 'I have a better idea.' She walked over to her desk, opened the drawer and returned holding two leaflets, which she handed to Kate. 'I've wanted to try these for ages. We could go together, then we'll both get fit and have fun into the bargain.' Jess looked pointedly at David.

Kate's expression brightened as she read the leaflets. 'I've always wanted to learn salsa,' she enthused, as David rolled his eyes in despair. She looked shocked as she read the second leaflet. 'But this one...' She looked at Jess, askance. 'I *can't!*'

Jess chuckled. 'Where's your sense of adventure? You'll love it! We're doing it! I'll sign us up for this week.'

Curious, Steven snatched the leaflet from Kate's hand. He looked astonished and then delighted. 'Belly dancing classes!'

Nick had been walking towards the door, and he stopped dead in his tracks. 'You're going belly dancing?' he squeaked. Kate's face felt hot under David's contemplative gaze. 'Don't you need a costume for that?' Nick asked hopefully.

From their vacant stares, Kate could see that the three men were letting their imaginations fill in the details for them. Jess snorted in disgust, took Kate's arm and led her from the room. 'We'll leave the boys to their fantasies while we go and get some coffee,' she decided. 'Nick, I'll be back in five minutes. Get your brain in gear!'

While Kate poured coffee, Jess used her phone to email the instructors of both dance classes to secure their places. She was determined that, as well as increasing her fitness levels, Kate would increase her self-confidence and learn to enjoy her femininity. Satisfied with her own efficiency, Jess then returned to Nick and the demands of her job.

As was their routine, Kate and Steven spent the morning preparing the notes and equipment for Friday's Egyptology class while David prepared future lecture notes. They worked quietly in the office, but Kate caught David watching her over the top of his computer screen several times throughout the morning. When their eyes met, David would hold her gaze for a moment, before returning to his work. Kate found him unsettling, especially after her dream of the previous night. At one point, she sought his advice on editing some of his notes; although he was as courteous as ever, Kate hid her trembling hand under the desk and tried to speak coherently rather than sound as flustered as she felt by his proximity.

The afternoon was spent checking more artefacts on display and making repairs where necessary. They finished their work early, as David and Steven had to attend a meeting with Adam Gray. It concerned the Katana sword which Kate and David had appraised at the grand house of Mrs Adams. Apparently the museum had agreed to purchase the Samurai weapon, but Mrs Adams insisted on a formal ceremony where she would donate the sword, albeit for a substantial sum, and receive recognition and gratitude for her selfless act. David was disgusted by the woman's narcissism, but was clearly overjoyed that the beautiful sword would be safeguarded by the museum and put on display for all to see.

As they walked back to the office from the workroom, David talking on his mobile, Steven leaned close to Kate and kept his voice low. 'Katie, I just want you to be aware that Professor Young meant what he said about getting fit,' he told her kindly. 'He takes it really seriously, and he's got no time for people who go to Egypt unprepared for the conditions. He has actually sent students home in the past because they couldn't hack it. He leads by example, and he'll expect you and me to do the same.'

Kate knew Steven was only trying to be helpful. 'I know, Steven. I think one of the reasons I'm going is so I can deal with the students' gripes and he won't have to bother with them. I will get fitter, but I can't do all those things he suggested. Let me try it my way.'

'Well, when the time comes, I can take you to the gym and we can train together. It might be a bit less daunting for you. In the meantime, why don't you try walking to work a few days a week? You could start by walking part of the way and building up. The weather's good right now and the fresh air and exercise will energise you.'

Kate smiled at her thoughtful ally. 'Thanks, Steven. You're very thoughtful. I won't let you down in Egypt.' She glanced back at David, who was putting his phone back in his pocket. 'Either of you.' She led the way through the office door and returned to her desk, planning to spend the rest of her shift on her archaeology studies. She felt David lightly touch her elbow and turned to face him.

'Kate,' he began uncertainly. 'I had Lewis bring something up from the archives for you to look at.' He walked over to his desk and picked up a large, leather-bound ledger. Setting the heavy tome on her desk, he stroked the old, scored cover. 'It's a collection of directors' letters,' he explained. 'This volume covers the time period when James Grahame was director of the museum. I thought you might like to read some of his correspondence.'

Kate placed her palm on the book of letters, astounded by David's solicitous gesture. 'That's kind of you, David. I had no idea the museum kept such things.'

'I don't know why they keep them, other than to mark the passage of time. Proof that these men were really here, and made a difference.' Kate glimpsed reverence in his eyes. 'You've done all I need you to do for today, so spend the rest of the day reading your ancestor's letters. They may give you some comfort, or at least some insight into his character.'

Despite her entreaties to keep their interactions professional, Kate laid her hand on his forearm. 'Thank you, David.'

'You're welcome. When you're done, call Lewis - I'm sure he'll be only too glad to come and take it back to the archives for you.' He gave her a teasing smile as he and Steven left for their meeting.

James Grahame had been the director of the museum for almost ten years, and it seemed that every piece of his correspondence was contained within the ledger's pages. Some of the letters were typed; others were in the man's own fluid handwriting. Each letter had been glued to a page of the book. Kate perused letters regarding staff appointments, noting that James had written kind letters to unsuccessful candidates, wishing them well in their future endeavours. There were letters pertaining to artefact acquisitions, letters to people wishing to donate or sell heirlooms to the museum, letters regarding staff disputes. They ranged from the mundane to the intriguing, until Kate finally reached correspondence from 1890 and her eyes fell upon the name of her soulmate. Edwin was mentioned in a letter to someone in the accounts department, who was ordered to add the archaeologist to the museum's payroll. She saw Edwin's name many times, as James

Grahame gathered the people, equipment and funding required for the Egyptian exhibition. In August of that year, James had sent a letter to the personnel department, announcing the appointment of Edwin Ford to the Art and Ethnography department upon his return from his honeymoon in Italy. Kate touched the letter, her fingers stroking the name of her once beloved husband and moving to her dear father's signature.

Turning the page, Kate was surprised to see that a personal letter had found its way into the book of professional missives. It was brief, handwritten and dated August 1890.

'My dear son,' Kate read. 'I hope this letter finds you and Katherine well. I trust you are enjoying your tour of Italy. My reason for writing is to reassure you that John has secured the house at Abercromby Place, as you instructed. We three have visited the property and find it most pleasing - the perfect first home for a young couple. We have spoken to the owner of the property and settled on a satisfactory lease. I took the liberty of paying the first month's rent, as part of our wedding gift to you and our dear daughter. I hope you find this acceptable.

'In addition, I have finalised your appointment to the Art and Ethnography department at the museum. We can discuss the details of your occupation upon your return to Edinburgh.

'Please convey our love to Katherine. I trust you are learning to manage her fiery temperament! We wish you a safe return journey, and look forward to seeing you both very soon.'

Kate smiled as she saw he had signed it, 'Your father (in-law), James Grahame.'

Images of her family's faces appeared in Kate's mind, but she was dismayed to find they were losing their clarity. The connection was fading. Suddenly full of self-pity, she started to cry, sitting back in her chair so her tears would not fall on the yellowing pages. It was then that David had the misfortune to return to the office. Bowing her head, Kate opened her drawer in search of a tissue. David acted swiftly, striding to her desk and gently pressing a tissue into her trembling hand. He leaned over to read the open page of the ledger.

'Ford and I worked in the same section,' David observed, his voice subdued. 'Although the job title and department name have changed since then. He got to live in a very affluent part of town with his beautiful wife, and had a honeymoon in Italy into the bargain! He had it all, didn't he?' He couldn't keep the acrimony from his voice. 'Did his in-laws get on well with him?'

'They loved him,' Kate whispered.

'As you did, in that life.'

Kate shook her head sadly. *As I did, in that life. And yet, I still know very little about his life before he arrived in Edinburgh, or how he lived after his wife died. What kind of man was he, when he wasn't with the woman he loved?* It struck Kate that she knew more about David than she did about her alleged soulmate.

'His *wife* adored him.'

'Then how did he suffer at her hands?'

Kate wiped her eyes. 'She didn't adapt very well to being a Victorian wife. She felt too confined.'

'Didn't he try to help her?'

'He was busy with his work, and sometimes had to travel.'

'I see.' David's disapproval was obvious. 'You realise that you can't feel bad about what happened to them? It's not your fault.'

'Perhaps not, but my own marriage had similar obstacles. I felt the same way as she did, and look what happened. I wish things had been different - in both timelines.'

'Do you still dream about the past?' he asked quietly. Kate shook her head. 'But you still yearn for Ford?'

She looked away, refusing to answer the question directly. 'I just want to feel whole again...'

'Oh, Kate,' David breathed, his eyes full of sympathy. 'Are you sure that only he can make you feel whole? Are you going to torment yourself with this forever?' She had begun wringing her hands, so he took one of her hands in his. 'It's holding you back, Kate!'

His vehemence made her pull her hand from his grasp and sit rigidly in her chair, her eyes downcast. David surrendered once again to the influence of his nemesis and returned to his desk, unable to comprehend why Kate still pined for a dead man. He heard Kate turning pages, reading about events which had occurred in a former life. A life he had evidently not been a part of.

Kate discovered that in April 1891, James took three days' holiday, and apparently left the running of the museum to his 'esteemed colleague', Edwin Ford. David heard Kate utter a small cry as she saw that the next few pages were filled with routine correspondence, all written in Edwin's familiar script. He had scribbled notes in some of the page corners, and one particular note caught her eye: 'Remember to pick up locket from jewellers. For Mrs Edwin Ford.' David looked up to see Kate weeping silently into her hands. He went to her, swung her chair round to face him and raised her to a standing position. Wrapping his arms around her, he pulled Kate against his chest. It wasn't long before her tears had soaked through his shirt.

'If I'd know it was going to upset you, I'd never have had the damn book brought from the archives!' His voice sounded harsh, but he hated to see her cry.

Kate turned her face towards the book. 'I thought he was gone,' she murmured. 'When I tried to find out about him weeks ago, I could find no trace of him. But he's there, in that book.' She pointed to the letter. David read the page, and the note scribbled at an angle in the bottom corner which referred to the engraved locket Edwin had presented to Kate on her twenty-first birthday. Reaching over, David flicked the pages and found Edwin Ford's signature on several letters.

'Every time I try to find my own path, he sends me a reminder to stay true,' Kate moaned, and her voice was full of anguish. David didn't understand what she meant, but he knew she felt tortured. He closed the book and guided Kate to the phone on his desk. With one hand, he called Lewis and asked him to retrieve the ledger. Kate started to protest as he put the phone down, begging him to let her read Edwin's correspondence.

'Is it going to make you feel better?' David asked her, his hands stroking her shoulders. 'Will it help you to read letters from the time when he died? Or from when James Grahame died? Or worse still, from when Kate Ford died?' Kate couldn't answer. 'You're torturing yourself with this! It's holding you prisoner!' He softened his voice as he stroked her hair. 'Enough now, Kate. I'm taking you home.'

Kate was tested again that week. On Tuesday, she had to talk about Edwin at another workshop but tried to ground herself by working extra hard at Tao Bo. On Wednesday and Thursday the museum hosted an exhibition of women's clothing through the ages, from the Roman toga to the mini skirt. Although most of the costumes were now on display at the National Museum of Costume in Dumfries, some were still held in storage in Edinburgh.

The Events team had set up the exhibition in the large space on the first level of the museum. A short film would be shown in the auditorium. Mannequins displayed the more fragile costumes and examples of lingerie through the ages. Replica costumes had been produced by local designers and students from the art college. These would be worn by members of staff, and Jess brought one to Kate on Wednesday morning.

Kate looked askance at the Victorian gown of midnight blue taffeta and lace. When Jess saw the pleading look in Kate's eyes, she felt deeply sorry that she had to ask Kate to wear it.

'I'm sorry, Kate,' Jess said sincerely. 'It's too small for anyone else.'

Her whole body drooping in resignation, Kate followed Jess to the small makeshift dressing room near the exhibition space. She tried to think of something positive to focus on, something to look forward to at the end of the day. When Jess produced an authentic corset, Kate gazed into the middle distance and allowed Jess to tighten the laces. She then carefully stepped into the gown, and Jess fastened the back. Kate sat awkwardly in a chair while her hair was tucked under a mesh cap. Jess carefully placed a wig over the cap, styled in the Victorian fashion and of a similar colour to Kate's own hair. The finishing touch was a pair of lace-up boots, which Jess had to tie because Kate couldn't bend over. Jess then had Kate stand and turn slowly so she could survey her handiwork. Kate's waist was tiny; the corset accentuated her slim hourglass figure. Jess remembered the wedding photo of Kate and Edwin, noticing the remarkable resemblance between the two women. She felt enormous sympathy for her friend and regretted putting her in such a difficult position.

'Can you breathe?' Jess asked, a crooked smile on her lips. Kate nodded wearily. 'If you start to feel uncomfortable, let me know.'

'Do I have to wear this all day?'

'I'm afraid so. But at least we can let loose at salsa class tonight!' Jess was relieved to see Kate smile. 'And at least you're not wearing the crinoline!'

Kate stood for the entire morning, promenading the floor between groups of visitors which were mostly women. Many stopped her so that they could touch the authentic costume, which had been authentically produced using tailoring methods from the late Victorian era. Kate found she was able to provide a little information of her own about the style of dress and the engineering of the corset which hugged her ribs. After a while, she started to feel comfortable in her gown. Even the scratching of the wig ceased to trouble her. Jess kept a watchful eye on Kate, noticing an almost serene expression settle on her pretty face. At lunchtime, Kate perched on a chair in a corner of the room and discreetly nibbled a sandwich. She looked across the large, light space full of people and spotted David and Steven weaving their way towards her. Steven's wide grin warmed her heart, especially when he handed her a fork and a slice of chocolate cake on a paper plate.

'We thought you might need your sugar and caffeine fix,' he explained, sitting next to her. David sat on her other side, holding a cup of coffee from the brasserie. He scrutinised her face for evidence of her mood. Kate smiled gratefully at both men, glad of their company.

'Are you wearing a corset?' Steven asked boldly. Kate gave him an incredulous look, and the young man flushed. 'I mean, can you eat? Your midsection looks tiny and squashed. Not that you don't usually have a really nice midsection. In fact, all of you is -'

David laughed as his intern became completely tongue-tied under Kate's amused gaze. 'Steven, please stop talking!' He studied Kate discreetly, remembering a sepia photo he wished he had never seen. 'You know Kate never refuses chocolate cake.' His green eyes twinkled as he caught her eye. 'Do you need me to feed you?'

Glaring at him, Kate shovelled a forkful of cake into her mouth. She made sure she chewed thoroughly, as indigestion would be most uncomfortable given the constriction of her stomach. Steven told her about their morning's work while she enjoyed her cake then handed him the empty plate. She turned to David and took the coffee from his hands, her fingers brushing his and her eyes silently imparting her gratitude for the comfort he was always ready to offer her.

'Would you two like to come for dinner on Saturday evening?' she asked tentatively.

'Are you making lasagne?' Steven asked with enthusiasm.

'I thought I would cook steak, if that meets with your approval.'

'That sounds great!' Steven's phone beeped as he received a text from his latest love. Kate watched his expression change to one of bashful pleasure. He stood up, the plate still in his hand. 'Have to go,' he announced. 'I'll bring you something to eat tomorrow, Katie.' He hurried off to a quiet corner in order to call Megan.

Kate smiled as she watched him leave. She turned to David, who was shaking his head at his sometimes impulsive intern. 'What about you?' she asked, referring to her dinner invitation.

'I'd rather take you out,' he replied bluntly, once again ignoring the rules she had tried to set. 'But I have to confess I love your cooking. Shall I come over early and help?'

'No, thanks. I'm going to ask Jess, too, so she'll probably come early enough to pitch in if necessary.'

'I see.' His eyes narrowed slightly. 'You're scared to be alone with me. Is that because you don't trust me, or yourself?'

Kate could see he was only half-teasing. She handed him the empty coffee cup. 'Thank you for bringing me coffee and cake. I have to get back to standing around now.' She stood with practised grace, smoothing her bodice over the rigid boning underneath.

'Kate - how are you?'

She saw concern in his eyes, and gave him a tentative smile. 'I'm better, thanks. I'm sorry about yesterday.'

David shook his head dismissively, watching her as she arranged her skirts. 'You look amazing,' he murmured.

Kate's eyes softened. A strand of dark blond hair had fallen over his eye, and she longed to push it back into place for him. 'Thank you,' she breathed, finding that a deep breath was a major effort. She smiled, remembering how much she had hated corsets in her past life. 'I'll probably have to wear this tomorrow as well, so don't be surprised if I turn up in jeans on Friday.'

David stood, towering over her once again. 'That won't do,' he told her. 'We have a function on Friday evening after closing time.'

Kate's eyes widened with surprise. 'Pardon?'

'Gray is holding a little soirée for Mrs Adams, in lieu of her donation. It will be held in the Bute room. It's just a small gathering to appease the woman, so it shouldn't last more than a couple of hours. I think Gray has asked someone from the Japanese embassy and a member of the press. I've been asked to go because I facilitated the acquisition.'

'Why do I need to go?' Kate had been looking forward to a quiet evening at home.

'You came with me when we went to see Mrs Adams -'

'That's not a good reason.'

'View it as a training exercise then, you difficult woman!'

Kate folded her arms and pouted. 'What do you suggest I wear?' She watched in satisfaction as he floundered.

'I like everything you wear!' he blustered. 'Especially those leggings and that huge jumper.' He chuckled as she swiped at his arm. 'Wear something nice, but conservative.'

'Boring, you mean?'

Feeling bold, David snaked his free hand around her small waist, feeling how the garment exaggerated the curve where waist met hip. 'Kate, nothing about you is boring. If you like, I can come round and help you choose something...'

Kate was scandalised and secretly thrilled at the same time. 'David, you're an absolute horror! Get back to work, you cheeky beggar!' She gave him a playful shove and flounced away. David watched the mesmerising sway of her bustled rear, before returning to an afternoon which would be empty and boring without her.

Kate and Jess hummed the same Latin dance tune as they made their way to the dressing room on Thursday morning. As they walked, they practised some of the steps they had learned at salsa class the night before. The steps were easy enough when moving slowly, but dancing at the correct speed proved challenging. The pair ended up giggling and bumping into one another in the hallway, just as they had during class the night before. When they reached the dressing room, Jess walked over to the rail of dresses and picked up a large garment bag. She unzipped it and revealed the most beautiful gown Kate had ever seen.

'It's occasion wear today,' Jess explained. 'And this is for you. It was created by an up-and-coming Edinburgh designer, so hopefully we can help her business.'

Kate touched the beautiful Victorian evening gown; the low cut neckline was edged with lace, as were the capped sleeves. The dress was aqua silk and had a sumptuous train. It reminded Kate of the dress she had worn to the Ramsays' ball. The memory made her wistful but thankfully not despondent. She found herself hoping that David would visit her at lunchtime again.

Jess smiled at the enthusiasm with which Kate stripped off her work clothes and donned the cruel corset. She held onto the back of the chair while Jess pulled the laces, asking her friend to tighten them further. The dress fit perfectly, although the matching shoes nipped a little. The wig had been brushed and restyled and was now adorned with tiny flowered pins. Jess handed Kate elbow-length gloves, thinking she had never seen Kate look as beautiful.Not surprisingly, Kate's gown was greatly admired by staff and visitors alike. The creator of the garment was also present, and Kate pointed out the talented young woman to everyone she spoke to, in the hope the seamstress might acquire some new customers.

When David and Steven arrived at lunchtime, they found Kate surrounded by gushing women, and a few men. Eventually, the group moved on to the next costume, and Kate was left standing in the centre of the floor, her face flushed. She smiled as her gaze fell on David and Steven; both wore dumbfounded expressions and had apparently lost the ability to move their feet. The plate in Steven's hand was slowly tilting sideways, a slice of lemon cake in danger of sliding to the floor. Giggling, Kate swept back her train and walked elegantly towards them. She was amused to see Steven hurry to find her a chair in a rare display of chivalry. David's eyes swept up from her satin shoes to the expanse of smooth décolletage, to the twinkling pins in the shining hair. *No wonder Ford fell in love with her - she's magnificent.* Kate was standing before him expectantly, her head tilted slightly.

'Words fail me,' he muttered, as she sipped from the cup of coffee still held in his hands. Anticipating the sweet cake Steven had brought, Kate unrolled her long gloves, unaware of the sensuousness of this simple act. She lowered herself carefully onto the chair, keeping her back straight, and took the plate from her dumbstruck friend. Steven sat down next to her, staring inanely. Kate blushed and nudged him playfully.

A middle-aged man approached them, well dressed and with an air of authority. David recalled him talking to Kate earlier. He fixed the interloper with a grave stare, but the man ignored David and Steven, his eyes fixed on Kate.

'Would you like a cup of tea to go with that?' he asked her, in a cultured voice. 'My group has a table over there, and we'd be delighted if you would join us.' He gestured to the far corner of the room.

'Katie doesn't drink tea,' Steven blurted rudely. The man raised an eyebrow, bemused but unruffled.

David cleared his throat and held up the cup in his hand. 'Miss Grahame has coffee,' he said, in a calm but firm voice.

Kate smiled politely at the man. 'Thank you for your kind invitation,' she said sweetly. 'But I'm only taking a very short break.'

'Perhaps later?' he asked. Kate smiled politely but did not offer a response. The man walked away to join his group.

Kate looked at her protectors in exasperation. 'Actually, I *do* drink tea occasionally,' she told Steven, a gentle reprimand in her tone.

'Aye, well he wasn't interested in any tea!' Steven retorted, glowering in the direction of the distinguished gentleman who watched them from across the room. Kate shook her head and continued eating, aware that David's eyes were still fixed on her.

'Steven,' David spoke up when Kate had finished her cake. 'Why don't you get started in the workroom and I'll join you in a little while? I need to talk to Kate.'

'Okay,' Steven muttered, clearly reluctant to abandon his self-imposed guard duty. He took Kate's empty plate from her hands. 'Katie, you look awesome today,' he said shyly, and dropped a brotherly kiss on her cheek. As he left, Steven passed the table occupied by the man who had offered Kate tea. Kate groaned when she saw Steven fire the man another dirty look.

'Perhaps I should join the territorial army or something,' she mused. 'Maybe then people would stop treating me as if I were helpless and in need of protection.' She discreetly slipped off her shoes, stretching her toes on the cool floor. Her feet were hot and aching.

'We can't help it,' David confessed as he handed her the cup of coffee. 'You bring out the best in us. And sometimes the worst.'

Kate gave him a puzzled look, unsure of his meaning. 'What do you want to talk to me about?'

David shrugged. 'Nothing...'

325

Kate pursed her lips, deciding it was time for them both to return to work. She slid her foot around the floor beneath her gown and realised she had pushed one of her shoes out of reach. Seeing her frown in consternation, David gave her a questioning glance.

'I've lost a shoe,' she explained quietly. To her embarrassment, David got down on one knee and felt under her dress for the missing shoe. He pulled it out from its hiding place, his eyes full of mischief as he reached for her foot.

'Allow me, Cinderella,' he murmured, slipping the shoe on her reddened foot. 'Your foot looks sore,' David commented with concern.

'My feet are killing me,' she confessed. 'But I love these shoes!' David chuckled as Kate slipped on the other shoe and stood up, pulling on her gloves once more. She patted her hair. 'Is my hair straight?' she asked David, and grinned at the ludicrous question.

David smiled. 'Everything about you is perfect,' he said quietly, deliberately aiming to unnerve her. 'Regardless of what you wear.'

Kate stared at him uncomfortably. 'Stop it, David. You promised you would stop flirting with me.'

'I promised no such thing. If I remember correctly, you asked me not to flirt with you and then you leapt into my arms.' He tried to look befuddled by her contradictory behaviour. Kate narrowed her eyes and pouted. 'You know when you do that, you're just asking to be kissed...' David grinned impishly and Kate couldn't help but giggle, astounded by his audacity.

'Sorry to interrupt,' Kate and David looked up as they were approached by Kate's latest admirer. 'Would you mind joining us for a little while, Miss Grahame? Some of my group are very keen to have a closer look at your dress.' He had the good grace to blush at his words as David's expression darkened menacingly. 'My name is Alan Soames, by the way.' He held out his hand to Kate.

Kate smiled graciously as she shook his hand. 'I can join you for a little while, Mister Soames.' She turned to see David's glare of disapproval. Then, before she could speak, David placed a hand lightly on her neck and kissed her cheek.

'I'll see you later, sweetheart,' he murmured, and left before she could publicly berate him. With pink cheeks, Kate gave Mister Soames a foolish grin and followed him to his table.

David ushered Kate into the Bute room in front of him, unconsciously admiring the green dress she wore and the way her curls bounced around her neck. As his gaze wandered to her shapely rear, he wondered how she had looked at her belly dancing class the night before. Steven had bounded into the office like an over-enthusiastic Labrador that morning, making a beeline for Kate's desk to ask about the class. As David had expected, Kate had been coy, revealing nothing except obvious pleasure in her new activity. But David thought that her hips had a more pronounced sway to them today.

Kate surveyed the beautiful circular room, which was situated in the new building and offered stunning views of Edinburgh Castle and the Old Town. A striking tapestry carpeted the floor, providing a depth of colour and warmth to the room. Two long tables had been set at one end, laid with drinks and canapés. There were perhaps twenty people in the room, and Kate saw Adam Gray holding court, with Mrs Adams standing next to him. She had a beatific smile on her face as she conversed with an immaculately-dressed Japanese man. At the other end of the room, a small table covered in white linen displayed the beautiful Samurai sword. Unable to resist, David approached the sword and admired its shining blade and carved hilt. Kate watched him fondly, but her expression changed when he was approached by a tall, curvaceous blonde. She was wearing a tight red dress, and ran her fingers through her long blonde tresses as she parted full red lips to speak to David. Gemma.

For a moment, Kate stood motionless, unable to believe her eyes. The woman who had stolen her husband was now turning her charms on another man Kate held very close to her heart. Resisting the urge to flee, Kate gathered her strength, donned her invisible armour, and strode purposefully towards David and Gemma.

'I understand you were responsible for the acquisition of this piece?' Gemma's voice was breathy and seductive.

David's face had reddened; he was looking flustered under the journalist's predatory stare. 'Actually, it wasn't just me,' he corrected her. 'I did the initial inspection of the sword with my assistant. Our job was to report back to the acquisitions team with our recommendation.' He looked at Kate as she came to stand beside him, his relief obvious. 'This is my assistant -'

'Katie!' Gemma looked shocked, embarrassed, and momentarily dumbstruck. 'How are you?' she stuttered, as her seductive demeanour dissolved.

Kate felt proud of herself as an icy calm descended over her. 'Divorced,' she replied. To Gemma's intense relief, the photographer called her to another part of the room to discuss what pictures would be required to accompany the newspaper article. David placed a protective hand on Kate's back, feeling the tension and rigidity of her muscles.

'Do you know that woman?' he asked quietly. When Kate turned to him, David winced at her cold, calculating stare.

'We used to be friends,' Kate explained, her voice ominously calm. 'Until she slept with my husband.'

David swore under his breath. 'Do you want to leave?' he asked, as Gray called for everyone to take a seat.

Kate's jaw twitched, and her eyes flashed. 'Hell, no!' she said vehemently. 'This is my territory.'

Discreetly, David squeezed Kate's fingers. Feeling proud of her display of strength, he led her to a chair.

Adam Gray began his speech, eager to get this ritual over with. It was his wedding anniversary, and his wife was furious that her husband was working late in order to appease another woman's demands. When he left for work that morning, he had been left in no doubt that special anniversary treats were now off the table. He silently cursed the overbearing Felicity Adams, even as he gave her a simpering smile and beckoned her to the podium next to the table which displayed the sword. She gave a mercifully short speech, since she had not taken the trouble to discover anything regarding the sword's history, or how her father had come to possess it. She then officially donated the sword to the museum, handing it to Gray with an exaggerated flourish. Gray accepted the box graciously, as he recounted the number of zeros written on the cheque he had handed her earlier.

Leaning towards Kate, David quietly excused himself and slipped out of the room. Kate hadn't really been listening to Gray rushing through his speech, as she had been thinking about Gemma and Mark. She watched the photographer manoeuvre Gray and Mrs Adams into conventional poses; two people shaking hands but smiling at the camera rather than looking at each other. A shot of them holding the box containing the sword as they grinned at the lens, rather than admiring the work of art in their hands. Gemma was supervising the photographer, examining every photo he took on his expensive digital camera. Kate felt deliciously smug at Gemma's lack of ingenuity. However, she was unable to refrain from comparing her own limited assets to Gemma's self-assurance and striking beauty.

Gray announced that they should adjourn to Hawthornden Court on the ground floor. There they would be treated to a display of Samurai swordsmanship by two members of staff. As security guards removed the sword to the safety of the storage area, Gray led them down the stone stairs and to the far end of the v-shaped gallery, where chairs had been set out in rows. At the wider end of the room, two black-clad Samurai warriors stood in full uniform. They held their gleaming

328

swords across their chests, waiting for Gray's signal to begin. Their faces were covered with masks, their heads protected by helmets. The armour they wore was heavy and cumbersome, even though it was a lighter replica of the armour on display in the Lady Ivy Wu gallery.

Kate watched Gray raise his hand like a Roman Emperor signalling the start of the games at the Colosseum. As he resumed his seat, the two warriors circled one another, their swords twirling with mere flicks of gloved wrists. Kate held her breath as combat began. Even though they were surely using fake weapons, Kate gasped every time she heard the clash of steel or saw a blade come dangerously close to one of the combatants. Despite their bulky armour, they moved with grace and surprising speed, almost as though they were dancing. At the end of the mock duel, they bowed to one another and then to their audience, who applauded enthusiastically. The warriors then left the gallery, their identity a mystery. The ceremony over, Gray gave a short closing speech and the guests drifted out of the nearby exit under the supervision of the security team. Gemma was first to leave, unable to face Kate again. Kate had never seen her look ashamed before, but felt immense satisfaction in the way Gemma scuttled past her with her eyes lowered. Kate walked triumphantly towards her office, feeling she was at last achieving closure in regard to Mark's infidelity. The museum was silent and empty, with only minimal lighting. Some of the galleries looked to be in complete darkness. Kate's newfound strength diminished a little as she realised she would have to pass both the Millennium Clock and Iufenamun. Her steps faltered.

'Hey! Wait a minute!' a voice called from behind her. She turned to see one of the Samurai warriors striding towards her, his voice distorted through the mask. With a gloved hand, he pulled off the horned helmet and the mask underneath. David grinned at her, his damp hair stuck to his head. Kate wanted to run joyfully into his arms - her knight in shining armour.

CHAPTER 19

Kate woke to the sound of the phone ringing in the hall below. Leaping out of bed, she ran downstairs, feeling slightly dizzy. Picking up the receiver, she mumbled something which was incoherent even to her ears.

'Happy birthday, Katie!' Ben yelled down the phone. 'Just wanted to speak to you before I go to work.'

'What bloody time is it?' Kate grumbled.

'It's six o'clock, so you have to get up soon anyway. Have a great day, Sis! See you for dinner on Sunday!'

'Thank you, Ben,' she sighed. 'I hate you!' She heard him laughing uproariously as he hung up.

There was no point trying to go back to sleep, so Kate shuffled to the kitchen to make some green tea and took it back to bed. As she sat in her large bed, she reminisced. One by one, Kate recollected and analysed each major event of the last year. Having forced herself to acknowledge the incidents which still pained her, she turned her focus to the positive changes she had made. She was enjoying her evening classes immensely; they were making her stronger, fitter and more confident than she had ever been. And the different types of exercise were giving her body a pleasing shape.

Her training with the upbeat Events team was sometimes more like recreation than work. She was involved in a variety of activities, from daily tours to corporate events. Arrangements for the December wedding were proceeding well, although Audrey received several calls each week from the controlling bride-to-be.

Working with David was often challenging. She worked hard, but carefully; Kate checked every detail of her work to ensure she made no mistakes. Although David dictated her schedule, it was Steven who provided most of her tuition. He and David were currently working on a practical assignment for her, which Kate was looking forward to.

She was still uncertain of David, whose moods changed with the Edinburgh weather. Kate had tried to avoid spending time alone with him outside of work, although she had invited him to dinner when other friends were also present. At times, he seemed to attempt to keep Kate at arm's length, but then his behaviour would become more ambiguous, as it had on the day she had worn the Victorian ball gown. She had resolved to treat his often audacious comments with a pinch of salt. Nevertheless, David Young was never far from her thoughts.

Kate wondered if Edwin would approve of the changes she had made. Would he confirm that she was heading in the right direction and that true happiness was within reach? Kate could not be certain, but felt content in the knowledge that she was developing into a better version of herself. She hoped that one day she would fall in love again, and experience the depth of emotion she had shared with Edwin. A part of her would always love him, but she controlled the pointless longing by filling her days with work and recreational activities. She only felt lonely at night, when the house was dark and quiet. She had taken to sleeping with a night light on and the curtains open slightly, but she was slowly growing accustomed to living alone.

Another long-stemmed pink rose had been placed on Kate's desk, its fragrance heady in the warmth of the room. She picked it up and held it to her nose, and as she inhaled the sweet scent, an image flashed into her mind. She was reaching out to accept a pink rose, her diamond engagement ring catching the light. Her fingers touched the fingers of the man holding out the bloom, and she looked up into the face of her fiancé, the love of her life. Edwin's eyes imparted all the love and passion he felt for her as he bent down to kiss her.

Kate jerked upright, shocked at the recollection of another past life event. Even though the memory had been fleeting, it had been vivid. Kate recalled the day when she had read James Grahame's letters, and had found Edwin's correspondence. Was she being reminded of him, by some supernatural force, so that she would not abandon hope of being reunited with him? Or was the past life memory supposed to discourage her from turning her attentions elsewhere? Stubbornly, she shook her head and refused to feel miserable. She forced herself firmly back into the present. *This flower has been left by someone of this world,* she told herself, as she walked to the kitchen for a mug of water. *I do not have a ghostly admirer.*

When she returned, her four room-mates had arrived and the room was noisy with chatter. David was on the phone and had his back to her, but she could tell by the tone of his voice that he was in a sombre mood.

'What day is it today, Katie Grahame?' Nick called over, a wide grin on his face.

'July twentieth,' she responded, placing the mug on her desk.

'And?' Nick continued, tilting his head enquiringly.

Kate grinned. 'It's the opening night of "The Dark Knight Rises"!' She had been looking forward to seeing the film for weeks, much to the amusement of her colleagues.

Jess came over, brandishing tickets. 'You'll be pleased to hear I booked our tickets for tonight, then.' Kate squealed like a child, delighted. Jess enveloped her friend in a warm embrace. 'Happy birthday, my hip-wiggling friend!

Nick kissed Kate's cheek as he handed her a beautifully wrapped present. 'Lucy chose it,' he admitted bashfully. 'And she wrapped it up, obviously.'

Kate carefully unwrapped the soft package and lifted out a wide turquoise chiffon scarf, embellished with rows of small gold coins and tapered at each end. Realising what it was, Kate blushed furiously and started to giggle with embarrassment. Jess started laughing, too, which brought Steven over to join them.

'It's to tie around your hips when you're...you know, belly dancing.' Nick's cheeks flushed above his beard. 'As I said, Lucy chose it. She said the colour would suit you.'

'I love it!' Kate enthused, shaking the scarf slightly to hear the coins tinkle prettily. 'Thank you, Nick. Tell Lucy it's my favourite colour and I'll wear it next week!'

Nick breathed a sigh of relief as he handed Kate an envelope containing her birthday card. 'Thank God! I thought you might skelp my ear!'

Jess put her arm around Kate's shoulders. 'I have your gift and card at the flat,' she explained. 'I'll give it to you before we go out. I've booked a table at that restaurant you like in Shandwick Place, and then we're off to see the Caped Crusader.'

Kate's eyes gleamed. 'Yum!'

'Is that for the food, or the man in the Batsuit?'

They both giggled. 'What do *you* think?' Kate muttered. 'My brother already bought me a poster for my wall!' Kate looked up at her friends. 'I made muffins,' she announced. 'They're in the kitchen - help yourselves!'

Jess and Nick raced each other to the kitchen, but Steven hung back. He looked at Kate, his expression crestfallen. 'I didn't know it was your birthday, Katie,' he said, sounding forlorn.

Kate gave him a sympathetic smile. 'Why would you? I didn't advertise it. I don't expect a fuss, at my age.'

Steven nodded towards the door. 'Jess and Nick know it's your birthday,' he pointed out, petulantly shoving his hands in his pockets.

Kate shrugged. 'Nick and Jess are close friends, and Jess is a very good friend of mine. She told him.' Sighing, Kate moved round her desk to link her arm with his. She looked up at him as beguilingly as she could. 'Now, it's my birthday. Stop being huffy and go and get a muffin. And get me some coffee while you're at it.' She reached up to kiss his cheek, which made him smile. Mollified, he bounded from the room and left her to face David. She saw him eye the rose on her desk and then fix his gaze on her.

'I'm sorry, Kate,' he said. 'I didn't know it was your birthday, either.'

'It doesn't matter, David,' she replied.

'It does to me.'

'It shouldn't.'

He moved towards her, purposefully. Kate took an involuntary step backwards, into the edge of her desk. David stopped in front of her, momentarily caught off-guard by her scent. She was wearing a new perfume; a hint of freshness, like summer rain on freshly cut grass, wafted insolently up his nostrils.

'You've changed your perfume,' he murmured.

Kate blinked, thinking he must have an extraordinary sense of smell because she had only sprayed a little on her throat. He, on the other hand, smelled scrumptious as usual. 'Yes,' she confirmed, but did not elaborate.

'Let me take you out for lunch,' he offered.

'I can't, I'm meeting my mother downstairs for lunch.' Kate's fingers fidgeted with the edge of the desk behind her. She considered inviting him to lunch, but knew this would give her mother the impression that she and David were a couple. Kate would know no peace thereafter.

'And you're going out tonight?' he questioned. 'A girls' ogle-fest, I believe?'

She grinned and nodded, making sure he saw her dreamy-eyed expression as she thought about the star of the film. He sighed impatiently.

'What about tomorrow then, or Sunday? Can't I take you out for your birthday?'

'I'm working tomorrow. And I have my birthday dinner with my family on Sunday.'

David's eyes narrowed suspiciously. 'Are you being difficult?'

Kate's eyes widened innocently. 'No!' she protested. 'It's the truth!'

'So you'll do nothing to make me feel better about missing your birthday?'

Kate's tone was haughty. 'It's not my responsibility to make you feel better. As I told Steven, I don't expect a fuss just because it's my birthday. I'm not a child, you know.' *I'm thirty. No husband. No children. Uncertain future.*

'You gave Steven a kiss to make him feel better,' David slyly pointed out. 'And you allowed Nick to kiss you.' Kate folded her arms and pouted. *He is so damned impudent!* 'Do you remember what I said about your pouting?' He leaned towards her with deliberate slowness.

Kate held her breath and felt a tiny shiver dart up her spine. Only seconds were passing, but they felt like long minutes. The sensible little voice in Kate's head repeatedly told her to move away, but her body cried out to her to move forward, to close the few inches between them.

'Here's your coffee, Katie!' Steven called as he strode back into the room. He stopped dead as he saw David and Kate standing very close together, Kate hemmed in between David and her desk. Her face was tilted up towards David's, whose head had dipped in her direction. Steven knew the position well enough; he swore under his breath, annoyed at himself for his rotten timing.

Kate straightened and looked at Steven with a relieved smile. 'Thanks, Steven,' she said briskly, stepping away from a peeved David. 'Once I've had this, we can go and get the seminar room ready for this morning's class.'

Kate was assigned to the Imagine gallery on Saturday morning. In this vibrant and colourful area, she helped children create stories and pictures, a cheerful smile pasted onto her weary face. The children kept her too busy to brood; she spent time playing on the floor with toddlers, making buildings with bricks. She also mingled with some of the older children, who made her laugh with their antics and outrageous questions.

After a quick lunch, she was put on floor duty and began by patrolling one of her favourite galleries. The Earth in Space gallery on the ground floor boasted a small cinema in the corner. Kate watched some of the short film about the Big Bang, which informed the audience that all life originated from stardust. Kate loved this notion, feeling that it put everything in perspective. The blackened back wall of the room twinkled with constellations, which provided a breathtaking backdrop for the displays of meteorites and instruments used by past astronomers to explore the heavens.

She roamed the small gallery, providing directions to a group of visitors looking for the guillotine which was displayed in the Kingdom of the Scots gallery. As she passed a display of minerals, Kate's eyes fell upon a sample of green malachite from Siberia, its beauty enhanced further by the darker striations in its smooth surface. Its neighbour was an irregularly-shaped piece of English fluorite of emerald green. A vision of David's eyes floated into Kate's head.

Walking away from the exhibit, she climbed the curving staircase to the Restless Earth gallery. Perhaps a seat beside the huge piece of purple quartz would calm her restless soul. Unfortunately, the seats were all occupied. The gallery was full of visitors sighing at the beauty of the vast collection of crystals and gemstones on display, especially the diamonds. Kate made a quick tour of the gallery, her hand stroking the freestanding amethyst crystal in the hope of receiving some of its purported healing energy, before climbing the stairs again and seeking refuge in the darkness of the Lady Ivy Wu gallery.

Kate secreted herself in the small passageway in the Lady Ivy Wu gallery, where the items salvaged from the wreck of the 'Diana' were displayed. She laid her forehead against the cool glass and closed her eyes, remembering her visit here at the beginning of April, the day she had first met Edwin's spirit in the museum. She remembered seeing dark eyes watching her in the reflected glass of the display case; she had assumed they belonged to the tourist who was wandering the gallery, but now she realised they had been Edwin's eyes all along. *I wish I could open my eyes now and find him beside me.*

Her birthday night out with Jess had been fun, the meal delicious and the movie exciting. Kate had returned home with her spirits buoyed, but her sleep had been disturbed by a nightmare. As she stood in the silence of the gallery, the details hazily returned...

She had been walking in a dark place, her hands stretched out to touch the stone walls which rose on either side of her. A damp, musty odour had filled her nostrils. Her feet had hesitantly shuffled along an ancient tunnel, testing the ground before taking each step. A pinprick of light had suddenly appeared some distance in front of her, growing larger as she moved quickly towards it. Eventually, she had been able to discern a blue sky and undulating golden sand stretching as far as the horizon. Then a man had appeared, standing at the entrance to the

335

tunnel, bathed in dazzling sunlight. Recognising Edwin, Kate had started to run towards him, her heart full of love and joy as she reached for his outstretched hand. But she had been unable to reach him, even though she had started to sprint. She could not close the distance and started to call out to him in panic. She had woken up sweating and panting, and overwhelmed with grief.

Hearing the heavy glass doors opening, Kate emerged from the narrow passageway and continued with her circuit of the gallery. A group of Asian tourists were noisily critiquing the artwork in one of the display cases. Kate admired the intricacy of the Japanese paintings on display. As she headed for the exit at the rear of the gallery, she passed the case displaying the impressive suit of Samurai armour. Once again, she thought of David. Sighing irritably, she left the gallery.

Inevitably, her tired feet eventually made their way to ancient Egypt. Compared to the rest of the crowded building, the softly-lit gallery was relatively peaceful. Only two visitors strolled quietly past the exhibits, as if the row of sarcophagi somehow demanded hushed reverence. Kate stood against the railing until they had left, then picked a small folding stool from the hook against the wall and took it to the Qurneh corner. She sat down, her gaze fixed on the burial display, her memory showing her the last time she had seen Edwin in this place. Her radio crackled.

'Reception for Kate Grahame,' said a female voice she recognised as belonging to a merry woman called Brenda. 'Can you confirm your current position, please?'

'I'm patrolling the Egyptian gallery,' Kate replied, reluctant to reveal her position, craving a moment's solitude. She stared hard at the display of pots and bowls, wishing one of them would move and announce his presence. When they stubbornly remained in place, Kate stood and looked at the stelae on the wall behind her. Steven had been teaching her how to read the hieroglyphs, and she now tried to translate the carved symbols on the slabs of stone. Steven had made it seem relatively simple, but Kate could fathom very little. Her eyes lost their focus for a moment, and she gazed at the reflection of her eyes in the glass. Her startled gaze flicked upwards as another pair of eyes came into view.

'Edwin -' His name escaped her lips as she inhaled sharply and spun round. Her voice had been little more than a whispered breath, and so David couldn't be sure he'd heard correctly. Still, he noted her fleeting look of disappointment and his jaw tensed.

'David!' Kate felt awkward, embarrassed and curious. She realised he must have asked Brenda to confirm her location. 'What are you doing here?'

'I was passing,' he lied, trying to sound nonchalant. 'I was on my way home from Annie's, and I realised I'd left something in the office. How was your night out?'

Kate wrung her hands nervously; she didn't feel up to jousting with him today. 'It was good,' she replied. 'I may go and see the film again.' *Since I was unable to focus on anything except how close I came to kissing you yesterday, you giant thorn in my side! Why can't you just leave me alone and stop diverting me?*

David pursed his lips, ashamed to be feeling jealous of an actor playing a fictional character. 'And your dinner?'

'Lovely. How's your day going?'

David shrugged. *I don't want to go riding alone anymore.* 'Fine. I had a nice canter along the beach. Zack was very disgruntled to be confined to the paddock.'

'Don't you ever ride him?' It suddenly dawned on Kate that perhaps Zack had been Diane's mount, and the idea unsettled her somehow.

'He's a bit small for me, and I don't give him treats. He's decided he prefers women.' He smiled wryly, and then decided to cast out a challenge. 'I've been thinking about selling him, actually.'

Kate said nothing, refusing to take the bait. She turned back to the display of stelae, her eyes falling on one particular stone which marked the final resting place of a husband and wife. David noticed the stool next to the burial display, correctly assuming that Kate had been seeking solace in a place where she could feel closer to Edwin Ford and be reminded of her vow of chastity.

'So,' David began. 'Why are you hiding in the corner? Skiving?'

Kate snorted indignantly and gave him a brief account of her busy day. 'I was taking a moment's respite before returning to walking the floor. I was just looking at this marker.' She pointed to the carvings of the husband and wife. While there were hieroglyphs and prayers relating to the woman, all reference to the man had been erased. 'See how the husband's name has been scratched out? It's not erosion - the hieroglyphs have been deliberately defaced. I wonder why…'

'Hell hath no fury.' David commented sardonically.

'Maybe,' Kate pondered, tilting her head. 'It just seems very…cruel.'

'Well, I'm sure your ex-husband will be relieved you hold that opinion.'

Kate turned to him, and David immediately regretted the remark when he saw her aggrieved expression. 'I have to get back to work,' she told him quietly. She folded the stool and returned it to its hook on the wall next to the display of shabtis. David followed her out of the gallery, blinking as his eyes were dazzled by the sunlight shining through the glass roof into the Grand Gallery.

'Kate,' he called softly. She stopped, hiding her face from him so he wouldn't see the hurt in her eyes. 'I bought you a birthday present.'

'You shouldn't have done that,' she murmured.

'I wanted to. It's locked in my desk.' David looked at his watch. 'It's nearly closing time. I could catch up on some work in the office, and then take you home. Or we could go for something to eat...'

Brenda's voice burst from the radio clipped to Kate's belt. 'Reception to Kate Grahame. Can you cover the Imagine gallery for another hour?'

'Yes, Brenda - I'm on my way.' Kate glanced up at David, who looked irritated at the interruption. 'David, I just want to be on my own tonight. Please don't stay here on my account.'

She wants to be alone so she can mope about a past lover, and a life she can never relive. And here I am, being pushed aside again for an ideal. 'What about your gift?' He felt like grinding his teeth in frustration.

Kate clutched the handrail, anxious to escape. 'It's not appropriate for you to buy me presents. You're my supervisor.'

David wanted to point out that Jess was also her supervisor, and even Nick had temporarily adopted the role. But he had suffered enough rejection. He would leave her to her fantasies and go home and lick his wounds in defeat. It was time for him to stop chasing her elusive affections. She was never going to stray from the isolated path she had chosen. 'You're right,' he snapped viciously. 'I've got just enough time to take it back to the shop and get a refund before closing time. I'll leave you to your work, and your romantic dreams of a man long dead.' He started to stride away but stopped and turned back to her. 'By the way, we'll be going on a field trip to Cramond on Monday. Make sure you dress appropriately.'

Monday was a cold, grey day. Kate cursed the typically Scottish summer weather as she selected jeans and a sweater to keep her warm on the trip to Cramond. In this picturesque area of the Edinburgh suburbs, modern buildings had been built over a Roman road. In Roman times, Cramond had been of strategic importance. The regiment of the Second Augusta had built a fort near the harbour, and modern visitors could now visit the remains of the sprawling ancient settlement.

Kate took a bus to Hanover Street and walked the rest of the way to the museum, where she immediately embarked on administrative tasks. Nick and Jess greeted her warmly when they arrived but, sensing she was immersed in her work and not in the mood to chat, they left her in peace. When David arrived, Kate kept her head down and did not speak to him, but she fancied the room grew colder and shivered in response. The office was silent except for the light tapping of her fingers on the keys. David swivelled his chair so that he did not have to face her and focused his attention on his work.

Jess was involved in a tour that morning, but made time to take Kate a mug of coffee before greeting the visitors at reception. As she walked towards Kate's desk, Jess became aware of the tension in the air and how Kate and David had positioned themselves to avoid making eye contact. As she set the mug on Kate's desk, she caught the younger woman's eye with a questioning glance. Kate shook her head and thanked her for the coffee. Jess patted her friend's shoulder and told Kate to call her in the evening if she needed to talk.

Around mid-morning, the phone on Nick's desk rang and Kate rose to answer it. David did not look up from the pile of papers on his desk. Kate rattled off her introductory spiel in her clearest voice.

'Hi, it's Sam at reception,' a cheery voice announced. 'I have Mrs Brodie here looking for Steven Brodie.'

'Oh,' Kate stuttered, at a loss. 'Can you ask her to wait a few minutes? I'll be right down.'

'Sure thing. See you in a tick.'

Kate looked uncertainly at David. 'Steven's mother is in reception,' she told him, chewing her lip. When David looked up, Kate nearly recoiled from his icy stare. 'Where *is* Steven?'

'Cramond,' David announced bluntly.

'Shouldn't you go down and talk to her?' Kate suggested, her voice sounding small and weak in her ears.

David raised an eyebrow. 'Me?' he scoffed. 'Why would I want to do that? He's in the field, not off to war.'

'You're Steven's supervisor. I'm sure she would like to meet you.'

'Yes, I'm his supervisor. Not his nursemaid. Apparently that's *your* role, so you go and meet her. Remind her that this is a working environment, not a crèche. And don't be all day - we'll be leaving within the hour.' He was treated to a withering look as she swept past him, muttering under her breath.

Kate spotted Steven's mother immediately. She was a smaller version of her son with the same bright blue eyes and dark hair. Eileen Brodie was not very tall, but had grown accustomed to having her husband and sons tower over her. Kate gave her a warm smile as she approached, her right hand outstretched in greeting.

'Mrs Brodie! I'm Kate Grahame. It's lovely to meet you!'

Eileen shook Kate's hand, mirroring her welcoming smile. 'Are you the Katie who works with my Steve?' she asked. 'He always has nice things to say about you!'

Kate laughed, thinking she was probably the bane of his life, with her incessant questions on archaeology. She invited Eileen to sit down on a bench, explaining that Steven was at Cramond. Seeing the woman's disappointment, she offered to buy Eileen a cup of tea.

'Och no,' Eileen replied with a brisk wave of her small hand. 'I was just passing. I heard you two were going on a field trip today, so I stopped at the baker's.' She handed Kate a small cake box tied with string. 'I thought I'd bring the pair of you a wee something. In case that slave driver doesn't let you stop for lunch.'

Kate swallowed a chortle. 'Do you mean Professor Young?'

Eileen shook her head disdainfully, her brows knitting together in a frown. 'Aye, him. He works my lad like he was a carthorse, the miserable beggar. Is he like that with you, love?'

Kate paused, wondering how best to answer the question. 'He likes things done properly,' she said diplomatically. 'And he does expect high standards. But he has taught Steven well, Mrs Brodie. Steven's brilliant at his job, and he's been teaching me. You should be very proud of him.'

Eileen patted Kate's hand and then took it in her own. 'I am, Katie. But I'm worried about him going to Egypt...'

'I understand. But I'm sure he'll be fine. And I'm going, too.'

'He told me. I think he's glad that you'll be there.' She leaned towards Kate conspiratorially. 'I think he looks upon you as a sister, dear.' Kate smiled at the admission. 'Tell me, have you met this Megan yet?'

Kate chuckled. 'I'm afraid not. But it seems Steven is smitten. She sounds nice.'

'Hmm,' Eileen murmured, pursing her pink lips. She sighed. 'Well, I'd best be off! Thanks for coming down to see me, Katie - it's nice to meet you, at last. I hope you won't get into trouble with His Nibs.'

Kate grinned, completely enamoured of this small, sharp-tongued woman. 'Thanks for bringing this,' she gestured to the cake box. 'I'm sure Steven will be very pleased!'

'There's something for you, too, Katie.'

Kate noticed she didn't mention buying anything for David. 'Thank you, Mrs Brodie. Listen, Steven can give you my number. If ever you want to talk about the trip to Egypt, you can call me.'

'Och, you're a sweetheart, right enough! I'll do that.' Eileen patted Kate's cheek and stood up. Over Eileen's shoulder, Kate spotted David descending the stairs and striding towards them. Kate bit her lip in trepidation. She touched the older woman's arm.

'Mrs Brodie, this is Professor Young.' The two women exchanged a meaningful glance as David halted before Steven's mother. Kate bit back a smile as Steven's formidable mother inclined her head proudly towards the much taller professor, defiant in the face of the tyrant.

David shook the woman's hand; he was well used to women casting him black looks. 'Mrs Brodie,' he said smoothly. 'It's a pleasure to meet you at last! Can we offer you tea or coffee?'

Eileen was taken aback; she had not expected the alleged despot to be charming, or so young and handsome. She resolved to have a few stern words with her eldest son about telling tall tales. 'No, thank you. Katie already offered - she's such a kind lass! I must be off.' She reached across to kiss Kate's cheek. 'Take care, Katie. We'll speak soon.' She turned to David, grim-faced. 'Nice to meet you, Professor. Good day.' Eileen Brodie strode out of the glass doors with her back straight and her head held high. Kate watched her go with a growing affection, a bright smile on her face. David turned towards her, disarmed by the rare appearance of dimples. He looked at her suspiciously; he could tell by the wicked glint in her eyes that he had been a topic of discussion. He hoped his appearance had at least surprised her.

'If you're quite finished socialising, we have to be going,' he told her gruffly. 'I'm going to get the car. I'll meet you out front in fifteen minutes.'

Kate gave him an insolent glance. 'Yes, Professor.' She hastily left the reception hall.

David remained in the driver's seat when Kate emerged from the museum, leaving her to open the door and climb into the car. He waited until she had fastened her seatbelt then started the engine, swiftly switching off the stereo when Jack Savoretti started to sing. Kate stared at David, realising that he had been listening to music she had recommended to him when he had called her from London. David's eyes were hard and cold as he drove towards the Mound, his expression stony. Kate knew she had hurt his pride, and he had every reason to be angry with her. He must think her ungrateful, stubborn and thoughtless. She wanted to apologise, but her own pride restrained her, reminding her that she needed to curb the intimacy which had grown between them. Glancing at his tense jaw and frowning lips, Kate sensed he was constructing a barricade between them, and it felt like a sheet of impenetrable ice.

Steven paced back and forth along the beach at Cramond harbour, pleased to see David's Land Rover finally pull into the car park on the bluff. He waved when he saw Kate walking along the path to the beach, but she could not summon a smile for her friend. David's arctic silence and displeasure weighed heavily on her drooping shoulders. As she drew closer, she surveyed the site Steven had created on the beach. He had used short poles and string to fence off an area measuring about two square metres. He stood beside a large toolbox and eyed her troubled expression as she stopped beside him. Steven tried to cheer her with a cheeky grin.

'Your practical assignment, madam,' he said, with a gallant flourish of his hand. Steven's smile faded as he saw David walking down the beach towards them, his expression solemn after the excruciating forty-minute drive to Cramond.

'Right,' David said curtly, addressing Kate without actually looking at her. 'Steven has buried ten replica artefacts in this relatively small patch of sand.' He gave Steven a reproving look, guessing that the intern had probably made the task easy for Kate. 'Use the tools and proper procedure to unearth them. When you've found them all, pack them up and return to the museum. I want them cleaned, dried and properly catalogued by Friday. There will be one item for translation. Once you have completed the translation, you should be able to date the item. Any questions?' He glowered at them both. Kate and Steven stood side-by-side, united in their resentment. They shook their heads. 'You have one hour. I'll be in the car park.' He strode back to his car.

Kate dropped her large shoulder bag on the sand and brought out the cake box. Steven rolled his eyes in despair when Kate revealed that Eileen had visited the museum; he had been living on his own for three years, but his mother still tried to baby him. Kate scolded his petulance as she opened the large excavation toolbox, which was filled with trowels of different shapes, a square shaker tray, packing materials and miscellaneous equipment. Steven assured her that she would not need a shovel on this trip. He sat on the sand and opened the cake box. His mother had bought them each a cheese pasty and a fudge doughnut.

'Have some lunch first, Katie,' he suggested. 'Before you get covered in sand.' He nodded towards the car park. 'He won't see us -

there's too much vegetation up there. He'll be hiding in his warm, comfy car with his nose in some report.'

They sat in companionable silence, looking out to sea towards Cramond Island. The tide was out, so a few people were braving the stone walkway which led from the mainland to the island. Kate remembered making the somewhat nerve-wracking trip with her father and brother when she was about seven years old. Christopher had built a small fire and they had shared a picnic, making the return journey before the tide came in again.

Kate finished her hasty lunch with a swig of water from the bottle in her bag and then set to work. She ducked under the barrier and began to dig in a grid pattern. Her tool of choice was a wide coal scoop. She filtered the sand through the shaker onto the ground outside the boundaries created by the barrier. Before long she found a small vase, which she placed in a plastic container lined with straw. When Kate moved methodically to the next grid, she unearthed an earthenware mug. When the coal scoop knocked against something large and solid, Kate reached for a pointed trowel and carefully cleared the sand from around the item. Using a paintbrush, she carefully cleared the sand from the surface of the object. Kate gave an involuntary scream when a skeletal mouth grinned up at her. Steven doubled up with laughter as Kate fell on her backside in the sand.

'Steven, you pig!' Kate wailed. 'That's not funny!'

'It's not a real head, Katie,' he reassured her, wiping tears from his eyes. 'But you'll have to get used to it. We'll be excavating cemeteries in Amarna.'

'Don't remind me,' she muttered. The thought of disturbing someone's grave filled her with dread.

Kate worked steadily, finding coins and pieces of jewellery at different depths in the ground. After a while, it started to rain, but Kate doggedly continued with her assignment. The hour had nearly gone by the time her trowel hit upon the last artefact. Using the edge of the trowel, she traced the shape of the object and found it to be almost square and not very thick. With the aid of a flat-ended trowel and the paintbrush, Kate uncovered a stone tablet engraved with hieroglyphs. Steven praised Kate's work as he helped her dismantle the barriers, pack their equipment and tidy the site. Now thoroughly wet, they jogged back to the car park and their po-faced supervisor, who brusquely ordered them to return to the museum and begin cleaning the artefacts. David seemed oblivious to the fact that his assistants were soaked and that Kate was shivering; he had been sitting in his car staring into space for the last half hour and listening mournfully to

Kate's favourite music. Without further preamble, he got back into his car and drove away.

'Is he mad at you, me or the world in general?' Steven asked as he walked towards his old blue Peugeot 206.

Kate declined to speculate as she helped him pack the tool box and containers of artefacts in the boot. The shower of summer rain had passed, and the sky brightened a little as Steven took out his iPad, and wandered over to the overgrown piece of land which bordered the car park. An information plaque explained how the fenced-off area housed the remains of the Roman bath house. As Kate joined him, Steven found online photographs of the excavations which had taken place in the 1970's, before either of them had been born. Kate was fascinated by pictures of the exposed walls which clearly delineated different rooms. The bath house had been covered over again, the plants encouraged to invade the area to protect the site from further erosion. If a plaque had not been erected, the large unkempt space would simply look like waste ground.

They returned to the museum, where they carefully cleaned the ten artefacts and placed them on a drying tray. By the time Kate had catalogued each item, it was nearly the end of the working day. Steven allowed Kate to take a photograph of the stone tablet so that she could translate it at home. Feeling somewhat abandoned by the man who was supposed to provide supervision and support, Kate and Steven returned to the refuge of their respective homes.

CHAPTER 20

Kate looked nervously across the desk at Audrey and waited for the Events team manager to speak. Audrey had summoned Kate to her office in the building opposite the museum, the nerve centre of Events Management. Now that Kate had worked for six months from the end of her probation period, it was time to appraise her performance.

Audrey perused the performance review in front of her, written by Jess and supplemented by Nick. Finally, she looked up at Kate with a reassuring smile. 'Well, Kate,' she began. 'How do you feel things are going?'

Kate was unprepared for the question, expecting Audrey to highlight further training needs and indicate where her performance could be improved. She tried to provide a positive response, despite having negative feelings about certain aspects of her work. 'I really enjoy working with the Events team,' she said with conviction. 'The team's enthusiasm is boundless, and I've received exceptional training. Although I still have a lot to learn, I feel more confident about things like managing bookings and speaking at workshops.' Kate's voice tailed off; she didn't want to sound as though she were gushing insincerely.

Audrey nodded. 'Your colleagues agree that you have made excellent progress.' She pushed the report across the desk to Kate, who scanned the appraisal as Audrey continued to talk. 'You'll see that Jess has some ideas for further training. How do you feel about leading workshops and tours? Your presentations at the ancient Egypt classes have proved very popular. I understand you researched and wrote the piece yourself?' Kate nodded. Audrey passed her another printed sheet, this time filled with emails from teachers thanking the staff for their outstanding delivery of Egyptian workshops. Kate's name was mentioned several times by teachers complimenting her on her presentation and caring attitude towards the children. Kate's face flushed with pleasure at this unexpected praise.

'I'm not sure I'm ready yet,' she said, in answer to Audrey's question. 'But I'm willing to take on more training.'

'I'm pleased with the way you handled Miss Michaels when she made her initial visit. Are you enjoying helping with the wedding arrangements?'

Kate bit her lip; as her wedding day loomed ever closer, the frequency of Miss Michaels' calls and emails increased. 'It's a challenge,' Kate replied diplomatically. 'But yes, I am enjoying it. I want everything to go well on her big day.' *Even if she is a nightmare.*

'Would you consider moving to these offices to handle large events exclusively?' Audrey's eyes narrowed slightly as she tried to gauge Kate's reaction to her offer. 'You have outstanding interpersonal skills, you're efficient and organised. I'm sure you would excel here.'

'Thank you,' Kate stuttered, unsure what to say because she didn't want to offend this influential woman.

'Have you considered your future at all?'

God, I think of little else! The past, the future. I barely have time to consider 'the now'. Kate took a deep breath. 'I love working with Jess's team. I like being in the museum and meeting different people. I enjoy being part of a team who are involved with the education of children. I admire the way they can engage the minds and imaginations of children - and adults - of all ages. And the work is so varied.' *But it's not enough to stop me from being utterly miserable.*

Audrey smiled. 'I understand you've volunteered to help Nick with his Halloween tour this evening?'

Kate smiled wryly. 'I'm not sure "volunteer" is the right word, but yes, I'm helping.' Nick had begged, pleaded and whined for her to don the dark blue Victorian dress once more and pretend to be a ghost. Kate hoped she could perform adequately, as Nick was depending on her to be a convincing spectre.

'And will you be staying for the séance at the end of the evening?' Audrey asked with interest. Nick had invited a well-known local medium to perform a séance in the Grand Gallery.

Kate's expression changed to one of uncertainty. 'I'm not sure,' she murmured. 'I'll stay if I'm needed, of course.'

Audrey sat back in her chair and seemed to reflect for a moment. 'How do you find working with Professor Young?' She thought Kate paled at the question. Jess had implied that the archaeologist had given Kate an unreasonably heavy workload which had forced Kate to take assignments home with her. Jess had also voiced her concern over

Kate's diminishing enthusiasm for working with Young. Audrey was aware that Jess was very fond of Kate, but that there was no love lost between Jess and the often arrogant professor.

'It's fine,' Kate answered carefully. 'I'm learning a lot, and I'm preparing for the trip to Egypt in December. It's keeping me busy, but I make sure there's no overlap between my work for Professor Young and my work with the Events team.'

'But you have taken some of the professor's assignments home with you, and you do work at the weekend sometimes. Am I right?'

'Yes, I take work home. But it's usually for studying, to help me prepare for the expedition. And it was Mister Gray who recommended I work extra weekend shifts.'

Audrey did not approve of Gray's insistence that Kate use her holiday allowance for the expedition, but she did not comment. 'Once you return from Egypt, do you still want to work part-time for Professor Young?' She didn't fully understand why Young had demanded Kate join his team, but hoped the arrangement would come to an end so that Kate could focus on her work in the Events department.

Kate looked down at her hands, which she had clasped tightly in her lap. 'No,' she answered quietly, and swallowed the lump which rose in her throat.

The last three months had been unbearable. David had been distant, treating her with an almost disdainful courtesy. Although he spent most of his time at the university, Kate was still working for him. As well as the recommencement of fortnightly evening workshops, she was now posting all his lecture notes online so that his students could access them. She had committed the expedition handbook to memory in order to deal with the sometimes ludicrous queries she received. David regularly treated her as a gofer, assigning her menial but time-consuming tasks. He was always quick to point out any perceived faults in her work, but never bestowed praise. David avoided dealing with Kate in person as much as possible, preferring to communicate by email. Kate knew she had wounded him with her behaviour in July, but he was drawing out his revenge and making her suffer. Every day she expected to receive an impersonal memo to say he no longer required her services, either in Edinburgh or Egypt.

Steven did his best to boost Kate's morale, but even he struggled with this new state of affairs. The professor's demeanour had returned to that of his former self, when he had been imprisoned in a toxic relationship with a manipulative diva. David rarely smiled, never joked and had little patience for his intern's youthful exuberance. Despite

Steven's attempts to heal the rift between David and Kate, the professor remained resolutely taciturn.

Kate's confidence and tenacity were wavering dangerously, and her unhappiness had forced her to consider resignation. She was no longer sure she wanted to go to Egypt, but knew her withdrawal from the team would cause considerable inconvenience to her colleagues. Besides, she was too proud to give David the satisfaction of knowing he had bested a weak woman, if that was indeed his intention.

She was still the recipient of the occasional pink rose, but now the gift felt like a mockery of the past. Jess had gently emphasised that the anonymous gifts coincided with events in the function rooms which required floral displays. Kate was no longer moved by the tribute, and now simply placed the rose in water and left it in the staffroom.

Kate also doubted she would ever find her soulmate, and feared that the trip to Egypt would prove futile in that respect. In moments of cold lucidity, she saw the absurdity of the whole concept. Even if she had loved him in her past life, surely souls evolve and change? Edwin Ford had loved Kate's great-great aunt, a different woman. And yet, in her darkest moments, Kate's soul still ached for him.

She was haunted, too, by the knowledge that she had hurt another man she cared about. She felt cursed, and desperately wished she could atone for her shortcomings.

Kate had never felt so low, or so alone. She now regularly declined invitations to social events. The Edinburgh Festival and the Olympics had passed in a blur, leaving her unaffected by the excitement the events provoked in those around her. She still enjoyed Tao Bo, and dance classes with Jess, but spent most weekends at home alone.

As Kate considered the muddy, indistinct path which marked her future, she was certain of only one thing: Once the expedition was over - regardless of how it turned out - her association with David Young would have to end. She would find another job, if she had to.

'Well,' Audrey began, watching Kate snap out of her reverie. 'You have a place with us, Kate. Is there anything else you would like to discuss?'

Kate shook her head, feeling stupid. 'I can't think of anything.'

'Okay. Well, we'll arrange further training for you. But you're making great progress, Kate. Be more confident. You have a lot to offer, so don't hide your light under a bushel. And don't be afraid to speak up when you feel things aren't going right -' Audrey stopped as the phone rang on her desk.

In the room directly below, Jess stood at the window. She watched life going on outside; cars causing congestion as they tried to park in the spaces which lined the centre of the road; groups of tourists blocking the pavement as they took photographs, impeding the progress of lawyers in striped suits who were rushing to the Sheriff Court. A little boy was running up and down the imposing flight of stairs at the front of the museum, laughing at his mother's warning to take care on the high, uneven steps. As he reached the bottom step, Jess saw him fall onto the pavement, his face immediately crumpling as he started to wail. His young mother ran to him and picked him up, enfolding him in her protective embrace and kissing his tears away. Jess wondered if the mother was also murmuring 'I told you so'.

Jess turned as she heard a light knock on the partially open door. Without waiting for her reply, a stern-faced David walked into the small, bare office. She had requested the meeting here, where they would not be discovered and their conversation would remain private. David closed the door and waited at the other side of the desk which took up most of the space in the room. He realised that, by staying at the business end of the desk, Jess was assuming a position of dominance in this meeting. Jess felt confident of her authority; she was a full-time employee of the museum, a senior member of the Events department, and about to discuss an employee who was under her direct supervision. Her expression inscrutable, she asked David to sit. He placed his shiny black iPad and some paperwork on the desk and lowered himself gracefully into the single chair on his side of the room. Jess remained standing, her hands resting on the desk. David noticed she held a folded sheet of paper in one hand.

'I want to talk to you about Kate,' Jess began. 'She is, at this moment, having her performance review with Audrey in the room directly above us.' She eyed his expressionless face, unable to tell what he was thinking.

'I'm sure you gave her a praiseworthy report,' David replied, his tone almost scornful.

'I gave her the report she deserved. As you can imagine, many of her colleagues sung her praises.' She leaned over the desk slightly, her eyes fixed on him. 'Did you?'

David did not flinch. 'I wasn't asked to comment.' He lifted a long finger to his lips, as if considering. 'But yes, I would say she's an asset to whichever department she works in.'

Jess wondered if he was mocking her. She frowned but kept her temper in check. 'I know that Kate is happy working with my team.

Can you say the same, Professor?' *Given that you treat her like your whipping boy?*

David looked uncomfortable as he realised that Jess and Kate were close friends, and as such she probably knew everything about his turbulent relationship with Kate. 'I barely see Kate these days, but I'm not aware of any dissatisfaction.'

'Really? Then perhaps you should look at this!' Jess unfolded the sheet of paper in her hand and slapped it on the desk in front of David.

David picked up the paper, noticing that it had once been crumpled into a ball. It was an unfinished letter, a first draft by the look of it, in Kate's neat script. David felt as if his world was crumbling about his ears as he read her letter or resignation. He looked up at Jess, and she was surprised to see the arrogance fall from his eyes and be replaced with something close to panic.

'I found it on the floor under her desk,' Jess explained. 'She must have missed the bin.' With rising indignation, she pointed an accusing finger at him. 'You've pushed her to this! Your treatment of her over the last few months has been abysmal. Did you think you could treat her badly and she would just accept it indefinitely?'

'Is she resigning right now?' David looked up at the ceiling, as if in the hope of seeing or hearing what was going on in the room above him.

'I have no idea,' Jess confessed, starting to pace back and forth behind the desk. 'She hasn't discussed it with me, but I know she's in a seriously dark place. I've never seen her so low, not even when she split up with Mark. She puts on a cheerful face at work and does her job. But she hardly ever goes out anymore, except to her evening classes. From what I can tell, she spends more time in Dean Cemetery with the dead than she does with the living. She has retreated back into her shell, and won't talk to anybody about how she's feeling.' Jess stopped and gave David a hard stare. 'This is *your* fault, and you need to fix it. All through spring the pair of you danced around each other, on the brink of starting something. You toyed with her feelings at a time when you knew she was confused and vulnerable; she didn't know what your intentions were from one day to the next. Since her birthday, you've treated her with something very close to contempt - all because she wouldn't accept a gift from you. You've beaten her down as surely as if you had physically abused her. Your behaviour is insufferable.'

'She was guilty of sending out conflicting messages, too.' His tone was defensive. 'But in the end her rejection was clear. After all, she's waiting to be reunited with her soulmate. How can I stand in the way of that? I can't compete with the sainted Edwin Ford.'

Jess stared at him in shock. 'She told you?'

David gave a short, derisive laugh. 'Oh, I doubt she told me everything.' He picked up his tablet and his fingers flew over the touch screen. Jess was incensed that he chose to play with a gadget when he should be figuring out a solution to this dilemma. She glared at the top of his head. 'But I suppose she felt obliged to tell me something when I found *this*.' He held up the pad to her, and Jess looked at the wedding photo of Kate and Edwin. David had taken the photo at Kate's house, using his phone when her back had been turned.

Kate snorted. 'So you're beaten by a ghost?' she asked in disbelief. 'By someone she might never meet in this lifetime? David, you're an idiot! Are you really jealous of a dead man?'

David smiled resignedly and slowly shook his head. Taking the pad back, he tapped the screen for another few seconds and handed it back. Jess nearly dropped it when she saw the photograph on display.

'This can't be right...' Jess murmured, staring numbly at the screen.

'That's what *I* thought.'

'Holy crap...' Jess read the information below the photograph. 'So she's going to meet him after all?'

'She's going to meet a version of him,' David corrected. 'He won't be the man she expects him to be.'

Jess's anger changed to sympathy. 'How long have you known?'

'Since the start of June.' David told Jess about his encounter with James Grahame's portfolio.

'Is that why you arranged for her to join the expedition to Egypt?'

'No. The arrangements were almost complete when I found the photograph. I had planned to surprise her once everything had been confirmed.' His smile was bitter. 'I keep asking myself, if I had known about this beforehand, would I have still arranged for her to accompany me to Egypt? But, they would have met eventually...'

Jess felt the need to sit down. The situation was worse than she had anticipated, and she could see no way forward. 'So why did you want her to go to Amarna in the first place?'

Normally, David would adamantly refuse to discuss his personal life. His instinct was always to retreat within himself and bottle up his emotions. But he needed Jess to understand that he could never knowingly be cruel to Kate. The look he gave Jess answered her question unequivocally.

'You love her,' Jess stated. 'And yet you're going to stand aside?'

'Jess, I can't stand in her way. I'm not sure how or why, but Kate believes she will meet Ford's reincarnation in Egypt. She believes she was a neglectful wife who hurt her husband, and I think she's searching

351

for absolution. She seems to be driven by the notion that if she saves herself for him, and meets him, she can somehow make it up to him.

'I've provided her with an opportunity to be with him, albeit unwittingly. I have to let her decide if she can make it work. I won't be a poor substitute for him. I'm trying to keep my distance because I know my behaviour confuses her - God knows, it confused me for long enough! But if I'm with her, and we're on speaking terms, I can't hide my feelings.' He ran his hands through his hair and hung his head. 'Believe me, if I'd never seen that photograph - and I wish to God I hadn't - I would have made my intentions towards her patently obvious a long time ago. But she won't let anyone else get close to her until she's made this journey. I've tried, but just when I think I've made some headway she shuts me down again. If I tell her how I feel, I'll just become a millstone around her neck.'

Jess was speechless; the story was so tragic it belonged in an Austen or Bronte novel. She struggled to find a way to help them, but a solution eluded her. Nor could she betray Kate's confidence by telling David about Edwin's ghost - not that the professor was likely to believe her. 'Will he make her happy?' Her eyes were full of desperate hope, but David's face was grave.

'Not as he is now. But Kate has a way of bringing out the best in people. I know that from experience.'

Having shared the burden he carried, David felt a lump rising in his throat. The futility of his feelings for Kate threatened to crush his spirit, but staying away from her was torture. His anger at her rejection had made him lash out at her, and he had used the only weapon at his disposal - cold indifference. But he had never intended to hurt her so badly.

'None of this excuses how you've treated her,' Jess told him firmly. David hung his head, ashamed. He looked so wretched that Jess's gaze softened. 'But there must be something we can do.'

'There's nothing we can do to stop them meeting. Nor should we even consider interfering. ' He looked up at Jess earnestly. 'But I'm sorry that I've hurt her with my behaviour. I will try to fix it. But, Jess - ' He looked out of the window as he tried to compose himself. 'I find it hard to be near her. Do you understand?'

Jess swiped at the tears welling in the corners of her eyes, nodding. Suddenly, she found a way to proceed. 'I have an idea,' she said, picking up the phone and dialling. 'Audrey?'

'Yes, Kate is still here. We're finished our meeting. Shall I send her down? Okay.' Audrey hung up the phone and returned her attention to

Kate. 'It seems that Professor Young would like to hold a performance review of his own.' She saw Kate's eyes fill with dread as the colour drained from his face. 'He's in the office directly below this one. He'd like you to join him now.'

As Kate rose from her seat, Audrey noticed the young woman's slumped shoulders and dejected expression. She wondered what had passed between Kate and the professor which warranted such desolation, but she hadn't heard any gossip which might explain Kate's reaction. Kate murmured her thanks to Audrey for her constructive comments and headed for the door.

'Kate Grahame,' Audrey called. Kate turned, her eyes questioning the stern tone in her manager's voice. 'Shoulders back and head held high. You belong in this place - you're related to James Grahame, remember.' She smiled as Kate blushed. 'It's common knowledge now, thanks to young Lewis from the archives. Be proud of your ancestry. And be proud of your own contribution.'

Kate gave her a grateful smile and left the office. As she descended the stairs, she started to tremble with trepidation. Her stomach flipped queasily. She knocked on the office door and entered when she heard him bark the command. She was surprised to see he had spurned his position of power by moving the chair from behind the desk so that he could sit opposite her without an obstruction between them. This brought her no comfort at all, but she sat down obediently at his polite invitation. Her gaze wandered, from the green carpet to his footwear; she looked everywhere but his face. David's eyes, however, observed the black outfit which hid her lovely figure. She sat in a tight pose, almost hunched over her crossed legs. Her dark brown hair was longer than it had been when they had met months earlier. The shining tresses fell in soft waves before settling on her shoulders in silky curls. The autumn sun which filtered through the window highlighted the vibrant coppery strands. But her hair was the only thing about her which exhibited vibrancy. Knowing he was the main cause of her pale complexion and lifeless gaze made David feel utterly miserable. He struggled to find common ground, a place where she could rebuild her faith in him but where emotions could be held in check, and they could respect each other's boundaries.

'I wasn't asked to contribute to your appraisal,' he began. 'But I wanted to let you know that I'm happy with your work.' *Please, Kate, look at me!*

'Thank you, Professor.' Her response sounded flat.

'I know I've given you a lot of work recently. Are you coping? I can reorganise your workload, if necessary.'

'It's not necessary. I'm coping.' She flicked him a nervous glance before returning her gaze to the carpet. His usually neat hair was in need of a trim. Thanks to the summer sun, light golden strands now blended becomingly with the darker blond hair underneath. His skin had also acquired a healthy golden tan, although his eyes were tired, wary and remorseful.

'Are the students in the expedition group bothering you much?' He already knew the answer to this, as Kate sent him copies of all correspondence.

Kate gave a small sigh. 'I can manage to answer most of their questions. Some of them have more questions than others...' Amy, for example, regularly harassed her. Kate suspected that the girl hoped her persistence might eventually earn her a conversation with David.

David was aware of his admirer's frequent emails, which probably exasperated Kate. Swiftly, he tried to recall normal appraisal procedure. 'What are your thoughts on your work and your training schedule?'

She finally looked up at him, but didn't answer with the words which were in her head. 'I'm doing my best, and Steven continues to provide excellent training. I've been focusing on Amarna, as you requested.'

'Tell me about it,' he urged gently, in the hope that he could somehow make her relax and talk to him. About anything.

Kate looked perturbed, as she knew David was monitoring her training programme. Nevertheless, she tried to organise her thoughts into a sensible order. 'I started by learning about Akhenaten's family,' she began. 'I thought it might help me to get into his head.' She stopped as she saw a smile playing on David's lips. 'I learned about Nefertiti, too, and discovered that some scholars maintain that she initiated the heretical new religion.' David watched her purse her lips, knowing that Kate would refute any defamation of her favourite Egyptian's character. 'I've studied Akhenaten's religious beliefs and the architecture of Amarna. There's so much information online, and a lot of it is contradictory, as you told me a while ago. I'm still trawling through it, but I'm trying to focus on recent and current archaeological expeditions.' She glanced at him, looking slightly guilty because she had resumed her search for information on Victorian expeditions to the area. Once again, she could only find the success stories of Flinders Petrie and Armando Rossellini. 'As you suggested, I've been using social networking sites to follow current excavations.'

David could see she was still tense. He wondered how to reach her without lapsing into a familiarity she would not welcome. 'Are you finding that useful?'

Kate glanced up, hearing scepticism in his voice and remembering his derisory comments about people who used social networking to record their every movement. 'The posts don't have a lot of information in them, but the photographs are amazing. It's a way to nurture awareness of the project, and it seems to be helping their fundraising efforts.'

He wanted to ask her to describe the photographs, to keep her talking until the anxiety left her lovely brown eyes. She sat rigidly, looking uncomfortable and unconsciously fidgeting with her fingers. David tentatively moved to more personal ground.

'I understand you were invited to Steven's graduation dinner?' He tried to catch her eye, but she looked down at her hands pensively.

Eileen had steadfastly refused to invite David to the family dinner celebrating Steven's PhD. Kate had enjoyed an evening with a warm and close-knit family and loved the proud look on Steven's youthful face when she addressed him as 'Doctor Brodie'. She nodded in response to David's question but did not volunteer any details of the evening.

'And he tells me he'll supervise your physical training for the expedition, if necessary. Although he claims you've increased your physical activities already. Is that right?'

'Yes. I've been walking to work regularly and swim more often.'

'And you're still going to your other evening classes?' David wanted to take her hands in his, to stop her from picking at her cuticles. But as she contemplated her dance classes, he thought he saw a hint of a smile on her beautiful lips. As she nodded, a wayward tendril of hair fell over one eye and she pushed it away absently.

David endeavoured to find more questions to ask her which would prolong their private meeting in this quiet room, but she provided such thorough written reports it would be pointless to ask for updates on her current assignments. 'Do you feel you need more training on any particular aspect of your work, to help you prepare for the expedition?'

'Doctor Brodie is very thorough,' she replied. 'And very approachable.' Her eyes flashed in reproach, before moving away from him again.

David welcomed her censure, glad to see a spark of vitality. He leaned towards her, his elbows on his knees, and looked at her directly. 'Kate,' he began carefully. 'Do you still want to go to Egypt?' He was surprised to see her hesitate, as if her determination had waned. When she spoke, her voice sounded unsure.

'Yes,' she replied, hearing her own uncertainty.

'Because, if you've changed your mind -'

355

Kate's eyes widened. 'Don't you want me to go?'

David sat back in his chair, his eyes fixed on hers. 'Yes, I do.'

'To act as nursemaid to your students?'

David was delighted to catch a glimpse of the feisty woman he loved. A smile tugged at the corners of his mouth, but he maintained an impersonal expression. 'You will have other duties, as well. Gray has given you assignments, too. And you'll have time to pursue your own interests, if you wish.'

Concerned that he was goading her, Kate glanced at her watch then looked boldly at David. 'I'm sorry, Professor - I have a tour to prepare for. Was there anything else?'

Yes. I've missed you, and I'm sorry I hurt you. You fill my every waking moment and a lot of the sleeping ones, too. Why can't you forget about Edwin Ford and let me love you? 'You're working on the Halloween tour this evening?'

'Reluctantly,' she admitted. She and Jess were peeved at having to miss their salsa class. Kate was dreading having to sit through a séance then go home to an empty house. In the past, she would have confessed her fears to David, but that was no longer an option. Even so, his benevolence in the last twenty minutes was already persuading her to forgive him. After all, she had hurt his feelings by treating him cruelly. His contrition was obvious, if unspoken. Kate felt a pang of self-loathing as she realised how weak he made her, how she longed to have him back in her life, how she scrabbled for the tiniest morsel of kindness from him.

David stood, heralding the end of their meeting. Relieved, Kate got up and headed for the door. 'Kate -' David began. She turned, her eyes guarded as he took a step towards her. 'I'll be working late in the office tonight,' he informed her. 'Please tell Nick that I can help out, if necessary.' She looked surprised by his offer. 'As long as I'm not required to dress up.' His weak attempt at humour had no effect; Kate's expression was blank, and she was clearly eager to escape. 'Thank you for your time, Kate. And thank you for your hard work, and your commitment.'

Kate ran from the small dressing room back to the office, in the hope of finding Jess or another woman to help her with the multiple fastenings and laces of her costume. She had removed the skirts and heavy petticoats, pulling on her trousers so that she could attend the séance. The fifty visitors were currently enjoying refreshments in the reception area, their nerves jangled by Nick's ghost tour. They had been split into two groups and led around the museum from different starting points so they would not overlap. The tour guides had regaled their guests with a selection of ghost stories; some of the tales were historical rumours, while others had been invented by members of staff. Nick had recruited colleagues to dress in a variety of costumes and alarm the visitors by jumping out from dimly-lit corners. Kate had been positioned on the top floor near the darkened archway which led to the Survival gallery. The guests learned of a young Victorian girl whose beau had worked in the museum and had cruelly jilted her. Bereft at the loss of her lover, the girl had allegedly thrown herself from the top floor landing, falling to her death on the Grand Gallery floor.

At a pre-arranged signal, Kate had flitted across the shadowy landing, wailing quietly. Kate's hands had been covered with dark gloves, her face hidden under a black balaclava of light cotton. From their position in the Grand Gallery, the visitors had caught a teasing glimpse of a dark figure moving above them. They had heard the faint rustle of heavy skirts, and a soft keening cry.

Kate had performed for each party of visitors, before running back to the changing room. She was expected to attend the séance as a member of the Events team, in case any of their visitors needed assistance.

Kate skidded into the office, but only David sat in the room. He was working on his computer, a desk lamp the only source of light. He was visibly startled when she rushed in.

'Have you seen Jess?' Kate asked, clearly agitated and wondering if her day could get any worse.

David looked at her inquisitively; she was wearing her own trousers and shoes, but her top half was dressed in a dark blue Victorian blouse. David recognised it as part of the gown Kate had worn during the exhibition of costumes. 'I haven't,' he replied. 'I imagine she's with the tour group.' He eyed her anxious face. 'Can I help?'

Kate looked at him nervously. 'I have to go to this séance in ten minutes, and I can't unfasten this stupid blouse. I think Jess has tied a knot in the corset laces, too, because I can't undo them. I was looking for a woman - any woman - to help me take the damn thing off.'

David stood, silently cursing Fate for taunting him yet again. He deliberately avoided her eyes. 'Well, you've got me,' he stated with a sigh. 'Come over here into the light and turn around.'

His commanding tone discouraged any protest, so Kate timidly obeyed. As she stood with her back to him, she wondered how it was possible that she could start the day resenting him and end it by allowing him to undress her. She cringed as David examined the tiny hook-and-eye fasteners which held the top together. Kate had managed

357

to unfasten the lower ones, and he could see the laces of the cream-coloured corset underneath. Jess had indeed tied a complicated-looking knot, and David wondered if the shrewd redhead had engineered this situation. He noticed that Kate was holding a black bundle to her chest, presumably her sweater and underwear. Deftly, David unhooked the blouse, trying to ignore the smooth skin of Kate's flawless back. As he turned his attention to the corset, she started to fidget.

'Hold still!' he ordered, and she stopped moving immediately.

'David?' Kate murmured hesitantly.

'Mmm...?'

'Why is it that, whenever we try to keep our distance, Fate throws us into situations like this?'

David exhaled, his breath tickling the nape of her neck. 'Fate's an evil bitch,' he muttered grimly.

The atmosphere in the room was thick with tension as he methodically loosened the tangled laces, concentrating on the garment to avoid thinking about the flesh beneath. When he finally untied the knot and began to draw the laces through the eyeholes all the way up the corset, Kate gasped. David felt her body tense, and stopped.

'You have red marks on your skin,' he said sympathetically. 'You must have been really uncomfortable. I'll wait outside while you get changed, then we can go to the Grand Gallery together, alright?'

Kate nodded and murmured her thanks as David left the room and closed the door. Within moments, she reappeared, looking sheepish. They walked in silence to the Grand Gallery, where the tour group were already taking their seats. Chairs had been placed in rows in the centre of the floor, facing a round table. Nick stood at the table with a short-haired woman who looked to be about forty-five. She was neatly dressed in a dark sweater and trousers and projected an aura of serenity. Kate sat down at the end of the back row and David sat next to her. They were joined by Jason, who greeted them quietly as Erin and Jess took their places at the round table. The remaining seats at the table were taken by Nick, the medium and members of the tour group. Once everyone was settled, the lights were dimmed even further. Lamps strategically placed around them provided soft lighting, which focused on the table and its occupants. The medium began placing items on the table, but Kate couldn't see over the head of the tall woman in front of her. She noticed Adam Gray slip into the seat at the end of their row, having brought his wife to the event. The audience hushed as the medium stood and introduced herself in a calm, authoritative voice.

At her invitation, the people round the table joined hands and the medium, whose name was Val, said a prayer for their protection and summoned only those spirits with good intentions. Glancing at Kate, David wondered if she hoped for a message from Edwin. He grew ever more sceptical of Val's abilities as the medium relayed a message from a maternal figure in spirit to someone whose name began with 'A'. The next message was for a woman who was at a crossroads in her life. A man was assured that his dearly departed dog was cavorting in heavenly meadows. It was evident that the audience were mesmerised, however. David supposed a ghost tour would put them in the right frame of mind to believe in communication with the dead. Nick had been very clever to hire a medium.

After a while, David stopped listening and let his mind wander. Inevitably, it only wandered as far as the woman sitting next to him, whose shoulder brushed his arm and whose knee touched his thigh briefly as she shifted restlessly in her seat. He considered his future, loving a woman who could not return his feelings. Would it be enough, just to be near her and watch over her? How would it feel to watch her fall in love with another man? David couldn't bear to think about it, but the thought kept returning to torment him. His reverie ended abruptly when he heard Kate inhale sharply and the arm leaning against his started to tremble. At the same time, he felt a change in the atmosphere around him, a chill pervading the air. As he inhaled, he thought he caught a whiff of cigar smoke.

'Katie Grahame!' Val's voice had changed eerily into a masculine bellow. 'Stand up, lassie!'

Those who knew her turned to gape at Kate as she stood up slowly, wringing her shaking hands. David saw terror in Kate's eyes as Val pointed straight at her. People in the audience murmured tremulously. David watched with growing apprehension as Kate's stare became fixed and glassy. He heard her whisper, 'Father?'

'You must not write that letter, lass!' Val commanded, in the same deep voice. 'You are where you should be.' Val's eyes grew more distant, as if she were listening to a voice only she could hear. 'Aye, I'll tell her!' she grumbled impatiently. 'Be patient, now!' She swatted something at the side of her head, but there was nothing there.

Val looked back at Kate, and the gruff voice softened. 'Those who love you are around you, Katie, lass. You're on the right road, but it's a rocky one. You are torn between two, but by the New Year you will have made your choice. Next year will be better. Remember you are loved, my lassie.'

The medium shook her head dismissively, returning to her normal tone of voice. She smiled kindly at Kate. 'You'll spend Christmas in a hot place, is that right?' Kate nodded. Val hesitated a moment, listening again. 'I have a lady here, too. A mother figure who passed away some time ago. She gives you her love and says she likes the colour of your bedroom.' A few members of the audience laughed nervously. Val nodded. 'They've drawn back now. You may sit down.'

Kate sat down slowly as Val moved on to someone else. She hung her head, her hair hiding her face. David heard her make a soft noise and knew she had started to cry. He offered her his hand and she grasped it tightly, their animosity forgotten.

After the séance, Erin and Jess hurried over to Kate, who had remained seated while the other visitors were ushered to the exits by security. Erin's face showed her concern as she noted Kate's stricken expression.

'I wanted to make sure you were alright,' she murmured to Kate as she crouched down beside her. 'You looked like you were almost in a trance state. Look at me, Kate.' Erin tilted Kate's chin upwards so she could look into her eyes. 'Are you feeling okay?'

'I'm fine, Erin,' Kate's voice quavered. 'I was just surprised, that's all.'

'Do you understand the message?' Erin asked curiously, reassured of her friend's cognizance.

'Some of it, I think...' Kate felt befuddled, and disappointed that the one she most wanted to connect with had remained silent. She felt comforted, however, that her Aunt Margaret had been able to communicate with her. And it seemed that James Grahame was keeping an eye on her. He did not want her to resign from her post at the museum; she would have to learn to live with the misery caused by having feelings for two men she couldn't have, one of whom had treated her with indifference, and now once again offered a strong shoulder to lean on.

'Miss Grahame?'

Kate looked up into the kind face of the medium, who had donned her coat and was about to leave. Kate stood and tried to smile at the woman, vaguely aware of David standing up behind her protectively.

'Miss Grahame, I'd like to give you my card.' She pressed a business card into Kate's palm as she clasped her hand between her own. She seemed to be reading Kate somehow, just by holding her hand. 'You should consider having a reading. Goodnight.' She gave David a thoughtful glance before following Nick to the exit. Gray and his wife were waiting at the stairs to the reception hall, in order to intercept Nick and exchange pleasantries with Val. For his part, Gray thought the whole idea of spiritualism was preposterous, but his wife was more broad-minded. At least this event would produce some good

360

publicity for the museum, which would put Gray in a favourable light with his superiors.

Jess looked at Kate, seeing her completely disconcerted by the whole experience. 'Do you want to stay with me tonight?' she asked her friend.

Startled from her thoughts, Kate turned to Jess. 'No, thanks. I want to go home.'

Jess looked up at David. 'Can you see she gets home?'

David nodded wearily. They would never be free of Kate's past life. It would always hang over them, an obstruction to any kind of relationship they might attempt to foster. 'Of course.'

Kate was too tired and distraught to argue. Jess and Erin kissed her goodnight, then left with Jason. She was left in the Grand Gallery with David, while members of staff cleared up the table and chairs around them.

'Go and get your coat, Kate,' David told her gently.

She looked up at him with childlike eyes. 'Will you come with me?' She didn't want to wander the silent museum alone. Without comment, David gestured for her to lead the way.

Kate was quiet on the way home, but glad of David's company. She wished she had accepted Jess's offer of a bed for the night as fear was creeping under her skin at the thought of spending the night alone. She looked at the business card Val had given her; she had clutched it so tightly it was crumpled now, the neat italic script creased and smudged.

'Will you go for a reading?' David asked carefully, as they sat at a set of traffic lights.

'No,' Kate replied firmly. 'I'm confused enough. I don't need any more people chipping in with "helpful" advice.'

'The message she gave you, was it from your father?'

Kate hesitated, reluctant to bring up the subject again. 'My own father never called me his lassie,' she explained quietly. 'Kate Ford's father did.'

David was thoughtful as the light turned green and he drove around the corner into Palmerston Place. 'So James Grahame is watching over you. And he wants you to stay in his museum.' *Which means that eventually, I may have to go.* Kate did not respond, her gaze fixed on the window. 'The medium didn't seem to say anything bad, though,' David pointed out, in an attempt to console her. 'What did she mean about your bedroom?'

Kate's mouth curved in a tender smile. 'I repainted my bedroom after Mark left. Val implied that my aunt approved of my colour scheme.'

When he parked in front of her house, David sensed her reluctance to leave the refuge of his car. He walked with her to the front door, and watched her open it and switch on the hall light without stepping over the threshold. She stood on the step staring down the bright hallway, feeling cold but not wanting to go inside. David saw her predicament, but wasn't sure what the sensible course of action should be.

'Don't take this the wrong way,' he began slowly, pushing logic to the back of his mind. 'But you could stay at my place if you'd rather not be by yourself. You've had an unsettling evening.'

She looked at him, grateful for his kindness and dismayed by her own lack of courage. 'No, I can't do that. This is my home. I shouldn't be scared here.' Her tone lacked conviction.

'Then I could sleep on your sofa,' he suggested. 'For the sole purpose of keeping you company.' He hoped his gaze convinced her that his feelings were merely platonic and he was only acting out of friendly concern.

She managed a dry smile. 'My sofa is not big enough for your unnecessarily long legs. I do, however, have a spare room. But only if you don't mind.'

'I have a spare set of clothes in the car.'

She narrowed her eyes suspiciously. 'Why?'

He smiled at her, amused that she would suspect he kept spare clothes in the car because he was in the habit of sleeping in different beds. 'Because sometimes I get dirty at work,' he explained. 'I *am* an archaeologist. I do have to do some practical work, now and again.'

'Except when you sit in your car and leave your students out in the rain.'

He knew she was reprimanding him, and fought the urge to kiss her impertinent lips. 'Archaeologists must learn to work in all weathers.'

He went to retrieve his sports bag, while Kate waited on the doorstep and hoped the neighbours wouldn't see him. She felt better; his smile and his comforting presence always made her feel better, and she had been denied both for too long.

Kate let David lock the front door as she wandered through the house, switching on all the lights as if to ensure they were alone. He followed her upstairs, where she showed him to the small bedroom next to hers. David looked around the neat, cosy room appreciatively; the walls were painted a soothing pale blue, the carpet a warm beige. A single bed was placed near the curtained window, a wooden bedside table next to it. A chest of drawers took up the opposite corner.

'I'm sorry it's so small,' Kate murmured, watching him appraise the room. For many years, Kate had pictured the room as a nursery for her child. Now the idea seemed like an impossible dream.

David gave her another reassuring smile. 'It's perfect.'

She led him across the hall to a beautiful bathroom, decorated from floor to ceiling with gleaming white tiles. The starkness was relieved by silver beading and occasional patterned tiles. Kate had added colour in the form of striped towels and rugs. There was a large bath, circular corner shower, and a wide wash basin.

'You created this, didn't you?' David asked, recognising her good taste.

Kate smiled proudly. 'Yes. A nice bathroom is of paramount importance to me.' She giggled, but the sound was half-hearted. 'But this is yours for tonight. My room has an en-suite.'

David refrained from asking to see it. He stood back to let her pass as she walked to the linen cupboard in the hall and drew out some bed linen and towels. She then returned to the bedroom and prepared to make up the bed. Frowning, he took the linen from her.

'I can do that,' he told her firmly. 'You don't have to run after me - at least, not when we're off duty!'

Kate chuckled then jumped as she heard a thud from her bedroom on the other side of the wall. The colour drained from her cheeks as she looked at David in fear. She followed close behind him as he walked to her bedroom door and opened it swiftly, switching on the light. As expected, the room was empty, although the window was slightly open.

'Did you leave the window open?' David asked.

Kate nodded in confirmation as he stepped into her bedroom and moved towards the en-suite. She heard him emit a soft whistle at the luxurious marble-clad bathroom. Her attention was diverted as she noticed Bastet lying on the floor in front of the dressing table where she had pride of place. With shaking fingers, Kate picked up the black cat. She remembered the day when the ornament had trembled on her bedside table, in response to Edwin's fierce anger.

'It was probably just a gust of wind,' David said softly, gently taking the statue from her and placing it back on the dressing table. He pointed to the curtains, blowing gently in the flow of air coming through the open window. He was acutely aware that they were standing at the foot of her king-sized bed, made up with pristine white linen.

363

Kate picked up the cat and gazed steadily into its blank eyes. 'I don't want this in here anymore,' she decided. David knew this was a momentous decision on her part. He gazed down at her, his eyes full of longing.

Sensing they were standing at the edge of a precipice, Kate walked slowly out of the room. She placed Bastet on the small table on the landing, and thought the cat gazed at her with disdain. Shuddering, Kate hugged herself.

'Are you hungry?' she asked David, unsure of what to do next.

He shook his head as he closed her bedroom door. 'No. I ate at the museum. What about you? A warm drink might help you sleep. Let me make you something.'

They made their way to the kitchen, where Kate sat at the table and watched David prepare some hot chocolate. He was calm and relaxed, but there was no banter, and no flirting. Kate felt relieved and disappointed at the same time.

'Would you like some whisky?' she offered, as he poured the pan of hot chocolate into a mug. 'My father always had a nip of whisky before bed after a long day.'

'Which father?' he asked, unthinking.

'My own father,' she clarified. 'He was a doctor.' She took the mug from him gratefully, warming her hands.

'Do you want some supper?' he asked, standing in her kitchen as if he belonged there.

Kate reflected on the lacklustre bagel which she had hastily consumed before changing into costume for the tour. 'I could eat some toast,' she replied, and David immediately set to work. Soon, he returned to the table with two plates of hot buttered toast and a glass of milk for himself. Kate ate with relish; it was nice to have someone else prepare a meal for her, even one as simple as this. And it was pleasant to have him sitting across from her, even though she knew their relationship would not be the same as it had been before her birthday. She hoped it would be better, more stable, and less volatile.

They chatted cautiously about work, Kate's training, and David's horses. Neither strayed into the other's personal life. David informed Kate that they would be returning to Cramond the following day for another practical assignment. Steven would act as her chauffeur while David would prepare the site. Kate realised that he would probably make the assignment more difficult than the dig Steven had set up.

They discussed the most recent updates from Amarna, and the questions Kate had dealt with from the students preparing for the expedition. David groaned when Kate laughingly told him that Amy had contacted her three times in the last week. The student had asked to speak specifically to the professor, the implication being that Kate was not qualified to provide information on which hiking boots and mosquito net were most suitable for their expedition.

When Kate finally glanced at her watch, she realised that they had been sitting for over an hour, and it was now well past midnight. She stood up quickly, exclaiming about the time. 'I have to get up at seven,' she groaned.

'That's plenty of sleep!' David admonished, automatically washing up the dishes and tidying the kitchen. 'I hope I'm not going to have to drag you out of bed every morning in Egypt?' Kate pouted, and then hurriedly changed her expression, remembering his past comments about her pouting lips. 'Off to bed, then,' he ordered. 'I'll finish up here and switch off the lights. Sleep well.'

Kate hovered in the doorway, feeling guilty because she no longer felt afraid and had no reason to ask David to stay. 'Do you have everything you need?' she asked him hesitantly, hoping he would not misconstrue the question.

'Sure,' he smiled, and watched her turn and head to her room. David made a supreme effort not to follow her.

Kate switched off the alarm and sat up in bed, feeling rested and more positive than she had in weeks. She had slept like a newborn baby, a luxury procured from David's presence. Hearing the front door closing, she jumped out of bed and looked out of the window. She saw David's car pulling away from the kerb and felt momentarily disappointed. Then it occurred to her that she would not have wanted him to witness her grumpy morning disposition anyway. She donned her fluffy dressing gown and slippers and went downstairs. Her heart melted when she saw that David had left a steaming mug of black coffee on the kitchen table, along with a folded sheet of paper and a dark blue gift bag tied with gold ribbon. Kate gasped when she discovered he had put his used bed linen in the washing machine and had started a wash on the correct cycle. In all the years of their marriage, Mark had never so much as loaded the machine. Smiling tenderly, she sat down at the table with her coffee and unfolded the sheet of paper. In an endearingly old-fashioned gesture, he had written her a letter…

Dearest Kate,

I decided to leave you to get ready for work in peace, but please call me if you would like a lift to the museum. Thank you for the best night's sleep I've had in months.

I want you to know how ashamed I am for the way I have behaved towards you during the last few weeks. I have no excuse other than my foolish pride, and I am deeply sorry to have hurt you. Please forgive me, and please accept my very belated birthday gift. By choosing this particular gift, I hoped to encourage you to follow your own heart, your own desires and dreams. Not those of a person long gone. Please keep it, and wear it when you feel the time is right.

I realise I have indulged in careless and sometimes despicable behaviour which has caused you pain and perplexity. Please be assured that from now on I will endeavour to behave appropriately and considerately. I will be whatever you need me to be.

Yours,
David

Kate touched his name on the page as she absorbed the words which had come from his heart. He was offering a truce, a second chance to form an association which would go no further than affection. He was trying to make things easier for her, as if he knew she had considered leaving her job because she found his coldness unbearable. He was not going to stand in the way of her quest to reconnect with Edwin, should she decide to continue with that mission. Kate had never met anyone as complex as David Young. She remembered Edwin's observations about David being in pain and shielding his emotions. Edwin had entreated her to be kind to David.

Kate's hand moved to the small gift bag on the table and untied the ribbon. Inside was a square velvet box in the same shade of blue. She opened it and stared at the beautiful heart-shaped locket engraved with folded angel wings. It was made of shining silver, and hung from a bright silver chain which twinkled as it caught the light. Kate knew she should not accept jewellery from David, but she couldn't bear to hurt him by rejecting his gift a second time. He had chosen it carefully, and she was impressed with his ability to select a perfect gift for her. But she could not wear it. Not yet. She closed the box and held it close to her chest for a moment, reflecting on the best course of action. She imagined David anxiously checking his phone for some response from her.

Kate ate some breakfast, showered, dressed and emptied the washing machine. Finally, she switched on her phone and sent David a text message: Thank You

David stood at the water's edge, looking south to where the River Forth met the sea. Seagulls flew lazily overhead, calling mournfully to one another as if complaining about a lack of fish. He had only four weeks left in Edinburgh. Then he and Steven would travel to London and meet Ethan. The three would attend several meetings at the offices of the EES, where they would be briefed on the objectives of the expedition. David had arranged to spend the weekend with Steven and Ethan, in order to help the young archaeologist settle in with his new superior. Steven would escort the company of students from London to Amarna, and would manage their acclimatisation before David and Kate arrived three days later. David had deviously arranged two nights at the Ramses Hilton in Cairo for himself and Kate. He wanted to show her the city and take her to the museum to look for Kate Ford's stone tablet. He wanted to keep Kate to himself for as long as possible. All the travel plans had been made with that single aim in mind.

He turned from the calm grey water to look in the direction of the car park. The trees displayed their warm autumnal colours, leaves falling from their branches in the chilly sea breeze. A graceful buzzard flew in a spiral pattern within a thermal column of air. People walked slowly along the wide promenade, admiring the view. Several dogs ran full pelt along the beach some distance away, barking in elation at being let off the leash. An optimistic ice cream seller had parked his van at the harbour mouth; the driver huddled in a warm coat as he sat in the front seat reading his newspaper.

David saw a figure running down the path from the car park, a taller figure following close behind. He peered, and recognised Kate and Steven. As they drew closer to his position, it became clear that they were cavorting and giggling like a pair of scatter-brained teenagers. Kate was walking on the edge of the walkway which led to Cramond Island, and Steven jokingly threatened to push her into the shallow water below. She squealed, and thumped Steven's arm as she berated him for his stupidity. Laughing, Steven put a fraternal arm around her shoulders and continued to walk down the cobbled walkway with Kate tucked under his arm. Clasping his hands behind his back, David looked out to sea once more, to give them an opportunity to regain their composure and don their work faces.

'We're here!' Steven announced, unnecessarily. Steven was in high spirits; in the last two days, David's mood had lightened considerably.

Kate also seemed happier, and Steven assumed that his two favourite workmates were mending their fences.

David turned to face the pair, who stood side-by-side with serious faces. 'So I see.' He eyed Kate's weatherproof jacket, gloves and cute woollen hat. 'And appropriately dressed, too.' David gave Kate a gentle smile, which she shyly returned.

David led them to the site he had prepared, which was larger than Steven's earlier efforts. Beside the boundary markers sat the large toolbox. Kate felt somewhat dismayed to see a shovel lying alongside the box. She looked up at David expectantly, awaiting instructions.

'Ten items in total,' he told her. 'Amarna grave depth. Let's see if your dance classes have strengthened your biceps. Have it done before the tide comes in.' His lips twitched in a smile.

Kate felt a little disconcerted by the word 'grave', but she set to work. At first she stood and looked at the area, trying to intuit where the objects might be. Opening the tool box, she laid out the equipment she would need. Her research had shown that, in Amarna, many graves had been unearthed relatively close to the surface. She might have to dig out a metre of damp sand before she found anything, and she would have to sift each shovelful of soil in the shaker. Hefting the shovel, Kate began to dig.

Satisfied that Kate had at least made a promising start, David walked over to a large black holdall he had left nearby. Steven watched with interest as David extracted a folding stool and sat down, stretching his long legs in front of him. With a slightly reproachful look at his professor, Steven sat down heavily on the sand and pointedly shifted about to find a comfortable position. Kate watched them out of the corner of her eye, and had to stifle her laughter when she saw David extract a flask from his bag and pour himself a cup of coffee. Steven's face displayed righteous indignation, which he wasn't quick enough to hide when David turned to him.

'I'm sorry, would you like some?' David asked innocently, successfully keeping a straight face.

'Do you have any milk and sugar?' Steven asked hopefully. David thought he looked like a dog begging for a biscuit. They both heard Kate snort with mirth as she continued to dig and sift.

'Do you think you'll have access to such luxuries when you're on the Amarna expedition?' David chided his intern. 'You'll be lucky to get black coffee. There are no branches of Starbucks in the desert.'

'I remember,' Steven said gloomily, and prepared to sulk.

David felt as though he and Kate had brought a querulous teenager to the beach, though Kate wasn't much better. He could see her shoulders shaking as she tried to contain her laughter. 'Well, if your partner-in-crime doesn't take all day with her assignment, I'll treat the pair of you to lunch.'

An elderly couple ambled up the uneven walkway, arm-in-arm. They turned at the end of the path and headed back again. Curious, they stopped to watch the little group on the sand for a few moments. As they moved on, the woman tutted at David and Steven in disgust and commented to her husband that they were a 'pair of lazy beggars' to sit there while the young lassie did all the hard work. Kate tittered at the sight of the two men blushing and hanging their heads.

'Can I help her?' Steven asked plaintively.

David gave him a stern look. 'No.'

The first layer of sand yielded no treasure, so Kate began digging a second layer from the site. David busied himself with the work he had brought on his tablet, occasionally checking Kate's progress. Steven quickly grew bored and started to sigh heavily. He turned his attention to Kate, who had her back to them while she worked.

'Nice bum,' Steven commented as she bent over.

Kate stopped digging and straightened. She turned slowly and glared at him. 'I've got nice boots, too. Want a closer look?'

Steven grinned wickedly. 'Sorry, did you say "boots" or "boo -'

'*Enough!*' David growled at the young man. 'Why don't you go for a walk or something?'

Steven jumped up. 'How long should I take?' he asked, his hand immediately feeling in his pocket for his phone.

'Be back in half an hour or so,' David replied irritably. Steven was barely out of earshot before they heard him talking to Megan.

'He was only joking, Professor,' Kate said tentatively, in Steven's defence. David had clearly taken umbrage at Steven's impudent comments. 'He didn't mean anything by it.'

'Maybe so, but he should learn some respect,' David remarked vehemently. 'You shouldn't let him talk to you like that. In fact, he shouldn't talk to any woman in such a demeaning manner. He should behave in accordance with his position. Like a gentleman.'

Kate leaned on her shovel as she looked at his grumpy face, her eyes and voice soft. 'He's young. And not everyone was brought up to be as gallant as you.' She watched a shy smile appear on his face. Happy to have appeased him, Kate returned to her work.

Kate had dug out nearly half a metre of sand when David's phone rang. He answered the call, a look of surprise crossed his face, and he scrambled to his feet.

'Dad!' he said in astonishment. 'Hi! Is anything wrong?' He listened for a moment. 'Hang on a second -' David turned to Kate. 'Kate, please excuse me. I have to take this.'

Kate nodded, and David walked towards the water's edge to continue his conversation. At that moment, Kate's shovel hit something hard. Ecstatic to be able to stop digging with the shovel, Kate cried out in triumph and danced a little jig in the sand. David looked over just in time to see her performing a very fluid undulation with her hips, which, even though she was wearing a heavy jacket, looked incredibly sexy. He grinned at the horrified expression on her face when she realised he was watching her. She quickly returned to work, pulling off her gloves to get a better grip on the smaller tools she would now have to use.

'David, are you still there?' his father asked, sounding slightly irritated.

David reluctantly turned away from Kate and continued to walk slowly along the beach. 'Yes, Dad. Sorry.'

Kate started to unearth artefacts similar to those found in the Qurneh burial site: Pots, bowls, some small bracelets and a necklace. She was grateful that David had buried it in fairly shallow ground, although the pieces were spread about the site. Once she had lifted and packed nine different items, she returned to the hole and dug a little more. David returned just as her shovel knocked against a large item. He watched in nervous anticipation as she used pointed and flat-edged trowels to dig around the edges of the piece, revealing a rectangular wooden box. As she prepared to lever it from the sand, she accidentally opened the unsealed lid. When her eyes fell on the small, mummified body inside Kate cried out in shock and stumbled backwards, cutting her hand on the sharp edge of a razor shell which protruded from the sand. Instinctively, she scrambled away from the remains and backed into David.

'It's alright, Kate,' he soothed. 'It's only a replica.' Without thinking, he put his arm around her to steady her. Kate was breathing heavily, trying to slow her racing pulse.

'Of course,' she said quickly. 'I'm sorry. It was just a shock. I'm fine.' She made no effort to step away from him.

'I didn't do this to be cruel,' he explained. 'I wanted to try and prepare you for what you will experience in Amarna. We'll be excavating a burial ground, and you have to be able to deal with this. If you unearth something which upsets you, you'll still have to appear calm and proficient. I can't protect you from it.'

'You won't have to,' she declared bravely. 'I'm sorry I was such a baby.' Kate moved towards the fake mummy. She conjured up an image of Edwin unearthing the child's wooden coffin during the Qurneh dig and wondered how he had felt, having lost his own child. She had suffered no such loss and could not claim that as an excuse for her cowardice.

'Compassion is not a flaw,' David told her, as she reached up to remove her hat. 'Kate, your hand's bleeding!' He took hold of her hand and saw she had cut the palm.

'Oh,' she said vaguely. 'I didn't notice.' She allowed him to lead her to the toolbox, where he pulled out a first aid kit. Taking an unopened bottle of water from his bag, he dowsed the cut and then used lint to pat it dry. Examining Kate's injury, David concluded that it was only superficial. Carefully, he applied iodine from the small bottle in the tool kit. Kate balked at the smell and the resulting sting in her hand.

'I'm taking a first aid class,' she informed David shyly, as he selected a large plaster and cut a small square of lint. 'I thought it might come in handy.'

'That's great,' David said. 'But don't overload yourself, or by the time you get to Egypt you'll be worn out!'

Kate glanced slyly up at him through her lashes. 'I can always sleep on the plane,' she teased.

'That's exactly what I was planning to do!' he retorted, smoothing the plaster over the square of lint he had placed over the cut. He stroked her palm absently.

'I'm back!' Steven called as he strolled towards them. 'And the tide's turning...' He nodded towards the sea, which was creeping steadily up the beach towards them.

David picked up the trowel, intending to lift the box himself. He moved into the hole Kate had dug, but she raced after him and took the trowel from him.

'I can do it!' she protested.

'You've cut your hand,' David replied patiently. 'You need to keep it clean.'

Kate lowered her voice. 'What I need, Professor, is for you to stop mollycoddling me. See, I'm putting my glove back on to protect my little scratch.'

'I wish you'd stop calling me that,' he murmured.

'What?'

'I hate it when you call me "Professor".'

'It's your well-deserved title. And I will address you as such while we're working. Now, shift!' Swallowing her distaste of its contents, Kate resumed her excavation of the makeshift coffin. Eventually, she lifted it from the sand.

'*Finally!*' Steven sighed, taking the box from her. He looked at David. 'Can we eat now?'

'Have you earned it?' David asked scathingly. Steven proceeded to clear the site, industriously dismantling the barriers and tidying the area. Between them, he and David carried all the equipment back to David's car. Kate followed them empty-handed, grumbling about their excessive chivalry.

They enjoyed a tasty lunch at a small restaurant which overlooked the harbour. Since it was too cold to sit outside, they huddled around a wooden table in a corner of the warm, low-ceilinged dining room. David cherished their time together that day. He looked on in amusement as Kate scolded Steven for flirting with their pretty waitress, primly reminding him he already had a lovely girlfriend. David hadn't felt part of a family for a very long time, until he met Kate. He would miss them, once they had both gone from his life. He could already feel their loss.

CHAPTER 21

Kate carefully checked her reflection in the full-length mirror; Gray wanted his staff to look smart but understated this evening. He had asked the men to wear evening dress, like the male wedding guests who were not in military uniform. Women were to wear black dresses if possible. Kate had decided to wear the dress she had only worn once, to her ill-fated anniversary dinner. David's locket hung around her neck.

The museum had remained open, although sections had been closed off to allow the staff to prepare for the wedding reception. Kate had immersed herself in the task of arranging floral displays and table decorations in the Grand Gallery. Now she enjoyed a brief respite before the arrival of the bridal party.

Through the mirror, Kate saw Jess entering the bathroom wearing a stylish black shift dress. 'Here you are!' Jess exclaimed. 'I've been looking for you.' Jess scrutinised her own reflection alongside Kate. 'Have you seen David Young?' she continued, glancing sideways at Kate. 'He looks good enough to eat!'

'David's here?' Kate asked brightly, and Jess couldn't fail to see her eyes light up.

Jess turned to Kate, pointing an accusing finger. 'Ha! I knew it!' she cried. 'You *do* have feelings for him, admit it!'

Kate and David had spent the last four weeks fruitlessly trying to prove their sentiments did not extend beyond friendship. They had avoided the heated, often flirtatious exchanges of the past and instead nurtured a more temperate relationship. While this was all very sweet to watch, Jess wondered if they were truly content.

Kate's face fell and she looked away. 'He's been a very good friend,' she mumbled. 'It's nothing more complicated than that.'

Jess reached for Kate's hand and squeezed it. 'Kate, are you blind?' she asked, gently. She was becoming increasingly frustrated by Kate's blinkered attitude. 'Haven't you seen the way he looks at you?'

Despite his busy teaching schedule, David practically haunted the museum. He attended almost every Egyptian workshop and preferred their cramped workspace to his private office at the university. Jess regularly caught him watching Kate as she worked at her desk, his gaze soft and wistful.

Shaking her head in denial, Kate wrung her hands. 'I can't,' she muttered. 'We have to work together in Egypt.'

'Kate, he's *taking* you to Egypt. I know you're great at your job, and you totally deserve to go, but he was supposed to pick someone with a degree in archaeology. Doesn't that give you a hint?'

Kate shook her head vigorously. 'No. I can't get involved with him, Jess. Please don't complicate everything.'

Jess took a deep breath, trying to find the right words. 'Is this because of Edwin?' Kate didn't answer, which was confirmation enough. 'Are you still being faithful to a ghost?'

Since Kate had ceased to mention Edwin, Jess had hoped her friend had moved past that particular obstruction to her future happiness. She had hoped that David would secure Kate's affections before they went to Egypt. Or better still, that Kate would decide to stay safely in Edinburgh.

'Jess, when I was Edwin's wife, I hurt him with my selfishness. Erin said that, if we don't learn our lessons in one lifetime, we have to learn them in the next. I made Edwin suffer, and I believe I should atone for that somehow. I'm scared of failing him again.' She looked crestfallen, because the message she had received during the séance was proving accurate: she was torn between two.

Jess hugged her friend, saddened to discover that Kate was still clinging to the hope of finding Edwin again. She wished she could prepare Kate for what was ahead of her, but David had pleaded with her to remain silent.

'You didn't fail him last time, Kate!' she cried. 'And don't you think that your premature death was atonement enough? When you were Kate Ford, you loved Edwin. It was your Victorian lifestyle which made you unhappy. What happened was nobody's fault.' She pulled back to look into Kate's miserable face. 'Kate, listen to me. You need to live *your* life. Remember what else Erin said? Just because you loved him in a past life, doesn't mean you'll love whoever he is in this one. If you are soulmates, why hasn't he found you? If he does exist in this timeline, he may not be as you remember him.'

Kate sniffed loudly. 'He said we weren't together now because I made the wrong decision somewhere in the past. He said we could be together again, but I have to go to Egypt.'

Jess silently cursed the over-possessive spirit. *Typical man, to blame a woman for things not working out.* 'I don't think we have just one soulmate, Kate. And you *are* going to Egypt - with a lovely man who cares about you. Don't waste an opportunity to be happy. Not on the off chance that you might meet Edwin Ford as he is today. Please, Kate, you have to think about this rationally. I know you care for David.'

Kate looked around the room, as if afraid of being overhead. She sighed, suddenly tired of battling her own emotions. 'Yes, I care for David. Very much.' Jess felt a surge of elation. 'I'm trying to keep my distance because I don't want to hurt him, but...'

Jess grinned. 'One soulful glance from those emerald peepers and you forget all your good intentions?'

Kate looked ruefully at her black shoes, unable to deny the truth. 'I'm not going on some crazy search for Edwin. I've decided that I'll go to Egypt and work, like I'm supposed to. If Edwin doesn't appear, then...' Kate shrugged helplessly. 'But I have to give him a chance - I owe him that much - and I can't commit to anyone else in the meantime. I promise, if nothing happens in Egypt, I'll come home and make a fresh start.' *But by then, David might have given up on me altogether.*

Jess patted her friend's arm and sighed, wishing that Erin had used her skills to suppress Kate's past life memories. Her friend was a prisoner, thanks to Edwin Ford and her own unfounded guilt. Jess prayed that Fate would intervene in Egypt, and bring Kate home with the right man. She reminded herself of Val's assurances that Kate would make the right choice. 'Alright. But don't chase David away.'

Kate smiled as she pictured David's boyish grin. Her confession had brought her immense relief. Every day she wrestled with feelings of disloyalty; she was supposed to travel to Egypt for Edwin's sake, but in a hidden corner of her heart, she suspected she was going to Egypt to be with David. Jess noticed Kate's doe-eyed look, and shook her head in resignation. *They're as bad as each other*, she thought in exasperation.

'That's a beautiful necklace you're wearing,' Jess commented, eyeing the silver locket.

Kate touched the angel wings, avoiding Jess's shrewd gaze. 'It was a birthday present,' she replied ambiguously.

Jess's eyes narrowed suspiciously. 'Oh? From whom?' she asked lightly, guessing that the gift had come from David. Kate pretended she hadn't heard and busied herself with tidying her hair, while Jess looked up at the ceiling in supplication. The redhead turned back to the mirror, smoothing her fitted dress and twisting to see the back.

'I have to say, all that salsa and belly dancing have really helped us!' Jess commented, making Kate laugh. 'We look totally hot!'

Adam Gray surveyed the line of staff like a drill sergeant inspecting his troops. The Grand Gallery was beautifully decorated for the wedding reception. Some exhibits had been moved to make way for the circular tables adorned with white linen, crystal glassware and silver cutlery. The dining chairs had also been draped in white linen.

The catering staff were well prepared. The bar was set up at one end of the gallery. At the other end, there was space for the disc jockey and the dancing which would follow the meal. Under his close supervision, all the arrangements were in place.

As well as staff to help serve drinks and canapés, Gray had asked a member from each department to be present at the reception to provide tours if required. Extra security personnel were on hand to patrol the museum; canoodling in the galleries was not permitted. The museum had an excellent reputation as a venue for weddings and other social and corporate events; today would be another feather in his cap. With a nod of approval for his staff, he strode forward to greet the bridal party.

David leaned on the railing of the first floor landing and observed the well-dressed wedding guests below. Military dress uniforms clashed with evening suits and expensive dresses. He and his colleagues had been kept busy for the entire event. Although he had not had to serve refreshments like some of the other staff, many of the guests had asked David for a guided tour of the Egyptian gallery. As always, he enjoyed talking about his work and the exhibits, but he was thankful when the meal began and he was left in peace.

The meal and speeches were over, the cake had been cut and the newlyweds had performed their first dance. David cringed at the thought of having to dance in front of people. For the first time in his life, he contemplated his own wedding. He felt he would prefer something small, intimate and meaningful. Then, out of the blue, he wondered what Kate's wedding had been like. The thought prompted his eyes to seek her out and he homed in on her quickly. She looked very beautiful tonight, in an elegant and understated way. The dress she wore showed off a toned but curvaceous figure. She had given up her Tao Bo class in November in order to join the expedition group at the university gym. David had watched her exercise with Steven, determined to keep up with the rest of the group. In fact, she was fitter than many of the others. David was certain she had attended the training sessions to gain the respect of the students who would be in her care. It had proved an insightful move.

Kate was smiling that lovely smile which revealed her dimples. David smiled then frowned as he watched a young officer approach Kate and start to talk to her, placing a hand lightly on her elbow in a manner far too familiar for David's liking. She was civil to the lieutenant, although she stood in a slightly defensive posture with her hands clasped in front of her. The young man gave her his complete attention, his face animated. He made Kate laugh.

The next dance had a Latin beat and David watched the man take a reluctant Kate by the hand and lead her to the floor. From his viewpoint, David could see her clearly. Kate was soon lost to the rhythm of the music and danced the steps she had learned with effortless grace. She was obviously enjoying herself and seemed quite unaware that the movement of her body was incredibly seductive. Her dance partner was captivated, and when the music changed from a salsa to a waltz he refused to let Kate leave the floor. Instead, he took Kate in his arms and began a clumsy waltz, holding her much closer than was necessary. David could see Kate was not enjoying this dance and left his post.

Kate was remembering other waltzes, with another man, a very long time ago. Closing her eyes for a moment, she recalled being in Edwin's arms and floating across the floor. She resolutely pushed the memory away. When she opened her eyes, David was standing behind her somewhat persistent dance partner.

'May I cut in?' David asked. The soldier looked as if he might refuse, but a pointed stare from the much-taller man at his shoulder made him relinquish Kate and walk away. David gently took Kate into his arms and stepped easily into a waltz. He glanced down at his partner. 'I owed you a rescue,' he said quietly, noting with pleasure that she was wearing the locket at last.

She looked up at him hesitantly, thinking that he had rescued her some time ago, despite their three-month estrangement. 'We shouldn't be dancing when we're supposed to be working...' She was painfully aware of his warm hand resting gently against her ribs, his other hand holding hers. He danced extremely well.

'Seniority has its perks,' he said, with mock self-importance. 'Besides, we've worked hard enough tonight.' He tilted his head towards hers. 'By the way, you look beautiful.'

Kate beamed at him, her cheeks turning pink. 'So do you,' she replied tentatively. He looked dashing in a perfectly-fitting black tuxedo. Kate was impressed by his bow tie, which he had tied himself; even the men in the bridal party appeared to be wearing clip-on bow ties.

As they moved past a table of women, Kate noticed them voraciously eyeing up her handsome partner. She heard one of them say, 'He looks like James Bond,' to the woman next to her.

'Better than James Bond, I should say!' her friend gushed, not bothering to lower her voice.

David should have felt amused to see Kate fire the women a somewhat menacing glance; he should have felt delight at her involuntary, possessive squeeze of his upper arm. But he just felt sad and defeated.

'It's a pity there's not a terrace,' David observed.

Kate looked up at him, bemused. 'Why would you need a terrace?'

He gave her a searching look, a mischievous smile playing on his lips. 'Have you never been danced out onto a terrace?' Kate stared at him in puzzlement as he led her around the floor towards the Millennium Clock. 'What about in your past life?'

Kate realised he had danced her into the relative quiet of the Discoveries hall. His eyes were playful as he moved towards the area where Iufenamun had been secreted behind wooden panels. He had made her speechless with his comments, and she struggled to find an appropriate response. She had no wish to discuss her past life with Edwin while she danced in David's arms.

'Did Victorian Kate get up to no good on a terrace?' he teased. The music stopped, and David reluctantly let her step back from his embrace.

'She most certainly did not!' Kate protested. 'What are you havering about?'

He grinned at her indignation. 'I found Armando Rossellini's autobiography, translated from Italian.' He drew her behind the escalator where they could not be seen. 'It describes his visit to Edinburgh in the spring of 1890. Apparently he was escorting some artefacts from Turin to our museum for the Ancient Egypt Exhibition.

'At first he found the people of Edinburgh to be welcoming and hospitable. He certainly had a lot of respect for Professor James Grahame. Naturally, Rossellini also had an eye for the ladies. He briefly mentions Professor Grahame's charming young daughter.' David paused as he heard Kate inhale sharply. 'But it seems everything went pear-shaped at a ball held by an affluent member of Edinburgh society, a Major Ramsay. According to Rossellini, there was a misunderstanding over a young lady. The lady in question had agreed to dance with him and had allowed him to lead her to the terrace for some "fresh air". She then changed her mind about him and caused a scene. Thereafter he was shunned by the women of Edinburgh, even though he claims to be innocent of any wrongdoing.'

David watched Kate's face, realising that she was reliving an event from that time. Her eyes were fixed on the middle distance as she recalled something which seemed to trouble her. 'It didn't end there,' he continued. 'Our blameless Italian was on the town one evening shortly after this mysterious event, when he was set upon by two ruffians, one of whom turned out to be a fellow EEF archaeologist who was working on the exhibition. This young man had taken offence at Rossellini's behaviour at the ball and punched him a couple of times before the second young man pulled him away. Rossellini complained to the EEF, and our young hero was grounded in Edinburgh for a year for his misconduct. Rossellini gloats later on about how he succeeded in finding Akhenaten's tomb, when his rival had failed and returned to Edinburgh with his tail between his legs.'

Kate's face displayed anger, surprise and sadness. David stroked her bare arm tenderly. 'The young woman was Katherine Grahame, right?' he asked softly. 'And it was Edwin Ford who defended her honour.'

'I never knew he did that,' she said quietly. 'I only remember that he and John were angry.' Kate wrung her hands. *Edwin should never have met me*. 'I didn't know he stayed in Edinburgh because he got into trouble with the EEF. Poor Edwin…'

'Kate, he probably didn't care about the EEF. Not when he had you.' He paused, waiting for a rebuke which was not forthcoming. 'So, what's the story about dancing on the terrace? Do you remember?'

Kate drew herself up, raising her chin in the air defiantly as she tried to envisage Rossellini's arrogant face. 'I recalled it during a regression. Rossellini was a pig! He inappropriately snatched me from another dance partner and steered me out to the terrace, where he made improper advances.' She stopped as she heard herself talking in the first person about a woman who was her ancestor. She had to stop doing that - it made her sound like a basket case.

David grinned at her outrage, noting how her language had altered as she spoke about her Victorian life. 'Did you thump him?'

'No, I did not! I was only nineteen and had no experience with men. Luckily, Edwin and John were in the vicinity. Most likely spying on me - they did that a lot.' She smiled wryly. 'But it seems that rumours about me were spread by the host's daughter, who had set her sights on Edwin.' Kate's eyes grew misty.

'So there was a big furore?'

'In those days, a girl had to behave impeccably. Katherine Grahame did her best to obey the rules. She tried hard to behave with propriety.' Kate remembered kissing Edwin in the rotunda, and on North Berwick beach. But perhaps not as vividly as she once had. 'Well, most of the time. There was gossip, for a while. She stayed at home, out of the line of fire, and didn't see anyone for a few days.' Kate waited to be overwhelmed with longing, but the disabling emotion did not present itself. She looked up at David. 'It all settled down, in the end.'

'Would you like to read the biography?' he asked.

'No,' she said firmly. 'The past is the past. Reading his lies would just make me angry. He would never have found the tomb if Edwin hadn't done all the groundwork. And Edwin hardly ran home with his tail between his legs...' She looked towards the Grand Gallery. 'I'd better get back to work.' She turned to leave the dimly lit area behind the Millennium Clock as a noisy group of soldiers gathered nearby.

David reached for her hand. When she turned back to him he smiled, his gaze pensive. 'I'm glad you're wearing your necklace.' Kate reached up to touch the silver wing feathers of her locket. 'Have you put a picture in it yet?'

Kate gazed at him steadily, unwilling to answer the question. David took this to mean that she had filled his gift to her with a picture of Edwin Ford. His tender smile left him.

'I'm going back upstairs,' he informed her gravely, eyeing the laughing soldiers. 'Where it's quieter.'

Her duties complete, Kate made her way to the Egyptian gallery. David stood in the centre of the arched entrance to the darkened gallery, like a guardian of the ancient civilisation. He was staring blankly in the direction of the Qurneh exhibit, a champagne flute in his hand. He looked up as she approached, and his mouth twitched into a half-smile. He handed her the glass.

'Aren't you having any?' Kate asked, taking the glass from him hesitantly. They were not supposed to drink alcohol on duty, but her mouth was dry. She had been busy helping to clear things away behind the scenes, as the wedding reception was almost over.

'I'm driving,' he explained. 'And before you say you can't drink at work, our shift is nearly over and I'm kind of your boss. If I say it's okay, then it's okay.'

Kate giggled and took a sip, the bubbles fizzing on her tongue. They wandered to the landing and looked down at the dancers. Still wearing her sumptuous designer wedding dress, the bride danced with her handsome new husband, her arms draped possessively around his neck.

'Are you pleased with your work?' David asked, referring to the floral displays and table centrepieces.

Kate nodded. 'The Grand Gallery looks beautiful.' She sounded wistful but happy.

'Every girl loves a big wedding,' he observed, testing her.

Kate gestured towards the Grand Gallery, the ornate flower arrangements and equally ornate guests. 'All this,' she began. 'It's not what's important.' She turned her back on it, leaning against the railing. 'As I found, to my cost.'

The music had changed; the DJ was playing romantic love songs for slow dancing. It was that time of the evening when the lonely make a last-ditch attempt to connect with another soul. Kate looked out of the roof windows, searching for stars in a clear winter sky of inky blue. She heard the opening bars of her favourite Jack Savoretti song; 'Without' always filled her with longing and often made her cry. During the weeks that she and David had been at odds, she had played the song repeatedly.

David took her glass from her and set it down on a nearby stool. Taking her hand he led her into the Egyptian gallery. Placing one hand around her waist he took her right hand in his and held it against his chest. Pulling her gently to him, he began to dance. A little surprised by his actions, Kate put her left hand on his upper arm, feeling the contours of his bicep under his jacket. She fixed her gaze on the lapel of his dinner jacket, floundering for something flippant to say to lighten the sudden tension in the atmosphere.

'This is one of my favourite songs,' she told his jacket, as they danced slowly around the gallery. The sarcophagi seemed to eye them with contempt.

'I know,' David murmured into her hair. 'I've heard you humming it - a lot.' *And I haven't been able to get it out of my head since. It could have been written for us.*

Kate felt him move his hand up her back, the action pulling her a little closer to him. Relaxing in his arms, Kate sighed. Her high heels enabled her to rest her cheek against his shoulder. She felt safe, content. When David leaned his cheek against her hair, Kate slid her hand from his shoulder to the back of his collar. It occurred to her that she had not danced like this with a man since her own wedding day. She asked herself which dance she preferred, then shied away from her eager response. David breathed in the faint smell of her perfume. It was exotic, mysterious, but not brash and overpowering. He recognised it as the same scent she had worn on the night of their doomed trip to the Usher Hall. He wondered where she had sprayed it, and if the scent was stronger there. Her hair was elegantly pinned up tonight, baring her smooth neck. He leaned down, searching for the perfume's point of origin, his lips almost brushing her skin. Kate quivered as she felt his warm breath on her neck.

'Can I take you home?' he breathed, his lips close to her ear. Her seductive scent wafted towards him, beckoning him closer. Kate looked up at his face, her eyes searching for the significance of his question. David forced himself to smile lightly, and the moment was gone. 'I mean give you a lift,' he said hastily. 'Obviously.' What had he just seen in her eyes?

Kate leaned her forehead against him so he wouldn't see the look of disappointment in her eyes. 'Yes,' she murmured. *Whichever way you meant it. I don't want to wait anymore.* She glanced up. 'I'm ready,' she whispered.

The song was over, but they still stood together, both of them afraid and feeling guilty.

'Let's go,' David decided. 'Where's your coat?'

'In my locker,' Kate answered in a small voice.

Ten minutes later they were in his car and driving home. The journey was torture for both of them. Kate longed to escape the heavy silence, but she didn't want to leave David. Her thoughts were tangled, and she felt appalled at herself for the desires and emotions which churned inside her. David was torn by indecision. He could remain noble and virtuous, and possibly lose her forever to another man. Or he could follow the screaming demands of his own heart.

He arrived in front of her house too soon. Viciously he pulled up the handbrake, angry at himself for so many reasons. Kate was reaching for the door handle, forcing him to get out of the car and open her door as he always did. She shivered as she climbed out into the cold night air, and huddled into her coat. She would not see him now for a week, for he was travelling to London with Steven in the morning. Kate told herself it would be good for them to be apart; they could begin their work in Egypt with clear heads. In Egypt, she would be too busy to act like a lonely, love-starved teenager.

Hope surged in him for a moment when Kate couldn't find her door key. She rummaged in her bag, finally finding it stuck in the folds of the lining. David followed her up the path and waited while she unlocked the front door and switched on the hall light.

Kate turned to him. 'Would you like to come in?' she murmured hesitantly. 'For a glass of milk?' She managed a weak half-smile.

David wanted desperately to cross the threshold with her and bang the door on the world and his obligations. Instead, he tried to rebuild the defences she had breached the first day they had worked together, when she had helped him with the Amarna lecture.

'That's not a good idea,' he said gently. Seeing the look of rejection which passed swiftly across her face, he stroked her cheek. 'I have an early flight in the morning, and I haven't finished packing.' David gazed into her tired eyes. 'Try to get some rest this week.'

Kate leaned her face against his warm palm. 'I'm working all week.' There had been no holidays since the summer. David had suggested that she use her last week's holiday after the expedition was over, as he planned to do. She had followed his advice, much to Adam Gray's displeasure, but she was exhausted from the months of relentless work and study.

'I know. But I want you to stop studying and working extra shifts. Try and have some fun this week.'

Kate shuddered as an icy breeze whipped her hair. 'Is that what you'll be doing?'

David shook his head. 'No. I'll be working.'

'But you'll be going out in London, with Ethan?' She couldn't help sounding concerned.

He looked deeply into her eyes as if he were searching for the secrets of her soul. 'You can rest assured that I will be on my best behaviour,' he smiled. 'I can at least try to set Steven a good example.'

'David,' Kate sighed. 'Steven worships you. Even when you're mean to him.'

David stepped back, beginning his retreat. 'I'll see you a week on Monday,' he told her, his voice husky. 'In the departure lounge at Heathrow.'

She tried to follow his example, folding her chilled arms against her chest. 'I'll bring the reports you asked for,' she said, sounding efficient. 'If you would like me to bring anything else, please let me know.'

Bring yourself, Kate. All I want is you. 'If you need me - for anything - call me.'

I need you right now, David. Please stay. Help me to forget. 'Enjoy your week away. And get some rest.'

Fighting the urge to kiss his cheek, Kate stepped into her hallway with the intention of closing the door. David smothered the desire to take her in his arms and hold her once more. He nodded briskly, and turned to walk back down the path. Kate closed the door, leaning against it as miserable tears coursed down her cheeks. She turned to peer through the spyhole in the door and held her breath as she saw David standing at the end of her path with his back to the house, as if

383

pondering what he should do. He stood there for several pounding heartbeats, before climbing into his car and driving away.

CHAPTER 22

David had chosen a seat in Heathrow's bustling departure lounge which would provide a clear view of the entrance from security. His eyes remained fixed on the area, his body tense with anticipation.

It had been a long week, filled with interminable meetings with people from the Egypt Exploration Society. David couldn't remember what half of them had been about. Once he had received his instructions for the expedition and once again defended his choice of assistant, he had tuned out. Even though he was in London, he still had to answer emails from students. He had even marked some essays, emailed to him because they were past their due date.

David's parents had graciously invited Ethan and Steven to stay with them while they were in London. Steven had been quiet and apprehensive throughout the week, even when Ethan had invited them out for a civilized drink in the city centre. On Friday evening, Steven had sneaked off to a quiet corner to phone Kate. David realised the young intern was seeking reassurance from his surrogate sister, and dearly wished he could talk to Kate himself. But he left Steven to his conversation, which lasted almost an hour. On Saturday morning, a more confident Doctor Brodie emerged to meet the students and fly out to Cairo, leaving David alone with his parents.

Spending time with his parents had been taxing, the conversation stilted. They didn't value the significance of his work and saw his job as financially insecure. His mother had been sorely disappointed in her quest to find out about his love life, and was now curious about his female assistant. In short, David was exhausted. He was at the stage where he could no longer focus on anything. Except the woman he couldn't wait to see.

There had been no work-related reason to contact Kate in the past week. He had hoped that distance might make his heart more prudent, in preparation for what was ahead. Unfortunately for David, a week without Kate had only made his feelings more intense. *I'm screwed,* he told himself despondently. *And it's all my own fault.*

His phone announced a text: she was through security and would be with him shortly. With butterflies colliding in his stomach, he picked up his newspaper but kept his eyes fixed on her point of entry.

Once through the stringent but reassuring security checks, Kate dived into the ladies' room. She was nervous and needed a moment to harness her self-control. She was concerned that David had not been in touch; he had not even replied to her text. Perhaps it was because of what had happened - or not happened - on the night of the wedding reception. Perhaps he regretted his decision to take an unqualified, untested museum employee on an important expedition. Kate gazed at her reflection in the mirror. Perhaps he was angry with her for some reason. Perhaps he was tired of the spectre of Edwin Ford and the shadow of her past life. Perhaps he just didn't want to be in her company...

Swallowing her rising anxiety, Kate assessed her appearance, hoping she wasn't looking too crumpled from her budget flight from Edinburgh. Jess had taken her shopping for Egypt-friendly clothing, although Kate was only taking a small suitcase. Today she was wearing nicely-fitting jeans, which Jess said made her backside look 'pinchable'. A white silk vest peeped out from her white cotton shirt. On her feet, she wore brown boots, which were the same colour as her brown suede jacket. Kate splashed some cool water on her face and tidied her newly-cut hair. She rearranged the printed cotton scarf which hung loosely around her neck. Then she smiled weakly at her reflection. She would do.

David's heart leapt into his mouth when he spotted Kate stepping into the departure lounge. She had changed her hair, he noticed. It was cut to just below the level of her chin, and was brushed off her face. Her loose curls caressed her jawline, and bounced as she walked. Her dark eyes swept the area, looking for him as she passed the duty free beauty shop. David smiled knowingly as he saw her slow down and her head swivel towards the bright, enticing shop. She stopped, took a couple of steps, stopped again. After looking around her with a slightly guilty expression, she fairly bounded into the store. She emerged a few minutes later, gleefully clutching a bag. David lowered his newspaper, unable to restrain the grin which lit up his face. He stood up from the hard plastic seat, his eyes greedily taking in her movement, her expression, her glossy hair. At last she spotted him and smiled in relief.

As she approached, David noticed that she attracted admiring looks from numerous men sitting in the vicinity.

Kate noticed nothing but David and his beautiful smile. He was wearing chinos and a soft blue sweater. Kate thought he looked tired and was immediately concerned. His smile reassured her that he was glad to see her. She stopped before him, wanting to hug him but not sure that she should. *What the hell*, she thought. *We're friends, aren't we?* Raising herself on tiptoe, she slipped an arm lightly around his broad shoulders. David closed his eyes and squeezed her to him for a brief moment, before stepping back.

'Have you done enough shopping?' he asked her, raising an eyebrow.

Kate giggled and held up her bag of treasure. 'I didn't want to waste an opportunity to stock up on my favourite perfume,' she replied with a smile.

'Which is?' *Because I still remember how delicious you smell when you're wearing it.*

Kate held the bag open so he could see a midnight blue box. 'Shalimar,' she breathed contentedly. 'But I'll keep it until I'm home again, because I don't want to get bitten by bugs. Oh, and I got some of Steven's favourite sweets.'

'Is that why he was on the phone to you for so long?' David grumbled. 'He was giving you a shopping list?'

'No! I met his mum for coffee last week, so I was telling him about that. I just wanted to buy him something nice.' She eyed his slightly miffed expression, and gave him a mischievous look. 'Shall I go and get you some sweeties, too?'

David had missed the wicked look in her brown eyes when she teased him. 'Was your flight okay?' he asked, now feeling self-conscious and aware that they were being watched by the man sitting near them. 'Did you get a big send off?'

Kate sat down. 'My brother dropped me off at the airport,' she replied as David sat next to her. 'I hate dramatic goodbyes...' She looked into his eyes. 'The flight was fine - I read a very trashy novel.'

'And what have you been up to all week?' David's eyes roamed over her soft hair. 'Apart from visiting a hair salon.' He smiled, as Kate blushed and automatically touched her curls. 'Lots of wild parties?'

'No!' Kate was indignant. 'We all went out for a meal during the week. It's not as if I've left my job forever. Jess took me for a wonderful spa day on Saturday.' Kate's eyes shone as she remembered their decadent day at a posh city spa, where they had swum in a rooftop swimming pool, giggled in a Jacuzzi and relaxed in the sauna and steam room. After a moderately healthy lunch, they had both gone for treatments. Kate had loved the facial, body scrub and massage. She had hated the extensive, painful waxing session. Kate grimaced at the memory and wriggled slightly in her seat. She looked up at David. 'What have you done all week?' *And why didn't you call me?*

David detected a slightly accusatory tone in her voice. 'I attended lots of meetings, and went out one night with Steven and Ethan. I spent some time with my parents...' He sighed and frowned. 'And I've still had to deal with students.'

Kate grinned mischievously. 'That reminds me, you had a visitor.' David looked nonplussed. 'Amy was looking for you.' He groaned, and Kate laughed at his chagrined expression. 'I told her you were unavailable and offered to help. It was another daft kit query, so I reminded her to read her guide. *Again.* I don't think I'll be on her Christmas card list!'

Kate rummaged in her small holdall. 'I've brought your mail, and the reports you asked for -'

David stayed her hand. 'Kate, we don't start work on this project until Wednesday.' He zipped up her bag and set it on the floor again. 'Let's just take some time...' He sat back in the uncomfortable seat. 'Talk to me. What else have you been up to?'

Kate's week had been busy, but she had found time to visit Dean Cemetery. The visit had produced no tears, this time, only a deep sympathy for Kate Ford. And a surge of resentment towards Edwin.

'I led my first workshop.' She smiled bashfully, and told him about the workshop on Romans. Nick had been there to help, but had allowed Kate to take charge of the group and the presentation. 'Oh, I got my first aid certificate,' she informed David proudly. 'And I stuck to my fitness regime, even though you weren't there to nag me.' She gave him a rueful smile. 'Gray is in a paddy about the Christmas programme, so he's driving the Events team insane. And Jess is seeing a teacher.'

David had been lulled by the musical sound of her voice, rather than taking in what she was saying. 'Oh? What's she learning?' he asked distractedly.

Kate snorted, but forgave his lack of concentration. 'I wouldn't like to speculate!' She laughed as he gave her a puzzled look. 'They're *dating*! They met when he brought a class to a Viking workshop.'

'That's scandalous!' he joked. 'Have you met him?'

Kate sighed dreamily. 'Oh, yes! He was at my farewell dinner. He's lovely!'

David gave her a reproving look. 'I see. And why was Steven muttering darkly about Lewis after he called you on Friday night?'

388

Kate blushed and averted her gaze, recalling the previous Tuesday. She had arrived at work early but was soon joined in the office by Lewis. He had obviously been waiting for her, and had not wished to be disturbed by their colleagues. The young archives assistant had presented a stunned Kate with a pink rose. He had then confessed to 'fancying her something rotten', and ended his attempt to woo Kate by clumsily asking her out on a date. Kate had handled the matter with her usual kindness, but left Lewis in no doubt that his affections would not be reciprocated.

Inwardly, she felt disappointed that her secret admirer had not been someone closer to her heart. And while Lewis had confessed to leaving pink roses on her desk, he had not claimed responsibility for the African violet. She had divulged the whole sorry tale to Steven, who had been less than complimentary about Lewis's actions.

Glancing up at David, Kate realised that Steven had shared the story with the professor, and probably Ethan as well. 'You already know!' she accused, and David tried to look contrite. 'Steven has a mouth like Vesuvius!'

David nudged her with his shoulder. 'I assume you let him down gently?'

Kate pouted. 'Yes, but I felt really sorry for him. Poor Lewis! I told him I was too old for him.'

Her pragmatism made him laugh. 'Well, I'm sure he'll have found a nubile young thing by the time you return to Edinburgh.' She fired him an indignant look. 'Did you have dance classes last week?'

'We went to the last salsa class of the year. The teacher invited some professional dancers as a special treat. So I got to dance with a man who knew what he was doing.' She glanced up at him coyly. 'Which I hadn't done since I danced with you…'

David cleared his throat. 'And what about your *other* dance class?' The man next to them was doing a terrible job of hiding the fact that he was eavesdropping. Seeing Kate blush, David couldn't resist teasing her. 'You know, the belly dancing class?' Their neighbour dropped the book he was pretending to read.

'David, hush!' Kate admonished.

'Did you ever buy appropriate clothing?' he continued, starting to laugh again. 'To go with the hip scarf Nick bought you?'

Kate scowled at him. 'I certainly did not!' she hissed. 'And that class has finished, too, although I'm supposed to practise every day to maintain the benefits.'

'Yes,' David sniggered. 'I'm sure there are many benefits!'

Kate nudged him in the ribs, but he kept laughing at her embarrassment. She rose from her seat, her lips pursed. 'I'm going to get some coffee,' she huffed. 'Do you want anything? Though I can't promise I won't pour it over your head!'

'No thanks,' he replied politely. 'But if you're craving anything, best get it now.'

He watched her walk away with her chin in the air, admiring the very nice fit of her jeans. As he turned back, he caught the eye of their neighbour.

'Is she your PA?' the man asked enviously. David gave the man a terse smile, revealing nothing. Deciding to join Kate, he picked up their luggage. The man shook his head in admiration. 'You're a lucky guy!'

David took Kate's near-empty laptop bag and effortlessly placed it in the overhead compartment of the British Airways Airbus, saving Kate the indignity of almost having to climb on the seat to reach. Kate had stuffed everything she would need in the seat pocket in front of her. The flight would take just under five hours, landing at Cairo International Airport around eight-thirty in the evening. Kate suddenly felt apprehensive about spending such a long time alone with David; supposing it was awkward, or she bored him?

'I don't mind if you want to read,' Kate said uncertainly as David fastened his seatbelt. 'Or listen to music.' Mark had always plugged himself into his iPod, read the newspaper or taken a nap.

'Are you bored with me already?' David asked, with a teasing smile.

'Of course not, I just -'

'I forgot to ask, are you okay with flying?'

'I love flying!'

'Good, because aeroplane sick bags are rubbish!' He smiled as she giggled and made a face. 'How do you feel about sailing?'

'I like that, too. Why do you ask?'

David looked smug. 'I've arranged for us to sail down the Nile to Amarna. It's much nicer than driving, and you'll see more from the river.' David's smile widened as Kate's eyes sparkled in delight.

David took his mobile phone from his pocket and quickly checked his emails, before switching it off for the duration of the flight. 'The students have found their way to Amarna,' he announced, as he read the email from Steven. 'Steven's getting them settled in.'

'Why didn't you travel with them?'

'Because I wanted to travel with you,' David replied, his attention now on the in-flight security leaflet. 'I'll see enough of them over the next fortnight. Which reminds me,' He turned to look at Kate, his expression sombre. 'When we're dividing them into work groups, can you make sure I don't have to work with a bunch of girls on my own?'

Kate laughed. 'You're joking! Why?'

His face flushed. 'This is a teaching expedition for me and practical experience for them. I don't want to be embroiled in...other stuff. There's not much to do around Amarna in the evenings. Boredom can lead to inappropriate behaviour.'

Kate gazed at him quizzically. 'You must really have to fight them off!' Her voice sounded as if she were teasing him, but Kate felt a stab of jealousy. 'Some men would take advantage...'

He gave her an exasperated glance. 'Please, Kate, just make sure I have mixed groups.'

'Should I also lock you in your room at night?'

He shrugged nonchalantly. 'I don't remember if there are locks. Perhaps you could take up sentry duty?'

Kate wondered exactly where she would be required to place herself in order to perform such a duty, but she remained silent.

They stopped talking as the plane halted at the end of the runway and prepared for take-off. For Kate, it was the most thrilling part of a flight, the moment when she was pushed back into the seat and lifted off the ground. Looking out of the window as the aircraft ascended, Kate watched London grow smaller and the sky change from grey to blue. She sighed with pleasure, marvelling once again at the skill of airline pilots and how lucky they were to have such an amazing job.

Almost as soon as the plane had levelled off on its flight path, the efficient and attractive air stewards brought their trolley up the aisle with an array of drinks and snacks. David and Kate had both bought water at the airport, so declined the offer of further refreshments.

'When will we be travelling to Amarna?' Kate asked David. She had left all the travel arrangements to him as he had requested, although she had booked and paid for her own flight to London.

'Very early on Wednesday morning,' David replied. 'I thought you might like to do some sightseeing and a bit of shopping. You wanted to visit the Cairo museum, didn't you?' Kate was looking at him uncertainly again. 'Don't look so worried. Steven will brief the students on the boring stuff like safety protocols and respect for the surroundings. They'll spend time getting to know the people in the other groups, and they'll tour the site. By the time we get there, they should be ready to work. And you'll be a bit more acclimatised.' He hesitated. 'Why the funny look?'

Kate's glowing eyes had softened. 'I can't believe how thoughtful you are, sometimes,' she said quietly, then narrowed her eyes. 'Or what a schemer you are! I'm beginning to understand why you wanted to make all the travel arrangements yourself!'

'I handled the travel arrangements because of all the funding issues. Navigating bureaucracy is complicated and frustrating.' David would never tell Kate how much of his own money he had used to ensure Kate would be at his side.

The television screens on the backs of the seats in front of them flickered into life, announcing the start of the in-flight movie. Kate squeaked in delight when the title flashed up on the screen: 'The Dark Knight'. David groaned in disgust. Although she had brought headphones which could be used on aircraft, Kate refrained from plugging them in to watch the film. She wanted to spend this time alone with David, without life and work getting in the way.

'Do I have to watch you drooling over your favourite superhero for the next two hours?'

She turned sideways in her blue leather seat and gazed at him brazenly. 'Who do you mean?' She was gratified to see him look flustered.

They talked quietly, enjoying each other's undivided attention. David told Kate about the discomfiture of 'quality time' with his parents, and Kate related the details of her latest family gathering. Both offered sympathy to the other. They created an intimate space around them, one which the stewardess was reluctant to disturb when she brought their in-flight meal. The meal was palatable; David commented that he ate similar food most of the time, except when Kate cooked for him. He was amused at the enthusiasm with which Kate opened her containers of food, as if they were surprise gifts to be relished. David ate the food because he was hungry, but Kate seemed to savour every bite, especially the dessert and mini chocolate bar.

After dinner, she pulled out the duty free magazine, as was her in-flight ritual, but nothing caught her eye in quite the same way as the man sitting next to her. She turned to look out of the window at a darkening sky streaked with red, orange and pink. She estimated they were about halfway there. Kate welcomed and feared the moment she would step on Egyptian soil for the first time in this lifetime. As she had confessed to Jess, her reasons for this trip had altered in the past few weeks. She would allow Fate a chance to intervene, to help her follow the 'right' path. But she was starting to believe Jess's theory that people had more than one soulmate. And she was already fairly certain of the path she wanted to take.

Kate turned back to David, who was reading a travel magazine taken from the seat pocket. Seeing her wriggling out of the corner of his eye, David glanced behind them.

'There's nobody sitting behind us,' he remarked. 'You could recline your seat if you want to sleep.'

Kate made a decision. Lifting the armrest positioned obstinately between their seats, she snuggled her head against his arm, feeling the softness of his sweater and the muscles underneath. She felt his arm tense momentarily. 'Is it okay if I lean?' she asked in a small voice.

David pretended to keep reading. 'You can lean, but if you start snoring I'll poke you in the ribs!'

Kate chuckled and closed her eyes, but the position was only comfortable for a short time. As her hips began to ache, she squirmed restlessly. Hearing David sigh, Kate opened her eyes to look up at his handsome profile. She sat up and away from him, but David lifted his left arm in invitation.

'I'll disturb you,' Kate murmured, chewing her lip.

David understood the reason for her hesitation. 'You won't disturb me. And if you're worried about propriety, just think of me as your big brother.'

Kate slipped under his arm and nestled against him, her head finding the perfect spot on his broad chest as his arm lightly circled her shoulders. Kate sighed contentedly, relaxing in the warmth of his body through the soft merino wool. 'I could never think of you as my brother, David...' she mumbled. She lay quietly, listening to his steady heartbeat. Within minutes, she had fallen asleep.

David closed his eyes, his heart full and at the same time heavy with the anticipation of grief. By the end of the week, she would be drifting away from him. For the thousandth time, he berated himself for not acting sooner; he had pushed his feelings aside for months, when he should have acted on them. If only he had realised that she had listened to baseless speculation about him, he would not have wasted so much time. If only he had not seen the photograph of Edwin Ford, he would have pursued her in blissful ignorance. They had both shown restraint, when they could have been building a relationship. Now it was too late, and he would have to let her go.

He buried his face in her soft, sweet-smelling hair. She made a little noise in her sleep and snaked her left arm around his waist. Her lithe body pressed closer against him. Carefully, he managed to recline both their seats. Tightening his arms around her, he kissed the top of her head and listened to her steady breathing. The plane was quiet; many of the passengers were taking the opportunity to rest before facing the chaos of Cairo airport. The stewards had stopped pacing the aisle, and the movie was over. David sat there, mentally torturing himself with what-might-have-been, until he dozed off.

'- landing at Cairo International Airport in approximately thirty minutes. Thank you.'

The pilot's indistinct voice invaded Kate's consciousness, pulling her from sleep. Slowly opening her eyes, she realised she was lying in David's arms, her own arms curled around his waist. For a moment, Kate thought she must be dreaming, but then a fellow passenger walked past, shifting the air about them as he made his way to the toilet at the tail of the plane.

Her slight movement woke David. Groggily, he looked down at the woman in his arms but made no move to release her. 'I'm awake,' he stated, more to reassure himself than her.

Kate gave him a crooked smile. 'Yes, you are. We'll be in Cairo in half an hour.' She didn't want to move. 'I need to freshen up.'

'Of course,' he muttered, releasing her and standing up quickly. Kate rose stiffly from her seat, suddenly feeling cold and bereft. She stopped in the aisle, leaning against him slightly, and touched his cheek.

'I had a lovely sleep,' she whispered.

'Me, too,' he answered, with a smile which did not disguise the sadness in his eyes.

Kate stood in the doorway of her room, awestruck. She had expected that their funding would provide rooms at a basic hotel, but David had booked two double rooms at the Ramses Hilton in downtown Cairo. Speechless, she had followed him into the bright marble reception area and then taken the lift to the eighteenth floor of the towering building. Kate's pristine room was spacious and luxurious. Large windows provided a spectacular view of the Nile, but Kate was more interested in sinking into the inviting king-sized bed.

The airport had been chaotic; they had waited an age for their luggage to appear on the carousel. They had then endured a somewhat frenetic taxi ride to the hotel, through busy streets packed with noisy vehicles. Although the city's landmarks were brightly illuminated, Kate had been too tired to notice. She had spent the taxi ride leaning against David's arm and dozing fitfully.

The porter set Kate's suitcase on the plush carpet, beckoning them into the room. In broken English, he pointed out the en-suite bathroom. With a slight leer, he showed Kate and David the door which connected their rooms. At that point, David hastily handed the man a tip and politely guided him back to the hallway.

'Do you have everything you need?' David inquired, as Kate slumped gratefully on the sofa near the window. 'Are you hungry?'

Kate shook her head as she ran her fingers through her tousled hair. 'No, I'm just really tired.' She looked up at him. 'David, did our funding pay for us to stay at the Hilton?' Kate saw him glance guiltily at the floor. 'If not, then I want to pay my share.'

David sat down heavily next to her but avoided her curious gaze. 'Kate, can't you just accept this without question?'

'I'm not a charity case!' she replied icily.

David sighed wearily. 'Listen,' he began. 'You've worked so hard for me at the museum, and in preparing for this trip. You've done more than I had any right to expect from you, and the hard work's not over yet. Please let me do something to show my appreciation. Besides, I always treat myself to a stay in the Hilton when I come to Cairo.'

'How much of my expenses will the funding cover?' she persisted.

'I don't remember,' he replied cagily. 'Stop fretting about it. Now, get to bed. If you want to go sightseeing tomorrow, we'll have to make an early start.'

Kate groaned. 'What time do I have to get up?'

'Seven thirty.' David smiled impishly. 'Unless you want to get up earlier and hit the hotel gym.'

Kate responded with a baleful look which made David chuckle as he stood up. He walked towards the bedroom door, pointedly ignoring the door which connected their rooms. With a tired smile, he said goodnight and sought the seclusion of his room.

David sat on the balcony, his feet resting on the low table in front of him, looking absently across the Nile. It was early, but already noisy far below. He could hear the sounds of traffic and market traders preparing for the day's business. Although the sun shone brightly in the morning sky, David felt as if a dark rain cloud hovered threateningly over his head. He sipped the coffee he had made by boiling bottled water in the small kettle provided in his bright and airy bedroom, and contemplated this final day with Kate. He resolved to ignore the despondency weighing down his heart and enjoy their day together. He would create a memory he could look back on later, when he was alone again.

Hearing a faint knock on the connecting door, he walked back into his room. Opening the door, he was greeted by a fresh-faced Kate, wearing blue trousers, flat shoes and a pale blue, long-sleeved blouse. Having researched Egyptian culture, Kate had ensured that all her clothes were respectable, and did not bare too much flesh. She thought she looked plain enough not to attract attention, but David thought she looked beautiful. He offered her his cup of coffee and Kate took a sip; it was dark, smoky and bitter, just as she remembered.

'I trust the bathroom meets with your approval?' David asked with a smile.

'It'll do,' Kate replied airily, with a dismissive wave of her hand. 'I had a wonderfully long shower and used all the complimentary toiletries!' She wandered over to the balcony and gasped at the breathtaking view. The wide expanse of the sparkling Nile stretched before them, bisected by a wide bridge full of noisy traffic. As Kate looked down to the ground, she saw vehicles everywhere, racing recklessly along the roads. There were even people driving carts pulled by donkeys, seemingly unperturbed by the haphazard conduct of the motorists. A couple with two small children all perched on the back of a motorcycle, weaving in and out between larger vehicles. She knew that Cairo was vastly overpopulated. The City of a Thousand Minarets was divided into the prosperous section where she now stood, and the older city which was occupied by the less fortunate. The western part of the city had been modelled on Paris and built by Ismail the Magnificent in the mid-nineteenth century. It was marked by modern architecture, gardens, wide boulevards and open spaces. Not surprisingly, hotels and grand government buildings had been erected in this area. The eastern area of the city, known as Old Cairo, was neglected in parts and consisted of narrow lanes, crowded tenements and hundreds of ancient mosques.

Kate looked across at the imposing Cairo Tower, the highest tower in Cairo at 187 metres tall. Constructed of granite, it had been inaugurated in 1961 but had recently undergone a complete refurbishment. Now a popular tourist attraction, it boasted shops and restaurants. More importantly, visitors could ascend to the top and admire the spectacular views of the city. On the journey to the hotel the night before, Kate had seen the tower illuminated by lights which changed colour. Through the heat haze, in the distance, Kate could make out the Pyramids of Giza.

The sun was shining, but Kate detected a smokiness in the air and deduced it was probably pollution from the considerable number of cars on the network of roads below. David came to stand beside her, thinking that she looked a little daunted by the sheer size and noise of the city below. Still, she would put on her brave face and stride through the streets like a diminutive Amazon warrior.

'We won't be able to see everything,' he told her apologetically. 'I could organise a bus tour, if you like.'

Kate wrinkled her nose in distaste, preferring a travel-free day. David smiled at her expression. 'We should go to the museum first, since it's just across the street.' Kate craned her neck for a partial view of the stunning building with the shallow dome in the centre of a flat roof. 'When you've had enough of that, what would you like to do?'

The answer which came into her head made her cheeks flush, and Kate glanced away quickly to avoid David's quizzical stare. 'We could just wander,' she suggested. 'I'd like to buy some little gifts to take home. I don't want to do any ambitious sightseeing on this trip. A little flavour of Cairo will suffice.'

'In that case, I need to lay down some ground rules.' Kate watched him don his adorable 'bossy professor' expression. 'Once we go into the street, we'll be mobbed by men who will try to sell us stuff, provide a tour of the city, or demand donations to questionable charities. They're relentless, and worse with single women. I suppose I don't have to remind you what some Egyptian men think about Western women?' Kate shook her head, having already received this lecture from Ben. 'When we're outside, please stay close to me and try not to make eye contact with anyone else on the street.'

'Should I just stare into *your* eyes, then?' she quipped, unnerving him by doing just that.

David frowned at her, while his hands itched to pull her against him. 'Do you have a ring?'

Bemused, Kate showed him the strangely-coloured band on the third finger of her right hand. 'It's a mood ring,' she explained. 'Rebecca gave it to me before I left Edinburgh. Apparently it has magical properties which will keep me safe, and help me meet my handsome prince.' She looked up at him meaningfully, but it was his turn to glance away. 'Actually, it changes colour according to my mood.' The ring had turned a pinkish colour.

'And what mood does it think you're in at the moment?'

Kate wasn't about to reveal what she was feeling at that moment. 'I'm hungry,' she told him evasively. Taking off the toy ring, she placed it in David's palm. They watched as the colour changed to an orange shade.

'Hmm,' Kate said thoughtfully, her eyes teasing.

'Please wear this on your left hand,' he requested awkwardly. 'You'll be harassed a little less if men think you're married.'

With an amused but calculating gaze, Kate held out her left hand, wiggling her fingers expectantly. Blushing, David took her right hand

and placed the ring in her palm. He gave her a reproachful look as she giggled and put the ring on as he had requested.

'I'll try to be a good, obedient wife,' she assured him, grinning mercilessly at his discomfort.

'I would hate that,' he muttered, holding the door open for her to pass through. David steeled himself for a day of being teased relentlessly. He could hardly wait.

CHAPTER 23

David's phone rang just as they passed through the tall iron gates of the Egyptian Museum. Kate admired the impressive façade of the building, with its arched windows and pillared entrance. Pretty gardens had been laid out at the front of the building. Even though the museum had not opened its doors, a throng of visitors had gathered in the courtyard. Kate took her camera from her canvas messenger bag and took some photos while David stepped away to answer his phone. As she took a surreptitious photograph of David, Kate noticed he looked perturbed. The call was short, and he soon returned to her side.

'I'm afraid I'm going to have to leave you for half an hour,' he said grimly, leading her towards the staff entrance to the museum.

'I thought we were supposed to stay together,' she grumbled, disappointed.

David showed an identity card to the man standing at the staff door, and they were ushered into the main gallery of the sizeable museum, which was still not big enough to house the 165,000 exhibits. Kate stared in awe at the treasure house of ancient Egypt; there were artefacts everywhere. She would never see all of the exhibits in one short visit. Display cases were crammed against every wall and lined the floor, but many of the exhibits were unlabelled.

Kate turned to David in dismay. 'Why do you have to leave?' she asked, sounding plaintive.

'I've been summoned to a meeting upstairs,' he told her, irritated by the intrusion. 'I'll try not to be too long. You'd probably rather look at the Amarna exhibit by yourself, anyway.'

Kate started to protest, but was interrupted by a small Egyptian man who greeted David noisily and gave him a fierce hug.

'Professor Young!' he exclaimed, ignoring Kate. 'How nice to see you again!'

'Yusuf!' David grinned. 'How are you? And how's your family?'

The man slapped David heartily on the back. 'All well! You are here for a meeting, yes?'

'Well, I am now,' David replied. 'Where is he?'

'Room two upstairs...' At last Yusuf turned to Kate, and she was annoyed to see his eyes appraise her from top to bottom.

David cleared his throat. 'Yusuf, this is Miss Grahame. Kate, Yusuf and I have been on expeditions together.'

Kate nodded in greeting but did not smile. 'Yusuf, Miss Grahame wants to look at the artefacts on display from the Amarna expedition of 1891. A member of her family took part in the expedition and found a particular piece - I'd be grateful if you could show her the exhibits and help her find what she's looking for. I believe it's a stone tablet.' He looked at Kate for confirmation, and she nodded.

'It would be my pleasure to help any woman of yours,' Yusuf gushed, oblivious to Kate's venomous stare. David stepped closer to her and touched her elbow. 'Try to be patient,' he murmured in her ear. 'I won't long.'

Kate watched David bound up the stairs two at a time, then turned back to a smiling Yusuf. He gazed at her speculatively for a moment, then led her down the main corridor of the museum.

As they walked, Yusuf pointed out various sculptures and artefacts, including the lid of a coffin found in an Amarna tomb. The Egyptian was courteous and well-informed, an interesting tour guide. Kate discovered that he currently worked for the Department of Antiquities, which controlled archaeological activity in the region to ensure the national monuments were treated with the respect they deserved.

Eventually, Yusuf ushered Kate into a small side room, where the Amarna exhibits were displayed. Statues of Akhenaten filled three corners of the room, each showing the pharaoh with a different persona. One of the statues looked disturbingly androgynous, while another showed the king with a rounded, almost maternal belly.

'Not all the items from 1891 are on display,' Yusuf told her, carefully enunciating his words. 'If you do not see what you are looking for, I could search on the computer.' He brandished his iPad.

Kate noticed some seats in the centre of the room, which was devoid of visitors. She imagined that most tourists would be more interested in the Mummy Room, or the treasures of Tutankhamen. 'I would like to sit here for a while,' she said assertively. 'I'll be fine on my own. Thank you for your help.'

Yusuf raised a bushy black eyebrow in surprise. 'I will be outside in the main hall, should you need my assistance.' He turned and left the room.

Kate sat down amid the display cases and closed her eyes. She breathed deeply, feeling the past like a mist which permeated the room and enveloped her. A warm, dusty breeze played on her cheeks, and she inhaled the thick air from within a canvas tent. The smell of tar-like coffee filled her nostrils, along with the smell of baking bread. A warm, familiar hand caressed her hair and she felt a presence near her...

Two noisy children ran into the room, and just as quickly ran out again. Kate opened her eyes, firmly back in the present and alone once more. Rubbing at the gooseflesh on her forearms, Kate walked over to the first display case and perused the contents. Although the items were interesting, she felt no spark of recognition and moved on to look at displays of desiccated food, figurines and small items of jewellery. An American couple wandered into the room and studied the exhibits in a perfunctory manner before leaving to seek out more sensational items. Kate continued slowly, taking her time to absorb the energy of each artefact. By the time she reached the last glass case, more than half an hour had passed. Her eyes fell on a small tablet of stone tucked at the back of the display. Its edges had crumbled, the hieroglyphs worn with age. She recognised the cartouche in the corner as that of Queen Nefertiti. Kate's eyes focused on her own reflection in the glass, then beyond. At the beautiful dark eyes staring back at her.

'Why aren't you at the dig site?' David snapped, too agitated to take the seat offered him. Ethan languished on the other side of the worn wooden desk, his feet propped on its surface.

'I've been begging, as usual,' he replied, disgust evident in his tone. Hearing David sigh impatiently, Ethan sat up. Clearly, his uptight friend was keen to be somewhere else. 'I've been doing some surveys around the rock cliffs, and I think there may be an undiscovered tomb out there. I was hoping for permission to start a proper search, but I'd need extra hands and equipment. The Powers-That-Be said no, of course.' He passed a hand over his short dark hair. 'I heard you were here, and I thought we could go out on the town tonight and travel down together tomorrow.' He gave David an inquisitive look. 'I'm looking forward to meeting your assistant.'

David pursed his lips. 'How did you know we were here?' He had been deliberately vague about their travel arrangements, fearing exactly this scenario.

'Your assistant texted mine,' Ethan smiled. 'They seem to be exceedingly close. Does she have a male harem then, this girl of yours?'

'She and Steven are friends,' David replied tersely.

'Oh, so it's just you she's got dangling on a string?' David did not reply. 'Where are you staying?'

'The Hilton,' David muttered.

'So you're treating her to a stay in the Hilton?' Ethan sounded flabbergasted. 'Be careful she's not a gold-digger, Davie. Does she have her own room, or are you at least benefiting from this arrangement?' David remained stonily silent, growing increasingly hostile towards his old friend. Ethan laughed derisively. 'Can I meet her over dinner tonight?'

David gave Ethan a grim, direct stare. 'We don't start work until tomorrow. Was there anything else, or can I go?'

Ethan grew more serious. 'There is one more thing. I'm going to lean on you a bit for the next two weeks.' He hesitated, knowing he was going to antagonise David. 'I'm really not feeling up to dealing with students.'

'You're supposed to be overseeing this project for the EES,' David reminded him. 'You have responsibilities, for which you're being well paid.'

'Yeah, and most of it is paperwork and red tape. I'm sick of it, Davie. I want to go out and be an archaeologist, not sit behind a desk and feign enthusiasm in front of students. I have no patience for it, and I don't want to be in Amarna...'

Sighing resignedly, David sat down and leaned on the desk. 'In the past you've practically pined for the place. Why have you suddenly changed your mind about it?'

Ethan shrugged, genuinely unsure. 'I don't know. Since I woke up from the coma, I haven't felt right about anything. It's as if I left a part of me somewhere else...' David said nothing, his mind working to rationalise his friend's behaviour. 'I can find no contentment, Dave. I thought that if you could look after things at camp then I could carry on looking for that tomb. Yusuf is coming down with us tomorrow, and if I could show him something tangible, I might get permission to launch a proper expedition.'

David exhaled heavily. 'Alright, I'll help where I can. But my first duty is to my students. And we're not breaking any rules.' Ethan rolled his eyes but smiled gratefully. David stood again, and leaned across the desk. 'I want to be left alone for the rest of the day, Ethan. I mean it.'

Ethan gave him an innocent look. 'Understood. Shall I pick you up in the morning?'

David walked towards the door. 'No. We're sailing down the Nile. I'll get Steven to pick us up.'

'How romantic,' Ethan commented sardonically. 'She must be really special.'

'I'll see you tomorrow, Ethan.'

'Did you find what you were looking for?'

Kate's gaze was fixed on the dark eyes reflected in the glass. She blinked and realised the eyes were green, not brown, and that David stood behind her. He moved closer as she pointed to the stone tablet almost hidden at the back of the case, his eyes scanning the hieroglyphs faintly visible on the eroded surface.

'You are more dazzling to my eyes than all the stars of heaven, the sun and the moon,' David read, and his eyes met Kate's. 'You are my heart, my life. I enslave myself to you for all eternity, my Queen.'

Kate flushed under his intense gaze. 'Kate Ford found it. The author's name appears to have been scratched out,' she commented, unable to look away from him.

'If he was caught composing love letters to a queen, he would have found himself in a lot of trouble. The poor man may have been executed, just for falling in love with an unattainable woman.'

A group of people entered the room, forcing Kate and David to move. 'Are you ready to move on?' David asked briskly, still bristling from his encounter with Ethan. Kate nodded, and allowed David to take her on a tour.

The museum was a fascinating place, a beautiful building which housed the world's largest collection of Pharaonic antiquities. David explained that over one thousand of the museum's artefacts had been donated by Flinders Petrie.

The collection from the tomb of Tutankhamen was spectacular. Kate was familiar with the famous pharaoh thanks to history lessons and further study at the museum, but to actually see the beautiful artefacts felt almost surreal.

David was selective about the pieces he showed Kate, as the museum's two storeys held too many treasures to see in one morning. He could tell that Kate was becoming tired of the crowds which had built up in a structure which offered no air-conditioning. When she adamantly refused to enter the Mummy Room, David suggested they return to the hotel and regroup in the Terrace Café.

It was only a short walk back to the Hilton, but they were accosted by traders several times. David was polite but firm in his refusal of their services, and did not stop to interact with the persistent Egyptians. Kate slipped her arm through his, grateful for his company.

After a short rest and a snack at the hotel, they set out again to explore the bustling streets which were within walking distance. Although it was not unbearably hot, it was quite humid. Kate relished every whisper of a breeze which blew across her face from the river. David planned their route, which took them past the Abdeen Palace, the Mosque of Al-Azhar, the Museum of Islamic Art and the Gardens of El-Azbakeya. Stunned by the beauty of the buildings, Kate took many photographs and frequently consulted the guide book she had bought in Edinburgh.

On the return journey to the hotel, David took Kate down narrower streets so she could buy some gifts for her family. These streets were packed with people in both Western and Arab dress. Women walked by with huge bundles atop their heads. Kate gaped in awe at two women in burkas as they walked by, carefully balancing a coffee table on their heads. It was noisy and claustrophobic, but Kate was dazzled by the multi-coloured fabrics hanging outside textile shops. Shop windows glittered with gold jewellery and gemstones. As expected, they were harassed by salesmen and restaurant touts. Kate walked with a purposeful stride, her messenger bag carried defensively across her body with the fastenings facing the inside. She browsed in several shops, becoming increasingly annoyed by the way the salesmen addressed David and ignored her. Their ill-treatment only induced her to leave their premises and look elsewhere. Finally, she found an intriguing shop which sold a huge variety of merchandise and before long she had spotted perfect gifts for her mother, Ben and the children.

Kate turned to David and lowered her voice. 'Is it alright if I do this myself?' she asked him, afraid he would feel emasculated in front of these Egyptian chauvinists if she made her own purchases. 'I'm sick of being treated like a bimbo!'

David grinned at his pintsized crusader and stepped back respectfully. 'Have at it - but be gentle with them!' He looked lovingly into her fiery brown eyes and watched her carry her items to the counter.

There followed a somewhat heated haggling session between the middle-aged salesman and his small but feisty customer. Kate did not even waver in her demands for a sizeable discount, given that she was making a significant purchase. The salesman was clearly unprepared for Kate's dogged determination, and David hid a proud smile when

Kate squared her shoulders and turned on her heel, prepared to leave the shop and take her custom elsewhere. The salesman hustled after her, caught up with her in the doorway and beseeched her to come to a reasonable agreement. With a triumphant glance at David, she settled on a price and politely asked the salesman to carefully wrap the items. Then, with a sweet smile, Kate paid and placed her hard-won loot into her bag. David gave the salesman a sympathetic smile as they left the shop.

Kate's final purchases were made at a tiny shop a few metres further down the street. As if under hypnosis, Kate drifted into the sweet-smelling store which sold dancing costumes in a rainbow of bright colours. Clothing of silk and chiffon hung everywhere. Seductive music played softly in the background. The smiling saleswoman was beautifully dressed in a modest belly-dancing costume of amethyst and gold, a gauzy veil covering her black hair and cascading over her curvaceous body. She welcomed Kate into the store as if she were an old friend, offering her coffee in a tiny cup. David hovered in the doorway, not sure if he were allowed in such a decidedly feminine place.

The woman showed Kate lots of flimsy clothing in beautiful colours, asking her in broken English if she knew how to dance. Kate nodded shyly, admitting she knew a little belly dancing. With a joyful exclamation, the woman turned up her music and began to dance playfully around Kate. Her gestures encouraged Kate to join her, but Kate reluctantly shook her head. David could see that Kate was itching to dance to the sensuous music, but he was still astounded when she removed her bag, raised her arms in the air and began to rotate her hips. The saleswoman clapped and encouraged Kate to perform an undulation. She then tied a green scarf around Kate's hips, bedecked by small golden coins. As the speed of the music increased, the saleswoman coaxed Kate to shimmy. The liberating movement had its usual effect on Kate, and she giggled with joy.

David was spellbound, his attention riveted by her movements and the flush of pleasure which crept up her throat to her cheeks. He shifted uncomfortably and cleared his throat, the sound catching Kate's attention. Embarrassed, she lowered her arms and her gaze. Praising Kate's efforts, the smiling saleswoman gave David a knowing look and returned to the business of selling.

Kate settled on a gold belly chain for Jess, encrusted with tiny crystals. She knew Jess would love the slightly risqué gift. In a fit of devilment, she bought a similar chain for Daniela. For herself, she bought a long chiffon scarf in her favourite shade of turquoise blue.

Kate didn't have the heart to bargain quite as forcefully with the kind saleswoman, but she knew that haggling was expected, so she made a perfunctory attempt to lower the price and reached a compromise fairly quickly. The woman embraced Kate and told her to come back for another dance.

Exhilarated, Kate looked up at David as he followed her into the street. 'What now?' she asked, her energy restored after only a few seconds of dancing.

David was still slightly dazed from the spectacle of her sinuous hips. 'Cold shower!' he blurted, making Kate laugh.

David settled for a refreshing swim in the hotel pool and attempted to re-establish his self-control with numerous lengths. He found the experience unsatisfactory, however, as the pool was small and irregularly-shaped. And so he was unable to erase the vision of a writhing Kate out of his head, his imagination providing additional scenarios where she was dancing in less clothing and in a more private location.

Kate had not emerged from the changing area, too shy to expose her body to his scrutiny. She waited until she saw him swimming away from where she hid behind a door, before running to the pool and descending the steps into the tepid water. A woman lay on a sun lounger near the side of the pool, her face hidden by sunglasses and a large hat; she watched Kate, amused by her bashfulness.

Feigning nonchalance, Kate started swimming lengths at the opposite side of the pool from David. Inevitably, she got bored quickly and languished on her back at one end of the pool, surreptitiously watching David as he swam relentlessly back and forth. She admired the way he cut through the water gracefully, his movements efficient. At last he caught sight of her and stopped swimming. Kate's jaw dropped when he stood up in the pool and waded towards her. His body was perfect, as though it had been sculpted by an artist. She let her eyes wander from his gorgeous wet hair to his broad shoulders and lean hips. His arms and torso were toned, the muscles well-defined, his skin a light golden colour. Kate wondered what it would feel like to trail her fingers over the smattering of hair on his chest and follow it down his body, where it disappeared into his black swimming shorts. She gulped, almost feeling her pupils dilate with the lust which suddenly rippled through her. She slid down into the water, hoping her long-neglected body would not betray her.

David gazed at her in amusement. She was hiding from him and blushing prettily, her wet curls clinging sweetly to her neck. Her respectable dark blue swimsuit showed off her assets no matter how she tried to hide them.

'Bored already?' he teased, dragging his wandering eyes to her face.

Kate had never experienced a predatory look from him before. She crouched lower in the water, so only her head bobbed above the surface. 'I did some lengths!' she said defensively. 'I don't want to strain anything.'

'You look pretty fit to me,' David murmured, floating on his back. He caught her pouting at him, and raised a warning eyebrow. Kate giggled, admiring his long legs stretched out just under the surface of the sparkling blue water.

He looked up at the blue sky, feeling the late afternoon sun on his face. 'Was there anything else you wanted to do today? An evening tour of the Pyramids, perhaps?'

Kate stood up, letting the sun warm her bare shoulders. 'No. I've had a lovely day. I'm going to have a very long bath before dinner.' She smiled at the thought of sinking into the large bath in her hotel room and then dressing up for dinner with David. She had bought a dress especially for this night, aware that she would not be dressing up during her stay in Amarna.

'How did you feel when you found the tablet in the museum this morning?' David asked lightly.

Kate considered her reply. 'I don't know. It was much smaller than I imagined. But then I suppose I wouldn't remember everything exactly as it happened. It made me feel sorry for Katherine Ford. She was so young...'

'Was she made to dig in the hot sun while she was pregnant?' David couldn't keep the resentment from his voice as he attempted once again to castigate Edwin Ford.

Kate sighed at his tone, but then smiled at the memory of the feisty woman she had once been. 'Katie Ford could not be made to do anything she didn't want to do! Her husband tried to keep her safe by giving her cataloguing jobs, but she got bored and insisted on joining the dig. She was pregnant when she found the tablet, but she hadn't seen a doctor and went to great lengths to hide her symptoms. Edwin would never have let her near a trowel if he'd known.' Kate's face fell. 'In fact, he was very upset when he did find out.'

'Didn't he want children?'

'Yes, but her pregnancy at that time was obviously inconvenient.' Kate's expression grew sad. 'Poor Katie. If only she had married a banker, she might have lived a long life.' She tried to recall the features of Alastair Scott.

'Ah, but would it have been a happy one?' David questioned. He turned his head to look at her. 'She fell in love with Edwin Ford. Love can make you do strange things…'

They were straying onto uncomfortable terrain. Kate changed the subject. 'What was your meeting about this morning? Shouldn't I have gone with you - to take dictation, or something?'

David stood up, and Kate's eyes swivelled to his washboard stomach. 'It wasn't important,' he assured her. 'It was just Ethan, that's all.'

'He's in Cairo?' she asked, alarmed at the thought. Her instincts told her that she and Ethan were not going to get along.

David moved towards her and laid a comforting hand on her shoulder, feeling her move a fraction closer to him. 'Yes, but he's not going to disturb us. At least, not until tomorrow.'

'Good,' Kate murmured. David's eyes looked into hers, questioning. She gazed at him, feeling brazen. 'I'm not good at sharing.' Tentatively, Kate reached up to push his wet hair away from his eyes. 'And I'm not sure we're going to be friends.'

David closed his eyes as he quelled a stab of pain. When he opened them again, he smiled gently at his beloved Kate. 'I'm sure you'll handle him,' he told her, tucking a strand of hair behind her delicate ear. 'You can beat down Egyptian salesmen, after all. And belly dance in public.' He watched her blush as she averted her gaze. 'That was possibly the most erotic thing I've ever seen.' His voice was low, his eyes dark.

'Yes,' Kate agreed in a weak voice. 'The lady was a lovely dancer. She made it look so effortless.'

'I wasn't talking about the saleswoman.'

David knocked on the door to Kate's room, hoping that ninety minutes had been ample time for her to bathe and dress for dinner. He had kept himself occupied by checking and replying to emails and reading reports from Amarna. The connecting door between their rooms had remained resolutely closed while Kate enjoyed a final, indulgent pampering session before travelling to the desert and the rudimentary facilities which awaited her. He was unprepared for the sultry beauty who opened the door to him, however, and gaped mutely at his dinner date.

With Jess's help, Kate had bought a long dress of midnight blue from a small boutique in the West End. It had a full-length slip of shimmering blue silk, held up by thin straps. The overdress was made of delicate chiffon and had long sleeves and a round neck edged with small blue bugle beads. It gave the impression of naked arms and décolletage, barely concealed by the thin layer of chiffon. The dress was not tight, but it flowed becomingly over Kate's body, accentuating her curves. She had frivolously packed one pair of heeled shoes, which consisted of an arrangement of thin silver straps, and had painted her toenails with bright pink polish. Around her neck, she wore David's locket, while her small ears were adorned with simple silver studs. For this one special evening, Kate had applied some make-up, but her abhorrence of mosquito bites had encouraged her to forego perfume.

Kate's face flushed under David's stunned gaze, and she tightened her grip on her small clutch bag. He had showered and shaved and looked handsome in a white shirt and navy trousers. He, too, had brought something smart to wear for their last dinner together. But now, he didn't want to go to dinner.

'Will I do?' Kate asked coyly.

'Yes...' David murmured, his eyes still avidly absorbing her appearance as he realised she had dressed this way for him. She had planned this outfit in Edinburgh, to wear for his benefit on this night. His eyes fell on the locket around her neck, and he reached out to touch it.

'I was hoping you would give me a photograph,' she began, her eyes wide and innocent-looking. He looked surprised, and Kate bit her lip to stifle her mischievous giggle. 'Of Zack.' She laughed as he looked mildly offended. 'I know I shouldn't have brought any jewellery,' she continued. 'But I couldn't help it. I promise to look after it. I'll wear it tucked under my tops, or if you have a safe in your room at Amarna I could leave it there.'

'It's fine,' David mumbled, replacing the silver heart against her throat. A chattering couple brushed past him on their way down the corridor.

'Are you going to be a man of few words all evening?' she teased, her eyes twinkling.

With a self-deprecating smile, he drew her into the corridor with a guiding hand at the small of her back. Kate deliberately leaned against him as he closed her bedroom door, breathing in his delectable scent.

As they walked slowly towards the elevator, David slipped Kate's left arm through his and placed his hand over hers. He felt proud to have her at his side, but was reluctant to take her to a public place where other men would undoubtedly admire her. Tonight, he wanted to keep her to himself, but he knew she was looking forward to visiting the famous restaurant on the top floor of the hotel, which boasted panoramic views of Cairo. Absently, he stroked her fingers as they waited for the lift, and found she still wore her ring on the third finger of her left hand.

Kate and David stood silently in the elevator, staring at the doors. They had enjoyed a perfect evening together and neither wanted to end it by stepping into separate rooms. David knew he could not cross that line, for to do so would provide Kate with a burden, an obligation she did not need. Kate had no idea how to proceed, or how to convey her desire for him without looking cheap or desperate. She was no seductress; to act like a temptress would feel false. With trembling fingers, she fumbled in her bag for her room key.

The doors opened, David waited for Kate to step out first and followed her along the empty and silent hallway. When her trembling fingers couldn't get the key to work, David took it from her and easily unlocked her door. He switched on the lights, glanced around the room then stepped back to let her pass. David remained steadfastly in the doorway.

'Would you like to come in?' Kate asked, nervously. 'I have chamomile tea.'

David smiled, but she saw the forlorn look in his eyes which was fast becoming a permanent feature. 'No, thank you. We have an early start tomorrow - we should pack. I've ordered breakfast to be brought to our rooms at five thirty.'

Kate laid her hand on his arm. 'Thank you for a wonderful day, David.' Standing on tiptoe, she reached up to kiss his cheek. Her kiss landed on the corner of his lips, which was as direct a sign as Kate could give.

'See you in the morning,' he said softly, before closing her bedroom door.

Kate listened to him opening and closing his own bedroom door, and the faint sounds of him moving about in his room. She stared at the connecting door, willing him to come through it. She didn't know what to do next, even though she felt sure of the chemistry between them. Perhaps he needed her to be his assistant on this expedition, and nothing else. He'd hinted at that on the plane, when he'd voiced his desire to avoid romantic complications with his students. Perhaps he was just tired. Naturally, Kate's mind turned to her physical flaws. As she wiped away her makeup, she looked critically at her face, wondering how she measured up to David's previous partners. Feeling sorry for herself, Kate reached behind her to unzip the dress she had felt beautiful in only minutes before. Just past the nape of her neck, the zip stuck. Cursing, she moved the zip one way, then the other. But it was difficult to reach and refused to move, and Kate was frightened of tearing the delicate fabric. She had only one choice.

'David,' she called hesitantly at the connecting door. There was silence then the sound of footsteps approaching.

'Yes?'

'I need help,' Kate rolled her eyes at the impending cliché. 'My zip's stuck.'

There was another moment's silence. 'Let me in, then.'

She opened the door for him and stepped back into her room. His shirt was open, and his feet were bare. He had removed his belt, so his trousers now hung loosely on his slim hips. His hair was tousled, evidence of him running his hands through it in frustration.

'Come over here,' he commanded, standing near the table lamp at the side of her double bed.

She obeyed, her eyes downcast as she remembered the last time he had helped her with obstinate clothing. David wondered fleetingly if this was an attempt to seduce him, but doubted Kate could be so devious. He examined the zip and saw that it had trapped some of the fabric. Very carefully, he began to tease out the chiffon from the fastener. Each time his fingers brushed her skin, Kate jumped. When she felt his breath on her neck, she shivered, her body taut with anticipation. Finally, David freed the snared fabric and slowly pulled the zip down. Kate held her breath, but David stopped unzipping her dress. He had reached the cream lace band of her strapless bra, and he would go no further.

'All done,' he murmured. Kate turned and gazed longingly into smoky green eyes. Her dress slipped down one shoulder as she placed her hands on his bare chest and moved her face closer to his.

'Stay,' she whispered. Summoning her courage, she reached up and brushed his lips with hers. She felt utter dismay when she felt him tense beneath her hands.

David cupped her face gently in his hands and shook his head. 'I can't.'

Kate looked up at him with wide eyes, her expression angst-ridden. 'Are you punishing me?' she whispered, dropping her hands from his chest.

'No, angel,' he said quietly, wishing he could tell her that he loved her, regardless of the consequences.

'Then you just don't want me...'

David measured his reply. Whatever he said would hurt her, whether he opted for the truth or a lie. 'Yes,' he breathed. 'Yes, I do. I just...can't.'

Kate gazed at him. 'I don't understand.'

'Kate,' he began. 'I know that in your heart, you're still searching for *him*. I won't be second best.'

She said nothing, too scared to confess her feelings for him were stronger than her desire to find Edwin Ford. Devastated by his rejection, her eyes filled with tears. David wanted desperately to hold her, to kiss her tears away, to stay with her this night and every night thereafter until the end of his life. But he had to give her the freedom to make her own choices.

His hands followed the contours of her neck and bare shoulders, gliding over her smooth skin. He took her hands in his. 'I could stay,' he said, kissing the palm of her hand. 'And I know it would be wonderful. But tomorrow, everything will be different.' She started to protest, but he placed a finger over her lips and looked deeply into her eyes. 'I couldn't bear to have you look at me with regret.' He leaned down and kissed her cheek, his lips lingering on her soft skin. 'Help me, Kate,' he breathed. 'When I leave, lock the door.'

Kate stood on her balcony for the last time, watching dawn turn to day. The Nile was calm, and the traffic was sparse. For Cairo, it was tranquil. Her luggage was waiting by the door, ready for the porter to take it to reception. A taxi would take them to their boat, and they would sail downriver to Amarna, a journey which was supposed to be a pleasurable, and possibly romantic interlude before their work began. Now they were fated to endure a long and uncomfortable trip, no doubt filled with stilted conversation about the weather.

She turned as she heard David knock on the connecting door. When she opened it, she could see he had suffered a sleepless night. Like her, he had paced the room before falling in an exhausted heap on the bed. Kate avoided his remorseful gaze, looking instead at his chest, covered today by a khaki t-shirt which showed off his biceps. Kate silently berated herself for still wanting him, even after he had rejected her.

'I have breakfast,' he stammered, eyeing her dejected countenance. 'Will you join me?'

Kate nodded and stepped into his room. David caught her by the hand, noticing her ring had been moved onto its proper finger. 'Kate -' He pulled her towards him. 'Please don't hate me.' Knowing it was unwise, David embraced her. 'I'm sorry, Kate.' He kissed the top of her head, breathing in the scent of her in case this would be the last time he held her.

Kate felt too humiliated to ask him to explain his actions. She had offered herself to him on a plate, but he had refused her advances. He had turned the tables on her. If his rejection had been out of misplaced chivalry, then Kate felt even more embarrassed by her behaviour. But she still had to spend the next two weeks with him. Somehow, they would have to put this episode behind them. She would have to repress her emotions, again.

'I don't hate you, David,' she mumbled, pushing gently away from him. 'It's best if we forget that last night ever happened. If anyone should be sorry about their behaviour, it's me. I apologise for my lack of inhibition.'

David gripped her upper arms firmly, his face grave as he forced her to look at him. 'Don't,' he told her, his voice strained. 'Don't do that. You are blameless.'

Kate pulled away from him and walked over to the breakfast trolley. Lifting the metal cover from one of the plates, she discovered that David had ordered pancakes. A small jug of maple syrup sat on the trolley, along with fruit and a pot of coffee. She smiled sadly at him, acknowledging his sweet gesture of ordering her favourite breakfast. Kate poured him a cup of coffee and handed it to him in a gesture of reconciliation, before drizzling syrup over her pancakes and taking her plate out to his balcony.

Standing on the front steps of the Hilton, Kate sighed with impatience. She had been waiting for fifteen minutes, while David settled their bill. Her pleas to be allowed to contribute had resulted in her being chased out of reception and told to wait on the steps beside their luggage. Taking her camera from her bag, she snapped a few more photos of the river and the vista beyond. A battered Range Rover drove into the hotel driveway and parked near the entrance. As Kate replaced the camera in her bag, she dropped her sunglasses and bent down to pick them up. As she blew the dust from the glasses and straightened up, her eyes fell on a pair of feet ascending the steps towards her. Her gaze travelled upwards from dusty brown boots to khaki trousers and a white shirt with the sleeves rolled up.

'You must be the famous Kate Grahame,' a deep voice drawled, as Kate's eyes travelled up a lean, strong body and stopped dead as she saw his face. 'At last we meet.'

David was intercepted by a chattering Yusuf as he left the hotel. He heard nothing as his eyes settled on Kate. The moment he dreaded had arrived too soon. David felt as if he had been kicked in the stomach, his heart ripped from his chest.

Kate would never see the look of desolation on David's face. She was rooted to the spot and suddenly felt sick. The man before her removed his sunglasses, and she stared into dark brown eyes. Those beautiful eyes gazed at her with an intensity which stripped her bare. His almost black hair was cut severely short. A sardonic smile graced the handsome face she had known so well in another life. She felt her soul lurch in recognition.

He held out his right hand to her. 'Ethan,' he stated, his voice deep and soft. 'Ethan Forbes.'

Lightning Source UK Ltd.
Milton Keynes UK
UKOW03f0038290414

230759UK00005B/484/P